CIRCLE OF LIARS

To Nat, Jack and Gemma

First published in the UK in 2025 by Usborne Publishing Limited, Usborne House, 83-85 Saffron Hill, London EC1N 8RT, England, usborne.com.

Usborne Verlag, Usborne Publishing Limited, Prüfeninger Str. 20, 93049 Regensburg, Deutschland, VK Nr. 17560

Text copyright © Kate Francis, 2025

The right of Kate Francis to be identified as the author of this work has been asserted by her in accordance with the Copyright, Designs and Patents Act, 1988.

Cover artwork by Daniel Prasad © Usborne Publishing, 2025

Palm trees © Pyzata / Shutterstock, 2025

Motel sign © antstang / Shutterstock, 2025

The name Usborne and the Balloon logo are Trade Marks of Usborne Publishing Limited.

All rights reserved. No part of this publication may be reproduced or used in any manner for the purpose of training artificial intelligence technologies or systems (including for text or data mining), stored in retrieval systems or transmitted in any form or by any means without prior permission of the publisher.

This is a work of fiction. The characters, incidents, and dialogues are products of the author's imagination and are not to be construed as real. Any resemblance to actual events or persons, living or dead, is entirely coincidental.

A CIP catalogue record for this book is available from the British Library.

JFMA JJASOND/25   ISBN 9781836042389   10093/01

Printed and bound using 100% renewable electricity at CPI Group (UK) Ltd CR0 4YY.

CIRCLE OF LIARS

KATE FRANCIS

PROLOGUE

The air in the bunker tasted bitter and dank. The kind of air you'd expect to take your last breath in, gasping for help as you tried to saw zip ties off your wrists with a rusty nail.

An arched, corrugated roof was lit by a string of bare bulbs, crudely nailed along the spine. The hum of a generator reverberated around and around, making the walls vibrate. It was not a place you'd want to spend time in.

But someone obviously had.

At one end there was a small kitchenette stocked with packets of ramen and a Nespresso machine. A camping toilet was discreetly tucked behind a plastic curtain; next to this stood an army cot, with weights and a chin-up bar set out underneath in a tidy row.

Further down, an eerie blue glow lit up the wall. A makeshift desk was propped in front of a bank of sophisticated monitors. The screens were all on, lit with colourful images of empty stretches of desert, a cluster of pink buildings, dark rooms. The screen in the centre showed a vintage road sign, winking on and off, over and over, its letters stark against a sweeping, empty skyline: *Motel Loba, No Vacancy.*

Eyes on everything. Nothing moved, yet.

A cork board hung behind the desk. Eight photos were pinned on it next to a crumpled twenty-dollar bill – school photos with a traditional green backdrop. Eight smiling faces, brimming with self-consciousness, heads cocked, posing for the camera. Attractive and well-groomed – these weren't kids; they were young adults, with one foot already out of the door of high school, ready to take on the world. Their futures ahead of them.

A small red light flashed on one of the monitors. There was movement in the corner of the screen. A bus pulled into view, caught in a sunset glow, slowing to a stop close to the flashing sign. The door opened and a figure slouched out, followed by another, then another. Teenagers, laughing, joking around, dragging bags and backpacks behind them. Chatting and jostling, oblivious.

Their photos on the wall watched them silently, smiling into the air; unable to speak, unable to warn themselves not to get off the bus. To go back to where they'd come from. To run before it was too late.

One by one they came, moving, spreading across the monitors, across the desert, into the motel. With each step, red lights flickered on, motion detectors woke up, cameras caught them. Silently tracking everything.

A loud creak cut through the heavy air.

A lone figure stood up and moved out of the shadows where they had been sitting – watching. The blue light from the monitors caught the edge of their dark clothes, momentarily outlining them; well-built, average height, a grey hoodie pulled low over their face.

Stepping close to the desk, the figure studied the screens intently, identifying each of the kids, counting them off against the photos on the wall. Everyone accounted for. All present.

Taking a deep breath, they sank into the desk chair. So, this was it. All these long months – all the planning and preparation had led to this moment. It was here at last. The first move had been made, and so far, everything was going according to plan.

After three hundred and sixty-four days, it was finally time.

Payback.

1 | Ana

Three hundred and sixty-four days.

Technically it was three hundred and sixty-three days since the hospital had declared Danny Reyes dead, though they were wrong. His heart might have kept going for an extra day, pushed along by all the machines at his bedside, but he was already gone.

Ana Reyes knew it; she'd felt the exact moment her twin brother had let go, curled up on the floor of the school locker room. Too much pain to bear, too little left to cling to. A softening – a gentle catch at the top of his breath, then gone. So quickly. So easily.

That was three hundred and sixty-four days ago, and tomorrow it would be a year.

Happy fucking anniversary.

Ana pulled her headphones down and stretched her arms out, shaking off the stiffness from the long bus ride. She looked around at her home for the next three days.

A vintage motel sign loomed over her, flickering on and off, red then yellow, the garish lights clashing starkly with the desert sunset sky.

Welcome to the Motel Loba.

The run-down old motel had obviously seen better days, if not better decades.

Two wings of baby-pink rooms stretched out on either side of a cracked asphalt parking lot with a cluster of lonely outbuildings scattered around behind. A lone palm tree stood sentinel over a fenced-off pool area in the middle of the lot. There were no cars, no people, no signs of life – only flat empty desert on all sides, the road they had arrived on ending just feet from the sign. Red dust coated every surface, weeds sprouted from the cracks. It had a post-apocalyptic appearance; all it needed was a zombie on the hunt for a busload of fresh meat.

Ana sighed.

The fresh meat had arrived ten minutes ago: seven restless high schoolers, now spread around the motel, loudly taking over the place as though they owned it. The whining had started before the bus even pulled into the parking lot. It was certainly not the fancy hotel they'd been promised in the invitation.

But she didn't mind. It was as good as anywhere.

There was no good place to commemorate the worst day of your life. The darkness travelled with her, now and for ever. The location didn't matter. Even home, the place where she had once felt safe and happy, was now heavy with pain and loss. The memories were everywhere – at the yellow kitchen table, in the shared bedroom, the empty bed – dark blue sheets untouched. A hollowness haunted her mother's eyes, the rift between them cutting through their small life together. The shared understanding that in some sick, karmic twist, the better twin had died. A silently acknowledged truth that it should have been her.

At least here, in the ass-end of nowhere, she could do the one thing that mattered most. She could give her mother space to mourn her dead son, without having to look at her living daughter.

Ana took a deep breath.

The desert air tasted different somehow, salt and sage. A wind was blowing across the darkening plains, whipping up small bits of sand and dirt, prickling the skin on her legs. A circle of light from the sign illuminated the ground at her feet, flashing on and off, like a police car warning her to get out of the way.

Time to check in – she couldn't hide out here for ever. It was only three days, she reminded herself. How bad could it be?

Hoisting her duffel bag onto her back, Ana turned her back on the desert and headed in the direction of the north wing of the motel and a dusty window with a red neon sign that optimistically declared:

REC P ION

"It's a shithole!"

Ana knew the voice instantly – she'd spent the last eight hours on the bus trying to avoid listening to it. Two figures were standing by the bus, their raised voices echoing across the empty parking lot. Keeping her distance, Ana watched them warily. She really didn't need to get involved in one of Ellis's dramas.

Ellis Locke was well over six feet of rock-hard, point-guard muscle and fancied himself the boss of St Francis High's senior class. He was standing next to the doorway, looming over the diminutive bus driver.

"This is meant to be a trip to a *luxury* desert retreat," Ellis shouted, thrusting a small black card in the driver's face. "Look at the fucking invite. This place is nothing like the photo. Where's the spa? Where are the yoga yurts and the stables? It doesn't even have cell reception!"

The driver, a short, middle-aged man with a stained grey uniform that stretched tightly in all the wrong places, did not seem impressed at being shouted at by someone young enough to be his grandkid.

"Sorry, kiddo. This *shithole*, as you call it, is where y'all are stayin' for the next three nights."

"Are you kidding me? This trip was the top prize in our school raffle. The *top* prize. Last year they went to Palm fucking Springs. *Does this look like Palm Springs?* We are clearly in the wrong place."

The driver pulled a rolled-up sheet of paper out of his back pocket and thrust it in front of Ellis, jabbing his finger at the itinerary.

"Look. It's right here, see? Motel Loba. Here's the map. I'm paid to bring y'all right here, and that's what I done. You got a problem with that, you take it up with the school."

"How am I supposed to do that, genius? We don't have *fucking cell!*" Ellis snapped in his cocksure, LA-royalty accent. He snatched the itinerary out of the driver's hands and pored over the words furiously. Not finding anything to help his case, he flicked the older man's name tag dismissively. "All right – well, Benny, is it? There has clearly been a huge mistake. This place is not acceptable. You need to get on that radio of yours and find us alternative accommodation immediately. Do you understand?"

Benny hiked up his belt and pulled himself up to his full, unimpressive height.

"Whad'ya think this is? The nineties? I don't have a radio, kid. I use a phone same as everyone else. You got no effing cell – I got no effing cell." Benny chuckled loudly, cascading into a hacking smoker's cough.

Ana walked on, suppressing the urge to smile. At least Benny the bus driver was giving as good as he got. Ellis was on one of his master-of-the-universe benders and unlikely to stop until he got what he wanted. No question, Ellis could be a spoiled brat, but a small part of Ana rooted for him. Yes, he was an asshole *and* rich *and* entitled.

But Danny had loved him. That counted for something.

The beautiful people had taken over the *rec p ion* – Danny's friends. They were sheltering from the end-of-day heat in the shade of the old motel building.

Jade Clark was posing on a worn and cracked pink pleather sofa, happily taking snaps, while her boyfriend, Jax Patel, pranced around in front of her, phone held high on the search for bars. Their designer bags and fabulous on-brand clothes were at odds with their shabby, dated surroundings, like a Vogue photo shoot in a dumpster.

Alex Cabrera was sitting by the window, his guitar propped next to him. He glanced up at the door when Ana walked in, peering at her through a curtain of floppy black hair. He looked off somehow – his usually tan skin was unnaturally pale.

Carsick. Ana knew it. She knew him. Like the back of her own hand.

At least – she used to. Before.

She turned away, shutting down the memories before they could take hold, and walked over to the reception desk.

Any hope of a speedy check-in faded as she looked around.

Something was off about this whole place. The desk was a relic from the eighties – floral, pink laminate with dark wood panelling. There were Christmas decorations hanging from the yellowed ceiling tiles over the counter, even though it was April; a thick layer of dust covered every surface. Behind the counter, a cracked glass door opened onto what looked like a deserted office.

A hand-scrawled message on a chalkboard behind the desk read:

LEFT FOR FAMILY EMERGENCY — CHECK YOURSELF IN

Ana wondered when the emergency had happened. 1985? There was no way this was still a functioning motel.

"Don't bother checking in. There's no one here. It's like completely deserted." Jade glanced up at Ana. "We're obviously in the wrong place. Ellis went to sort it out with the driver." She sighed, a long, world-weary sigh and examined her nails. Jade had perfected the art of sounding bored at all times. Enthusiasm was for lesser mortals.

"No cell in here either," Jax muttered, waving his phone at Jade. "This whole place is a total dead zone."

"Seriously? Can you even call yourself a motel if you don't have Wi-Fi? Is that legal?" Jade monotoned. She sat up, her perfectly straightened hair swinging behind her in a glorious golden arc. "What is taking Ellis so long? Low key, I need a shower so badly."

"Don't worry, babe." Jax threw her one of his easy smiles. "Ellis said he's gonna sort it. I reckon we'll be leaving soon enough." He cocked his adorable head and grinned at his phone camera. "So, hey, guys, I'm in this creepy, abandoned motel…"

Jade rolled her eyes, and looked around for another source of amusement, locking in on Alex.

"I'm so bored. Play something for me, Alex," she cajoled, flopping forward onto the sofa, draping herself across the length of it.

Ana felt a flash of something uncomfortable. She hated that Alex had crossed to the dark side, that he was one of the popular kids now, invited to all the hottest parties, sitting with the cool crowd at lunch. It wasn't the Alex she knew. The kind, gentle boy from the apartment next to hers.

Danny's best friend.

"If we're gonna be stuck here, I need cheering up." Jade peeked at Alex over the back of the sofa, pouting like a toddler in a shopping cart. "Pleeeease."

Say no, Ana willed him. *Tell her you're carsick. Just tell her no.* She didn't want to watch Alex playing for Jade Clark, performing like he was the paid entertainment.

Alex looked miserable, but he reached for his guitar case. His eyes flicked up for the briefest moment, catching Ana.

She swallowed and looked away, her cheeks flushing. It felt as though they were still at school; the entire air space was dominated by the St Francis royals. They had staked their entitled claim to this trip already – to the bus, to the motel…to Alex – pushing everyone else to the edges. Same old, same old.

"I'm, er…just going to see if there's a landline…or something…" Ana mumbled to no one in particular, heading for the small office. "In case we need to call someone…about the mix-up…or whatever…"

Anything to get out of there.

* * *

The office looked just as abandoned as the reception area. Dust motes floated lazily in the stale air, catching strips of evening light through the blinds before settling on the rows of filing cabinets that lined the walls.

Ana scanned the room but there wasn't much to see. Apart from a boxy, outdated computer on the desk, it was pretty much empty, with a thick layer of dust on every surface. Ana walked over to the desk. If there was ethernet, at least they could email the school. She tapped on the old keyboard, then reached around to switch the monitor on, hoping for signs of life, but nothing happened.

Musical notes drifted through from the reception. Chords. Alex was tuning up, getting ready to amuse Jade. Ana wished she'd shut the door behind her.

Where the hell is Raya? she thought irritably. There were seven of them on this trip, but Raya Mori was the only one she was remotely close to. At least, she had been before the fire – they had barely spent any time together this past year – it had just been too messy, too sad. As soon as they'd arrived, Raya had predictably disappeared. No doubt she was smoking weed behind some random building with Caden Loftus, St Francis High's resident drug dealer. They were probably making up for lost time and getting their vacation started with a bang. This trip was awkward enough as it was; if her only friend was going to be missing in action the whole time, it was going to suck.

Sighing, Ana turned to leave, when she noticed a small pink rectangle on the corner of the desk. She picked it up; it was an envelope addressed to *St Francis High*.

So, they *were* expected.

For a moment she was tempted to rip the envelope open, but then thought better of it. She would let Ellis and the others deal with it. They were the ones who had a problem with staying – they could sort it out. All she wanted was to keep her head down and stay below the radar for the next three days. She would give it to them, then go dig out Raya from whichever hole she was hiding in.

As she walked back into the reception, she was relieved to see that Jade had lost interest in Alex and was staring sadly at her useless phone. Jax was squatting on the vintage linoleum floor, taking artful photos. Alex glanced over, guitar balanced lightly on his knee.

"I, er…I found this in the office," Ana said, holding up the envelope. No one responded. "It's a letter or something, addressed to us. I guess we're in the right place after all?" This made the others look up.

"Did you open it?" Jade looked mildly interested, for the first time. She rolled herself lazily off the sofa and walked over. "So, what does it say?"

"I didn't open it. I ju—"

Ana never finished the sentence.

A brilliant flash of white light hit first, almost immediately followed by a deafening boom that rocked the building to its foundation. The windows shuddered, the door smacked open; clouds of dust and plaster fell from the ceiling.

Ana flinched and dropped to the floor beneath the reception desk, instinctively burying her head in her hands.

For several moments she didn't dare move – her mind was reeling. What had just happened? She listened, holding her breath as dust sank heavily around her, settling on the floor, her clothes. Her heart was beating wildly.

What had just happened?

A cough snapped her out of it.

Alex. She scrambled to her feet, looking around, finding him. He was on the floor by the window, dusting himself off. Their eyes met – there was shock in his expression, and something else. Something familiar. Just like a year ago. *It was happening again.*

That look was all it took – as though someone had shaken her hard, waking her up. Instantly all senses were firing.

Alex was okay. She could see Jade and Jax moving around, coughing. The reception was still standing, still intact. The explosion had come from outside, from the parking lot.

She ran around the desk and out through the open door, Alex following close behind. The desert air pulsed with heat as they turned to face an immense cloud of black smoke towering over their heads. Underneath they could just make out a burning shell of twisted metal, flames licking through the frame.

The breath locked in Ana's throat as she stood, watching the fire crackle, consuming everything. Alex moved next to her. Slowly she turned to look at him, her shock mirrored in his eyes.

They both knew what this meant. Their bus was gone. Their ride home was gone.

Over their heads, the road sign winked at them through the thick smoke – red and yellow lights catching the edges of the dark cloud. On and off. Over and over. Never-ending.

Welcome to the Motel Loba. No vacancy. Enjoy your stay…

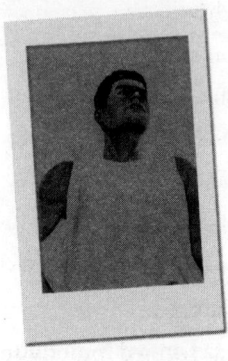

2 | Ellis

What the fuck?

One moment, Ellis was walking towards the reception. The next – a wall of hot air smacked him in the back so hard it lifted him off his feet and threw him face down in the dirt. His ears were ringing; he could still feel the searing heat on his skin.

He knew this feeling – from a year ago, standing on the basketball court, watching as the gym lit up around him, flames coursing across the roof. He felt a tightening deep inside his chest – a hard, fist-sized knot. Fear, maybe? Shock? Who knew? Those were all just words. It was the sensation he remembered – the pure, physical sensation of danger.

He was all right, he told himself sharply. He was alive. Instinctively, he rubbed his shoulder; the rough, patterned burn scars on his skin were sensitive to his touch, the nerves still raw after a year.

Shake it off. He pulled himself up. *You're fine. Get the fuck up.*

He could hear a voice. Someone was coming.

"Jesus – Ellis, are you okay?" Hands reached for him. Black fingernails. Raya Mori. He brushed her away roughly.

"I'm...fine," he managed to say. "The driver...he was back there..." Ellis waved his hand in the direction of the bus. He just needed a moment; everything was still spinning.

Heavy, grey smoke billowed out from the bus frame. Deep in its shadow, a dark outline moved towards them – Benny.

Ellis watched as Raya ran to him. He could make out someone else too, someone big – maybe Caden? The two of them grabbed the driver and dragged him a safe distance from the flames.

Benny was coughing over and over but seemed otherwise unharmed. He slumped on the ground, his hands planted on either side for support, a comical expression of shock on his red face.

"My...my bus!"

"Are you all right? Are you hurt?" Raya kneeled next to him, her hand resting on his shoulder. Caden lurked over them both awkwardly, shuffling nervously from foot to foot. Benny was obviously fine and loving the attention.

"Yeah, yeah. I'm all good...but my bus! What am I gonna do? I'll lose my job, for sure." What little hair he had left was standing on end, ash covering his face and hands.

The shock was loosening its grip on Ellis now, giving way to a surge of pure anger. How could something like this happen? He could have *died*.

"You *should* lose your fucking job," he snarled. "Buses don't just explode for no reason, do they? A few minutes earlier and we would have all been killed." Clearly, someone was to blame. Someone had to be guilty. That was how Ellis's world worked. Bad things didn't just happen to him.

"Ellis, back off," Raya snapped. "We don't know what happened. Maybe the bus overheated on the drive or something? Just give

Benny a freaking break – he nearly died."

"*I* nearly fucking died!" Ellis clenched his fists tightly. He did not like Raya Mori. Plain and simple. He hadn't liked her before she transitioned, with her ridiculous mullet and oversized jorts. He didn't like her now with her short black hair, kohl-ringed eyes and piercings that shouldn't be legal. *Emo witch.*

He was simmering dangerously; he could feel it. The adrenaline from the aftershock was taking over. His self-control was slipping.

The others were approaching, running over from the reception. He pulled himself up. This was not the time or place to lose it.

Think of Father in court, he told himself. He pictured the calm poise and sheer magnificence of his father – Grant Locke, the brilliant criminal defence lawyer, stalking around a courtroom, controlling the air, commanding everyone's attention. He was magnificent, like a real-life Avenger. On the raw edge between handsome and cruel.

Pull yourself together. Be like Father. He reached down and touched his expensive-looking Rolex, his fingers stroking the smooth watch face.

By now, the others had arrived in a cloud of hysteria. Jade was freaking out loudly. Jax was filming everything. Danny's twin sister and Alex hovered near the bus driver, who was prattling on in his ridiculous accent about his "poor dang bus". Ellis blocked them all out, only half-listening while they got it out of their systems. He turned his back to them and watched as the fire burned itself out, until his heartbeat slowed to normal, until the panic subsided.

Now that the imminent danger had passed, the reality of their situation was sinking in, and one by one they fell quiet. Ellis nodded to himself, flexing his hands. There was no question in his mind about who was in charge. Benny – the only adult here (and he used the term loosely) – was clearly incapable of managing himself, let alone seven teenagers trapped in a deserted motel with an exploding bus. No – it was go time. The situation called for a real leader and Ellis was ready.

He turned to face the group.

"Is anyone hurt?" He had a natural, easy authority, and knew it. No one said anything, a few heads shook. "All right, good. Is everyone here?" Heads nodded. He looked around, double-checking. All seven plus Benny. All present.

"Ellis, what are we supposed to do?" Jade dusted off her tiny Lululemon shorts and checked herself on her phone camera; her carefully curated perfection was firmly back in place now the shock had worn off. "Seriously. How are we going to get home? We can't even call an Uber. This really sucks!"

There was a murmur of agreement.

"There's not much we can do. The bus is gone, it's almost dark and the nearest town is miles away. We can keep looking for a cell signal. But in the meantime, we might as well check in for the night and make the best of it." He kept it direct and simple – commanding. A chip off the old block.

"Wait, you don't mean we're staying *here* tonight?" Jax said, a flash of panic in his beautiful green eyes. "I have to upload today. Like, for real."

The chorus started up.

"I won't stay here," Jade said flatly. "It's filthy and—"

"There's no Wi-Fi," Jax added unhelpfully.

"No food," Caden grunted.

"Anyone seen *Psycho*?" Raya grinned.

"All right, enough!" Ellis barked. He looked around at the expectant faces. "We don't have any choice, do we? Like it or not, we have to stay – for now, at least. We'll leave in the morning. *Are we clear?*"

There were reluctant stirrings of assent.

"So unfair," Jade griped, under her breath.

"*Fuck's sake,* Jade," Ellis snapped, the last of his patience gone. "Get over yourself. It's not my fault the driver drove us to the wrong motel."

Benny muttered a half-hearted squeak of protest.

"Actually...we are in the right place," a small voice cut in. It was Danny's twin sister, his dull little shadow. What was her name again? Emma? Anna? Ellis honestly couldn't remember and cared less.

"What do you want, Danny's sister?" he said sharply. She wilted a little under his glare.

"It's just that...I found something." She held out a small pink envelope. "This was in the reception office. It's addressed to us. We were expected."

Ellis glared at her. Even though she was boring, quiet and totally irrelevant, there was a touch of *something* about her. A small flash of Danny in her eyes, her voice, maybe the way she turned her head. Like an after-image, a living reminder.

He snatched the envelope out of her hand, noting the distinctive scarring across her palm – he wasn't the only one marked by the fire. Quickly he turned his back to her, preferring to look anywhere else, as he tore open the envelope.

Inside was a card with a picture of pink roses bathed in a sickly, yellow light. It looked perfectly innocent, if a little tacky. As he opened the card a twenty-dollar bill fell to the ground. He bent down and picked it up.

A shadow crossed his face.

"What is it already?" Jade asked impatiently, her voice sounding a touch less bored than usual.

Ellis rubbed his face, then held the card out for everyone to see. Printed inside was a generic message: *Happy 1st Anniversary.* Someone had handwritten a message below it: *Only the truth will set you free.*

"Seriously?" Jade scrumpled up her nose in confusion. "What's that even mean? And what's with 'happy anniversary'? *Happy?* I'm sorry but that's messed up."

She had a point. Tomorrow would be exactly one year since the fire. If someone knew they were from St Francis High, then they had to know about the fire – about the deaths, didn't they? Ellis looked around at the worried faces.

"Look, I don't know. It's nothing. Probably the only card they could get on short notice." He suddenly needed to get away from the smouldering bus – from these idiots. He handed the card back to Danny's sister, discreetly slipping the twenty-dollar bill into his pocket. His hands were starting to shake a little. He folded his arms before anyone could see. Show no weakness. "Let's go and check in. First come, first served," he added.

That got them going. Jade grabbed Jax by the hand and practically took off for the reception, closely followed by the others.

Ellis waited until they'd all left, turning to look at the bus; red embers glowed through the hollowed-out windows, like a row of fiery eyes glaring back at him. The truth was, he didn't know what was happening here. Maybe the bus had overheated. Maybe the motel was just a cheap rip-off, and the card was an unfortunate coincidence. Maybe there were perfectly logical explanations for all of this. It was just…it didn't feel right.

He put his hand into his pocket, his fingers playing with the twenty-dollar bill, pulling at the edges. He swallowed nervously.

Clearly, someone wanted them here. They were stumbling forward, figuring things out as they went. But the inescapable fact was – they were trapped at the Motel Loba. Maybe tomorrow things would sort themselves out. But for now, for tonight, they were playing someone's game, and they didn't know the rules.

3 | Ana

"Hey, neighbour."

Ana froze. This was not good. She glanced up to see Alex unlocking the door next to hers. What were the odds he'd be in the room next door? She'd waited until the others had chosen their rooms before grabbing a random key. Mentally she kicked herself for not paying more attention.

"Destined to always be neighbours, right?" Alex said. He seemed nervous.

"Looks like it." Ana bit her lip, avoiding eye contact. This was going to be awkward. She had spent the best part of a year listening at her door every time she went out, just to be sure she wouldn't run into Alex in the hallway between their apartments. Now here he was, front and centre, for three whole days. Unavoidable.

"Want help with that?" Alex nodded to the key. She was violently jamming it into the lock. Damn thing wouldn't budge.

"No, er…I'm good." This was the closest she'd been to him in months. He was taller than he used to be. She hadn't noticed from a distance, but standing here she could sense the change. The angles were all wrong. She had to crane her neck to look up at him.

That wasn't the only thing that had changed. After a year of hanging out with the beautiful people, he'd started to look like one of them. His chest and arms had filled out, his Lakers T-shirt was stretched tight in all the right places, his face was squarer – there were still traces of the boy she knew, but they were impermanent, brief flashes. He wasn't a kid any more. He really wasn't.

Ana blushed.

"Hey, um, I won't keep you," Alex said. "I just...I wanted to ask how Carmen's doing? I haven't seen her about much these days."

"Er...good. Fine. Mom's fine. Yes. Thanks for asking."

Ana used the term "fine" loosely, as in "still functioning, despite the death of her only son, loss of her job and an over-reliance on antidepressants". Her mom wasn't the same person that Alex used to know. But then, who was?

"Okay, sure. That's good." Alex's voice was quiet. He knew Ana wanted to get away from him, it was obvious. The hurt registered in his eyes. His eyes – the only thing that hadn't changed about him. The same soft brown, gentle eyes. God, everything about him hurt. Everything stirred up stuff she couldn't face.

The stupid lock wouldn't open. She yanked hard on the door, pulling it towards the jamb and tried the key again and again.

It was starting, the way it always started. A noise, a roar was beginning somewhere in her head behind her ears. With all the drama – the bus exploding and the creepy card, she could feel how close she was to the edge. At least a year of therapy with the incompetent school psychologist, Mr Dankman, had taught her one useful thing; she knew when she was hitting her limits.

It would be okay. She could handle this, she told herself. She'd done it before, too many times to count. She just *really* needed to be alone, now.

"Hey, some of the guys were thinking of meeting up by the pool later," Alex said, nodding in the direction of the fenced area in the middle of the parking lot. "You know…blow off some steam, make the most of this whole situation. I thought I'd go for a bit. I don't really want to be sitting alone in my room tonight, tomorrow being the anniversary and all. I thought you might want to come…if you wanted company or something?"

Alex had managed to say the entire thing without looking up at her. At least that was one thing. If he'd seen her face, he might have noticed it in her eyes. The memories.

Danny and Alex.

They used to be inseparable, the scholarship kids who rode the bus for an hour every day from Receida to the posh suburb of La Cholla. Always hanging out after school in the kitchen, Danny goofing off, Alex writing songs for their band, Trash Dogs. Laughing, easy, together. All that ended the day Danny died.

The roar was getting louder. It was now or never. If she hurt his feelings, she'd have to make up for it later. Better than letting him see her have a full-blown panic attack.

"Okay, sure. Yeah, I'll come…thanks," she mumbled. With immense relief, the key finally clicked, and she swung open the door, pointedly stepping inside.

"Great." Alex smiled.

"Sure." Ana nodded.

"See you."

"Yeah."

"Okay, bye."

"Bye."

Oh, god. Ana pushed the door firmly shut and for a long moment stood, her back to the jamb, listening to her heart beating fast and hard, willing it to slow down.

The room was dark; strips of faint light from the road sign flashed through the crooked blinds, alternating red and yellow lights catching the edges of the bed, the nightstand, a single chair backed against the wall. It was basic, utilitarian stuff, dated and unbearably stuffy – but private, nonetheless. Grateful for the space, Ana switched on the lamp and pulled the blinds shut.

Flinging her bag onto the floral bedspread, she headed for the bathroom. A blisteringly hot shower should fix her right up. She just had to keep busy. She could do that. She was an expert at keeping busy.

Turning on the shower, she adjusted it to the hottest setting she could bear. Then she flung her clothes in a pile and stepped into the steaming water, gasping with shock as it singed her skin. It was good; it was what she needed.

Ana tilted her whole head back under the water and let it form rivulets down her face, along the sides of her nose, her chin. She stood like that for a long time, until the heat made her body protest, weakly, tempting her to slump down and melt onto the tiled floor. But she wouldn't. She had spent enough time curled up on the floor, this past year. She was stronger now. The grief had forced her to grow up.

Leaves, broken glass, a can of green paint. The vivid images caught her, flashing before her eyes. She pushed them away.

Keep busy, her head warned her.

She stepped out of the shower and wrapped up in a stiff pink towel. Wiping the steam off the mirror, she looked at herself. Her distinctive hazel eyes stared back.

In all ways but one, the twins took after their mother. Carmen Reyes had grown up in the Dominican Republic, moving to California the day she turned eighteen, in search of new adventures. She got one more than she planned for when, shortly after arriving, she fell pregnant and began her brand-new life as a single mom.

The twins had inherited their mother's easy nature and good looks – thick, wavy hair and a wide smile. But their eyes were the one thing they owned from their father. Every time Ana looked in a mirror she saw a piece of him – a reflection of the stranger from a lost night seventeen years ago. Unlike their mother's warm brown eyes, his legacy was absorbing and ever-changing – brilliant hazel eyes that took on the myriad colours of the world around them, blue, green, gold. Danny's eyes.

Ana looked away.

Turning on the faucet, she filled her cupped hands with refreshingly cool water. The hot shower had irritated the burn scars on her palms, turning them a brilliant red. They appeared raw and angry, the way they'd looked in the hospital when the bandages had first come off. She held her hands under the running water for a few long moments, turning them around and around until the painful itching subsided.

The mirror had misted up again, making her reflection a blurry haze of pinks and browns. Something dark caught Ana's attention, at the top of the reflection. She turned around and checked for the source.

There it was, in the top corner of the bathroom wall. A small black dot, no bigger than a pencil eraser. Whoever had put it there wasn't very subtle. Against some trim or behind the shower, it would have been impossible to see, but in the corner between the pastel walls, it stood out easily.

A bad feeling in her stomach, Ana walked up to the corner, clambering onto the rim of the tub for a better look. Light reflected off the small round object recessed in a tidy hole. Its black mesh surface was shiny, and unlike everything else in the motel, appeared to be new. It wasn't a camera – maybe some kind of tiny microphone? It was carefully embedded in the wall, silently listening to everything she was doing, to every sound she made. She recoiled, almost losing her balance, instinctively pulling the towel up tight around her.

This was not good – not good at all. It could only mean one thing.

Someone was spying on them.

4 | Alex

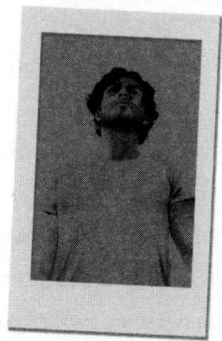

The night air was working its magic on Alex.

Several long hours after arriving, he was starting to feel human again. He was a lousy traveller. It didn't matter if it was a car, bus or boat. It was embarrassing. Once he'd even vomited on a roller coaster in front of half his grade. Danny had never let him live that down.

At least he wouldn't have to go back on the bus again, Alex told himself, even though it was small consolation. Pausing outside the pool area, he looked across at the black outline of the burned-out bus and shivered slightly.

Adjusting his guitar strap over his shoulder, he pushed the rusted pool gate open and stepped inside.

Maybe once, a long time ago, this place had been the main attraction of the motel – somewhere to escape the day's harsh heat and cool off under the shade of the lone palm tree. But as with everything else in the Motel Loba, it was a shadow of its former glory. The small pool was completely dry, red sand accumulating in the corners under rusted pieces of broken loungers and sun umbrellas. Discarded pool furniture and faded blue tiles were strewn around the enclosure. Strings of broken Christmas tree lights hung off the fence like barbed wire.

A fire was burning in the bottom of the pool; dancing shadows lit up the walls, flickering in and out of focus, creating golden ripples. Ellis was sitting on a diving board high above everyone, talking loudly, but no one was paying much attention. Jax was standing by the fire, throwing pieces of old, desiccated wood into the flames with one hand while simultaneously filming himself with the other. Jade was lying stretched out on a beach towel nearby, wearing a white micro bikini, despite the chilly air. She was the spitting image of her beautiful movie-star mother, the rom-com queen Jennifer Clark, and she knew it, flaunting her second-hand celebrity every chance she got. She waved at Alex and smiled, dropping her head coyly to one side.

He swallowed nervously, grateful that it was dark. Walking to the pool edge, he lightly jumped in, settling himself a safe distance from the fire, on the far side to Jade.

Carefully, he unclipped his guitar case. He was the entertainment, and that was fine by him. It was simpler this way. When he was playing he didn't have to make conversation.

These were Danny's friends. Alex understood that. But they were pretty nice and seemed to like him well enough. After the fire, after the news stories and rumours about him had started circulating and people began to avoid him in the hallway, they'd been good to him – they'd kept him around. Having somewhere to go and people to hang with had meant more than he cared to admit.

"No cars, no one here, no other guests. All very convenient, right?" Ellis muttered to himself, a line of empty minibar vodka bottles stacked neatly beside him. He was flipping a coin high in the air and catching it easily, over and over. "Something is very wrong about this – you mark my words."

"What's the big deal, Ellis?" Jade said with a sigh. "Seriously. Tomorrow we'll get out of here and we'll never have to think about this awful place again."

"As usual, your tiny little brain is not seeing the big picture, Jade. The bus exploding, the anniversary card…something is off about this." Ellis stood up and started bouncing up and down on the diving board. The bottles scattered and rolled off.

There was a pent-up, dangerous energy about Ellis tonight. Alex had seen it at parties plenty of times over the last year. Ever since the fire, he always seemed to be angry, as though there was still something smouldering, slow-burning inside him, looking for a way to explode.

Ellis's steel grey eyes roved restlessly around the pool enclosure, pausing on a dark corner under the solitary palm tree. He smiled.

"Well, well. Caden Loftus. There's something I've been meaning to ask you."

For the first time, Alex noticed Caden lurking in the deep shadows by the fence. He must have just arrived. He had his hands in his pockets and was kicking at pieces of broken furniture. He looked up when Ellis said his name – a deer in headlights.

"Why are you on this trip, Loft-ass? Weren't you expelled from St Francis last year? Let me see, what was it…oh, yes – didn't you sell Karl Hunt drugs, right before he got off his face and set fire to the whole fucking school?"

Alex felt sick hearing *that* name.

Caden didn't respond. He just shifted slightly on the spot. The flickering firelight lit his face from below, contorting his features into a fierce expression.

"Of course," Ellis continued, "even *you* can see why that would be confusing for us. I mean, you get Hunt high, right before he decides to burn the school gym down during the biggest game of the year. He kills himself and *two* of our friends. Then you get expelled, and now...you're here on a school trip with us?" Ellis's eyes were firmly locked on Caden – he was enjoying himself.

"I wasn't expelled," Caden growled. His voice was low and dangerous. "I did a semester at military school."

"Is that what they're calling juvie these days?"

"Screw you, Ellis. There's no proof..."

"No, screw you, Loft-ass. We don't need proof, do we? Not really. Because everybody knows what you did. The press released Karl Hunt's autopsy. He was toasted, and there was only one person selling pills at the game that night." Ellis could smell blood. "Danny and Maia *died*, and I've got to live with these for the rest of my life." Ellis yanked his jersey up, revealing hard ridges of burn scars across the side of his chest and his shoulder.

"*Hunt* started the fire. *Not me*," Caden bellowed. He was roving around the tree like an angry bear, agitated. "I hardly knew him. He was one of *your* friends, Ellis. One of your stupid Wolves."

"One of *my* stupid Wolves?" Ellis unfolded like a snake.

Alex winced. Caden had made a rookie error, insulting St Francis High's legendary basketball team, the Wolves, in front of its star player. Even Jax turned the camera away from himself for once, so he could film the confrontation – just in case things got good.

"Karl Hunt was a murdering psycho who got thrown off the team for being a junkie loser. He didn't buy drugs from *me*, Loft-ass. He went to *you* – another junkie loser. Game recognizes game."

"It wasn't my fault! You got something to say, come here. Say it to my face," Caden yelled. He picked up a metal chair frame and flung it hard against the fence.

Ellis laughed.

It was too easy. Ellis was spoiling for a fight. He obviously hadn't had enough exercise sitting on a bus all day. There was no gym here, so he would get his cardio beating the shit out of someone – a bit of light stress relief.

"Oh my god, get over yourselves," Jade snapped. "Ellis, just chill. We've got enough problems being stuck here in this stupid motel without you two acting like a pair of toddlers. Right, Jax?" Jax was standing by the side of the pool, phone propped on the tiled edge, filming Caden from a safe distance. When he didn't answer, Jade sighed deeply. "Hey, Alex. Play something happy. Ellis has been on *such* a downer tonight."

Alex already had his guitar on his knee, his floppy hair tucked behind his ears. As he started playing, he felt instantly calmer, instantly better. He could sense the tension lifting as the notes floated on the air. With the skill of a seasoned performer, he worked his magic, switching it up, catching the mood. It wasn't long before the music took hold of the moment; the pent-up, angry energy diffused, fading away into the darkness.

Soon enough, Caden turned away and started kicking at the furniture again, the argument forgotten.

But Ellis didn't move. He remained fixed to the spot, head down, glaring around him. Alex felt a sharp tug of anxiety. He'd been around Ellis long enough to know that this negative energy had to go somewhere, to blow itself out; if it didn't happen here and now, then it was sure to come out later.

Turning back to his guitar, Alex's fingers uncharacteristically fumbled the notes. He made a mental note to stay away from Ellis on this trip; he was a live wire waiting to be tripped.

Drunk, angry and dangerous.

Primed.

5 | Ana

It was almost midnight.

Ana and Raya were walking slowly towards the pool, playing Spot the Dot. Ever since she'd found the microphone in her bathroom, Ana kept noticing more and more small black dots everywhere – in corners, under lampshades, behind picture frames, in plant pots. The dots in the bathrooms were microphones, but more worryingly, the rest of them looked like cameras. The whole motel was wired.

Raya was completely unconcerned.

"How can someone be spying on us if there's no one else here?" She was mugging around in front of the newest discovery – a tiny black dot above the pool gate. "Think about it, Ana – all this spy shit is probably ancient and hasn't worked in decades. I reckon the motel was a skank brothel in a past life. That would explain the cameras, not to mention the pink roses and ick everywhere."

Ana laughed and pushed the pool gate open.

Raya had a point. Creepy spyware in a remote motel didn't seem like a stretch; some past, disgruntled employee making a little side cash at the expense of the guests. This whole place was abandoned, the cameras along with everything else. There was no reason to worry about it. It probably had absolutely nothing to do with them. Probably.

Everyone else was already at the empty pool. Ellis was sitting sullenly on his diving-board throne. Jade was lounging by the fire, Jax next to her – one hand on the small of her back, one hand on his phone. Caden was lurking in the shadows, watching everyone silently. Alex had his back against the tiled wall and was playing his guitar, his profile illuminated softly by the firelight. His face was still, almost restful – he was in the zone.

Ana tried to look anywhere else, but her eyes kept coming back to him, seeking him out. Raya must have noticed.

"Gotta say it. Your Alex has had a major glow-up," she said, just a little too loudly. "I was checking him out on the bus. I'm totally digging his whole if-Timothée-Chalamet-was-Mexican-and-played-a-guitar vibe."

"He's not *my* Alex," Ana protested, willing Raya to shut up. She pointedly headed to the shallow end, and they sat down on the pool edge, which was as far from the others as they could get in the undersized pool. "If anything, he's one of *them* now." Ana nodded towards the beautiful crowd.

"Come on, Ana. You know Alex couldn't give a shit about being popular. He's just too nice to say no to anyone, and the cool kids have decided he's talented enough to make them look good." She nudged Ana with her shoulder. "If you went up to him now and said 'hi', he'd follow you around for the rest of the trip like a lost puppy."

"I don't want him to follow me around."

Raya gave a sharp laugh and pulled out a mini bottle of gin that she'd pilfered from Ana's fridge. She cracked it open and took a sip.

"Just sayin'."

Ana sighed and checked her phone: 11.58 p.m. Two minutes to go. Part of her wanted to leave and run back to her room – just hide away until tomorrow. But a bigger part needed to be here, to feel the light, to see people, to hear Alex play. When it got to midnight – when the anniversary finally arrived, she didn't want to be alone.

She pulled her hoodie close around her. There was a chill in the air that she hadn't felt before.

"You holding up all right?" Raya nodded at her phone. She must have noticed the time. "Tomorrow's going to be a rough day for all of us. But it's got to be worse for you."

"It's just a date, right? Just another day. I mean who cares if it's been one year, or a year and a day, or ten years?" Ana tried to brush off the conversation.

"I know, but still. I can't imagine what you must be feeling. You lost so much…"

"I'm fine," Ana said shortly. They didn't need to go there. There was nothing anyone could say. She shifted slightly away from Raya, hoping she'd let it go. Ever since they had dated briefly in sophomore year, Raya had a knack for knowing what Ana was thinking, sometimes even before Ana did.

A deep tiredness was settling over her. Maybe she should have just stayed in her room. It might have been easier. No need to talk. No need to pretend.

She checked the phone screen again: 11.59 p.m.

It wasn't like anything would change just because it had been a year, she told herself. This was her life now and nothing was ever going to fix that. Nothing was going to turn back time or bring

Danny back. There were no second chances. She watched dispassionately as the last seconds counted down, ticking away the worst year of her life.

It doesn't mean anything. It's just a date – just a jumble of stupid numbers. Nothing more.

12.00 a.m.

And there it was. Finally.

The anniversary. She was still breathing, wasn't she? *Life goes on.*

Ping.

The alert made her jump. A message? How was that even possible? They didn't have any phone reception.

On cue, there was a roar from the deep end.

"Oh my god, we have cell!"

"I got a message!"

"Me too."

"Yaaaaasss!"

The elation was short-lived, the voices dropping off one by one as they studied their phone screens.

"Wait, I don't have any bars."

"This doesn't make any sense..."

"What the hell?"

Ana clicked on the notification and opened the message. The formatting was off. It wasn't a text or snap. The font was different, the background was black and the letters green and oversized. What was clear, was the message:

**KARL HUNT LIT THE MATCH,
BUT YOU ARE ALL GUILTY.**

"Did you get the same thing?" she asked. Raya nodded. Ana glanced around to see if someone was secretly texting, but no one was.

"I don't understand…I'm not getting any reception. How did we even get a message?" Raya's voice had an edge to it.

"Maybe it's a mistake?" Ana asked, though she already knew it wasn't. "Or perhaps it's an old message that just came through." She was reaching, they both knew it.

There was another *ping*. Another message. They looked at each other briefly before turning to their screens.

I KNOW WHAT YOU DID A YEAR AGO. NOW IT IS TIME TO PAY THE PRICE.

"What…I mean…why?" Ana was lost for words. Who would do something like this? Who would send creepy messages today, on the anniversary? She felt a rising wave of panic.

I know what you did…

It had to be a prank, or a sick joke. Didn't it?

She turned to Raya, but before they could speak there was another *ping*. Ana jumped, almost dropping her phone. The new message was longer – much longer and much worse. She read it slowly, carefully, rereading parts as she took time to process.

When she was finally done, she put the phone down on the pool edge, pulled her hood up and wrapped her arms around herself, a feeling of cold, blind fear stealing through her.

Ellis was the first to speak.

"What did I tell you all?" he said. "Didn't I say it? We're in trouble. We're in so much fucking trouble."

TODAY AT 9.58 A.M. YOU'RE GOING TO PLAY THE BALLOON GAME. EVERY HOUR YOU MUST CHOOSE WHO IS THE GUILTIEST AMONG YOU. BEFORE THE HOUR ENDS, THAT PERSON MUST LEAVE THE CIRCLE WHERE THEY WILL BE SHOT. IF NO ONE LEAVES, ALL OF YOU WILL DIE. ONLY ONE CAN SURVIVE. HAPPY ANNIVERSARY.

6 | Ana

"It can't be right. I mean, what freaking circle?" Raya wondered out loud. "There's no circle here. It must be a mistake. Right?"

All seven students were gathered around the fire now – all needing to be together, to be a part of whatever came next. Only Benny was absent; he hadn't emerged from his room since he'd got the key.

Ana shivered, despite the heat from the flames.

"Why the fuck do you think it's a mistake?" Ellis blurted out. He was squatting close to the fire, fidgeting with a quarter, rolling it across his knuckles, one way and then back again. "Look around. There's no one else here. Our bus has been destroyed. We're in the middle of nowhere. This message is clearly not a mistake."

As Ellis said it, Ana knew he was right. Nothing about this was accidental. They were being played – some strange, twisted game.

You are all guilty.

Guilty. The word burned through Ana. Had someone found out what she'd done? How could they? There were only two people who knew what really happened a year ago.

Danny couldn't have told anyone. He never woke up after the fire.

The other person wouldn't tell anyone – not without betraying patient confidentiality. In a moment of stupid weakness, a few weeks after the fire, Ana tried to talk to Mr Dankman during one of their mandatory therapy sessions, only to have him paraphrase it as "survivor's guilt" and send her home with a prescription for Zoloft and the unhelpful suggestion that she get some sleep. Even though she had a pretty low opinion of Dankman's skills as a therapist, she couldn't see him intentionally revealing her confession. Though, to be fair, he might have said something by mistake. Maybe to another patient or student, or one of the teachers? There was just no way of knowing.

Or maybe someone had found out another way? Had someone seen her? Had someone else been there a year ago? The thought made Ana feel physically sick. She looked around at the others. If she was actually guilty, then what did that mean about the rest of them? Were they all guilty too? What secrets were they hiding?

Seven survivors on this trip. Was it possible that a year ago, *each* of them had done something. Something bad enough to die for?

The shadows from the firelight were dancing across their faces making their expressions morph and contort, rendering them unrecognizable. How well did she even know them? Any of them? What were they capable of? What had they done? Ellis, Jade, Jax, Caden... She looked around at the ring of faces. Raya. Alex.

No.

She shook her head, as though the thoughts might fall away. She was playing into the trap, allowing herself to think that way. Whoever sent the message was manipulating them, wanting them to doubt each other, to feel afraid. She had to be stronger than that. She had to do better, think clearer. Whatever this was, it was just getting started and she was going to need her wits about her.

"It's gotta be a joke, right?" Jade asked. Her voice sounded small and childlike. She was pushed up against Jax, his arm around her.

"Yeah, for sure. It's a prank. It's gotta be a YouTube thing." Jax was nodding vigorously to himself, as though that would make it true. "Loads of content creators post stuff like this all the time. Last one to leave the circle wins a suitcase of money. We're probably being filmed right now."

"I found a microphone in my bathroom," Ana said quickly. "And there are hidden cameras all over this place." As soon as the message arrived, she'd ditched Raya's theory that the small black dots were a relic from the past. From now on, she would assume that they were being watched – at all times.

"Oh my god, me too!" Jade added. "I found a mic over the mirror – it totally creeped me out."

"There were cameras in the reception," Alex said. "I saw, like, maybe...three?"

"See?" Jax said, vindicated. "Someone's trying to record this from every angle. We're totally being filmed. It's a prank."

"Just because there are cameras doesn't mean we're being filmed. It means we're being watched, doofus," Ellis said. "Do you honestly think anyone would be stupid enough to take a group of school-fire survivors and publicly torture them for fun? You'd get cancelled if you tried to pull that kind of shit."

Jax scrunched up his face in thought as he tried to follow Ellis's reasoning.

"Maybe it's some kind of secret government experiment?" Raya piped up. "I bet there's like some hallucinogenic shit in the air that's messing with our heads. Or some bored motel employee who's been hitting up the home-brewed mescalin and decided to play a twisted mind game on a busload of heteronormative rich kids." Raya laughed. She seemed to be enjoying herself far too much.

"For fuck's sake, Raya," Ellis cut in. "You need to lay off the weed and grow up. Mescalin? Jesus Christ." He kicked a piece of burning wood.

"Dude, *you* need to cut down on the steroids," Raya retorted, her tone instantly hardening. She could flip on a dime, from guard down to defensive warrior queen. Ana got it. Raya had learned to protect herself; it hadn't been easy being the only openly trans kid in the whole high school.

"Don't tell me what to do," Ellis growled.

"Roid rage getting to you?"

"No. *You* are getting to me," Ellis snapped back. There was no humour in his tone. He was angry and getting angrier by the second.

"Maybe we need to focus on what we *do* know, not what we *don't*, okay?" Ana cut in, moving between Raya and Ellis. "I think I know what the Balloon Game is. They played it on the debate team."

As part of her scholarship deal, Ana had been roped into joining the hugely unpopular debate team, aka social death in an orange-and-grey striped polo shirt. Other than Maia Walsh, the team captain, Ana had been the only girl on the team, alongside a group of nerdy boys, and a handful of slackers who were forced to participate as punishment for various infringements. Karl Hunt was one of them.

"It's a morality game. You imagine you're on a hot-air balloon and there's a leak. The balloon is sinking, and you'll all die unless you throw someone overboard. Each round, you have to debate who deserves to live, and who doesn't. Then you vote. Each round, another person dies."

She stopped, suddenly aware of what she had just said. The real-life implication of her words was not lost on them.

"So, you're saying the motel is the balloon? We're all trapped here, and some psycho wants us to vote who leaves the motel every hour? They want us to choose who dies?" Raya said, her tone incredulous.

Ana nodded. This was insane.

"Wait! It's *Survivor*!" Jax declared loudly. "Holy cow, we're playing *Survivor*! Who will leave the island? I told you! It's a game. It's all a game. I'm so into this. Where's Jeff? Show me the money! I'm totally gonna win this one." Jax was shouting now.

"Seriously, Jax – you're so right. It's *Survivor*. *Desert Survivor*. Oh my god, it *is* a game." Jade clasped her hands in delight, immaculate nails clattering against each other. "Got to say it, babe, I was a little worried, you know?"

Ana watched in disbelief. How had they joined the dots and come up with *Survivor*? Someone had set up the structure for them to self-destruct. They had provided the rules for murder.

"Look, whether it's a game or not, we know that someone went to a lot of effort to set this up. We know that we were all chosen to come here for a reason – all seven of us." She hesitated before saying the next part; she didn't want to throw Benny under his bus, but anything was better than standing around listening to conspiracy theories all night long.

Besides, the one thing they needed more than anything else right now was information.

"The other thing we know for a fact is that only one person here has no connection to St Francis High. That might be a good place to start looking for some answers. I think it's time we talked to Benny."

7 | Ana

On the scale of scary things that wake you in the night, seven angry high schoolers bashing on your door was right up there with creepy clowns and broken-necked ladies. At least it was for Benny.

When he opened the door, his red face had an almost comical expression – somewhere between abject terror and resignation. But, to his credit, he rallied quickly.

"Whad'ya think y'all doing banging on my door like a pack a banshees? I was gettin' my beauty sleep," he grumbled, his eyes watchful, uncertain. He was still wearing his uniform, belt undone now.

Ellis didn't stop to explain, he pushed his way past Benny and led the charge into the motel room.

The room was just as dated and funky as the rest of the motel, but oddly it suited Benny. He looked like he was in his natural environment. Shabby and stale. The air reeked of cigarettes and alcohol; clearly, he'd raided his minibar too; several bottles were lying empty on the bed.

"We need answers," Ellis said, thrusting his phone in front of Benny's face.

Benny squinted at the screen, mouthing out the words as he read:

"*You are all guilty...play the Balloon Game...* What's going on? What's all that about, then?" He scratched his bald spot, looking flummoxed.

It took a solid few minutes of explanation to get him to catch up. He kept asking for bits of information to be repeated and then squinted his eyes as though that would help it seep in. Finally, he seemed to get it.

"Phew," he muttered, sinking down on the end of the bed. "I dunno, but that sure don't sound good."

"Really? You think?" Ellis said coolly. He was unnaturally still, arms folded across his chest, studying Benny's face. "Show us your phone."

"My phone? Why? All this ain't got nothin' to do with me. What you wanna see my phone for?"

"Why do you think? To see if you sent the fucking messages!"

Benny looked around at the expectant faces and shrugged resignedly. The banshees outnumbered him. He nodded at the dresser. An old-style flip phone was charging next to a pile of change, an orange keychain with the letters "HT", and a box of Lucky Strike cigarettes resting on top of a folded piece of paper. Jade snatched the phone up and flipped it open.

"Passcode?" she demanded.

"6969."

"Ugh, seriously?" Jade unlocked the phone, holding it gingerly, as though she might catch something from it. She tapped on the screen several times. "There's no message, and nothing recently sent or deleted either," she said.

Well, at least that was some information. Benny hadn't sent the message, but he also hadn't received it. Whatever was going on, he wasn't invited to play this game.

"Look, I dunno what y'all got yourselves into here, but I ain't no part of any of this. I'm not responsible for y'all. Whatever kinda trouble y'all are in, ain't nothin' to do with me. I ain't no babysitter. I was hired to drive y'all here and that's what I did. Just doing my job." Benny looked on edge.

Ellis laughed drily.

"Really? *Your job?* Well, it turns out your job involved kidnapping a group of teenagers and trapping them in a remote motel."

"*Kidnap!* I didn't kidnap...I...this ain't fair! This ain't my fault! I got nothin' to do with all this...I'm a bus driver is all. Just drivin' my bus..."

Ellis was clenching and unclenching his fist; he looked about ready to lose it, and Benny was in the line of fire.

Ana stepped forward quickly.

"It's okay, Benny. We're just trying to figure out what's going on. Do you have any idea who might be behind this, or who hired you to drive the bus?"

"I don't know nothin'!" he said, turning to Ana imploringly. "Look, someone emailed me a work order – they need themselves a minibus and a driver for three days. The money's real good. I mean, *real* good. More than I make in a month. They drop the itinerary in the mailbox and you're good to go – easy money."

"Do you usually take commissions from people you've never met?" Ellis cut in.

"*Commissions?*" Benny gave a short bark of a laugh. "It ain't no *commission*. It's work, payin' work – and, yes, I take any work that comes my way and I'm grateful for it too. Not everyone's rich like y'all. Man's gotta do what a man's gotta do…put food on the table… pay the bills," Benny grumbled.

"Yeah, right. Real salt-of-the-earth stuff. Come on, think. You *must* know something about all this," Ellis said, clearly frustrated.

Benny stood abruptly, chest pushed forward: "You reckon I drove y'all here for what? So's I could blow up *my own bus*? Like I wanna be stuck out here with a bunch a stuck-up, no good, TikTok-lovin', self-obsessed teenagers?"

"Who the fuck are you, Benny-boy? Why should we trust you? We don't know you. You're just a loser with a bus and a messed-up accent. *What's up with the accent?* Trying to pretend you're a New Yorker? Oh, hey, I'm just some regular guy? Well, you're not fooling anyone."

"A New Yorker? Now that's insulting. I'm a bus driver…just a dang bus driver!" Benny was spluttering.

Ellis's fists were firmly clenched, his arms tense. Ready.

This was not going to end well.

Ana wasn't sure what she could do to defuse the situation, but she knew she had to try. They needed more information and beating people up was not going to help.

"I'm sorry, Benny. We're not accusing you. We're just scared." She could feel the electrical presence of Ellis close by, his tight, angry energy filling the room. "Can you think of anything that might help us? Anything at all?"

Benny scratched his head thoughtfully, then reached over to the dresser and picked up the folded piece of paper. Shaking it open, he held it out in front of them.

"Look, here's the work order. I brought a copy in case." He pointedly spoke to Ana.

Ellis snatched the sheet out of his hand and unfolded it. It was a printout of an order placed a month ago and sent to the *Happy Travels Bus Co*. The instructions were clearly entered, just as Benny had described: services of one driver for a three-day trip, a description of the bus, route information to follow. Payment in the amount of five thousand dollars. Deposit of two hundred dollars paid immediately. An additional five hundred for driver expenses.

There was a name at the bottom of the sheet. Order placed by N. Bates.

"*Fuck!*" Ellis snapped, flinging the paper down. "Are you *fucking* kidding me? N. Bates?"

"Wha—" Benny asked, hands raised in confusion. "Y'all know this Bates guy?"

Raya picked up the sheet and scanned it quickly. She started laughing.

"Benny – you got a work order from N. Bates to go to a remote desert motel with a busload of random strangers? *Norman Bates? A motel?* No alarm bells there?" she said, grinning.

"Why would there be? What aren't y'all telling me?"

"Wow. Okay." Raya passed the sheet around. "I guess you're not a fan of old movies. Have you seriously never seen *Psycho*?"

Benny's face fell as he put the pieces together. Clearly, he *had* seen the murderous horror movie set in the remote Bates Motel. The implications weren't totally lost on him. He plonked himself on the edge of the bed and scratched hard at his bald spot.

"It's a joke, right?" Jade said as she read the sheet. "I mean, this just shows that someone's messing around. Like a prank or something..."

"Or we're trapped here by a nutjob with an ironic sense of humour and a taste for vintage movies," Raya said.

"No, listen. Jade's right." Jax snatched the sheet out of Jade's hands. "Think about it. *Psycho*'s a movie, right? A movie – that's gotta be a clue. We're playing a so-called 'game'. We got cameras everywhere filming everything we do? Guys, this proves my point. It's YouTube! It has to be. And whoever's doing this spent serious money on this set-up. Trust me, this isn't some small wannabe influencer. Not naming names, but this is big. I'm talking like a hundred-million-subscribers kind of big, if you know what I mean." Jax lit up, proud of his wayward logic. He beamed radiantly for the invisible cameras. "Guys, smile. We're about to get famous."

"Oh my god. Jax, you're so right," Jade said, all smiles suddenly. "It makes perfect sense. I was wondering why *I* was invited, but now I totally get it."

The mood in the room lightened instantly. At least this half-baked explanation didn't involve getting murdered.

Jax was practically bouncing up and down with excitement.

"This is brilliant," he shouted, turning around to random corners of the room, and flashing his full-kilowatt smile. This was his fantasy, the push he needed to project himself into the social media A-list. If he made a good impression in front of millions of viewers worldwide, he would get verified. "Game on. Let's do this."

"Oh my god, tomorrow is going to be so much fun." Jade was glowing with excitement. "Wait, I need to pick my outfits and my make-up – it's got to be perfect. There's so much to do. Jax, come!" The two of them hustled over to the door, on a mission.

"Norman Bates…cool," Caden mumbled, following them out.

"So, y'all figured it out. Now can I get some sleep?" Benny grumbled, pushing himself back on the bed and plumping up his pillows.

The conversation was over. Time to go to bed.

But as they stepped outside into the cool night air, Ana looked at the remaining people. Raya and Alex were quiet. Ellis was deep in thought. Were they thinking what she was thinking?

It would be so easy to choose to believe Jax's theory. After all, maybe he was right. Was it any more ludicrous than the idea that someone was planning on killing them off one by one?

There was just one small problem.

What if Jax was wrong?

What if they all went to bed, then woke up bright and early, put on their cutest clothes and counted down to the start of the game, only to find out that it wasn't a prank? What then?

They'd have thrown away their one chance to escape.

"I still think we need to leave," Ana said quietly.

"Agreed." Ellis stepped forward and turned to face them; authority restored. "Maybe Jax is right, maybe it's a game – but I for one am not staking my life on his theory."

"Do you think someone will come for us?" Raya asked. "What about our parents? Someone's going to wonder where we are, aren't they?"

Ana shook her head: "It was on the invite. It said that the retreat would have limited cellular, so not to worry if we are out of contact for a while. Whoever brought us here made sure we won't get rescued for at least the next few days."

"Fine, so what's the plan?" Raya asked. "Head off down the road now? Walk through the night? See where we get to?"

Ana did the math in her head.

"The last thing I saw along the road was an old gas station, about half an hour back. At about seventy miles per hour, that would be about thirty-five miles from here. It would take us maybe eight, nine hours if we walk fast. Plus, there are no guarantees it would even be open – it looked kind of deserted."

"No freaking way!" Raya declared. "No way in hell am I walking thirty-five freaking miles. Especially at night in the middle of nowhere, with who knows what kind of wild beasts waiting in the dark to eat us. We'll probably get lost and die out here. They'll find our bones picked over by vultures…"

"Fine. We'll do it in the daytime." Ellis glanced around at them. "Let's go to our rooms, clear out any cameras and get some sleep. If you're worried, you can sleep together. In the morning, anyone who wants to leave can head out early with water and supplies. It'll be a long walk, so rest up. As long as we are out of here before 9.58 a.m., we should be fine."

The others nodded. It was a solid plan. Anything was better than staying in the Motel Loba for another day.

As they walked back to their rooms, Ana briefly considered asking Raya to sleep over. But no one else seemed bothered and she didn't want to look like she was making a big deal out of things. After all, it was going to be okay. They would leave in the morning and never look back. Nothing to worry about.

She paused at her door, and looked around at the road sign, still endlessly flashing. The letters L and the B were off sync, alternating with the O and A: MOTEL L B, MOTEL O A, MOTEL L B… Over and over. Welcome, come and stay, vacancy, a cosy bed for the night – false promises.

"See you in the morning." Alex was back at his door, key in the lock. Despite all the drama, he still had his guitar with him, slung low over his shoulder, his hand resting on it. Like a security blanket. Same old Alex.

Ana forced a smile.

"Yeah. Crazy day, right?"

"Yeah."

"Who'd have thought…"

"I know…"

The words tailed off until there was just space between them. But it wasn't empty, the air felt charged with something electric – something that pulled Ana in. She wanted to lean into it, lean into him, but held herself back, feeling the draw, the need, the desire to move closer, to succumb.

Did he feel it too? He must feel it. There was something. She couldn't be imagining it.

"Well, goodnight," Alex muttered, turning the door handle, and pushing his door wide open.

Ana snapped out of it. She stepped back, reaching in her pocket for her key.

She must be tired and imagining things. Weakness. That's all it was. It had been one hell of a day. Tomorrow was shaping up to be even worse. She just wanted connection. It didn't mean anything.

"Night, Alex," she said briskly.

He went into his room; the door closed.

The moment was gone. Ana opened her door and stared into the musty darkness. How could she sleep? It wasn't possible. There was too much in her head.

She stepped inside and pulled the door shut, locking it carefully behind her. Then she headed to the bathroom and peered around the door at the tiny black dot, high up in the corner. Still there, still listening, the beady little bug – capturing everything.

Picking up a bar of soap, she held it under the faucet until it was foaming. Carefully, she climbed up on the bath surround and wedged the soap hard into the microphone, filling the hole.

No one would hear anything now.

Slowly and systematically, she searched the entire suite, end to end. There was another bug taped to the frame above the mirror, and one more on the bedside lamp. She plucked them out and dropped them into the toilet, flushing them away for good. Next, she dragged the chair over to the door and tipping it at an angle, wedged it under the handle. Finally, she plugged her phone in to charge, ready for whatever tomorrow would bring.

Feeling a little stupid, she lay down on the bed, fully clothed.

She could see the road sign through the gaps between the blinds; the letters lit up red and yellow, stripes of garish colour illuminating the walls around her. The two out-of-sync letters, L and B, were a different font from the rest – more modern-looking, as though they had been recently replaced but no one had bothered to try and match them. They flickered on and off – a lazy, half-assed repair job, uncared for and neglected like everything else in the motel.

There was something oddly relaxing about the discordant rhythm of the winking lights, the contrasting colours flashing on and off like a dangerously irregular heartbeat. For several minutes Ana lay there, silently watching as a deep weariness settled over her. Her eyes felt heavy and the soft mattress pulled her in – but she knew it wouldn't be enough. She wouldn't be sleeping tonight.

Her thoughts wandered.

Was she overreacting? What if Jax was right and this was all some prank?

But then…what if he wasn't right?

Her mind was racing. Alex, the card, the bus exploding, the

message. She couldn't just pretend that everything was okay. Jax might be able to switch off his brain and go with the flow, but she couldn't.

Because there was one thing that wouldn't fade away, that kept playing over and over in her head. One part of this that made her feel, in her heart, that this was not a game. One single inescapable truth:

You are all guilty.

Someone knew what she'd done a year ago. Someone knew what she was capable of. Someone had decided that it was time she paid the price.

8 | Ellis

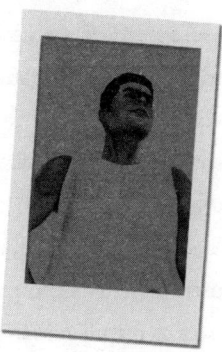

Ellis was up early and pissed.

He didn't care if the whole deal with the message was some sick joke. He was done. He was packing food and water and hitting the road. When he got cell coverage, he was going to call his father and get a ride home.

Fuck this for a laugh.

He dragged his rolling suitcase violently across the red dirt, bouncing it hard into the air as he headed over to the reception. There had to be some food somewhere in this godforsaken hole.

It was early – all pastel colours and deserty blah-blah everywhere. Very beautiful, no doubt. Also, very boring. Ellis had zero interest in scenery. He had set his alarm for an ungodly hour with a plan. He would leave before anyone else woke up. Then he could enjoy a peaceful hike without having to talk to some imbecile, and he would get to be the hero of the day – the brave kid who hiked solo for thirty-five miles to save his classmates. He grinned to himself. His father would like that.

In the reception, he nosed through cabinets and around the counter. Nothing edible. Next, he tried the small office. Just a desk and empty filing cabinets. Useless. He headed back outside and walked around the side of the nauseating pink building. His stomach was rumbling, and he was hangry as all hell by the time he found the snack machine. It was half-stocked with candy bars and chip bags that looked like they'd been there since the previous millennium.

Grabbing the machine by its sides, he shook it hard in an unsuccessful attempt to free some of the snacks. Frustrated, he tried sticking his arm through the slot – a nerdy obsession with magic tricks in middle school had made him remarkably adept with his long fingers, but they barely brushed the corner of a lonely bag of Doritos. Pulling his arm out, he gave the machine a solid kick, squatted low and ran at it, toppling it over sideways with an immense crash.

Smug, it took him all of a minute to realize his mistake. Now the snacks were stuck down the back of the machine.

He was not going to be defeated.

Ellis stood on top and jumped up and down on the surprisingly resilient Plexiglas.

A snickering sound behind him made him stop. Jade and Jax were watching him, amused expressions on their faces. Jax had his camera out and was filming the prince of St Francis beating the crap out of a junk-food machine.

"Delete that," Ellis said, pulling himself to his full don't-mess-with-me height.

"Okay...okay. Chill." Jax made motions to delete the video. "No big deal. We're just hungry too."

"Then help me," Ellis shouted, turning back to the machine, irritated. What were Barbie and Ken even doing up this early? Weren't they missing their beauty sleep?

It took ten minutes of combined effort, but soon they had most of the stock of Chex Mix, Starburst and Gatorade packed in Ellis's suitcase, along with several dusty bottles of water.

"I'm leaving. Are you coming?" Ellis asked as they sat in the shade munching on Doritos.

"Hard pass," Jade said, glancing dismissively across the desert stretching out on all sides. Even this early in the day, heat waves were shimmering and warping the distant mountains – it was going to be unbearable.

"Why would you want to stay in this place?" Ellis asked incredulously. It was inconceivable to him that anyone would voluntarily be here a minute longer than they had to. A quick image of the message shot through his mind, along with a brief, hard flash of panic.

"We're not missing out on the game. Are you kidding me? This kind of exposure is the best thing that could happen at this stage of my career," Jax stated enthusiastically.

"Besides, we don't hike," Jade added flatly. "Send someone for us, okay? I'm going to my room to pick out the perfect outfit to 'die' in. It's really hard – you have to stand out, without looking like you tried too hard. You know?" She swept up a handful of bottled waters and stalked off around the building.

Jax filmed her leaving, head cocked on one side appreciatively.

"Aww, man, just look at that walk – damn, my girl's hot! Gonna add this cut to the final edit – keep the subs sweet." Jax must have caught Ellis's look. He pulled up defensively. "What? Jade *likes* me posting her. It boosts her stats too. Plus, she always approves the edit. If she doesn't like the way she looks, she can pull it. Jade totally gets it – she's the coolest girl I've ever dated. I'm not even kidding you. We're in sync, like soulmates, know what I mean, bro?"

Ellis gave Jax a clear do-not-bro-me glare. Jax was hot, undeniably, but boringly straight and about as interesting as cardboard. Not Ellis's type. He liked sporty boys. All those endorphins just made them easier to get along with. No drama. No commitment. Yup – if they hadn't made varsity, Ellis wasn't interested.

Apart from Danny, of course. The one exception to every rule.

Ellis stood up quickly and brushed himself down. Time to get the hell out of this place.

"Later." Ellis walked around the front of the motel, dragging his snack-filled suitcase behind him. He checked his Rolex. It was close to eight already. He'd lost his head start. Better hit the road before it got any hotter.

As he cornered the pool fence, he stopped in dismay. A figure was standing at the edge of the road behind the burned-out shell of the bus. Fuck. Now he'd have to share the credit for saving the day.

Worse still, as he got closer, he recognized the emo witch. Raya Mori was staring at the ground. He could just make out something white at her feet.

"Good morning," he announced as he got close. He'd already decided he wouldn't tell her about his snack supply. Maybe he could outlast her and leave her along the roadside. "Are we escaping together?"

"Ellis, come here. You've got to see this," Raya called out. She was pointing at a thick, white line that had been spray-painted on the red dirt. It stretched out in both directions on either side of them. "Weird, right? I don't remember this being here when we arrived. Why would someone paint a white line in the middle of nowhere?"

Ellis stopped. His eyes followed the line off towards the horizon on one side, only to see it curving back on itself. A feeling of dread started in his stomach, creeping up slowly as he turned to look at the Motel Loba.

"It's not a line. It's a circle. Look." His voice was tinged with tension.

Both of them faced the cluster of pink buildings. From their vantage point it was clear what Ellis was talking about. The white line formed a perfect circle around the motel, the bus and all the random sheds and outbuildings. The only part of the Motel Loba that wasn't inside the circle was the road sign, which stood a solid ten feet outside the line.

"Jesus, it's starting…isn't it?" Raya half-whispered. She wrapped her arms around herself.

Ellis didn't say anything. He got the message. Yeah, very scary. So, they were trapped inside the circle. Maybe Jax was right, and it was some stupid online prank. Don't cross the line, win a million pretzels. If some idiot YouTuber did show up, Ellis would get his father to sue the hell out of them. Some fucking joke.

He walked up to the edge of the white line and nudged it with the tip of his neon green Kobe sneakers.

Whoever painted the line had made one small miscalculation; Ellis Locke wasn't into games. They could spray-paint all over the place. No one was keeping him here another minute, and if they thought a stupid line would stop him – well, he was the king of crossing fucking lines.

He was about to step forward when a black-fingernailed hand caught his arm.

"Wait," said Raya. "We should think about this first. The message said—"

"I don't give a fuck what the message said. Some fucker is playing with us," Ellis snapped. "Someone thinks this is some great game. Very funny. Well, I'm not playing."

"But what if the message was right? You heard it. It said if you leave the circle—"

"Jesus Christ, Raya. It's just a line – it's *spray paint*! I'm not afraid of a damn line." Ellis turned away from her dismissively. This was not the time for overthinking.

He checked his watch again. It was eight a.m. now and the air temperature was creeping up steadily. It was time to get going. The game wouldn't start for almost two hours. He had a head start and a bag full of snacks. He was leaving, and as far as he was concerned, Raya Mori could do whatever the hell she liked. She wasn't his problem.

Raya stepped away from Ellis.

"Fine. You go for it, Ellis. Knock yourself out there, big guy. I'll just stay here and watch from a safe distance," she said, smiling.

"Whatever." He rolled his eyes. He *definitely* wouldn't get her rescued.

This conversation was getting old. In fact, this whole drama was getting old. In fact, this whole motel was…well, already old. Grabbing his suitcase, he marched across the line, not a flicker of worry. He was going home. A few steps in and nothing bad had happened. He couldn't resist gloating, just a little bit. Turning back, arms outstretched as if to say *I told you so*, he smiled.

"See. Nothing to worry about. Nothin—"

Bang.

A sharp crack made him cower. Dirt flew up inches from his feet. He froze in shock, his mind processing what was happening.

Bang. Another report, just behind him.

Gunfire.

His warrior instincts kicked in this time and in one bound he leaped back across the line, stumbling and falling to his knees. Hands grabbed him. Raya pulled him back from the edge, both scrabbling to get away.

Somehow, they made it to the wreckage of the bus and fell, panting, in the dirt behind the warped metal frame.

Ellis looked around wildly, catching Raya's eye. There was a familiar look there. One he had hoped he would never see again, not in this lifetime. It was more than fear. Not the hollowed-out look of shock or grief. It was more basic, feral. Like a cornered animal. He'd seen it in the school gym a year ago. He'd seen it in the eyes of his friends when the roof fell, flames crashing around them. He saw it in the mirror, for weeks after the fire, staring blankly back at him, taut with shock.

This was really happening.

Someone was shooting at them.

9 | Raya

Raya's mind was reeling. She pushed herself hard against the burned-out shell of the bus; the soft grey ash coated her clothes, her arms, her face. She didn't care. She squeezed her eyes shut, willing herself to breathe – willing her heart to slow down.

Ellis was talking, but she couldn't make out his words. There was too much in her head. *Someone was shooting at them.*

Panic rose up inside, overwhelming her.

Instinctively her fingers reached out for her wrist, pushing her long black sleeve up, feeling for the scar. It was there. It was always there. It was a part of her; it would never leave her. She touched it gently, the jagged surface stretched across her pale skin.

I survive. She squeezed against the line hard. *No matter how bad things get. No matter what happens. I survive.* She could feel her life's blood, her heart beating through her fingertips, through the skin. *No matter what happens. I will survive.*

The panic receded. She breathed out slowly, a long shaky breath. Then forced her eyes open. Ellis was still talking, but she blanked him out. She had to hold onto her own thoughts. The bus…the metal. It would stop bullets, wouldn't it? They weren't in any immediate danger. They had time. It was okay. It had to be.

"We've got to get inside the motel, with the others." Raya nodded to herself as she said it. "We'll be safe there."

"Fuck that." Ellis sounded subdued, his natural authority shaken. "There's no way we can make it from here to the building without getting shot. It's a solid fifty-foot sprint."

"You can make it," Raya said. "You're fast."

"Faster than a bullet? It would be suicide." Ellis shook his head.

"Maybe we could make some kind of shield?" Raya looked around. The only likely piece of metal was the bus door, which was still dangling off the frame precariously.

"I'm not staking my life on a piece of metal," Ellis snapped. "We don't know if it would stop a bullet."

"What are we going to do? Maybe…maybe the others will see. Maybe they'll rescue us." She was reaching, but she didn't know what else to do.

"I can't believe this. I can't." Ellis was clenching his fists. "We're stuck here. We should have left last night. Such *fucking idiots*."

"How could we have known?" Raya said.

"I don't know, but we should have. I knew this was off. I could feel it. I should have trusted my instincts. Not listened to Jax and the rest of you."

"Don't blame us, Ellis. You're a big boy. You make your own choices, unless your daddy makes them for you…"

"*Don't*." Somehow Ellis managed to fill one syllable with menace. Raya raised her hand placatingly and backed off. Enough lines had been crossed today.

They both fell quiet.

Jesus, she didn't want to die here, with Ellis of all people. What an ending. Shot dead in the arms of the school's biggest jock-douchebag. She'd rather run across the line and go out in a blaze of independent glory.

"S'up?"

The voice made her jump. Pulling herself out of her thoughts, Raya looked around.

Caden was standing in the open near a prickly-pear bush, completely unprotected, staring at them.

"Oh my god, no," Raya gasped. "Caden, get down! Run! There's a shooter." She stood up, waving her arms violently in the air.

Ellis jumped up too.

"Get back! You'll get shot. Run!" They both waved desperately, trying to steer Caden away.

Caden squinted back at them, then gave a short wave. His eyes were red; he was swaying slightly – clearly high. He must have spent the night sampling his way through his merch.

"All right, all right…I'm coming." Oblivious to the danger, he started walking towards the bus, mumbling as he went. "I'm coming already."

He was in the open, the shooter could take a shot at any time.

"Stop! Get back! Run!" Raya and Ellis shouted, but Caden kept walking, oblivious, zigzagging slowly towards them.

"You jackass!" Ellis picked up a stone and threw it at Caden's feet. Caden didn't even flinch. Nothing worked. He kept shuffling closer. *He just wouldn't listen.*

Raya sank to her knees, closing her eyes, pushing her hands over her ears. There was nothing she could do. *Nothing.* She wouldn't listen for the shot, if she focused, she could blank it out. Like it never happened. Any second…she willed herself to block out the sounds around her. Three, two...

"Yo."

The voice was right next to her. She opened one eye.

Caden was standing behind the bus. Alive.

Raya and Ellis both jumped to their feet. Without thinking, Raya leaped on Caden and hugged him, her arms barely making their way around him. Even Ellis threw a manly arm across Caden's shoulder, patting him awkwardly.

"You made it! Jesus, that means...the shooter's gone. We're safe, right?" Raya was delighted. "C-Dog, you are a legend. You just saved us a whole heap of heartache."

"Okay," Caden grunted, even though he clearly had no clue what was going on, his red eyes crinkled a little with what might have been pleasure.

Ellis seemed less enthusiastic.

"Not quite safe." He tentatively stepped out from behind the bus, arms raised slightly. He turned around in clear view of a possible shooter. Nothing happened. "Don't you see what this means?"

Raya moved next to him, nervous at first, muscles tensed.

"It means we're alive, Ellis. At least for now," she said, her voice flashing with irritation. "What could possibly be bad about this? The shooter's stopped. We're in the clear."

"It means we're trapped." Ellis spoke slowly, like he was explaining to a child. "We're safe inside the circle. But if we try to leave and cross the white line, then we'll be shot. It means we aren't going anywhere."

"Fuuuuuuccck," Caden whispered.

"No kidding," Raya added. It was sinking in. No walking through the desert. No escape. They were well and truly caught. "So, what the heck do we do now?"

This time Ellis had an answer for her.

"What do you think we do? We have no fucking choice." He slammed his hand against the bus, frustration simmering through him. "Norman has us right where he wants us. When 9.58 a.m. comes around, like it or not, we do what this psycho wants – we play the Balloon Game…"

10 | Ana

"We're in a *circle*?" Benny said, as though his mind was two steps behind the words coming out of his mouth. "And if we go outta the circle, then we get shot at? So, we're...trapped?" He was chewing methodically on a piece of gum, staring at the vintage linoleum floor as he spoke.

The sound of gunshots had kicked Ana into high gear. She felt alert and on edge as she stood by the window in the reception, listening to the others talking. Everyone was gathered together, blinds drawn, dust drifting lazily in the heavy air. She focused on one speck of dust, watching as it was swept up in a current of air from Ellis's manic stomping up and down, back and forward. The guy was never still.

"Yes, Benny. Well done," Ellis snapped. "Everyone else keeping up?" He glared around the room.

His usual sarcasm wasn't enough to hide the fact that Ellis looked scared. Ana watched his body language as he paced the room, shaking out his hands over and over.

No one could blame him. Someone had just tried to kill him. Of all the people in this room, he knew what that felt like. He'd been there. A year ago, Ellis had been the big hero of the day. He had been the first to react when the fire started, running across the basketball court towards the flames, while everyone else ran in the other direction. He'd dragged several students out of harm's way before the fire finally caught him, paying for his courage with nasty burns across his chest and shoulder.

Raya also seemed subdued. She was perched on the pink pleather sofa and had barely said a word, letting Ellis do the talking.

"So, this isn't a prank? This is all real?" Jade's voice sounded uncharacteristically high-pitched, far from her usual monotone drawl. Her make-up was immaculate, her outfit perfectly put together, ready for her moment in the spotlight.

"No, babe. No, it's not real, okay? We're fine." Jax spoke up, manfully protecting his *wo-man*. All he had on was a pair of jeans, his perfectly toned six-pack glistened with a sheen of sweat.

"So, who's shooting at us?" Jade asked.

"No one! Can't you see?" Jax said. "It must be part of the game. It's probably special effects. It's genius."

"Didn't you read the message?" Ellis spluttered. "*Karl Hunt lit the match, but you are all guilty.* Someone brought us out here to punish *us* – not some random kids. Us! Isn't it obvious? This is no prank."

"Look, Ellis." Jax was committed. "You can believe what you want. But you're going to look like such an idiot when it turns out to be a prank. Just saying…"

"And if it's not a prank, you're going to look fucking dead," Ellis snapped back.

This didn't feel like a prank, simply because it wasn't funny. Any way she looked at it, Ana knew it didn't make sense. Taking a group of survivors, kids who had been through one kind of hell, and torturing them for amusement was beyond reason. No successful YouTuber would touch this. They'd get cancelled at the very least, and most likely arrested for reckless endangerment. No – this wasn't a bad joke.

Oddly, the thought didn't scare her. She felt wired and focused, but not afraid. Maybe she was numb and the reality hadn't set in yet. Or maybe…maybe she didn't care enough. She glanced across at Alex. His hair was tousled with sleep, and he still had the imprint of his pillow on his cheek. He caught her eye and gave a resigned half-smile. He looked sad and worried, his arm wrapped around the neck of his guitar protectively. Ana felt a pull of something inside.

No. She cared.

"I want it on the record that whatever happens, I ain't responsible for any of y'all," Benny said emphatically. The guy looked terrified. As the only legal adult within a thirty-mile radius, it wouldn't look good if all the kids died on his watch. "This ain't nothin' to do with me. I ain't gettin' blamed for y'all getting shot, just cos I'm the only grown-up. I'm just a dang bus driver!"

"Yeah, that's not really a good legal defence, is it?" Ellis said with a half-laugh. "If we all die and you're still standing…negligence, accessory to murder, second-degree manslaughter…"

"How about we look at the facts?" Ana cut in, surprising herself. She held up her phone. "It's already nearly nine-thirty. We can spend the rest of the time arguing, or we can try to figure out what's going on."

"Fair point." Ellis stopped pacing and moved in front of Ana, taking over the room. "We need to share everything we know and gather as much information as possible." Heads nodded in agreement.

Ana felt a small flash of irritation. Wasn't that what she'd just suggested?

"Let's start with the invites." Ellis pulled the black card out of his pocket.

A couple of other cards were produced and for a few minutes, they stood around studying them. The images were clearly cobbled together from random photos; a yurt with a woman meditating, a close-up of a mud-covered face with cucumbers over the eyes, a horse with a smiling rider. The most interesting image was in the background. It looked like the Motel Loba, only sleek and modern. Everything was in the right place, the reception with its angular carport roof, the wings of rooms, even the palm tree.

"Photoshopped!" Ellis declared. "Someone made all of these invites and set this whole trip up. Think about it. Every year some super-rich parent donates a trip as the top prize in the school fundraiser, right? So, this year, whoever is behind this must have pretended to be a school donor and arranged all of this – the invites, the bus, the motel, just to bring us here. That's a hell of a lot of effort."

"But who…and why us?" Jade asked. "We won this trip in the raffle, which is random, right? I mean, that's the whole point of a raffle – you buy a ticket and it's luck who wins. So, what? We're just really, really unlucky?"

"No, the message was clear. It said we're all guilty. Clearly the raffle wasn't as random as it was supposed to be. Somehow Norman figured out a way to rig the results. He must have known it was mandatory to buy a ticket, so we'd all have at least one entry. Which meant he could pick who he wanted to win – and he chose us. All of us."

"How's that possible? I can't have been *chosen*. It doesn't make any sense. I'm not guilty of anything!" Jade's voice kept getting higher and higher.

"I know. Me either." Everyone knew Ellis wasn't guilty – he was the big hero. "The only thing I'm guilty of is not getting fried into a charred hunk of dead meat."

Ana felt like she'd been slapped in the face. She quickly turned away. How could he just casually throw out something like that? What was his problem? Images swept into her mind before she could mount a defence. She closed her eyes, willing them away.

"Don't say stuff like that, Ellis. You're not the only victim here." It was Alex's voice – one of the rare moments he'd chosen to speak up. Ana didn't need to look at him to know that he'd done it for her.

"All right, I'm sorry." Ellis sounded contrite. Probably surprised by Alex's uncharacteristically sharp tone. It took a lot to provoke Alex, and Ellis backed off.

There was an unpleasant silence. Ana opened her eyes and looked around. Alex was standing next to her, his guitar momentarily discarded. Her protector. She was touched by the gesture, but she didn't need protecting. She could look after herself.

"What I don't get is *who* would do this?" Jade carried on, oblivious to the tension. "I mean, who would want to hurt *me*? Seriously, I'm not like overstating or anything, but people generally like me. Wait, unless it's like a stalker…"

"Look, whoever this Norman is, it's not some low-level stalker," Ellis said. "They're a rich, organized and determined—"

"YouTuber," Jax muttered in a stage whisper.

"Fuck's sake, Jax! This is going in circles." Ellis sounded exasperated. He rubbed his hand hard over his head.

As Ana looked from face to face, she could tell that the mood in the room was sinking. They could guess all they wanted, but it didn't change the fact that they had no idea who was doing this, or why.

But maybe they could start with *how*.

"What if we'd said no?"

A row of faces looked back at her blankly.

"What if one of us had decided we didn't want to come...or we couldn't make it? Norman's plan would have been ruined."

"Good point," Ellis added. "What are the odds that all of us would accept the invitation – that we'd all be free this exact weekend?" Ellis was talking fast now. "I wasn't going to come. I had a game on Sunday night, but it was cancelled the night before the trip."

"Jax and I were going to skip the trip too," Jade chimed in. "All my college friends were throwing this really cool party in the hills. I'm like not even kidding you – 24kGoldn was set to play. I *so* wanted to go."

"Yeah, but then I got this DM...but I'm not supposed to talk about it," Jax said with a faux-humble smile. "You know, non-disclosure and all that," he added mysteriously.

Jade paused for a respectable five seconds before adding: "Let's just say *someone's* PA reached out and said that *someone* thought this whole trip would make a cool story, seeing as how it's on the anniversary of the fire and all. And that *someone* might be interested in having Jax and me on their show to do an exclusive when we got back. But don't share that, okay?" Jade was air-quoting furiously.

"Yeah. You don't say no to *someone*, right?" Jax added emphatically as if this was a no-brainer. Jade nodded enthusiastically and slipped a proprietorial hand into Jax's back pocket, pulling him close.

"If it was a DM, how do you know they were really *someone's* PA?" Raya asked, one pierced eyebrow raised archly.

"Because she told us – duh," Jax said as though he was stating the obvious.

"Well, then, it must be true," Ellis said, rolling his eyes. Raya coughed pointedly. "Okay, moving on. What about the rest of you?" Ellis looked around. There was a tight knot developing in Ana's gut. "Alex?"

Alex looked embarrassed.

"Someone called my abuela about it." He blushed awkwardly. "They told her I'd won this special trip, and it was the chance of a lifetime. We've never been on a vacation, so she was really happy about it. I had to go...for her."

The thought of Norman calling sweet old Mrs Cabrera to manipulate her into sending Alex was sickening. It was a violation. Norman had reached into each of their lives, poking around and stirring. The knot in Ana's stomach was getting bigger by the minute.

"Caden – what about you?"

"None of your business," Caden said grumbling.

"It's kind of our business, don't you think?" Ellis said.

Caden shuffled from foot to foot awkwardly. He seemed to be weighing up his options. Finally, he cleared his throat and spoke.

"This sophomore on the cheer team DM'd me and said she was going on the trip too. Wasn't gonna say no to that. She's a solid ten. But then she never showed, did she."

"Ever heard of catfishing?" Raya said drily.

Ana felt her face go red. It would be her turn soon. Everyone would turn to her and ask her why she was here – how had Norman manipulated her into coming? Why had she started this whole conversation? She should have just kept her damn mouth shut.

"I got an email from Dankman saying I would be excused from all detentions this month for showing 'school spirit' if I came. Seemed like a good deal." Raya grinned, but her eyes were on Ana.

Everyone turned to look at Ana. The final piece. Positive proof that they had all been lured here by some crazed psychopath (or very well-organized YouTuber). She chewed her lip nervously. The knot in her stomach was so big now she felt like she might vomit.

She could just lie. She could make up a story. *My mom got a call*, or *the school said I had to come*. But what good would that do?

The truth was, she was the outlier – the only one who hadn't been manipulated into coming on this trip. She hadn't needed manipulation. She'd come voluntarily to the Motel Loba, not because she wanted to – it was quite possibly the last thing she wanted to do. But she'd come because she had to.

She had to get away. Now – on this day. She couldn't be at home, staring at the blue sheets across the room, the white trainers lined up underneath, the Lakers hat over the bedpost. Untouched, unmoved. She couldn't walk into the kitchen and see her mother at the stove, look her in the eyes and see that expression. That pain. That resentment. She couldn't feel that roaring, devastating guilt. The shame of knowing that the universe was upside down. That it had made a huge, terrible mistake. That she was bad, and Danny was good. *That she should have died.*

No one made her come. She was grateful for an excuse to run away from everything for a few days. There was never a question of whether she'd say yes to this trip. She had no choice.

The thing was, Norman hadn't even tried to force her hand.

He hadn't set some story in place to ensure that she would be here. She was the only one who hadn't been lured into this terrible trap.

Which could only mean one thing. Norman knew she'd come. With complete certainty, he knew. In two steps she made it to the door, swung it open and ran outside, giving in to the knot, to the nausea.

Norman knew her. Whoever he was, he knew what she'd done; he knew what she was thinking. He was in her head.

He was in her head.

11 | Ana

Life goes on.

Ana was hiding out behind the corner of the building. She'd found a shady spot on the sidewalk and was sitting, knees hugged to her chest, on the edge of the kerb. A weed sprouted through cracks in the pavement, optimistically fighting for dominance over the man-made concrete; a small white flower on top danced happily in the breeze.

Life goes on.

The reception door banged shut and footsteps clumped towards her hiding spot. Raya plumped herself down next to Ana, puffing a little from the exertion. Raya always sounded out of breath, like someone five times her age. She rooted around in her pocket, pulling out a Zippo lighter with the letters RM etched into it.

Raya's recent efforts to cut back on smoking had unlocked a new nervous habit. She flipped the lighter open and thumbed the flame to life before slamming it shut again. Fidgeting, over and over, on repeat.

Ana watched for a while in silence. *Open, shut, flick, flick.* Raya's black thumbnail working the silver lighter vigorously. There was something soothing about it. Something reassuringly predictable.

"Raya, I'm sorry I ran out like that. I panicked. I'm fine now. I promise."

"Come on, Ana. You don't have to apologize. This whole situation is messed up."

"I know. But still. I need to do better."

"Wanna talk about it?"

Ana shook her head. How could she explain? How could she tell Raya that she was the only one who hadn't been manipulated into coming here? That somehow Norman knew she would come? That he knew her?

Raya pulled out her phone and propped it up on her knee in front of them both. 9.50 a.m.

"Eight minutes to go."

"I wonder why it's 9.58 a.m.," Ana said, changing the subject. "It's so specific. It must mean something. Everything here is so carefully set up, so thought out."

Raya shrugged.

"Maybe. Maybe not. I mean, Norman's clearly off his nuts. Perhaps it's just a bunch of random crazy shit. Some strange idea in the warped brain of a freaky psychopath."

Ana shook her head. None of this was random. She was thinking back to a year ago; 9.58 a.m. didn't mean anything to her. It was just a regular morning at school. It wasn't until the evening that everything had changed. She knew *exactly* where she would have been at 9.58 p.m. The hospital. The green-walled hallway. Waiting.

No. She shook her head again, harder. She couldn't think about that now.

"What about the messages?" she said. "How are we getting messages when there's no Wi-Fi or cellular? I thought maybe

Bluetooth, but it has a pretty short range, and it would need the same app on each device." Ana scratched her cheek thoughtfully. Raya just listened, without trying to keep up. "What app would we have in common? The big ones – Snapchat, TikTok, Instagram? I mean, they'd be almost impossible to hack, right? No, it would have to be something more basic. But what? What would we all have in common?"

"Oh, wait. That's easy! I can answer that one." Raya sat up. "Nada. Nothing. Zilch. I can promise you, hand on heart that the only thing I have in common with Jade Clark is that we go to the same freaking school – unfortunately."

Ana laughed outright.

"Raya, you're brilliant."

"I am?"

"Yes! That's it. The school app. It has to be." Holding up her phone, Ana flicked through the screens until she saw it – the letters SFHS in green letters on a yellow background over the faint outline of a wolf's head. The St Francis High student portal used the same font as the messages. *Norman was using the school app to send them messages.* "Of course! It makes perfect sense. Norman must have figured out how to hack into it!"

"Jesus, are you sure? He's starting to sound less like a psycho and more like a freaking criminal mastermind."

Raya had a point. If Ana's theory was right, Norman must have serious tech skills, or be rich and motivated enough to hire someone who did. Whoever was behind this had built a meticulously-crafted trap, and they had walked right into the middle of their web. But who? Who could possibly hate them enough to set all this up and lure them here? Who could know about her, about all of them?

Ana felt a dark stirring of anxiety. She put her phone down and wrapped her arms around her knees. Things just kept getting worse.

Raya must have picked up on Ana's mood. She nudged her gently with her shoulder.

"So how do you think this works? We get to 9.58 a.m. and the sky falls in on us? Or maybe some rando YouTube prankster paraglides into the pool with a suitcase of money?"

"I hope he knows it's empty."

They both grinned and looked out across the desolate landscape. The mountains seemed to change colour constantly. Right now, they were almost blue, merging into the sky. They seemed further away than they had yesterday, now that the white line lay starkly between them.

"Well, whatever happens, I really hope it involves food. I'm so hungry." Raya resumed her fidgeting, taking out her hangry thoughts on the little lighter. *Flick, flick, flick.*

Ana sat forward, reaching her fingers out to the tiny flower – gently, almost tenderly touching the delicate white petals. The flower could survive against impossible odds. So could they.

"Raya." Ana paused, trying to find the right words. "I know I've been…distant this past year. I'm so sorry. Really, I am. I just… I couldn't…"

Raya reached over and took Ana's hand.

"Again, you don't have to apologize, doofus. You know I love you, don't you?"

"Yeah. I love you too," Ana said quietly. There was love and there was *love*. What they shared fell between the two. Ana felt tears in her eyes. "I want you to know that whatever comes next, I won't let you down. I promise. I will do whatever it takes to keep you and Alex safe…"

Raya pulled her hand away and turned to face the desert, her short hair falling across her face.

"It must be time." There was a sharp edge to her voice that hadn't been there before.

Ana looked at the screen: 9.57 a.m. She held her breath.

Whatever was about to happen next was inevitable. Time was moving them towards their destiny – good or bad. They could only bear witness. They both watched in silence.

It seemed to take for ever, and then suddenly, there it was.

The lock screen disappeared and a black screen with green numbers took its place. The numbers were counting down, the seconds racing backwards.

59:59

It was at once terrifying and yet anticlimactic. No great bells and whistles, but real at the same time. The countdown had begun. The game had started. They had an hour before one of them had to cross the line.

Without saying a word, they both stood and turned to walk back to the reception, back to face whatever came next.

At the corner, Ana paused on a whim. She turned to look at the kerb, the crack, seeking out the little flower, the small hopeful survivor. But it was gone, crushed under Raya's Docs. A few matted petals remained, ground into the concrete, its small, plucky fight for survival ended in one moment. Dead.

Despite the heat, Ana shivered.

12 | Alex

42:17

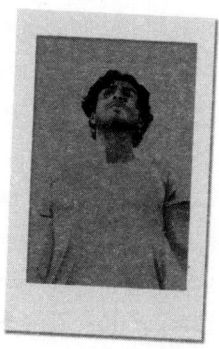

A small, rusty windmill was propped crookedly on top of what might have once been a well. The blades spun loudly as they caught the wind, clacking and squeaking in a whirring burst of action, before falling silent, waiting for the next gust.

Alex stood, transfixed. There was music everywhere if you took the time to listen. The whirring started up, clacking rhythmically before fading. He thought he might record the sound; he'd been doing that a lot recently – listening, recording, sampling. It wasn't the same as when he'd been in Trash Dogs and writing songs in every spare minute; that had been the best time of his life. But still, it was fun just to listen and play around with sounds. Music made him happy, however it came to him.

He pulled out his phone, intending to save an audio file, but when he saw the green countdown on the screen he slipped it back into his pocket, changing his mind. He didn't want to record this. He didn't want to remember any of this.

They had decided to break up into groups and search the motel to see if they could find anything that might help them get out of this predicament – a weapon, a functioning landline, maybe a fully gassed-up, vintage convertible locked away in one of the random sheds (if they were really lucky). Alex was standing around the back of the reception building with his group: Jade and Jax. He'd rather have been with Ana, but Jade had grabbed him and hustled him out of the door before he could change his mind.

They hadn't done much of anything useful. Mostly just kicking around and grumbling. Jax was filming what he called "transitional footage" that he could cut into the final edit. He said it made the product more professional. Jade wouldn't leave the shade of the building as she was worried about the UV. Which left Alex to wander around and look in a few random sheds. He wasn't sure what he was looking for, but everything he came across seemed rusted beyond use.

He headed back to Jade, who was perched on top of an upside-down snack machine, drinking water. She patted the machine next to her.

"Hey, Alex. Come sit in the shade for a bit. It's like seriously hot already." She dropped her head to one side and peered up at him, squinting against the light; a curtain of platinum blonde hair fell across her face.

"Um…I'm…we should, you know…maybe, keep looking around?" His hands were sweating.

"Seriously, Alex. Just sit down. Save your energy. We're not going to find anything out here." Jade waved her hand at the dismal surroundings. She had a point.

Reluctantly, Alex sat on the furthest edge of the machine. Jade shuffled over and reached a hand around his arm. He couldn't help it, but somehow those fake nails with pink tips reminded him of claws.

"So, what do you think is going on?" Jade said, lowering her voice, her tone soft and unnervingly personal.

"I think, maybe..." Should he say it? He knew exactly what he thought, and he was with Ana on this one. No one would be stupid enough to run this scenario as a prank. Plus, there was the fact that Norman had said they'd all been somehow complicit in the fire a year ago. He couldn't speak for anyone else here, but he certainly knew that he was guilty as charged. Everyone knew what he'd done.

"Jax is totally convinced it's all a prank." Jade continued, not waiting for his answer. "Don't get me wrong – I love Jax and all. It's just, sometimes he's so wrapped up in his whole YouTube thing, it's like he doesn't even see what's right in front of him...or *who's* right in front of him. I'm not complaining, but being his girlfriend can be a bit – you know...lonely." Jade paused and looked at Alex probingly.

"Um...yeah," was all Alex could manage. He looked at the windmill longingly; it seemed quiet by comparison.

"It's like, out here, with everything that's going down...I'm kinda scared, Alex. But Jax doesn't understand; he almost seems to be enjoying it. I just wish we were on the same page. I wish he could get what I'm feeling. Whatever's happening here, I don't want to face it by myself." Jade shifted infinitesimally closer, and dropped her head onto Alex's shoulder, her claws reaching around to rest on his stomach. He flinched slightly. "You know, it's weird, but somehow...I feel safe with you."

Something close to panic hit Alex squarely in the gut. He would be the first to admit it, but girls scared him. Especially cute ones. The only girl he'd ever really felt comfortable with was Ana. Jade on the other hand was like an animated Victoria's Secret model. Absolutely terrifying. If only he had his guitar for moral support.

He'd reluctantly left it in his room when the timer started, hoping it would be safe in there – that it might survive, no matter what happened out here.

"I think it'll all be fine," he managed to stutter. He wasn't sure where to put his free hand. It felt odd having her wrapped around him with his hands behind his back. He decided to go for a comforting pat on the back, but she pulled into him, and somehow, before he knew it, he was sitting with his arms around her, and she was practically in his lap.

Nervously, he looked around for Jax, only to see him standing beside a small lean-to shed. For one horrible moment, Alex was sure that Jax was watching them. But then his hand went up, camera attached, and he turned away, heading back behind the shed in his endless quest for the perfect angle.

Alex breathed out, but his relief was short-lived when a voice said: "Well, well. What have we here?"

Raya and Ana were standing by the corner of the building.

Why now? This was all wrong. Alex looked down, assessing the damage – arms everywhere, blonde hair everywhere, golden skin pushed up against his T-shirt. Not good. Jade lifted her head, smiled at Raya and Ana, and with a casual informality that was not appropriate, pulled Alex even closer, taking ownership. Alex blushed bright red.

"Find anything useful?" Raya's tone was dripping with sarcasm.

"Um, no…we were…um…" Alex mumbled. No way was he going to make eye contact with Ana. Not like this.

"Yes, we can see what you were doing. Jade, does your *boyfriend* know you're moving on? Or are you going to keep that a secret in case he decides to throw you across the line?"

"Oh my god, Raya! You are such a bitch! Alex was just making me feel better." Somehow, the way Jade said it made it sound as though "making me feel better" was a full-service deal.

"We're not...I'm not...this isn't..." Alex protested, daring to look up. Ana was facing away, towards the mountains. Strangely, it felt worse than if she'd been glaring at him. As though he'd been dismissed somehow.

"Whatever, bitches." Raya nudged Ana and turned to go. "We just came to tell you that Prince Ellis has summoned us to the reception. We need to come up with a plan for staying alive, in case you forgot what's going down."

And they were gone.

Jade unfurled herself, managing to envelope Alex in a heady cloud of Daisy perfume, brushing lightly against his arm, chest and hand while doing so. As soon as he was liberated, Alex jumped to his feet.

"I'm gonna go and tell Jax we're all meeting, okay?" He backed away, tripping awkwardly over a discarded piece of bedding. "I'll see you in the reception."

As he ran towards the shed, all thoughts of the timer and the line were momentarily suspended. There was only one thing that was looping through his mind.

What would Ana think of him now?

13 | Ana
29:44

The reception had become their de facto meeting place. The blinds were pulled down all the way and the large room had taken on the appearance of a battle HQ – chairs pushed to the side, the desk from the office dragged into the centre of the room with various papers strewn across the surface.

Ana sat quietly, watching the others.

Ellis was pacing. Jade was whining. Jax was filming. Benny and Caden had gone outside and were sitting by the window in the shade of the carport roof, smoking. Alex had followed them, looking grateful for an excuse to leave. The mood was foul. No one had eaten anything since Ellis had deposited all their snacks on the far side of the line in his suitcase. They were hungry and scared – not a winning combination.

Every corner of the motel had been searched for anything that might help them escape, but they had come up empty-handed. Other than the motel itself, there were just piles of junk and discarded furniture, the rusty windmill, some random sheds, a handful of old farm vehicles with no engines and three large, corrugated metal outbuildings, each of which was firmly chained and padlocked and would take some time to break into. Right now, time was not something they could spare. The clock was ticking.

Figures moved outside the window, their shadows catching the light through the blinds. Ana recognized Alex's outline, his distinctive hair, his slight slouch.

No matter how hard she tried not to, Ana kept picturing Jade on Alex's lap, all satiny and perfect. It had caught her by surprise, to be honest. She could see why Jade might be interested in Alex since his glow up. What surprised her was that Alex would feel the same. The Alex she knew wouldn't have liked someone as shallow as Jade. Then again, maybe he'd secretly wanted that all along but thought that Jade was out of his league. Maybe Jade was *exactly* his type. Wasn't she everyone's type?

Not to mention the fact that Jade already had a boyfriend. Jax was easily the hottest guy at St Francis and high-school famous – perfect for Jade. So why was she mooching at Alex?

Ana stood up and started pacing.

This was pointless. Why did she care who Alex hooked up with? It had nothing to do with her. They weren't together; they weren't even friends any more. Alex was free to do whatever he wanted. Alex deserved to be happy. He was good and kind and gentle. If Jade was his type, then good for him. If that's what he really wanted, then fine.

Even if Jade would shamelessly use him, posting photos of them together with his guitar strategically placed next to them, bathed in golden light and fake tan and—

Gah! Snap out of it.

They were in a potentially life-or-death situation. Why was her brain spiralling on something so inconsequential? The stress was getting to her. She had to pull herself together and focus.

She chewed on her lip and walked herself through the situation mentally for the hundredth time. Twenty minutes left. When the hour was up, it came down to two choices: go or stay. No one wanted to cross the white line and risk being shot at, like Ellis. But if they stayed, the message said they would all die. Great choices, if they could even be called that. At the rate they were going, they would still be sitting in the reception staring sadly at their phone screens when the timer ran out.

A tapping at the door startled her. Benny was outside, waving at them. He seemed uncharacteristically excited, a red flush on his smiling face.

Ellis pushed open the creaky door.

"What?"

"Y'all need to see this," Benny puffed breathlessly. "Caden and I, we reckon we got ourselves an escape plan." He checked around for a response, but no one moved.

Clearly disappointed that his words hadn't had the impact he'd expected, Benny hoisted his pants by the waistband, pulling them up high, in what was likely intended as a manly gesture.

"Didn't y'all hear me? I said we got an *escape plan*! Y'all coming or you gonna sit around and wait to die?"

He had a point.

Ellis made an expansive, eye-rolling gesture, but headed out after Benny. Ana quickly followed. Anything was better than sitting in this stuffy room. One by one the others came too.

It was already baking hot. Ana blinked, her eyes adjusting to the glaring light. Benny jogged ahead of them, waving them on, heading behind the motel strip to the outbuildings around the back.

He stopped by a small pile of debris – an old mattress with ungodly stains, a fridge door, several bits of broken cabinetry. Caden was already there, collecting more bits and pieces to add to the pile.

"So, Caden here knows about guns and military and stuff. He had an idea. Why don't you tell 'em, Caden?"

Caden looked like the ground had better eat him up and spit him out before he would volunteer to talk in front of his peers. But Benny kept nodding and nudging him until he finally spoke.

"High-velocity rifle, range would be three hundred, maybe four hundred yards, and that would be a decent shot. I reckon, if there's one shooter, they'd be over there." He pointed out past the road sign to a small cluster of rocks in the middle distance.

"So's if there's one shooter over there, and y'all make a big hoo-ha out front, then while they're distracted, one of us can escape around back and go get help!" Benny threw his hands up, clearly satisfied with his own plan.

There were *so many* holes in the plan, Ana didn't know where to start. *If* there was one shooter. *If* they were hiding in those rocks. *If* they didn't see this coming. She glanced at Ellis to see what the prince was making of all this.

He was silent, his hand stroking his chin in thought, watching Benny and Caden.

"Look, I know it ain't risk-free, which is why we make ourselves some armour, see! Like this," Benny said as the two of them launched onto the pile of junk at their feet.

Caden picked up the old mattress and tried to wrap it around Benny, who had dug out an old rusty bucket, and was wearing it as a makeshift helmet. Despite their situation, Ana almost laughed. It was like watching Mario and Luigi play dress-up.

"Who would go?" Ellis said quietly. He was still stroking his chin.

Benny and Caden looked at each other as though they hadn't made it this far in the conversation.

"It's a decent plan. Of course, it only works if someone is brave enough to volunteer," Ellis said smoothly.

Ana knew exactly where this was going. This was not a good plan. If the shooter was hiding out there waiting to kill someone, then anyone streaking across the desert dressed in a mattress and a tin bucket was volunteering to die.

Ellis knew. It was obvious. He was too smart to think otherwise. But this was a way out. The inescapable clock was ticking the minutes of the hour away. If one of them was stupid enough to volunteer, it would kill two birds with one bullet; they would test if the shooter was serious, and if they were, it would reduce the competition by one.

Win-win.

Of course, Ana thought, no one would be foolish enough to actually do it. Would they?

"I'll go," Benny said, trying and failing to look heroic. "Seems only right, me being the only responsible adult and all."

"Wait, Benny, are you sure?" Ana blurted out. It really seemed like Benny was operating on half a tank and it would be wrong to take advantage of him. Ellis turned his full attention to her, and she withered a little under his icy stare. "I'm just... I mean. We should really think about it, you know? It's just if the shooter's serious, you could..."

"Benny knows what he's volunteering for," Ellis cut in sharply. "Benny, you are quite right, your plan is fucking genius and you, as the only adult, are a hero. When we get out of this, we will make sure everyone knows what you did here. You can start a fundraiser page, probably make a fortune and never need to work again."

"Yeah, my mama always said I'd be good for something," Benny said, laughing. He actually seemed to be enjoying himself.

"Are you sure, Benny?" Ana asked again, stepping to the edge of the pile of junk, nervously kicking at an old piece of a toilet bowl.

"Abso-effing-lutely," Benny said. "Caden, my man, pick up that mattress. We're gettin' outta here."

14 | Ana
08:12

Raya was by the prickly-pear cactus near the road, Ellis and Alex were outside the reception and Jade and Jax were near the road sign. The plan was in place.

They were watching the countdown on their phones.

When the timer got to five minutes, they would all leap around, shout, bang things and create all kinds of chaos at the front of the motel. With the distraction in place, Ana and Caden would help Benny to the edge of the line and see him off. Ana had volunteered to stay behind to help. She wanted a last chance to reason with Benny without Ellis getting involved.

Benny tried a little jogging in place to see if the makeshift strapping tied from torn bed sheets was up to the job.

"Benny, do you really want to do this?" Ana moved in front of him so she could be sure he was listening.

"I'm all good, girl. Don't you worry about ol' Benny-bear," he said, smiling.

Ana nodded. "Just remember, if you change your mind, it's okay. You really don't have to go. We can figure something else out."

"You got a good heart, kid." Benny paused, his expression

serious. "Now listen – you take care of yourself, okay? Those kids aren't so nice." He nodded in the direction of the others.

It felt so wrong. Ana didn't even know the guy, but she was fully aware of just how dangerous a risk he was taking – even if Benny wasn't. He was putting his life on the literal line. Maybe this would be a prank, and everything would turn out fine, but then again, maybe it wouldn't.

Benny must have sensed her concern. He leaned towards her, his armour clunking awkwardly.

"Listen, kid. I'm gonna be fine." He smiled his big-bear smile and patted her gently on the shoulder. "All of you are going to be just fine. I promise you that. Okay, kid? *I promise.*"

The way he said it...somehow, she believed him. She wanted desperately to believe him. She needed to.

There wasn't much more to say, Benny had made his decision. His big red face grinned at her from under the rusty bucket.

"Almost time, Benny," Caden called out.

So, this was it; this crazy idea, the best and only escape plan they had managed to come up with, was actually happening.

Ana tried to smile.

"Then just...be careful. You're a hero, Benny, and I won't ever forget what you're doing – what you're risking for us."

A flicker of something crossed Benny's face. Ana caught the look but couldn't make it out. Fear? Doubt? Sadness, maybe? Before she could question it further, it was gone. The moment passed and Benny broke into a wide grin.

"It's all good, kiddo. It's all good." He shook out his hands and did a few old-man warm-up stretches, reaching around behind him as far as the mattress would allow.

"Ten, nine, eight…" Caden started the final countdown.

Benny adjusted his bucket and squatted as low as he could manage, like a sprinter on the blocks. His toes were on the line.

"Seven, six, five…"

A loud banging and shouting started up at the front of the motel. Great whooping noises and hollering ripped through the air.

"Four, three…'

Ana felt her whole body tighten with nervous energy. They were really doing this.

"Two, one…"

Launching himself across the white line, Benny was off.

Benny was fast, even weighed down with his makeshift armour. He headed straight into the desert at a good clip. Ana and Caden stood on the line watching, holding their breath.

He made it past a scraggly bush, then on to a cluster of cacti, then a half-dead saguaro.

So far so good. No shots. Nothing. Ana felt a spark of hope. This might work.

Benny started slowing a little, his initial burst of adrenaline dying out, he puffed to a walk, then stopped. Turning around, he reached up and took his bucket off. He was panting from the exertion, sweat dripping down his face. He stretched his arms out wide, grinning.

"Yay, Benny!" Caden shouted, fist-pumping the air.

Ana sank back slightly, releasing her breath. He was a good fifty feet out. This was good. This was really good.

Benny waved, then turned to face the open ground ahead of him, ready to keep going, ready for his big escape. But he didn't move.

The *crack* echoed around them. Ana gasped.

Benny's head snapped back violently. His hulking form appeared suspended for one long second before he teetered over sideways, crashing into the dirt. He flopped onto his back, his arms falling limply on either side of the mattress as his face rolled towards them.

Eyes open, mouth open, dark red blood pouring down across his face, pooling onto the sand beneath him.

Benny was dead.

The game had begun.

15 | Ana
59:22

Ana fell to her knees. This was real. This was happening. It was happening *again*.

Vaguely she was aware of the others running up. Everything sounded distorted, as though she was listening through a long tunnel. There was crying, shouting, voices raised in pitch. Slowly fading away. One by one, falling silent. The aftermath. She knew the sounds too well. She closed her eyes.

Leaves, broken glass, a can of green paint.

Someone put their arm around her, but she didn't know or care who.

Leaves, broken glass, a can of green paint.

Her body felt disconnected, like a broken limb. She was being pulled into someone; she slumped against them her head falling against their chest. Alex. She could feel him, smell his clean linen-fresh smell as she buried her face into his T-shirt.

She remembered this moment. At the hospital, the bitter smell of disinfectant, red plastic chairs bolted to the wall, waiting to be officially notified of what she already knew, waiting to be told Danny was dead – it had been Alex who had sat through the night with her, his arm tight around her shoulders, holding her up, until she couldn't bear it any longer. Couldn't breathe with his gentle care and love. *Love she didn't deserve.*

The thought made her snap into focus. This was not the time to remember.

Ana pulled back from her memories, extricating herself, untangling the barbed wire of pain inside her head. She forced herself to her knees, moving away from Alex.

She looked out across the sand, at the lifeless dark outline. Red dust was blowing across Benny's body, pockets of it accumulating in the folds of his clothes. The bucket was rattling as it wobbled backwards and forwards in the wind.

Benny was dead. The clock had reset. And in an hour, someone else would have to cross the line – someone else would have to die. She looked around. Everyone was here. They were all standing on the white line.

"We can't leave him like that," Raya whispered.

"How are we going to bury him without getting killed?" Ellis snapped back at her.

"I don't know." Raya was shaking. She couldn't take Ellis's assault right now. "It's just...wrong. Leaving him like that." She turned her face away from the desert, from Benny.

Ana knew Ellis was right, but the thought of Benny lying out there in the dirt, for all to see, as the hours ticked by, was horrifying. Once again, they were helpless. Just like last time. Just like a year ago.

How could this be happening again? How?

She turned to look at Alex. He was bent forward, hands on knees, head down. His hair was covering his face, but she didn't need to see it to know what he was feeling. He hadn't been in the gym a year ago. He hadn't seen, first-hand, the searing flames tearing at the walls, at people, shadows falling over each other, screaming. He hadn't seen death. This was his first time.

A powerful impulse swept over her. She wanted to walk over to him and hold him, to push his hair back and look him directly in his soft eyes and tell him everything would be okay. Even if she knew it wouldn't. It couldn't be. But her feet wouldn't move. It was as though she was frozen in place. Locked down inside. Useless.

A loud grunt made everyone jump.

Ana had almost forgotten Caden was there. He had been lurking off to one side since the shooting. He was staring into the distance, one hand shading his red eyes.

He grunted again, and raised a hand, pointing towards the horizon. Far away, by the mountains, a cloud of dust was forming, growing larger by the second.

"What the fuck is that?" Ellis muttered to no one in particular.

The dust cloud was blowing to the right, stretching out across the desert. There seemed to be a red dot at the centre of it, some kind of car maybe.

"Oh my god. Help us. *Help us!*" Jade shouted. "Someone's coming, they'll rescue us. We've got to signal them. Come on." She started waving her arms in the air. Jax followed her lead, and before long the others joined them, shouting and waving.

Only Ana and Ellis stood still.

There was something wrong. The red dot wasn't coming from a road. It was driving cross-country, barrelling at high speed, headed directly for them. Whoever was coming knew exactly where they were going and why.

The dot grew, forming the clear shape of a red truck. They could make out dark outlines behind the windshield. It looked like there were at least two people inside.

One by one, the others fell quiet as they realized that the truck was coming whether they shouted or not, whether they wanted it to or not.

Closer and closer, the trail of dust was forming a mighty cloud above the truck, several storeys high. Like an approaching sandstorm. Dangerous.

As the truck neared Benny, it swung around, skidding to an abrupt stop just feet from the body. A fan of dust settled over everything. The doors opened and two men got out, bandanas over their faces. They looked like they were in their twenties, wearing indistinctive flannels and jeans, with matching cowboy hats pulled low.

No one called to them. No one waved. Something about their efficient, businesslike manner warned the group to stay quiet and watch.

Without a glance in the direction of the motel, the men walked over to Benny, one standing at his head, one by his feet. They stared down. There was no surprise or concern in their movements. They had known he was there, and they knew he was already dead.

Ana felt nauseous. What were they going to do to him? What did they want?

One of the cowboys pulled something out of his pocket and held it up to his bandana. It appeared to be some kind of hand-held radio. He listened intently, nodding, then slipped the radio into his pocket and bent down to grab Benny's outstretched arms. He said something to the other man, who picked up the feet. Benny's grey shirt pulled up, exposing his belly; the ignominy of it felt like a slap in the face.

"Leave Benny alone," a loud voice shouted, making them all jump. Caden stepped forward, his face flushed an angry red.

He picked up a stone and flung it in the direction of the truck. It fell short, rattling along the ground.

"Leave him!"

The men *must* have heard Caden but didn't so much as glance in his direction.

Something released inside Ana – suddenly she could move again. She bent down and grabbed a rock and flung it as hard as she could in the direction of the men.

"Don't touch him!" Her voice sounded puny and distant, but she didn't care. "Leave him alone!"

"Stop it!"

"Let go!"

"Put him down!"

Everyone was shouting now. They followed Caden's lead, grabbing anything they could reach and throwing it at the two cowboys. Caden rooted around and grabbed an entire fridge door and with a roar flung it over the line. It crashed loudly onto the ground.

The men didn't even acknowledge their efforts. They lifted Benny's body easily between them and carried it towards the truck.

Helpless again.

Ana looked around desperately, noticing Ellis standing off to one side, watching. She walked over to him, grabbed a sharp rock off the ground and held it out. He was the Wolves' all-star point guard. Fifty feet was nothing to him.

"Ellis," Ana said. "*Please,* do something."

Ellis nodded, understanding. He grabbed the rock, balanced himself, took aim and launched it high into the air.

It was a perfect throw, smacking one of the men hard on the back. The cowboy dropped Benny's legs, and for the first time turned to face the motel.

Ellis smiled and bent for another rock, aimed, and threw it. This one hit the truck inches from the second man.

Caden cheered. The barrage picked up, led by Ellis. Infinitely more dangerous now they had their captain.

"Stop it."

"Don't touch Benny."

Ellis kept up the attack, gauging the distance and getting closer and closer to his mark. The men were forced to take cover behind the truck.

Now both the cowboys faced the motel. One of them pulled out the radio again. He spoke briefly into it, then nodded to the other cowboy.

They didn't seem worried; their movements were relaxed and easy. They took up their positions behind the truck, leaning on the back, arms resting over the sides of the flatbed. What were they waiting for?

Ana paused, rock in hand. This felt wrong. They looked too comfortable, just standing there, faces hidden smugly behind their matching bandanas.

She looked around and caught Ellis's eye. He had stopped too, a worried expression on his handsome face.

Who had they called on their radio? What was going on?

It didn't take long before they found out.

One of the sheds close by suddenly exploded. It felt like the air was sucked up as a wave of burning heat whacked them.

Ana fell to the ground, momentarily disorientated. In a second, she was back in the gym. Back in the burning hallway. Her ears were ringing; she shook her head trying to clear it, pushing herself up to sitting. She looked around.

The others were spread out, some on the ground, some on their knees. They all seemed cowed, shocked. Raya was trying to stand, shaking dust off her arms. Alex was already standing, staring at the fire that was burning on the spot where the shed had been just seconds ago.

Dirt and ash fell from the sky as an immense cloud of black smoke spiralled up into the air over them.

Ana turned back to look at the truck. The two men had thrown Benny's body in the back of the flatbed. They slammed the tailgate shut and calmly walked to their doors. Not so much as a glance in the direction of the motel.

The truck pulled away, swerving fast, heading back to the nowhere it had come from. It was over. Benny was gone.

So that was it.

The motel was wired to explode. That's how they would die if they tried to hide out – if they didn't send someone over the line. They were in a cage, a trap, and there was no escaping, no running. Play or die.

They had been warned.

16 | Ana
47:23

The second hour of the Balloon Game was counting down.

With its pink blinds pulled firmly closed and the ancient air conditioner rattling loudly, Ellis's room gave the illusion of safety, hidden away from whatever was outside waiting for them.

After the explosion, they had somehow found their way here, running from the line, from the truck, from the place where Benny had died, the place where it had finally hit them; *this was real*. This was really happening. They'd followed Ellis inside, slamming the door shut and locking it behind them, and were now hiding in various corners. Their drawn faces carried the shock of what they had just witnessed. The horror of what was to come.

Ana's hands were shaking so badly she couldn't hold her phone steady enough to read the countdown. She tucked them under her arms and squeezed tightly. *Breathe.* She knew the drill. She'd been here before.

Leaves, broken glass, a can of green paint.

Push it away. Push it out of her mind. Just breathe. In. Out.

There were voices. Some of the others were talking, some crying.

For now, she needed to hold on to her own space, her own thoughts. Eyes closed. Focus.

For several precious minutes she sat on the cream-and-brown swirled carpet fighting the rising wall of panic inside. If anyone could do this, she could. She knew it. She had been here before and survived. She could do it again. Somehow, she would find the strength. She just had to believe.

Of course, that was easier said than done.

She could hear voices around her, becoming clearer with time. One voice stood out. A familiar voice. She focused in on the words, reeling herself back from the dark thoughts in her head.

"What do we do?" More mumbling voices. Then the same soft voice again. "So, what now?"

Alex.

That was all it took. It was as though a key unlocked her. Her eyes opened and she looked around, seeking out Alex first and then Raya. They were here, they were safe and alive – for now. Alex was standing by the dresser, arms folded around him. Raya was sitting on the floor by the window, hugging her knees to her chest, rocking slightly.

Alive for now. That was enough. That was all she needed to believe, to hope. As long as Alex and Raya were alive.

Ana stood up.

What would Danny do? She tried to focus her thoughts. What would he do if he were stuck here instead of her? She tried to imagine Danny standing in the room in his white trainers and scruffy Goodwill jeans, hands in pockets, calmly taking charge. He'd lead because that's who he was – a leader. He would be proactive, move them forward and come up with a plan. Ana wasn't a leader, but she could certainly come up with a plan. She'd never run short of ideas.

"Is there a camera or a microphone in here?" Ana spoke calmly. Her hands dropped to her sides. They were not shaking any more.

A few faces looked up at her. Ellis nodded his head.

He had been pacing up and down like a benched player on the sidelines of a title game. His steely eyes were narrowed. There was intensity and tension there, but Ana didn't see fear. He was ready to do what was needed next. He was ready to fight.

"I found two last night. There was a camera in the corner by the door, and a microphone in the bathroom. I smashed them both." Ellis pointed to a small pile of black debris on the nightstand. It looked like crushed beetles.

"Okay. Let's keep looking for them and get rid of as many as we can. We have to assume whoever is doing this is watching every move and listening to us too." Ana looked around. They needed to act, not sit around, and give up. Anything would be better than that. "We can light a signal fire, in the pool. If we throw on damp wood and leaves, it'll smoke. We can use a blanket or towel and send smoke signals. And we need to think. If we can figure out who's doing this to us, we might be able to find a way to stop them."

"She's right," Ellis said, stepping forward and somehow placing himself between Ana and the others. He was taking charge. "We split up. One team to disable the recording devices. One on the smoke signal. The others can break the locks on those three outbuildings – there were some pliers in the pile of junk Caden and Benny collected. We've searched every other corner of this fucking motel. We need to get inside and see if there's anything that we can use to get the fuck out of here." He looked at Ana. "And while you're at it, start thinking. I want each of you to come up with a list of possible suspects. Who knew you were coming? Who might want to hurt you? Anyone you can think of. We need to know who we're dealing with here."

"Wait, maybe those two cowboys are behind this?" Jade said, pushing herself up from a giant pile of pillows. Jax and Jade had commandeered the entire bed on arrival.

Ellis shook his head: "They were getting instructions from whoever was on the other end of that radio. That's the person we need to find. That's the one who's doing this to us."

Ana nodded, racking her brains for anything that might help.

"We can build a bomb shelter," she said, thinking as she spoke. "If we collect as many old mattresses and pillows as we can, we can pile them up somewhere, just in case the timer runs out and we need to hide."

"Too risky." Ellis shut her down. "You saw the shed explode. We've been warned. The whole motel will blow up if we don't play the game. A pile of old blankets won't protect against that. Face it – if this place blows, we all die. Anyone got any serious suggestions?" He turned away from her. Ana couldn't help feeling she was being put firmly in her place.

"We'll search for the cameras and bugs and stuff," Jade offered, nudging Jax. He nodded and reached over to the bedside table, where he'd left his phone charging – always ready for action.

"I'll take the fire," Raya said, pulling her Zippo from her pocket and flicking it.

"Alex, Caden – why don't you take the outbuildings?" It was phrased as an order. He checked his phone. "Okay, we've got forty-plus minutes left. We'll meet back on the line, near the road sign, twenty minutes before the hour is up. That leaves about twenty minutes to figure out how to get the fuck out of here. Let's go, people!"

Ana was shut out. Her punishment for daring to threaten Prince Ellis's rule.

"I'm going to build a bomb shelter." Ana said it quietly.

There was a long silence. Ellis turned his cold eyes on her, tilting his head to look down.

"We discussed that. It wouldn't work. I told you..."

"*You* discussed it. I disagree." Ana had no idea where it was coming from. She didn't have a confrontational bone in her body. But something about the stress of the situation was pushing her into the line of fire.

Ana knew full well what Ellis was thinking. He'd suggested meeting on the line for a reason. The odds of them finding something that would save them were slim, to say the least. Ellis wasn't going to take any chances. One of them would be crossing the line before the hour was up, whether by choice or otherwise, and it wasn't going to be Ellis.

"I told you that a shelter wouldn't work," Ellis said, his voice tight with barely contained frustration. "We all saw the explosion. We wouldn't stand a chance."

"Unless you build it somewhere that's already been detonated." Ana turned to the others. "Think about it. The explosives were planted before we arrived. If we wait on a spot that's already been set off, we should be safe."

She looked around. A few of them were nodding.

"That's ridiculous. If we sit on the spot where the shed used to be we'll be sitting ducks. It's completely exposed, there's no shelter.

And assuming we miraculously survive the explosion, we'll get shot – picked off one by one. It can't work," Ellis protested. He was not liking this one bit.

"I wasn't talking about the shed," Ana said. "We can make a shelter in the bus."

It made perfect sense. The shell of the bus was a metal core. They could pull out the remaining seats and build a decent bomb shelter. It would be hot and tight, but it just might work.

"I'll help," Alex said quickly. "It's a great idea."

"Yeah, I'll help too," Caden mumbled.

Ellis looked like he'd been slapped. Outmanned. Outgunned. He looked from Ana to Caden, and finally Alex; his eyes narrowed.

"All right, fine. I'm not going to waste any more of our precious time arguing about it. Do whatever the fuck you want. We'll meet by the bus, twenty minutes before the hour is up. Let's go!"

Ana smiled, relieved that the moment was over. The confrontation had ended. They had a plan. She could duck back out of the spotlight and get on with doing what she was best at – watching and thinking.

With a little shuffling around they all got into their teams and tentatively opened the door. The bright light was blinding. Ana squinted through half-closed eyelids as she stepped into the hot sun. Jax and Jade headed off one way, Raya the other. Caden lolled off by himself, on a hunt for things to pad the bus shelter.

As Alex stepped out, Ellis caught his arm.

"Things are going to get nasty around here really fucking fast. You might want to remember who your friends are, Cabrera," he said quietly.

Alex looked at him, then Ana. He flashed a quick smile at her.

"Thanks, Ellis, but I think I just did." He brushed Ellis's hand away and walked off towards the bus.

Ana watched Alex's back, a wave of gratitude and optimism sweeping through her. Alex had stood up for her. Alex was on her side. They could do this. The bomb shelter could work. If Norman exploded the whole motel around them, just imagine how much smoke that would make. Someone somewhere would have to see it. They'd have to wonder what was going on, wouldn't they?

Someone would come.

They just needed to stay alive long enough to be rescued. They just needed time.

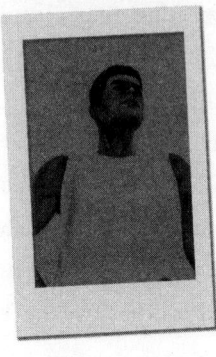

17 | Ellis
40:54

"Danny's sister. A word." It was a command. Ellis had mastered the art of dominating with the minimum number of syllables. It was essential in sport, and pretty damn useful in life too, as it turned out. He walked up to Ana, looming confidently over her, placing himself between her and the sun.

She looked up nervously at him, squinting awkwardly into the light.

He'd planned this, waiting until the others had gone. She'd challenged his authority in front of everyone with her whole bus-shelter plan. He couldn't afford to lose his position as leader, not with so much at stake. Time to set boundaries.

"You do realize what you've done?" He dropped his voice, projecting calm control with a dash of barely concealed irritation.

Ana bit her lip and looked down, forced to by the harsh glare.

"You've given them hope," Ellis said. "That's a dangerous thing when we're fighting for our lives."

"I think—" Ana mumbled.

"You think you're helping. I get it. But the truth is, your little plan is only going to delay the inevitable. Maybe it'll get us through this hour, but when Norman figures out what we're up to, he'll find a way to destroy the bus and anyone cowering inside it. Your little shelter plan will kill us all."

"But what if—"

"What if we get rescued? Come on. Think! We're over an hour's drive from the nearest town. That gives Norman plenty of time to pick us off one by one. By the time help gets here, it'll be too late – we'll all be dead. You read the message. It's play or die. If we don't play, *we die.*"

She shook her head, frowning as though trying to formulate her thoughts before speaking.

"I know it's risky, Ellis…but what's the alternative? If we don't even try, then when the hour's up someone must cross the line."

"And your point is?"

Ana didn't respond. Ellis didn't like the way she was squinting up at him, with Danny's bright hazel eyes. She was a mousey little thing, but Ellis could sense something beneath it. Something unbendable.

"Listen, Danny's sister, I understand. We're trapped between a rock and something fucking harder. But we have no choice, we need to play the game if we want to have a chance of getting out of here alive. We need to buy more time. When the hour's up, if we haven't figured out a way to get out, someone needs to cross that line, as brutal as it sounds. Then we reset – a new hour, more time."

Her face was unreadable. No tears, no drama, just that annoying, watchful expression. Taking him in, processing. Ellis was starting to feel uncomfortable.

"But…we can't just…"

"Let someone die? We are fighting for *our lives* here! If we have to…lose one person to save everyone else, then that's what we have to do. This is not a time for weakness. There's no place for cowards here. Don't you get it? *We're at war.*"

She winced when he spoke – he'd struck a chord.

Ellis had made his point, there really was nothing she could add. It was a no-brainer. Hiding out in the bus would be a death sentence for all of them. They would do everything they could to escape or be rescued. But if they were still trapped by the end of the hour, they would have no choice. There was no way around it. Someone would have to cross the line.

Worst case, they would play out the whole game, and only one of them would be going home. Ellis didn't want to think that way, but at the same time, he was a realist; if he wanted to walk away from this alive, he had to face the terrifying truth. Winning the game was his best shot at surviving, and he wasn't going to give that up for anyone or anything.

He adopted a conciliatory tone. "Look, someone will notice we're missing or see the smoke signal. Jax's fans will raise all kinds of hell without their daily post. We will be missed. People will come looking for us eventually. Until then, we buy time. We play the game. We stay alive. Trust me, I'll take care of everything."

Problem handled. He was so fucking good at this. A natural born leader, like his dad. Not someone who was going to wind up dead in the back of a red pick-up truck. He turned to walk away.

"Ellis?" Ana's voice stopped him in his tracks. Weren't they done here?

"What?" He was impatient and didn't bother to hide it.

"Who dies first?" Ana looked at him directly for the first time. There they were…Danny's eyes. Ellis almost flinched. Almost. "In your plan. Who crosses the line first?"

Who was she? He was getting a bad feeling about her. Danny was something – everything. He had been top of the St Francis food chain. People had loved him – no one more than Ellis. Maybe the twin was more like her brother than he'd thought.

He needed to end this. No more wasting precious time. He'd been watching everyone from the moment the bus exploded. It was a useful skill – sizing up the opposing team. Ana had given her weakness away at the pool last night.

"I think you know the answer to that." He looked pointedly towards Alex and Caden's retreating backs. "We're playing the Balloon Game after all, aren't we? A morality game. Who's the guiltiest? Who most deserves to die?"

Ana followed his stare; her face dropped, eyes widened. For the first time, Ellis could read her expression clearly. Fear. He had her.

"That's right." Ellis's voice was matter of fact. "When it comes to guilt, we have our first two volunteers. Caden got Hunt stoned off his face before he killed himself. *Guilty*. As for Alex – we all know why he's here, don't we? We all know what happened a year ago. *Guilty*. It's a pity, I quite like the guy."

Ellis turned to face the pool. A thin line of smoke had appeared. Raya must have lit the fire already. His eyes narrowed.

"As for who *deserves* to die…well, let's see. Anyone who has attempted suicide in the past would be bumped right to the top of that list. I mean, clearly, they don't value their life if they've tried to kill themself before. Tragic, really."

Ana had been warned. He could tell from the shocked expression on her face that she understood his message very well. *Challenge me and I will hurt the people you love. I will see to it that Alex and Raya cross the line.* He hadn't wanted to play hardball, but she'd pushed.

"Now, Danny's sister, forgive me if I stop wasting what little time we have left," he said, turning his back on her. He walked away; relief coursed through him. That had been harder than he'd thought. He hadn't gone ten paces when her voice stopped him again.

"I have a name, you know."

Slowly, he turned. There was something in her tone that set off his alarm bells. She was standing still, head dropped, eyes locked on him. There it was again. Danny. He could see it. As if he was standing in front of him. Danny, the rock star, the hero. The king to Ellis's prince. His Danny.

The little mouse was gone.

"It's Ana," she said, her voice low and dangerously calm. "My name is Ana. You'll want to remember that."

With that, she turned her back to him and walked away.

Ellis watched her go. He tried to smile, but there was a new feeling in the pit of his stomach, fluttery, nervous. They'd played their cards. Shown their hands. He'd pushed. She'd pushed back. He was going to have to be careful. Very, very careful. He had a possible challenger. Ana Reyes was the unknown factor. This was about to get interesting.

Well, fine. Ellis could do interesting. He was his father's son.

Game on, little mouse. Game on.

18 | Ana
31:06

There were two dusty bottles of water and an expired Twix bar in Ana's mini-fridge. Score!

She dropped the bottles into the heavy crate next to her – it was already loaded with random drinks, snacks and out-of-date sodas she'd collected from other rooms. She was stocking the bus shelter – who knew how long they'd be stuck there for.

Carefully, guiltily, she ripped open the Twix wrapper. There was no point in saving it – it would just disintegrate in the heat, she rationalized.

Holding the chocolate close to her face, she breathed in the intoxicating, sugary scent. How many hours had it been since she'd eaten? Too many – that was for sure. She reached out the tip of her tongue and gently, oh so gently, licked the already melting chocolate. This was as close to heaven as she was going to get today – hopefully.

A shuffle behind made her jump.

Alex was standing in the doorway, his arms full of a random collection of pink bedding and pillows. He grinned. Ana blushed.

"Oh…er…hi. I didn't see you there…" she mumbled. "Twix?" She held out the second bar, with a small pang of regret.

"Hell, yes," Alex said. He dropped the pile of sheets on the bed and sat on the cream-and-brown swirled carpet next to her. "Thanks." He took the precious Twix, balancing it lovingly in his fingers. He had musician's hands, long and fine.

They sat, side by side, and munched away in contented silence.

It was weird. After an entire year of avoiding Alex, in this moment, there was no one she would rather be with. Even in this godforsaken hellhole, he made things feel normal – better.

"So, what do you really think about the shelter?" she asked at last.

"I don't know." Alex rubbed his nose thoughtfully. "I mean…it's good. It's a great idea and all, you know… It's just…"

"It's okay. I get it," Ana cut in. There were a thousand ways it could go wrong. She didn't want to hear all the potential flaws in her plan – she was already stressed enough. What if it failed? What if everyone piled into the bus and it exploded anyway? Or if they got trapped there, out in the open and cooked to death? It would all be her fault. She bit her lip nervously.

"I keep thinking about Benny," Alex said. His face was turned away from her, towards the open door. "He thought it was all a prank, didn't he? He had no idea he was actually going to…" Alex's profile was outlined against the blisteringly blue square of sky through the door frame. His hair had flopped forward; he chewed his lip, searching for words. "I just wish…I wish I'd said something more. We shouldn't have let him go, Ana. We should have stopped him." He crumpled up the Twix wrapper and threw it at the wall.

Ana didn't say the usual platitudes; *he made his choice, he didn't suffer, it was quick* – all the things people tell themselves to justify the incomprehensible. It was too soon – the shock was too real.

They had just watched Benny die, right in front of them. They were hurting and she couldn't fix that.

Without thinking, she leaned over to Alex and wrapped her arms around him.

Alex dropped his head towards her and buried his face in her hair. She closed her eyes and breathed in his warm familiar scent. Alex.

They sat in silence, pressed against each other as though the world might, just for a moment, fuck off and leave them alone.

Ana felt a mess of words, thoughts, feelings. It was overwhelming. The fear of the last few hours and of what might come next was mingled with something else, something she couldn't understand. It was like a small fire was burning inside. Hope? Love? She didn't know, she couldn't read it. But as she held Alex, she felt it. There was a deeply buried strength that was stirring in her heart.

They would make it. Somehow. They had to. This feeling couldn't just disappear. It was too powerful, too pure. It had to be enough.

Didn't it?

"There's something I can't get out of my head." Alex spoke so softly that for a moment, Ana wasn't sure if she'd even heard him. "I keep thinking that it should have been me."

Ana let go of him and pulled back, studying his face, his eyes. Was he really saying that?

"I mean, if you're talking about guilt, about who deserves to die first, I'm right up there. I should have gone. I should be next." He said it too quickly, giving himself away. He'd obviously thought this through.

Ana felt a flash of irritation at him. It was his *life* at stake.

He couldn't just give up like that. He had to fight if he was going to make it out of here. *He had to.*

"You know it wasn't your fault," she said.

"Wasn't it? I mean, let's be real, Ana. A year ago, Karl Hunt drove up to the gym in his truck, playing Trash Dogs at full volume, singing along to my song – 'Burn'. My song, Ana. Not Danny's or anyone else's. A song *I* wrote, the words *I* wrote."

"What Hunt did was on him – no one else. He wanted to die. Your song...those were just lyrics. You're not responsi—"

"*I will burn you down. You will scream my name. There's nowhere to run from me. Your blood will turn to flame...* Ana, how am I not responsible?"

"It was just a stupid song. You didn't *mean* for anyone to get hurt."

"I dunno. Maybe I did?" Alex mumbled the words so quietly Ana barely caught them. "When I wrote those words, I was thinking about my dad and what he did to my mom and me. My head was really messed up about stuff. I wanted to hurt him, like he hurt us. I had so much anger, just like my dad. Ana, I think I'm like him. I think maybe inside I'm the same. Bad."

Ana slipped her hand into his without thinking.

"You're not like your dad, Alex. You're the sweetest, kindest person I know. But you're also human. You've *never* hurt anyone, even if you wanted to. Yeah, you wrote a song about it, an angry song. But that's not weakness, or a sign that you're bad. That's a good thing to do. You turned your anger into music. That's strength. Your dad couldn't have done that." She faced him, her bright eyes intense. "What Karl Hunt did with your song. That's on him. Not you. Alex, you can't blame yourself."

"But I do. My song, my words, my anger...they meant something to Karl, they inspired him. People died because of it. How can I ever forgive myself?" Alex looked directly at her. "I *am* guilty, Ana. I deserve to be here, and maybe...I deserve to die here." She could see the guilt in his eyes, like a reflection of her own guilt. They stared at each other, words lost between them.

This was the moment. Ana knew it. This was her time to tell him the truth about what had happened a year ago, about what she'd done. The reason why she had been brought here. Why, if anyone deserved to die, it was her. She faltered. Her mind struggled to find the words.

"Alex...there's something I need to tell you." She could do this. He needed to hear it, to understand that what he'd done was nothing; his own guilt and shame paled when compared to hers. She pushed herself to speak. "You're not the only one who feels guilty for what happened. All of us were brought here for a reason. You just don't know what the rest of us did, not yet." She stared out of the doorway, across the enviable emptiness of the desert.

How could she tell *him*? How could she let him down?

"What do you mean?"

Ana looked back at him, his soft eyes, his kind face, worry written across it. The words were on her tongue. She could say it. Say the words. Just be done with it. Once and for all.

But even as she thought it, she knew she couldn't. Not now. If he knew what she'd done, she would lose Alex for ever, just like she'd lost Danny. If he knew the truth, he would despise her. He would walk away and never look back. With everything they were facing, she just couldn't take that. Not yet.

"I just mean...it'll be okay. I promise."

She dropped her eyes. She had failed him. A coward, once again. He deserved so much better. It was time to shut this down, to stop playing with dangerous feelings like hope and love. Those weren't for her.

"We should go," she said abruptly, jumping to her feet. "Time's running out and that shelter won't build itself."

Alex nodded. He looked confused and hurt by her sudden coldness. But it was for his own good. It was better this way.

He stood up and walked over to the bed, scooping up the pile of bedding.

"Okay, sure. Are you coming?"

"You go. I'll be right behind," Ana said, turning away from him. She needed a moment. A reset.

"I guess I'll see you by the, er…shelter."

Ana closed her eyes and waited until his footsteps had faded. She could still feel him in her mind, in her arms, his warmth through his T-shirt. It hurt; the feelings cut into her. It was never worth letting her guard down. Never. Every time she opened up to someone, life would turn it around and shred her, like a punishment for her weakness. No. This wasn't her path. Her path was alone.

But not for her friends. They had a chance for happiness – if they could just escape the motel.

It was time to remember her promise. She had one job here – to keep her friends alive. Nothing more.

The water ran cold over Ana's scarred fingers. She caught it in her cupped hands and splashed it over her face and neck. It felt good in this heat.

Ana stood at the beige bathroom vanity, stained and crusted after decades of motel service. Her chat with Alex had kicked off some things she didn't want in her head.

Triggers was the word Mr Dankman had used.

Watch out for triggers. Let the bad thoughts into your head, then let them drift away. Give them permission to be released.

The seventies strip light gave her reflection a bluish tinge – a morbid thought flashed through her mind. Was this what she'd look like when she was dead? She quickly gave herself permission to release *that* thought.

Instinctively she glanced at the corner of the room, searching for the soapy microphone.

But what she saw stopped her cold.

Her breath caught, held tight as she blinked, trying to make sense of it. Something told her not to react. She made herself reach for the faucet and go through the motions of washing her hands again, moving on autopilot as her brain raced, finally allowing her eyes to turn upwards and study the corner carefully.

There it was. The tiny black dot listening to her. The bug was back. It looked like the soap had been carefully wiped away and the device had been polished clean. Which meant that someone had been in here, climbed up and fixed it – someone had stood in her bathroom, in her motel room.

If she was right, then Norman was inside the circle.

If she was right…they were not alone.

19 | Caden
23:51

Scratching his sunburned nose, Caden looked out across the desert. Something had been bothering him since Benny crossed the line. He struggled to rewind his thoughts and play back the moment Benny was shot. He pictured him standing, arms outstretched, the sound of the gunshot as he fell, his uniform riding up as he lay in the dirt.

Any way that Caden played it, things didn't add up.

He scanned the middle distance. The nearest shelter was a small pile of boulders, maybe three hundred yards away. Nothing else. Just flat, dusty emptiness and a couple of scraggly weeds. Pointing at the rocks, he closed first one eye, then the other, peering along his finger like a gun scope.

If there was one thing he'd learned about in military academy, it was guns. To make a clean shot from that distance would take a high-velocity rifle – the kind of gun that would do serious damage. Benny was too clean.

"Hey, C-Dog. How's it going?"

Alex had come up behind him, carrying an armful of pink sheets and pillows. Caden glared at him. It was nothing personal – he didn't mind Alex, but he preferred to be alone. Simpler that way, and a hell of a lot quieter.

"I'm thinking," he grunted.

"About anything in particular?"

"Benny."

"Yeah, I know – me too. I'm sorry, C-Dog." Alex stepped forward and for one horrible moment, Caden thought he was going to hug him. Alex clearly had the wrong idea. He wasn't sad. He had to shut this down before Alex thought he was a pussy.

"There were no brains or guts and stuff. Should have been way more blood and chunks of skin, stuff like that."

"No brains…and, um…guts…er…?" Alex looked taken aback and a little queasy. He seemed to be struggling to say the words.

Caden grinned. Alex was the pussy.

"It was too clean – didn't look right. There'd be splatter over that distance. High-velocity rifles will mess you up."

"So…what are you saying? Benny wasn't shot with a high-velocity rifle?" Alex asked. Caden nodded. "So, that means what… the shooter's close by?"

"Yup. Fifty feet or less is my guess. But it's weird. Can't see anywhere you could hide that's close enough."

They both turned to stare out across the desert. There was nothing but the distant rocks, shimmering slightly in the heat. The white line stood out starkly near their feet.

By now, Caden's attention span had reached its limit. He glanced at his phone. It was almost time. The others would be coming soon to build the shelter. He rubbed his sweaty neck. It was too darn hot. Way too darn hot. His empty stomach hurt. He was a big guy and needed regular meals. He hadn't eaten all day and was starting to feel sick with hunger. Time for a little pick-me-up.

Settling himself on the bus steps in a small patch of shade, Caden reached into his pocket, feeling for the comforting crinkle of plastic. He pulled out a small Ziploc bag containing several treasured pink pills. These were his pride and joy – premium quality, top of the range. Each pill sold for twenty dollars a pop at school, but there was no point in saving these for resale. Not while he was stuck in this hole. Just one little pill would do more than take the edge off. He took two and dry-swallowed them both.

"You should go easy on those." Raya had arrived. She walked up to Caden and squatted down in the shade next to him. "Remember last time you took too many and went skinny-dipping in Ellis's pool – mid-party? Trust me, no one needs to see that again." Raya grinned, clearly enjoying the memory.

Caden nodded at her grumpily.

"Not your business, Mori," he growled. Raya just laughed.

"Check out my fabulous signal fire." She nodded towards the pool enclosure. A weedy stream of smoke trickled out over the top of the fence, dissolving instantly into the strong desert wind. "Impressive, huh? Somehow, I don't think that's going to be our ticket out of here." She looked around at the large pile of bedding and raised a pierced eyebrow. "Let's hope we have more luck with this lot."

Figures were appearing around the corners of the motel, heading for the bus. Caden groaned. People – the reason he took pills and anything else he could get his hands on. If he was the only person on the planet, he'd be stone-cold sober and happy, just hanging out in the school parking lot in his affectionately named Candyvan. No noise, no bother.

Sniffing loudly, he wiped a grubby arm across his pink face and stood up. Break time was over. He picked up an armful of bedding and dragged it over to the bus, hefting it over the side.

Ellis and Jade arrived first, closely followed by Jax. They were arguing.

"...it's means, motive and weapon. Seriously." Jade tossed her shiny, golden hair back as though to emphasize her point. Caden kept his eyes averted. Girls like Jade made him uncomfortable.

"Fuck's sake, Jade. You're thinking of *Clue*," Ellis said sharply. "It's *opportunity*. A suspect has to have means, motive and *opportunity*."

"Okay, whatever, Ellis. I just don't get how that's going to help us figure out who's behind this."

"I'm saying we start with motive. Who would go to all the effort to set this up and lure us out here? Why? They're going to have to have a damn strong reason, strong enough to kill."

"Unless it's just some batshit crazy psycho," Jax interjected, green eyes flicking up briefly from his phone screen.

"Jesus...can we focus for half a fucking minute? I'm talking about *real* suspects, *real* people. Who has an actual motive for setting this game up? It has to be something to do with what happened a year ago. But not just anything – something really fucking bad."

"Wait, I got it," Jax piped up. "Maia and Danny, right? They have a *really* good motive. They both died."

"Oh my god. Seriously, Jax? How can they do this if they're dead?" Jade snapped.

"No, wait, Jax has a point," Ellis said, rubbing his head thoughtfully. "Maybe not Maia and Danny, but what about their families? They've got motive. Weren't Maia's parents high-up, genius NASA nerds? I bet they were destroyed by the death of their precious little pooky – gruesomely murdered and no one held accountable. Maybe they decided to avenge Maia's death. They'd be smart, resourceful and rich. Now that's a motive."

"You don't really think so? They seemed so sad and lost at the funeral. Though I guess you never really know people, do you? It's always the quiet ones." Jade's eyes flicked up and caught Caden watching her. He grunted and dropped the pile of embarrassingly stained sheets.

"Didn't they move back to Canada?" Jax added unhelpfully.

"Well...maybe they came back? I don't know." Ellis suddenly grinned. "Besides, there's always Danny's family. We've got motive right there."

"Stop it, Ellis!" Raya shouted, jumping to her feet. "There's no way Ana or her mom have anything to do with this."

"I'm just saying...if we're talking motive, they're at the top of our list. What was the other one...oh, yeah – opportunity." Ellis was enjoying himself. "No better opportunity than being right here with us, inside the motel. Pretending to be trapped..."

"Don't even go there, Ellis." Raya stepped forward; her fists clenched at her sides.

"Go where?" Ellis said innocently.

"You know exactly where..."

Yadda, yadda. Caden pulled out his phone. Seventeen minutes and counting. These losers were going to waste the whole hour talking. He sighed and turned away, heading over to the bus steps. They could argue all day if they liked – not his problem. He'd check back in if things got real, and they started fighting. Time to start building the shelter. He climbed onboard the bus, careful not to touch the hot metal frame.

As soon as he stepped into the aisle, he was hit by the smell – ashy, burned plastic mixed with the pungent stench of something else. He pulled the neck of his shirt up over his nose to stop himself from gagging.

"What the—" he grunted. Liquid coated the floor, mixed with the ash forming ominously dark, shimmering pools. It looked toxic and smelled worse.

He squatted down, rubbing his thick fingers into the gloop. Sniffing them tentatively, he recoiled; he knew that smell. "You've got to be kidding," he muttered. Could this day get any worse? He looked across at the others, but they were all still squabbling.

"Oi!" he bellowed. One by one they turned to face him. He held up his hands, the oily black liquid dripped off his fingers. "Got a problem."

This was not good. Not good at all.

The floor of the bus was completely soaked in gas.

20 | Jade
16:04

"*Gas?*" Jade felt her stomach drop. "Are you serious right now?"

The sickening stench of gas was everywhere, spread around by people's hands, their shoes, their clothes. It was inescapable – nauseating. Jade's thoughts were jumping all over the place, fuelled by a flurry of blind panic. How was this even possible? The bus had exploded – all the gas should have burned off. What were they going to do? The shelter plan had failed. There was so little time left...so little time...

She looked around; the others were just as lost. The only one who seemed capable of functioning was Ellis. True to form, he climbed onto the steps of the bus and took charge: "All right. Let's stay calm and think this through." He rubbed his hand over his head, hard, his face creased with worry. "How much time have we got left?"

"About fifteen minutes," Jax called out, eyes on his phone.

"*Oh my god.* Ellis, what are we going to do?" Jade's voice sounded odd, even to herself – unnaturally high and tight. *Fifteen minutes.* Nausea swelled in the back of her mouth. In fifteen minutes, someone would have to cross the line. She pictured Benny, the blood, the truck.

"I say we do nothing," Raya spoke up, her sharp voice silencing the others. "It's hot. The gas will evaporate. We can wait and go on just before the hour's up. Odds are we'll be far enough from the explosion that the bus won't catch fire."

"That's your plan, Mori?" Ellis looked incredulous. "The gas is obviously leaking from somewhere. Do you seriously think it's a good idea to lie down on top of a gas leak and hope we don't catch fire? We will burn to death. Do you get it? *Burn*."

That did the job. They'd been at the gym a year ago. No need to go into details.

"Well...maybe we can hide out somewhere else? We could grab this lot and run." Raya gestured at the now useless pile of bedding. "What about the pool, or the reception?"

"Have you forgotten that the whole motel is wired to explode? The bus was our only safe bet."

"Out of the fire into the frying pan. We just can't catch a freaking break," Raya muttered.

Jade could taste the vomit now; she swallowed hard, folding her arms tightly in an effort to steady herself. There were bad pictures and ugly thoughts circling in her head. The reality of her situation was both obvious and terrifying. She could actually die. She could be dead soon – *dead, like Benny.*

Footsteps momentarily pulled her up. Ana – the mastermind of this shitshow, had finally bothered to show up. Alex caught her up on the situation, pointing to the bus, talking in a low voice. Probably explaining how spectacularly Ana's shelter plan had failed, how someone was going to die because of her.

Maybe it should be Ana. It seemed only fair.

Jade was considering the politics of suggesting this when Ana stepped forward.

"I found something." Ana spoke directly to Ellis. "I think someone's inside the circle with us." Jade only half-listened to the mumbled story about a cleaned microphone and soap, how if they weren't alone, maybe they could find Norman and *blah, blah*.

She was relieved when Ellis called it.

"Just *stop*! We don't have fucking time for another of your stupid ideas," he snapped. Ana recoiled, shocked. "We can't make another shelter. We can't go on the hunt for some goddamn microphone-cleaning psycho. Don't you get it? If someone doesn't cross the fucking line when the timer runs out, *we are all going to die.*"

Oh, god. Did he have to say it like that? Jade sniffed, desperately holding on to herself, trying to be strong, trying to be brave.

"Listen, we have no choice." Ellis turned to face them, arms spread wide. "There's only one option left. I know this is fucking hard, but we have to do what we have to do, if we want to survive this and go home." His handsome face was sincere, honest. He was their leader – no question, and he was right. There was only one way this was going to play out. Only one terrifying, horrific way.

Everyone knew what was coming next.

"Like it or not, if we want to live past the hour…we have to play the Balloon Game. When the hour's up, we vote. The loser crosses the line."

Jade dug her nails into her palms, willing herself not to cry.

So, this was it. No way out. In less than fifteen minutes, they were going to decide who was guiltiest, and then another one of them would be dead – *dead like Benny*.

The problem was…it could be her. If anyone here remembered what she'd posted a year ago, on the day of the fire, she could lose the vote. She could be the one. *She could die.*

She pictured the red truck. Oh, god, the truck. Those men, grabbing her by her toned ankles, slinging her body onto the flatbed, like a piece of meat. It was just too real. Too close.

Panic smacked her viciously in her gut. Whatever happened next, she couldn't survive this alone. She needed help.

She turned to look for Jax, but he was squatting in the shade of the bus staring at his beloved phone screen, seemingly oblivious to their predicament. Useless. Delusional. The stakes were too high to rely on Jax.

No, she knew what she needed to do. She needed strength and power on her side. She needed to win this game, and to do that – she needed a winner.

She needed *the prince*.

11:18

Ellis had already gone to the reception to collect a random assortment of pens and drink coasters from the desk drawer. They would use them to vote. Jade sprinted after him, slamming the reception door open so hard, she almost smacked him in the face.

"Ellis. We need to talk – *now*."

Ellis was irritatingly calm, as though he was above all this. Normally it would have annoyed the hell out of Jade, but his arrogance implied confidence, and confidence meant he could help her. He nodded.

"Go on."

"Ellis, I can't do this. I can't just…*die*. You have to help me," she said, her voice low and urgent.

He watched her dispassionately, his pale grey eyes giving away nothing. How could he be so damn cool? The minutes were counting down and her *life* was on the line.

After what felt like for ever, he nodded and pushed his way out of the door, motioning for Jade to follow. The wind was kicking up, blowing unpleasantly hot air and dust in Jade's face. She kept having to tuck loose strands of blonde hair behind her ears as she trotted along behind him, frantically talking to his back.

"We're friends, right? We've been friends for a long time. You know we always hang out at parties and stuff. I mean, we're the same. Our parents are famous. We're A-list, right? You, me and Jax."

Ellis didn't slow down.

"Ellis, please. We need to help each other out. I have money. My mom would pay anything to keep me safe. People like us, we need to stick together. Ellis, *please!*" She was begging but didn't care.

Ellis stopped abruptly and turned to look at her with a calculating expression. She tried to hold his gaze, but the panic was becoming overwhelming again.

"I'm not going to die out here!" she blurted out. "I can't. Not like this." Tears were welling up.

"What makes you think you're going to die, Jade?"

"Because…because…" Jade's bored pout had been replaced by a steely, tight expression.

Ellis narrowed his eyes.

"Because…of your video, maybe? Your little bullying prank that bought you a one-way ticket to the Motel Loba?"

"You…you've seen it?" Jade stuttered. Her skin turned bright red under her carefully applied foundation. She'd only posted it on her private story and taken it down right after Karl's suicide and the fire. But what was she thinking? These things had a way of spreading. She knew that better than anyone. Of course he'd seen it. Of course he knew – and the odds were, he wasn't the only one.

Ellis gave a short laugh: "Yeah. I saw it. Can't really forget that one. Brutal."

Oh, god, the video. She could picture it now.

It was filmed in the St Francis locker room – the day before the fire. A group of heavily made-up blonde girls giggled next to a shower curtain. Jade was in front of them, mugging for the camera. She held up her fingers: three, two, one. They whipped the shower curtain back and there was Karl Hunt, in the middle of the locker room, naked. A cacophony of mocking laughter ensued as the person holding the camera raced forward, closing in on Hunt's nudity, the girls surrounding him.

It had been a mistake. She knew that now. But what could you do? What was done was done.

"It wasn't bullying, Ellis. People have no idea what it's like to have a celebrity mom. Everyone wants a piece of me. Hunt was a creep. He was always lurking around my locker and staring at me over his lunch tray. Everyone noticed. It was embarrassing. It was sexual harassment. I had no choice. I told him I was hot for him and to meet me in the locker room and get naked. So, he did – what kind of loser even does that? He deserved it. People like him deserve what they get."

"You don't see what's wrong with that?" Ellis said, raising his eyebrows.

"No. I don't! I was doing a public service," Jade said flatly, folding her arms over her crop top. She looked around desperately. "Any self-respecting feminist would have done the same thing.

I don't deserve to die for this, Ellis. I don't. If they vote for who's guilty, I know someone will have seen it. Someone will remember. Please…you've got to help me. I can't die out here, like this. *Ellis, please!*"

After a brief pause, Ellis nodded, as if making his mind up about something. His expression softened.

"Okay, Jade. I can help you. On two conditions."

Jade felt like throwing her arms around him but knew better: "Yes. Anything, Ellis. Anything."

"First, if I tell you to do something, even if you don't understand it, you've got to do *exactly* what I say," Ellis said, watching her response closely.

"Yes, yes. I do, I mean, I will. Yes!" Jade smiled. The prince was on her side. *The prince*. The point guard was on her team. She felt an intense wave of relief.

"Secondly, you have to promise you've got my back," Ellis said in a measured tone. "If we stick together, we can survive this. But only if we stick together…and you bring your lapdog with you." Ellis nodded to where Jax was standing by the bus with the others.

"You got it, Ellis. Whatever you say goes. We're a team. You, Jax and me. We will do whatever you say. Thank you." Jade tried to stop. Gushing was never a good look – right up there with begging and brown-nosing. They were signs of weakness and Ellis didn't respect weakness. She pulled herself up, wiping at her streaked mascara with the back of her hands. She must look ridiculous. Nothing good in life came from looking bad. Her mom had taught her that.

Ellis held out his hand. It was a slightly odd, old-fashioned gesture, but Jade was past caring. She took it, and they shook on it.

It felt good – real somehow, a silent contract that would guarantee her survival. They would win this game because that's what Ellis did. He won things.

Jade could breathe again. She liked being taken care of. It felt good.

Ellis turned and started jogging towards the bus. Jade trotted along behind him feeling much better – almost hopeful. Without realizing it, she started humming quietly to herself.

I will survive…

I will survive. For the first time in hours, she smiled.

21 | Ana
08:39

A handful of coasters were stacked near the bus, a faded image on the front – a pink rose over a dated photograph of the motel in its former glory. The reception, the shiny road sign, the pool filled with water – umbrellas and sunloungers lining its side. A different time. Holidays and sunshine. Who would have imagined what this place would become, what horrors would unfold here?

Next to the coasters was a pile of used biros from the reception desk. Ready for the vote.

All seven of them stood in a silent circle like a western showdown, guns at the ready. One person wouldn't walk away from this, one person was going across the line. Ana could picture Benny, the look on his face when the shot rang out, falling – eyes open.

Was this really happening? Were they actually going to vote someone to their death? It felt remote somehow. Unreal. Should she even write a name? Wouldn't that make her a party to murder, an accessory? A murderer, even?

But as she looked around at the ring of faces, she knew the answer. There was no choice. She had to do this, because if she didn't then she'd be throwing away her vote. A vote that might save

Raya or Alex from crossing the line.

"So, like, how do we do this...?" Jade was shuffling slightly. She kept pushing her hair back; her perfect make-up was running at the edges, making her face oddly blurry, as though she was melting. "We just write a name?" Ana narrowed her eyes. Jade was acting strangely. She kept looking at Ellis. The two of them were up to something. Which would mean, the *three* of them were up to something – Jax would do whatever Jade told him to do.

"Yes. We all get one vote. The person with the most votes must leave the circle. If there's a tie, we toss a coin." Ellis's voice was calm. "You all heard the rules of the game. I think it's pretty clear how we choose. We start with the guilty." Ellis looked pointedly at Caden, then Alex – his expression dark.

Everyone knew what he meant. Or almost everyone. Caden seemed abnormally unconcerned, partly because he was swaying on the spot grinning and humming to himself, clearly off his face.

"No," Ana blurted out. "We're all guilty. The message said it. We all did something a year ago. All of us, even if we don't know..."

"Are you volunteering, Danny's sister? Is there something you'd like to confess to the group?" Ellis said.

Ana kicked herself. She'd played right into his hands. If she confessed to save Alex, then Ellis would get both of them voted out. She fell silent.

Nodding to himself, Ellis turned away dismissively and faced the others.

"Listen – I know this is fucking hard, but it's not our fault. Whatever happens here is not on us. It's on Norman. Got that? He's making us do this. *We have no choice.*" Ellis cast his pale eyes around at the anxious circle of faces.

No one moved, no one spoke. The windmill spun wildly in a sudden gust of wind, clacking loudly into the air. They could all feel it; time was moving away, escaping beyond them, out of reach.

Ellis stepped forward and picked the first coaster off the top of the pile.

"It's time to vote. My advice, for what it's worth...vote with your conscience." He took a pen; his hand was steady. He knew he had no skin in the game. He was safe, for now.

"Ana?" Alex looked at her, worried. Raya moved closer to them, her eyes round with fear.

"What should we do?" Raya whispered. "I don't know if I can..."

"I know," Ana said, keeping her voice low. "But we don't have a choice. If we stick together, the three of us, we'll be okay. We just have to stick together." She walked up to the steps and picked up her coaster. One by one, the others stepped forward; even Caden, going through the motions though he clearly had no idea what was going on.

It was obvious what they needed to do. If the three of them voted for Caden, they would just need one of the others to vote for him too. Caden wouldn't vote for himself. So that left Ellis, Jade and Jax. They'd vote for Caden, of course. Alex was their friend. It would be a sure thing.

But as Ana looked around at the ring of faces, something didn't feel right. She couldn't put her finger on it.

Ellis was standing loosely, pen in hand, Jade and Jax on either side of him. His wingmen. He wrote something and threw his coaster down on the ground. The first vote was cast.

Jax followed, casually chucking his coaster on top.

They were running out of time. Hands shaking, with a queasy

feeling in her stomach, Ana printed a name. Raising her chin almost imperceptibly, she held out the coaster angled to the right so that Alex and Raya could read the name. Raya gulped nervously but nodded.

Jade took longer: she was clearly struggling and kept pausing to push her hair behind her ears. Finally, she placed her coaster down next to the others. There were tears in her eyes. Why was she so upset? She didn't even know Caden. Ana frowned. She hadn't thought Jade would care so much as long as she knew she'd be safe. Maybe she'd underestimated her.

One by one, they all placed their coasters face down on the ground. Even Caden managed to somehow scribble something and drop his card on the floor.

When all the votes were in, Raya walked over to the pile of votes. She had lost the toss and it was her job to count the votes. Ana was relieved it wasn't her; her hands were shaking too much.

Raya collected the cards, mixed them up and then held out the first and carefully flipped it: CADEN.

Ana recognized her own writing. She looked down, avoiding eye contact.

The next card: CADEN. Caden stopped giggling.

The next: ALEX. It must be Caden's vote. But the letters were neatly printed; how could someone as off his face as Caden write that neatly? Ana felt nauseous, a dark knot of fear was growing inside her. She turned to Alex, but he was oddly calm, just standing, hands in his pockets, watching. *How could he just stand there?*

The next card read: CADEN.

"Hey, that's me!" Caden slurred, confused. He had no idea what was happening.

Three votes for Caden. No surprises there. They just needed one more.

Raya flipped the next card: ALEX. The letters were written in round cursive. This shouldn't be happening. Who else had voted for Alex? *Why?*

Ana looked around at the circle of faces desperately, and that was when she saw it. It was the smallest of things. Jade looked up, her eyes, flicked to Alex, then back down. It lasted a second, but that one sad, little look – her guilty expression – gave her away. Jade had voted for Alex. Which meant Jax and Ellis had too. Three votes for Alex. *Three.*

Which meant with Caden's…it would be four.

A wall of sheer, blind panic hit Ana. *How had she let it come to this?* Of course, she should have thought. *She should have thought!* Ellis was two steps ahead of her. If they voted out Alex, then next time, Ellis would have the majority.

She had fucked up.

Two cards left. Raya looked at Ana, her face wrought with worry. Carefully she picked up one of the cards, holding it like it was poisoned. She flipped it.

ALEX. Printed in large, neat letters.

Ana's knees felt weak. The familiar buzzing noise was building in her head. She reached her hand out to Alex. He took it. Their fingers roughly entwined.

There was one card left. Three votes each. One card remaining. Alex was going to lose.

Oh, god. Ana wanted to turn away. It was like watching a crash in slow motion, her heart thudded painfully in her chest. She couldn't help herself. She looked at Ellis.

Slowly, lazily, his eyes drifted upwards maybe sensing that he was being watched. He found Ana and met her intense gaze. All the power was in his court now. She still had everything to lose. He cocked his head almost imperceptibly, his dark expression locked in. He'd won and he knew it.

Raya picked up the final card.

She would go – Ana knew it with one hundred per cent certainty. She would take Alex's place. He'd try to stop her, so she'd have to act fast. She'd just run for the line. No stopping, no thinking. It was better that way. Much better.

Ana willed herself not to close her eyes. Raya held out the card, her hand shaking. She counted:

"Three…two…"

Ana heard Alex take a sharp breath in, his hand tightened on hers. She focused on the feeling of his fingers, the warmth of his skin. It had to be okay. It had to.

"One."

Raya flipped the card.

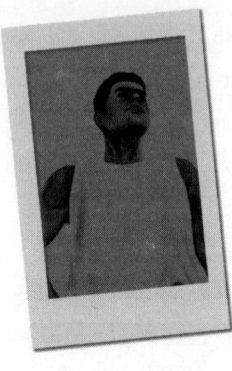

22 | Ellis

04:07

The final coaster lay in the dirt where Raya had dropped it.

Ellis looked at it dispassionately. There it was, just a small square of cardboard – a piece of trash that for one brief moment, held the power to take a life.

The scruffy letters on the back of the coaster stood out clearly. CADEN.

It was done. It was over. Caden was going over the line.

No one dared to look up. The wind gently danced around them, stirring their clothes, their hair.

"I win. Right? So…what's that mean…I mean, wha—" Caden was slurring so badly it was hard to make out his words. He was shuffling from side to side like a preschooler. Whatever was going on inside his head, it wasn't making any sense. "Imma…I'm…" He sniffed and rubbed hard at his nose.

"It means it's time for a drink," Ellis said quietly. He pulled a mini bottle of vodka out of his pocket and cracked the top, holding it out to Caden. Ellis's hand was oddly still. No shaking, no weakness.

Caden took the bottle and knocked it back in one gulp, flinging it on the ground when he was done. It rolled next to the coaster.

Ellis passed him another. He was recalibrating, the vote hadn't gone as planned. But it was okay, he could pivot. After Caden went, he would reset, come up with a new plan. After Caden...

There were minutes left to do this. Ellis took a deep breath and forced himself to look up. He needed to know what he was dealing with here. Caden was confused and fearful; he'd over-medicated and was barely holding himself upright, but it would be a mistake to underestimate him. He'd had military training. He might still be dangerous.

The others were in varied states of shock. Jade was hopeless – her face was frozen in a grimace of fear. Raya was crying. Alex looked like a puppy in headlights. None of them would have the balls to do what needed to be done.

That left Danny's sister and Jax. They still looked functional. But when push came to shove, would they help?

"Hey, Cade," Ellis said, moving closer to him, positioning the bus at Caden's back. There needed to be one way out of this. Only one direction to go. Across the line. "Time to go, buddy. Let's go find a place to hang out and get off our faces, okay?" He reached his arm out and gently nudged Caden towards the line.

Caden nodded – he was always up for getting higher. He turned slightly towards the line.

"That's it, buddy. That's it." Ellis pointed out across the line, at the empty road. "I reckon we passed a bar, just up the road there. No way they'll card us after all this. Let's head out and get a cold beer." He nudged him, a little harder this time.

One step, two. Caden stumbled closer to the line.

"Oh, god..." It was Jade's voice. There was sobbing too – Raya, maybe. Ellis silently cursed the others. If they weren't going to help him, they could at least shut the fuck up and stay out of his way.

"Imma...not sure..." Caden turned back to face Ellis and the others. "I'm gonna...stay."

"No, no, buddy. We're going. It's safe now. It's time to leave. We're going to head out and get a nice cold beer. It's all good." Ellis stretched out both arms wide. He had the wingspan of a point guard. He could cover a lot of space. He edged forward.

Caden stepped back. His heels were on the line. He looked around, his red eyes taking in everything, struggling to focus.

"Imma...I'm stay."

This wasn't working.

"Jax!" Ellis said sharply. He didn't call on Danny's twin. He didn't know how far her morals would let her go.

Jax moved forward and positioned himself behind Ellis's right shoulder. The two of them formed a wall. There was nowhere for Caden to go. Just the line.

"Go!" Ellis said firmly. There was no time left for games.

"Oh my god! Ellis, we only have two minutes left." It was Jade's voice, hitting a new shrill note of alarm.

"Go!" Ellis commanded. He moved forward, pushing into Caden.

"I don't wanna...I don't..." Caden's face turned red. His big mouth opened into an O and he wailed. "I don't. I don't. Don't make me." He looked like a scaled-up toddler. A full-scale tantrum was settling in on him, cutting through the fog in his head. Maybe he didn't understand what was happening, but some instinct was telling him to stay. He started moving, pushing back against Ellis. "I don't wanna go...I won't."

Ellis held fast, he grabbed onto Caden's camo T-shirt, locking him in place. Caden was making a high-pitched keening sound, his movements were becoming wilder, more violent. If this turned into a fight, Ellis could lose. He had to end this quickly.

"One minute! Ellis, you have to do it. Now!" Jade's voice cut in.

This was worse than he'd ever imagined. Could he actually do this? Ellis faltered. He knew what this meant. He was about to kill someone. Physically throw them to their death. He edged forward, but Caden was reeling around now, he was clearly hitting his limit. This was not good. If Caden lost it, they could all die.

"Caden, it's okay. It's okay." It was Danny's sister – she was standing by Ellis's left shoulder. She reached her hand out and gently touched Caden's arm. Caden turned to her, imploringly.

"I wanna stay. Please…" he begged. "I'm…scared."

"You don't have to be scared. It'll be okay." Her voice was soft. "It's okay, Caden. You can do what Ellis says. It'll all be okay."

Caden looked behind him, across the line. Ellis shuffled forward incrementally.

"It'll be okay?" He rubbed hard at his nose, then turned to face her. "You promise?"

She paused; her hand dropped from Caden's arm. Would she be able to end this?

"*Ellis! Twenty seconds!*" Jade's voice cut in.

"D'you promise?" Caden asked again. His fists had dropped, he was focused on Ana.

This was it – the moment. Caden had calmed down. He was distracted. Ellis had to act now. He had no choice. There was no time. No one else was going to do what needed to be done. He had to. *He had to.*

He pushed.

Just a small, firm shove, releasing his grip on Caden's shirt as he stumbled across the line, one step – two, three.

Caden lost his balance and fell hard, momentarily disorientated, confused. He reached up and rubbed hard at his eyes, trying to focus. Slowly taking in what had happened, where he was.

He saw Ellis, Ana and Jax standing in front of him. He saw the burned-out bus. And he saw the white line, between them.

That was the last thing he saw.

He never heard the gunshot.

23 | Ana

53:31

Ana sat on the burning hot ground in front of the bus, her knees hugged to her chest; the sockets where the headlights had once been glared out blindly on either side of her. She kept her eyes down, away from the white line, away from the trail that Caden's army boots had left when the cowboys dragged his body away.

There had been a moment – one brief moment – when she had been tempted to make a desperate run for the red truck. Caden's body had fallen so close to the line, the truck was maybe twenty feet away at most. But clearly she wasn't the only one aware of the danger. One of the cowboys set himself up behind the open truck door with a rifle pointed at them, an ominous red dot making its way across them. The message was clear. You run. You die.

The others had left, desperate to get away from the scene of the crime, disappearing off to their separate corners of the motel. She'd needed to be alone, just for a precious minute, before facing the next hour and whatever horrors it would inevitably bring.

The wind gently danced around her, stirring her dark hair, mocking her with its playfulness. She knew it was her fault Caden had died. She accepted responsibility for her part in sending him across the line. There was blood on her hands, again.

But she didn't feel a thing.

Nothing.

It was as though her emotions had shut down and left a numb emptiness in her core. Something inside her was blocking her thoughts from going too deep, too dark. The turning of the final card, Caden's bloodshot eyes, his body spreadeagled in the dirt: nothing was registering. Nothing other than her relief that Alex was safe.

Something tapped against her foot, pulling her reluctantly back to the present. She looked down.

A small pink square, caught in the wind, had blown up against her trainer. The final coaster – the final vote.

As she watched, the wind tauntingly whipped it up, carrying it into the shadows under the bus. It flipped over, burying Caden's name deep in dust. The faded pink rose on the card rested on top, like a dead flower on a grave.

She reached under the bus and softly, almost tenderly, picked up the coaster.

Gently she blew on it to clear the dust off Caden's name. The letters were crude, almost childlike and barely legible – it was Caden's writing. It had to be. Jesus. He was so off his face he'd voted for himself. He hadn't understood what the vote was for; he had just wanted to win.

"I'm sorry," she whispered. "I'm so sorry. I won't forget."

Taking a deep breath, she slipped the coaster into her back pocket.

That was when she saw it. The smallest thing. A flash of bright red in the shadows, deep under the bus. Ana squinted, trying to adjust her eyes to the darkness, to make out the source. But the contrast was too strong. She pushed herself forward on her hands and knees, crawling under the burned metal frame.

The stench of gas was overwhelming. The ashy liquid had seeped through the floor of the bus and was dripping on top of her, down her neck. She almost turned back. Almost.

Her eyes adjusted and, at last, she could make out a corner of something red and plastic, buried under an old tarpaulin. She dragged herself the last few feet and pulled the tarp back revealing a gas can, lying on its side. Behind it, she could see several more cans, lids open, all empty.

Her first thought was that she had found the source of the gas leak. But it didn't make any sense. How could the cans have survived the explosion? It wasn't possible. The heat would have melted the plastic in an instant, even if they were empty.

Slowly, another thought made its way through the fog in her head. It was obvious, wasn't it? The cans had been moved here *after* the explosion, *after* the fire.

Fuck. Ana backed out from under the bus as fast as she could and jumped to her feet.

All senses were functioning now. This wasn't a gas leak or an accident. Someone had poured gas over the bus deliberately. Then they had hidden the empty cans here so they wouldn't get caught. Which could only mean one thing.

Someone had sabotaged the shelter.

45:38

"This proves it. I was right – Norman is here! He's inside the circle and he's sneaking around while our backs are turned, doing whatever the hell he wants to stop us from getting out of here." Ana was pacing up and down the patio outside her room with barely contained excitement. She'd been talking non-stop since she'd arrived; about the gas cans, the cleaned microphone, Bluetooth. How it all fitted together, it all made sense.

Raya was sitting at one end of a concrete kerb, her head buried in her folded arms. Alex was standing in the shade, back against the wall, hands in pockets. No one wanted to go inside – not after Ana told them about the mysteriously repaired microphone.

"So, what do we do now?" Alex peered at her through a curtain of hair. He looked worn – exhausted.

"There are only a handful of places where someone can hide. We already searched all the motel buildings and the sheds. The one place we didn't look was in the outbuildings. Norman has got to be lurking in there somewhere, or maybe there's an entrance to a bunker or some underground tunnels, or…I don't know." She was talking too fast, barely pausing to breathe. "We'll split up. Two of us can search the outbuildings, while the other one can stay out here and keep a lookout – maybe on the roof. They can keep an eye on Team Ellis and watch for signs of Norman sneaking around, now we know he's here." The gas can discovery had kicked off that dangerous feeling inside her again – hope; now it was out of the box, she just couldn't put it back in.

"What do we do if we find him?" Alex asked, frowning.

"Look…I don't know. I don't have all the answers. But I know one thing – Norman knows us. He knows all our worst secrets. Somehow, in some way, he has to be close to us, or connected. If we can find him – just get to him, we can figure this out. I know it."

Alex nodded and chewed on his lip. Raya didn't speak or move.

Ana felt a wave of frustration.

"Guys, this is our chance to get out of here. Our first real chance. If we figure out where Norman is hiding, then he's not untouchable any more. *We can stop him.*" Why weren't they more excited? "*We can't just ignore this!* We have to try. Otherwise, we might just as well give up and line up for our turn on the red truck—"

"Don't say that!" Raya shouted, speaking for the first time since Ana had arrived. Her black-ringed eyes had a hollowed-out, empty expression.

"I'm sorry, Raya. I'm just trying to…"

"How can you even stand here and talk like that – planning and…and…going on like this is all a game? *Caden is dead.* He was murdered in front of us. I voted for him. And *you* – you lied to his face, Ana. You told him he'd be okay. *How could you do that?*" Raya turned away. "You're just like him, you know? You're just like Ellis."

The words were out there in the hot, dry air. Ana closed her eyes.

Maybe she was more like Ellis than she wanted to admit. Caden had just died in front of her, but she was already thinking about the next hour and how to survive. There was a disconnect. The reality, the horror, wasn't fully sinking in. It was stopping at a level, blocked from going deeper by the numbness. Maybe Raya was right. Something was wrong with her and Ellis – they'd already broken.

"It's not Ana's fault," Alex said. He shuffled uncomfortably.

"Right. Step in and defend her," Raya snapped. "Caden didn't deserve that. He didn't…" Raya stopped. No tears. Just raw grief. She buried her head in her hands and turned away from them, again.

There was truth in Raya's words, even if it was tied up in pain and shock. She hadn't been at school a year ago. She'd gone to hang out at the mall. The first she heard of the fire was when the sirens started wailing past, one after another. This was her first time on the front lines. She had to do what she had to do to get through this moment, to get through this day. Ana got it.

"Alex, can you give us a minute?"

There was no point in talking with Alex present. Raya and Alex barely knew each other, and at least from Raya's side there had never been any love lost. Alex nodded, looking relieved.

"I'll wait by the outbuildings," he said. "Don't take too long, okay?" He touched Ana's arm and walked away.

Ana sat down on the other end of the kerb. She felt a pull inside as she looked across at her friend. Suffering. It had been such a part of both their lives. The time they were dating seemed like a million years ago. Such a stupidly innocent moment, with nothing to think about other than crushes and band gigs, all the regular teenage stuff she had put behind her.

She would have given anything to go back to those days. To be lying on her lumpy old bed, Raya's head in her lap, listening to their old, thrifted vinyls. Laughing and gossiping, nowhere to go, nothing to do.

As though she'd heard her thoughts, Raya shook her head, and wiped her sleeve across her face hard, turning to look out across the harsh red streaks of desert stretching all around them.

When she spoke, her voice sounded flat and lifeless.

"I'm sorry, Ana. I didn't mean what I said…"

"It's okay." Ana took a deep breath. There was something she needed to say to Raya, something that had been worrying her for hours, but she dreaded bringing it up. It felt invasive and wrong, but it had to come out, one way or another. Before it was too late.

"Raya, I need to ask you something," she said. Reaching out she placed her hand next to Raya's. Their pinkies touched. Her voice must have given something away. Raya's eyes narrowed suspiciously.

"What?"

"I need you to promise me that you won't give up. No matter what happens. No matter who dies. Even if you want to..." Ana paused, catching her words. No drama, she reminded herself.

"Why would you even say that?" Raya said, an edge of irritation creeping into her voice.

Ana had kept their hands close together, and before Raya could stop her, she pushed up Raya's sleeve. The white line was clear against Raya's skin. Stark. It had lost its violent red edge over the last few years, slowly turning into a mark of history.

Raya pulled away angrily and yanked her sleeve down over her hand. She stood up, avoiding Ana's eyes.

She'd overstepped. Ana could feel it. The cutting, the suicide attempt – they were *Raya's* path, *Raya's* truth. Not Ana's or anyone else's. It wasn't something to be put out there in the open like this. Not unless Raya wanted to.

"I'm sorry," Ana said quickly. "But here, now, with all this... I need to know that you won't give up...again."

"Really? You want to go there?" Raya said, her voice unnaturally cold.

"I'm sorry, it's just...you're my best friend..."

"You think?" Raya gave a short bitter laugh and turned away; her arms folded defensively across her chest.

"Look, we don't have to talk about it, okay?" Ana said, backing off. She held out her hands, palms up – her scars from the fire exposed in the bright sunlight. "I get it. When Danny died, things were seriously messed up. There were times I didn't know how to get through another minute, feeling the way I did. I just wanted everything to go away. I do understand, Raya. Really."

"*But you don't, Ana.* You don't understand. You don't know what it's like to grow up feeling different from everyone around you, just because of who you are inside. I was so freaking alone, for so freaking long." Raya squeezed her eyes shut for a moment. "Look, things have been really bad for you, I know. But just because you're hurting doesn't mean you understand how everyone else feels. You have no clue what it's like to be me. And at the end of the day, no matter how shit it got when Danny died, you didn't try and end it all, did you?" Raya turned to face her now, squarely. "So don't say that you understand – because you don't. You can't. You never will."

Ana was lost for words. She'd never heard Raya talk like this. There was so much anger and pain. She wanted to put her arms around her, hold her tight until the feelings faded. But she knew she wasn't welcome. She'd crossed a boundary.

"I'm sorry," Ana said quietly.

There was a long silence. Raya glared at the desert, furious at Ana, furious at the world.

Ana kicked herself mentally for screwing up and hurting her best friend.

It took a while before Raya spoke again.

"One moment of weakness. That's all it was. One hour, one minute of one day when it all got too much. One bad decision, and I will have to live with that for the rest of my life." Raya pulled her sleeve up and held out her wrist – no hiding now. "But that was a long time ago, before the fire. I've changed. I've grown into myself, and I'm not about to quit. So, if you think this makes me weak, you are so wrong. Anyone who has been there and made it back is not weak or vulnerable. We don't deserve pity. We're the survivors. We have faced our darkness and lived."

Abruptly Raya turned and walked into the shade of the porch. Squatting down, she pulled out a rolled-up joint. Ana could feel the tension lift. Raya had said her bit – the topic was shut down.

Raya held out the joint and her Zippo lighter – a peace offering. Ana walked over to her and took them; for the first time in a long time, she lit up. Did it matter any more, if they were all going to die anyway? Did anything matter? She took a long drag, then held them out, but Raya shook her head.

"Keep them, you might need it. You want someone to worry about, Ana? Worry about that guitar boy of yours. Have you seen the way he plays? I swear there's nothing but rainbows and kittens inside that man-child. If anyone's in danger of going across that white line – it's Alex."

It was a classic Raya redirection. Changing the subject and ending the conversation once and for all. But Ana didn't want to hear this. There was already so much fear.

"No. That won't happen," she said, shaking her head. "You and Alex will be going home. You're going to get out of this alive. Both of you. I promise."

"You mean, all three of us? Right?" Raya said quickly, her eyes narrowing.

There was a slight pause, before Ana spoke.

"Sure. All three of us." She forced a light smile, turning her face away from Raya. She squinted as her eyes followed the tracks of the red truck, disappearing into the unreachable distance.

Last year, after the fire, she'd wished she could go back in time and do things differently. Eventually, she had accepted that life doesn't work like that. But the future hadn't been written yet. This was her second chance, and this time, she wouldn't fail.

When it came to her turn on the red truck, her two friends would be standing behind her, safe and well – *inside* the line.

24 | Ellis

38:18

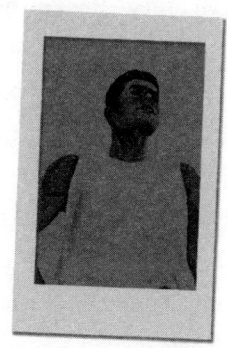

Finally!

It had taken a solid ten minutes to throw a loop of rope over the large metal arrow at the foot of the motel sign, but Ellis had done it. He gave himself a little mental cheer – few mortals could make that throw.

Time to test it out. He picked up the other end of the rope and pulled hard. It went taut, stretching out across the white line, all the way to the road sign and back. Ellis pulled even harder, throwing his full weight onto the rope. He needed to be sure it could take the weight of a person, especially one struggling against it. The rusty metal arrow creaked, but held fast, welded firmly to the signpost. Nothing was going to budge it.

This was going to work. Ellis nodded to himself. When the next hour was up, things would go smoothly. Much better. Not like last time.

No. The thought of his hands on Caden's camo shirt, the cheap sweat-stained fabric between his fingers. Caden's voice, begging not to go...fuck it. No way was he doing that again. It was so easy for the rest of them – *the sheep*. They just sat back and let him save them all, let him do their dirty work. Not again.

He flexed his hands. His fingers were stiff, probably from all the failed throws. He shook his arms out.

"Ellis!" He heard the stomping of little feet and sighed. Jade was approaching, Jax in tow. He made a mental note to be patient. He needed them on his side – for now.

"Jade. Jax." He nodded at them. Jax did the *dude nod* back. A small grunt of welcome. They looked different, flattened somehow. Their golden sheens hung like a fake veneer over their worried faces.

"So? What's the plan? For the next vote?" Jade's voice was carefully modulated but contrived. It was obvious she was trying to convey a kind of confidence that she just didn't have. "You do have a plan, right?"

Ellis sighed. Here it comes – *save me, Ellis*.

He knew her type well – nepo babies. They weren't bred for real life, just mild drama, like bad hair days and chipping a nail. Any hard problems and they would run away and hide behind their mommy and daddy's chequebook. The Jades of the world breezed through life under the impression that everyone else was born to serve their rich, gym-toned asses.

"Of course I have a plan." He nodded towards a large rusty tractor. He'd found it under the windmill and rolled it over. "Help me move this closer to the line."

Obediently they followed Ellis and the three of them dragged the ancient machine to the edge of the line.

"So, like, what is it for?" Jade asked, walking over for a better look.

"It's... Let me show you." It was hard to explain in words without sounding somehow...dastardly. "First, we flip the tractor upside down. Then we take this..." He held up the rope. "We wind it around the front axle on the tractor; maybe six or eight times should do the trick. Then we'll have a clear loop of rope from the tractor to the sign and back."

"Across the line?" Jade muttered, her eyes following the rope trailing in the red dust.

"*Exactly!* It's a pulley. Pretty basic, but it should do the job. You turn the tractor's front wheel and it moves the rope. We just have to tie someone onto the rope by this knot, and the pulley will drag them over the line." He held out the pre-tied knot as if it would explain everything. Jade and Jax were both still staring vacantly across the line. At some point they'd get it, wouldn't they? *Would they?* Ellis sighed and tried again, speaking slowly as though he was teaching a kindergarten class: "When the hour ends, we won't have to push someone over the line. The pulley will do it for us. Do you get it now?" He described it calmly, not a hint in his tone that he was talking about murder – he was simply describing a game-winning play. All he needed was a white board and marker.

Jade recoiled from the tractor in horror: "No...no way. No." She shook her head violently, backing away.

So now she got it.

"Whoa! It's a death machine!" Jax said, impressed.

Ellis gave a short laugh. It was a bit brutal, but it worked.

"Don't just stand there, help me flip the tractor," Ellis said to Jax. No point in asking Jade to help; she was clearly not invested in this. The two of them stood on one side and on the count of three, hefted the rusted old machine up, crunching it loudly over on its side, then rolling it onto its back. A wheel spun wildly in the air. Ellis grabbed one end of the rope.

"Are you *serious*?" Jade had finally found her voice.

"Yes, I'm fucking serious! I don't plan on throwing everyone over the line, and I don't see you stepping up to help," Ellis snapped. He passed the rope under the front axle and looped it around tightly, several times. "If you don't like it, you can go and join the other team."

Fucking sheep. No way was he taking on their moral judgement. They could pretend to be better than him, but if it was Jade's turn to cross the line, she would happily strap her own mother to the rope faster than she could do a gym squat. Ellis knew it, even if Jade didn't – yet.

Taking the rope in both hands, he pulled hard. It snapped tight, all the way out to the signpost. Keeping it taut, Ellis knotted it securely, and there it was – the death machine, ready to go. All they needed to do was tie someone on and turn the wheel.

"Want to test it?" He glanced sideways at Jade, throwing her a dark smile.

"I will," Jax shouted, raising his hand to volunteer.

"No!" Jade quickly stepped in. "No, Jax. For once in your life don't be an idiot."

Ellis laughed.

"Smart move. Let's test it on that," Ellis said, pointing to a plastic orange-and-white traffic barrel lying upended near the roadside.

"This will look so cool on film." Jax nodded happily.

The two of them kick-rolled the barrel over to the rope. It must have weighed about forty pounds. Much lighter than a human, especially one resisting being dragged over a line to their death. They scooped sand into it, lifting it up from time to time to estimate when it was close to a human's weight.

Finally ready, Ellis pulled a handful of plastic zip ties out of his back pocket.

Jade recoiled. "Seriously, Ellis?"

"I know, right?" Ellis said, smiling. "I found these in a shed back there. Very serial killer." He looped one through a hole in the barrel and tightened it.

"Wait," Jax shouted, running to the line. "I've got to film this. This is going to look great." He squatted, cocking his head, checking his phone screen. "Okay. Go ahead, Ellis."

Ellis grabbed the wheel and turned.

There was a creak and crunch as the barrel fell sideways, rolling and smashing hard against the ground. Sand spilled out as it flipped around, dragged slowly, inevitably towards the white line.

Ellis turned faster. It took all his strength to turn the wheel, but it worked. The barrel crossed the line, pulled further and further out of the circle.

There was a crack. The plastic split and the barrel finally dropped off the rope, rolling across the desert, red sand spilling like blood onto the ground.

Jax cheered. Ellis smiled, relieved he'd removed all the nearby cameras – he didn't want a record of his death machine in action. The test run was a success. Next time, it would be a person. An *actual* person was going to be zip-tied to the machine and dragged across the line. Ellis felt an odd thrill of exhilaration.

Clearly the same thought had occurred to Jade. She jumped up and started walking around in a tight circle, clutching at her chest, gasping.

"Oh my god…can't breathe…I can't…"

"Babe, it's fine." Jax walked up to her and put an arm around her waist. "You got this. Just breathe – like Dankman showed us. Like a box or something. Nice and slow. In…hold…out…hold…" He was holding his phone out, low-angle, capturing his manful, supportive boyfriend move. He flashed a quick smile at the camera. "Doing good, babe. The death machine isn't for us. It's for the others. When they lose the vote."

"*What if we lose the vote, Jax?*" Jade shouted. "What if…they know about the video and…and…" Her face had turned red; she pushed Jax's phone away.

"C'mon, babe. I won't let that happen. I'll protect you."

"You? Protect *me*? Wait…are you being serious right now? You do know you are just as guilty as me, or have you forgotten? In fact, if anyone knew what you did…maybe I'm not the one who should be worried."

"Yeah, but I'm safe, babe. No one knows what I did. That's all I meant…" He put his phone away for the first time all day.

"You're *safe*?" Jade's hands went straight to her hips. "Oh, no, no, no. You do not get to be *safe*, while my life is on the line. I am not going down alone. No fucking way!"

"Babe, don't be like this," Jax entreated; his voice had an edge to it. He tried to slip an arm around her waist, but she smacked him away, hard.

She turned to Ellis. "Do you remember the video Jax filmed of the school fire?"

Ellis nodded. Of course he remembered. How could he not? Jax's silent footage of horrific waves of flame engulfing screaming bleachers full of students had been posted on every news feed. Jax's face was constantly on the screen as he'd staggered backwards through the gym – pushing through the desperate crowds trying to escape. His handsome, distraught expression lent the film a slightly remote, movie-like quality, as though he was an actor and none of it had been real. It was a winning mix of gruesome-but-safe, easy to watch without having to feel too much and yet sick enough to scratch a perverse itch.

Ellis had only watched the video one time. That had been enough.

"Jade, please don't...c'mon, babe. I didn't do anything wrong. I was just filming stuff. That's what I do. It wasn't a big deal." Jax was sweating now.

"Oh my god, are you serious?" Jade turned on him. "You were going to post the whole video, *unedited*. I was the one who stopped you. I made you delete the audio before you shared it. I saved you, Jax. If anyone had heard the uncut version, being cancelled would be the least of your worries!"

"It wasn't like that, Jade. It wasn't that bad. I don't do well under pressure, y'know? Filming stuff makes me feel better. People would have understood..."

"Oh, right – because social media is so forgiving. I get trolled for posting a beach shot with the teeniest bit of cellulite. You honestly think ignoring Maia Walsh screaming for help would go down well? She called out your name, Jax. She begged you to do something, to help her. You *literally* stepped over her and walked away because you were too busy filming yourself. Big fucking hero!"

Ellis was mentally filing everything away for later, just in case. This was better than Netflix.

"What could I have done?" Jax's cocksure voice sounded smaller. "I'm not a firefighter...or a doctor. I couldn't help her or anyone..."

"How do you know that, Jax? You didn't even *try*. Maybe you could have put the flames out, wrapped her in something. I don't know. Something. *Anything*. She *died*, Jax – and you did nothing. *You filmed her!* Are you going to film me next? Are you going to film me die? Because you'd damn well better lose the fucking audio again."

"Babe, please…I'm not…I would never let you get hurt. *Never.*" Jax's green eyes welled up with tears. He ran his fingers through his shiny hair. "I love you, babe. We're not going to…to…fuck, this can't really be happening. I can't do this, Jade. I can't."

"You don't get to choose," Jade said; her voice dropped, her tone softened. "Look, Jax – you can't just stare at your phone and pretend this isn't happening. Not this time. It's real. *I'm* real. I need you, Jax. More than ever. I love you and *I need you.*" Jade had started crying too; streaks of mascara tracked down her face. She reached out and took Jax's hand. "I can't do this alone…"

"Babe…" Jax pulled Jade closer. She fell into his arms, her face pressed against his chest. "You're not alone, babe. I love you too." They snuffled into each other, lip gloss and hair products slathering into their golden sweat as they kissed desperately.

Ellis sighed. Sometimes he was astounded by the lies straight couples fed each other, covering the blatant cracks with the catch-all Band-Aid: *I love you.* Even if he survived the balloon game, he would never say that to anyone again. Ever.

Enough. He shook his hands out. He'd enjoyed the little show up to now, but needed to draw a line under things before they went too far. The clock was ticking.

"All right, look, neither of you has anything to worry about. The death machine is just an insurance policy. Just in case." Ellis gestured at the rusted tractor. "I didn't build it for us." *Yet*, he added silently.

"What do you mean, Ellis?" Jade said, reluctantly pulling away from Jax.

Ellis grinned.

"I mean...we don't have to lose the vote." He reached into his pocket and pulled out a quarter. "Heads or tails?"

Jade scrunched up her button nose in confusion.

"I mean, like, heads, I guess?"

Ellis flipped the coin in the air and caught it easily in his closed fist, then slapped his hand on top of the other. He walked up to her and lifted the top hand. Heads.

"Jax? You want to call it?"

"Tails," Jax said, walking over to watch, his emotional outburst forgotten.

Ellis flipped the coin, revealing tails. They tried it a few more times. Every time, it matched the call. He let them inspect the coin – no tricks, an ordinary, everyday quarter.

"That's brilliant," Jax laughed. "How do you do that, Ellis?"

"A magician never tells." Ellis smiled mysteriously. It was satisfying – showing off his favourite party trick. It never failed to get attention. He just hadn't thought he'd be using it to kill someone.

"When it comes to the vote, we all vote the same. It'll be our three votes against theirs. It'll come down to a coin toss – which we will win. Next round, we're three against two. We win again." Ellis stopped there. No need to take it further and have them thinking about what would happen after the last of the others went. That's when it all broke down. No more coin tossing then.

Jade took a dramatic yoga breath, in and out.

"Seriously, I was like so scared. Ellis...you're a genius."

He knew.

It was chess. Always plan three moves ahead. He had caught out Danny's sister and the others in the last round. If Caden hadn't been such a fucking idiot and voted for himself, he would have had the luxury of a few safe hours. But it didn't matter now. He'd get them at the next vote. He wasn't worried.

His hands spasmed again. He rubbed them together, then placed his palms flat on the hot rusted metal of the tractor's underbelly. The burning heat helped; he could feel his muscles unlock, his skin protesting.

"So...who do we vote for this time?" Jade asked awkwardly. Jax instantly lowered his camera.

There was no question, really. Alex wasn't a threat – he was too nice. Raya was unpredictable but acted on impulse; she'd be easy to manipulate. The biggest threat going forward was Danny's sister. No matter how hard he tried, Ellis just couldn't get a handle on what she was thinking. The way her mercurial eyes watched everything – it was unnerving. She was dangerously smart, and when she'd stepped up on the line to handle Caden, she'd shown that she wasn't afraid. Pity she was batting for the other side – together, they would have made a killer team.

"It's obvious, isn't it? There's only one person here with a possible motive to hurt us all." Ellis didn't believe for a second that Ana was behind any of this, but he wanted her gone.

For a second, Ellis pictured Danny, standing by the bleachers in the gym, smiling at him in his laid-back, easy way. If he knew what Ellis was about to say...if Danny was somehow up in the sky, watching him...

Ellis's hands seized again, tighter this time. He shook them out hard. Not now. He could worry about all this later when the game was over. When he was safely home. He'd have the rest of his life to worry about it. He turned to Jade and Jax:

"There's really only one choice. When the hour's up, we vote for Danny's sister – we vote for Ana Reyes."

25 | Raya

33:17

Paper. How could paper lose three times in a row? The gods were not on her side, Raya thought grumpily.

She was standing outside the middle of three corrugated metal outbuildings playing Rock, Paper, Scissors against Alex. They had found some rusted bolt cutters and hacked the chains off the metal doors already.

The loser got to go first. Great.

There was no avoiding it. Raya kicked herself for volunteering to search the outbuildings. It had sounded easier than spying on Team Ellis, less mental effort involved. But now it came to it, anything had to be better than sweating your shorts off in an oven-like building, searching for a potential psychopath lurking behind some discarded paint pots. Next time, she'd take the Jason Bourne shift. If there *was* a next time…

Sighing dramatically, Raya gave the buildings a quick once-over.

The outbuildings were built close together, almost touching. The style was identical, arched corrugated roofs like an old-school aircraft hangar – dirt floors, piles of rusted junk and old bits of machinery strewn around them. There was nothing distinctive about any of them. At least, nothing that indicated the presence of a hidden dungeon or a creepy clown's sewer lair.

Raya shot Alex her finest stink eye, and walked up to the metal door, creaking it slowly open. Recoiling from the fetid air inside, she forced herself forward, stepping into darkness. Her eyes took an unnervingly long time to adjust.

Rows of heavy-duty utility shelves lined both sides of the arched walls. They were stocked with dusty boxes and large tubs. As Raya got closer, she could see faded labels peeling off the boxes: Froot Loops, Lay's, Pepsi. All sorts of heaven. She'd found the motel food store.

Score.

Raya quickly walked along a long row, scouting out the supplies and checking the corners for lurking axe murderers. All clear.

"Doofus, look," she called out to Alex, who was standing in the doorway.

For the first time in several hours, Raya felt something close to happy. She reached for a solitary box of Ritz Crackers, lovingly stroking the cardboard. How had she not realized how hungry she was?

"Whoa," Alex said, his jaw dropping as he took in the rows of goodies.

Raya ripped open the box of crackers and started munching loudly as she squatted down on the concrete floor, keeping the box protectively stashed behind her. Some things just weren't for sharing. Alex was still hovering in the doorway.

"You just gonna stand there and watch?" she said sharply. "It's *food*, Alex. Actual, real food. Come and eat."

Alex wandered over, eyes growing bigger as he read the

tantalizing labels. He wasn't a dick or anything and Raya didn't hate him *exactly*. It was just that she couldn't see what Ana liked about him.

Yeah, he was kind, a nice guy, and he had that whole music thing going for him. But Ana was quite possibly the coolest person Raya knew – whip-smart and super-hot in a girl-next-door way. Alex was…just Alex.

"Sit," Raya ordered, pulling up a crate between them. She reached up and collected a small feast of raspberry jelly, peanut butter and squeezable cheese.

It didn't take long before she started feeling a warm glow inside as the food went down, accompanied by some fuzzy feelings. She even caught herself smiling at Alex.

He must have been feeling the same.

"Raya, can I ask you something?"

"Alex, let's just eat, okay? Whatever you're going to say is probably going to spoil my appetite, and right now I'm enjoying my food too much," Raya said, looking mournfully at her cheese-and-peanut-butter cracker. Time was so short, the last thing she wanted to do was waste it talking to Alex.

"The thing is…I need to ask you something while Ana's not around."

Raya's interest was mildly piqued. She nodded shortly and stuffed the whole cracker in her mouth, sitting back, arms folded defensively across her chest.

"I've been thinking…I know you still love Ana, even though you broke up. She's your best friend and all." He glanced up at her as though hoping for a sign of acknowledgement.

Raya didn't move. He could think what he liked.

"Well, the thing is...so do I." Alex glanced nervously at Raya. "I really do. For a long time now. You know, Danny was my best friend, but Ana was always...more. To me."

Raya looked at him and archly raised an eyebrow. This wasn't news. Before the fire, Ana had always had a little shadow. Alex: irritatingly ever-present, sending loving glances, ready to jump up and help at a moment's notice.

The only mystery was how Ana hadn't noticed that her twin brother's ever-present bestie was crushing on her – hard.

"Where are we going with this, Alex?" Raya worked to keep her tone neutral, even though he had her full attention.

Alex's expression darkened. He put a box of Cheerios down and brushed crumbs off his jeans thoughtfully.

"I...want Ana to live."

"Duh. So do I," Raya said, watching him closely, trying to figure out what he would say next.

"I mean...*whatever* it takes." Alex's voice was quiet.

Raya was taken aback. It wasn't what she'd been expecting. His words were plain, but his message was loaded with subtext.

She looked at Alex, but his hair was in front of his face, hiding his eyes. His arms were tan and toned, resting lightly on his jeans, his hands knotted together as he struggled to find his words.

"It's just...none of this makes sense – Danny's death, the fire, this place. None of it means anything if there's nothing to hope for. If Ana makes it, then there's a kind of justice in the world. An order. I want her to live and live well. To get out of here, to find love, have a family...grow old. I want her to get over Danny and whatever happens here today – to prove that this whole mess isn't all there is left."

Alex glanced up. For the first time, Raya felt the force of something behind the soft brown eyes. There was more there, a depth she hadn't seen before: love and strength of character intermingled in equal measure.

So, this was Ana's Alex, the person hiding behind the floppy hair. It felt like they were meeting for the first time. This was the person who had stolen Ana's heart away from her.

It was starting to make sense.

"Just say it, Alex."

"If…when it comes to it, I'm okay going. You know? I'll do it. I'll cross the line if it means that she has a chance. I just want…I need to believe she can make it. I need something to hold on to. Something to hope for. I thought…you might feel the same way too?"

Raya was surprised to feel a dampness on her cheek. She reached up and quickly brushed it away.

"Yeah, all right. No need to be dramatic," she said brusquely. "So, what are we talking about here? Making a secret pact or some shit? When it comes down to it, we make dang sure Ana is the last one standing?"

Alex looked up. Her bluntness had cut through his thoughts.

"I…I'm sorry." He looked genuinely mortified. Spelled out like that, the reality of what he'd just asked hung heavily in the dusty air. "I barely know you… I should never have said that. It's not right… I don't even know what I was thinking."

"Nah, it's okay. We're good. If you can't be honest when you're about to die, when can you?"

Alex nodded, his expression sober. They faced each other, no pretence, nothing hidden. Raya didn't warm to people easily, but once you'd got into her heart, she was loyal for life. In this case, that might only be an hour or two. But for that short time, Alex made the cut.

"Okay, then," Raya said, holding out her hand. It wasn't a hard decision.

"Are you... Do you mean it?" Alex said, his eyes round with surprise.

"D'uh." Raya grinned.

They almost laughed. The situation was ludicrous. Here they were, sitting on the dirt floor of a shed among a pile of half-eaten Ritz Crackers, agreeing to sacrifice their lives if it came down to it. Agreeing to die.

Alex took her hand and shook it once, firmly.

Deal done. Enough said.

Raya reached into the box of Ritz and pulled out a handful, then stood up. She very reluctantly forced herself to check her phone:

25:27

Jesus, where had the time gone? They needed to do their freaking job, already. She looked around, there was a whole section at the back of the outbuilding that they hadn't searched yet. She'd start there.

"Here, hold these for me. Don't eat any!" Without warning, she chucked the Ritz box in Alex's direction.

"Huh?" Surprised, Alex flubbed the catch and managed to swat the box away. It slid across the floor under a shelf.

Raya sighed, downgrading her opinion of him a notch.

She scrambled to her knees and crawled under the shelf in the direction of her beloved crackers, swearing loudly as she went. If she was going to survive for the next few hours, she was going to need every available crumb of comfort food. Alex hadn't batted the box too hard, it had to be here somewhere.

"Raya…there's something I always wondered." Alex's voice sounded a little hesitant. "Why did you and Ana break up? You seemed so good together, so happy. When you ended it, she cried for a month straight. I never got it. I mean, it just seemed like you were still into each other."

Was he seriously asking? Raya felt a flash of irritation.

"That's none of your business," Raya muttered grumpily, sweeping her hands over the dirty floor hoping to locate the box.

"Sorry." Alex sounded lost.

Raya paused and sighed deeply; her hand buried in a pile of cobwebs. Now she felt like she'd kicked a sweet, innocent puppy. She considered answering him, but what would be the point? Hadn't they just shaken hands on their own deaths? Wasn't the plan to let Ana live – to give her a chance to forget them and move on? What good would it do to tell him now?

But even as she thought it, she knew the answer.

There were things in the universe greater than death and red trucks and lines in the sand; things that transcended everything else. Love was one of them. Maybe telling him wouldn't change the future or stop them from dying on the line. Maybe it wouldn't help Ana let go of them after they were gone. But maybe it would help Alex. The stupid, floppy-haired kid could sacrifice himself knowing that in his short time on earth, he had been loved.

"Okay, you want to know why I dumped Ana? I'll tell you." Raya stayed buried in the shadow under the shelf, where Alex couldn't read her expression. "I dumped her because she was hopelessly, head over heels, crazy-stupid in love with someone else. It didn't matter how great we were together, and we were freaking awesome

– she could never feel the same way about me, and I wasn't stupid or insecure enough to stay in a relationship where there was no hope."

Had she said enough? Had Alex joined the dots, or did he need it spelled out in big neon letters? Raya waited, listening to the wind rattling on the metal roof.

Nothing. If Alex understood what Raya was trying to tell him, he was taking it very quietly.

Raya sighed again, her thoughts wandering back to the sweet-saltiness of the lost crackers. She slightly hated herself for craving them so badly. But, hey, if you're about to die, alone and unloved, no need to worry if you're a junk-food junkie. She would cross that freaking line with a mouth full of Ritz, dang it. She would die her way.

"Ana barely spoke to me all last year," Alex said at last. "I thought she blamed me for what happened. It was like she didn't want to know me."

Raya knew exactly what he was talking about. After the fire, Ana had changed. They all had. But for Ana it was different. When Danny died, a wall went up between her and the world. She faked being okay, but no one was giving that girl an Oscar any time soon.

It had hurt Raya deeply, being on the outside, but grief and depression are like that. They consume you from the inside and push away the light. Raya had been through enough struggles to know. She also knew that since the circle had been spray-painted around them, the old Ana was back. There was a light there that Raya thought had gone for good.

"Look, I just know what I know, okay?" Raya was done hand-holding. "Talk to Ana and do it soon. If we don't find this creep hiding under a crate of peanut butter, we are going to be out of time."

"Thanks, Raya." Alex said it so quietly it took Raya's brain a moment to process.

So, he got it. Raya smiled to herself. He understood, finally. The girl he was prepared to die for loved him too. Had always loved him. Too little too late. But, hey, it worked for Romeo and Juliet.

Raya pulled out her phone and switched on the flashlight. Her work here was done. She just needed to rescue those crackers and find a psychopath before they ran out of time. How hard could that be?

Something caught her eye in the far back corner. She reached out, hoping to feel the cardboard box. But instead, her hand wrapped around something hard. A cold metallic tube, reflecting the light. She shuffled closer.

The box had slipped under what looked like a small vent. The shaft made a clean right angle and disappeared directly into the dirt floor below the outbuilding. As Raya's fingers scrabbled around, she could feel the sensation of cool air whistling through the vent louvres.

She gasped, instinctively putting a hand over her mouth. Slowly, quietly, she edged backwards, out from under the shelf, bumping into Alex, who was still sitting staring at the floor, lost in thought.

Alex looked up at Raya, smiling.

"Got what you wanted?"

"Yes…" Raya said, shaking her head slowly and shooting him a clear, warning look. She held her multi-ringed finger to her mouth and pointed in the direction of the vent, then nodded to the door.

In the seconds it took them to scramble outside, Raya's mind had processed her discovery. The impact hit hard, and she found herself struggling to catch her breath, to find the words.

It took a few attempts before she managed to speak.

"Alex...I found something...I think someone's in there...I found an air vent at the back, underneath the shelves. It's working. There's cold air coming from it!" She grabbed Alex by his T-shirt, her excitement uncontainable. "Alex...we found him! The psychopath who's doing this to us – I think we've found where he's been hiding out. I think we've found Norman!"

26 | Ana
11:09

Ellis, Jade and Jax were waiting by the road sign. They were in a conspiratorial cluster, next to an old upside-down tractor, looking shifty. Probably plotting the next person's demise.

"I thought you might chicken out," Ellis said as Ana, Raya and Alex ran up. He eyeballed them suspiciously. "Where have you been hiding all this time?" His contempt was open-faced. There was no place for niceties in a war zone.

"Not hiding, Ellis. We've been trying to get us home. All of us," Ana added. "Raya found something."

It took a few minutes to explain. About the microphone and the gas cans, about the air vent leading underground, below the outbuildings. They finally had what they needed – physical proof that someone could be hiding right under their feet, and a place to start looking for them.

Ellis questioned every statement, verifying facts and challenging assumptions.

When they'd finished, there was a long silence. It wasn't the reaction Ana had expected. Had she not explained it right? Why wasn't everyone excited? Whoever the cowboys were, they were safely out of reach beyond the line. But if someone was *inside* the line – *inside* the motel with them, then they could get to them, which meant they could stop them. They had a chance.

Ellis turned his back on them and started pacing, agonizingly slowly, up and down the white line. He stroked his chin pensively, precious moments falling away as he took his sweet time.

Was he really going to argue about this? This wasn't a game. It was the best lead they had – the *only* lead. Ana's eyes found the upturned tractor, the long loop of rope stretching out across the line – the upturned barrel. She felt a sinking sensation in her stomach. *What was he up to?*

Abruptly, Ellis stopped pacing and turned to face his captive audience.

"Not good enough."

"What the hell, Ellis?" Raya said, her face reddening. "Haven't you heard anything we said? We might be able to get out of here, or at the very least try. What is your freaking problem?"

"It's too risky."

"*Risky?* What's riskier than dying on the line?" Raya was shouting, incredulous. She threw her hands up and turned away from him in disgust.

If they weren't together on this, there was only one way forward. In less than fifteen minutes, another one of them would have to die.

Jax was filming everything, right up in everyone's faces, pulling his stupid expressions for an unseen audience. Constant. Like a buzzing fly.

"Let me be clear," Ellis said, pointing his finger in their direction. "You're asking us to waste the little time we have left searching the motel, because of a half-baked theory that the person doing all this might be hiding inside? Do you know how naive you all sound? What if we don't find Norman? Clearly, he doesn't want to be found, and we have minutes left. Where's the margin for error before we're all blown to hell and back? Even assuming we *do* miraculously find Norman in time – what are we going to do then? I think it's safe to assume he'll be armed and fucking dangerous."

Raya stood her ground:

"Well, then, let's spread out and wait for Norman. He's going to have to come out of hiding if he's going to shoot one of us when the hour's up. We can catch him by surprise, then…"

"Jesus Christ, Raya. He's probably already outside waiting for us. He might be watching right now. Besides, who's to say he doesn't have several hidey holes, or a whole underground network of tunnels? We've been here since last night and no one has seen him yet. We've got little to no chance we'll just happen to catch him wandering around before the hour's up. Stop being so fucking ridiculous. You'll get us all killed."

Ridiculous?

Enough. Ana felt an uncharacteristic wave of anger. Ellis couldn't just stand there and dictate their future, insult Raya and send another one of them over the line to die. He did not have the right.

She stepped forward.

"You want to know what's ridiculous, Ellis?" The words flowed easily, as though someone had raised a creaky locked-down floodgate deep inside her. "What's *ridiculous* is having a chance to get out of here alive and not even trying to make it happen. What's *ridiculous* is throwing another one of us over the line – *executing* one of us, just to buy yourself more time…" She looked pointedly at the tractor and rope.

Ellis stormed up to her, towering over her small frame. His powerful athleticism was wound up dangerously tight, and for a moment Ana thought he might take a swing at her.

"You like my death machine, do you? What – you thought I was going to happily throw someone over the line, every time another one of your plans fucked up?" Ellis spat the words with barely controlled anger. "Who the *fuck* do you think you are? No one gives a shit about what *you* have to say. You're not your brother. You're not Danny. Not even close." He shook his head, raw contempt in his cold grey eyes.

Dismissed. Taken down. Ana's thoughts faltered. There was the familiar crack inside her. The crack that had become a chasm since Danny died. Insecurity and self-doubt reared up to fill the void. The thing was…he was right. She wasn't Danny. *She wasn't even close.*

Ellis was watching her. It was as though he could see the crack inside her, sense her weakness. He would stick his fist into it and rip her open if she made him.

Her eyes dropped. It was the smallest of movements, but it was enough.

Ellis nodded and turned away from her. Dismissively. Victoriously.

"We vote. Now. If it's a split vote, we toss a coin. One of us goes and we live past the hour. End of discussion."

Jax circled him slowly, catching a flattering upwards angle. The hero. The leader. The MVP.

Who made him *the prince*? Ana thought angrily. Why did he hold so much power? He was just another seventeen-year-old boy, not to mention an arrogant, self-serving jerk who would sell his own grandmother to get what he wanted. Why him? Why was he a leader when he so clearly didn't care about anyone other than himself?

Maybe Ellis was right. Their plan was weak, there were holes. They might be wrong, and, yes, they could be making a terrible, fatal mistake. But at least they had a plan. At least they had hope. Right now, that was all any of them had.

It came in a wave: fiery, bitter anger. Pure and unrelenting. This day's fear and grief closed in around her. She was done. She was over this. Over Ellis. Over the white line. Over constantly being afraid and sad and hopeless. She was done being a victim.

Without noticing it, Ana stood taller, her hands clenched into tight fists at her sides.

"No." Her voice was clear, all doubt gone.

Ellis looked at her again, surprise and irritation vying for space in his dark expression.

"No?" he said patronizingly.

"You heard me. I said no. I might not be my brother, but I know this much: no one else needs to die today. We'll find where Norman's hiding. If he's there, we'll fight him. If he's not, we'll take over his hiding place. It won't be rigged to explode, and if he's in contact with those cowboys, he must have a way to call out of this place. We'll barricade ourselves in and wait to be rescued. We have a chance now – all of us here. Maybe it's a small one, but that's a risk we have to take."

Ellis fixed her with a powerful stare. Ana stood her ground, meeting his eyes squarely. For the first time all day she felt utterly calm. She knew what needed to be done and was going to do it.

It was clear that Ellis was re-evaluating her threat level. Moving her up the pile, from Danny's nobody sister, to something else –

something much more dangerous. There was a look on his face that hadn't been there before. Respect? Fear? She couldn't place it, but she knew what it meant. He would be coming for her next.

She smiled at him.

Bring it.

Jax was circling the two of them, wedging his phone into the centre of the confrontation. He had a talent for sniffing out cinematic moments, she had to give him that. But this time, he flew too close to the sun, and Ellis smacked him away.

"Get the *fuck* out of my face, Jax."

"Jeez." Jax rolled his eyes and retreated to Jade's side. He started filming himself and Jade, mouthing "WTF" dramatically and pouting.

"Oh my god. Seriously?" Jade pushed him away. "Just stop filming me, Jax. Stop it! STOP IT!"

The focus had shifted. Ana felt the tension of the moment release, though she kept Ellis in her peripheral vision, just in case he decided to grab someone and throw them over the ever-present white line, while they were all distracted by *The Jade and Jax Show*.

"Babe. C'mon," Jax said, holding his phone up as though this made everything okay. "We talked about this. Filming stuff makes me feel better, y'know?"

"I DON'T CARE." Jade was losing it. Her face had turned red. "*I don't want to be filmed*. Don't you get it, Jax? This is not good. We don't want anyone to see this, ever. Even if we…"

Jade stopped, catching the word in the air before she could say it. Her arms folded defensively across her chest. She looked imploringly up at Jax.

"I don't want...I don't want to be *remembered* like this. Oh, god..." She broke off, pushing her fist into the corner of her eye, trying to hold the tears inside.

"Aww, babe," Jax said, putting his arms gently around her. She snuffled into his shoulder.

Off to the side, Ana noticed a movement. Ellis had sat down on the old tractor and was watching the show, a laconic smile on his face. All he needed was some popcorn.

Jax was kissing Jade on the top of her blonde head. They stood wrapped together, a genuine warmth between them.

Briefly.

"SERIOUSLY?" Jade pulled herself away, hands planted on her hips with all the ferocity she could muster. Jax grinned sheepishly, lowering his phone. He had been filming their tender moment.

"You look really hot...?" he offered tentatively.

Jade seemed like she was about to burst. Her mouth dropped open, fury pouring off her. Ellis was grinning now. The entertainment had just got good.

Jade was taking violently deep cleansing breaths, glaring hard at Jax all the while. He withered a little, flashing her a weak version of his kilowatt smile, cocking his head cutely on one side.

It fell flat. Jade took two steps towards Jax and, quick as a whip, snatched his phone from his hand.

Before Jax could stop her, she swung around and flung the phone across the white line. It landed with a sickening crunch a good fifteen feet from the line.

There was a long silence as all eyes turned back to Jax.

"*Why did you do that?*" Jax turned to Jade, shock and betrayal written deeply on his face. "How could you do that to me? Everything

I have is on that phone. My whole life is on it. Jesus, Jade. How could you?"

He walked up to the line, his toes on the edge as he stared longingly at the small black rectangle. So near and yet so far.

Jade folded her arms again and raised her chin defiantly.

"Look, I'm sorry, but if you had just stopped filming us when—"

"Don't you get it? When I post the footage from this place, can you imagine what's going to happen? I'll blow up. I reckon I'll get over a million followers. Easy. I'll get sponsorships, collabs and money. So much money…"

He was talking to the phone. His voice as loving and affectionate as he'd ever sounded talking to Jade. His toes pushed forward into the white spray paint.

There was something in his manner, his body language. Ana felt a jolt of nerves run along her spine. Jax wasn't that stupid, was he?

"Without that film, I got nothing. It all goes away. I'm nobody." Jax glanced over his shoulder at Jade. "I thought you understood, babe."

"I do. It's just so irritating. You're always on your phone, always filming."

Jax had turned back to stare at his phone.

"I reckon it's only eight, maybe ten feet."

Jade looked like roadkill. Her mouth was open again and her eyes had grown rounder. The realization of what was going down hit her firmly. She panicked.

"Wait. Jax, what do you mean? You're not nobody. It's just a phone. Okay? Look, we'll follow Ana's plan. We'll find Norman and get out of here and I'll buy you a new phone. Just come here. Come away from the line." Her voice was tinged with desperation.

"It's not the phone, Jade. I need the footage. I got everything on there. The voting, the deaths, it's all there. It's gold." Jax had turned back and was staring at the black rectangle again. "If I wait, it'll be fried; there'll be nothing salvageable. Looks like maybe ten…twelve feet to me. Yeah. I'm fast. I can do this."

"No! Jax, please. It's just a phone."

"Why don't you get it? *Why?* It's not just a phone. That's my whole life out there. My future. I got nothing without it."

Jax's whole body leaned forward, his weight over the line, his feet still firmly planted on the white dust. Ana held her breath, half expecting a shot to ring out.

"You've got me," Jade said. Her words hung in the baking air for a moment. Jax paused, his forward momentum stopped. "Don't do it, Jax. Please. I love you."

Jax's head dropped to one side as he listened, his eyes still locked on his phone.

They all stood frozen in place, watching things play out before them. A cricket struck up a loud whirring from somewhere beyond the line. The death machine creaked as the rusty metal expanded in the harsh heat.

Ana didn't breathe, her heart was beating hard and fast, she could feel her pulse in her fingers. *Don't do it. Don't do it.*

Jax straightened, turning to face Jade. He smiled, his beautiful face lit up with his perfect white teeth, his achingly deep dimples.

"Love you too, babe," he said, cocking his head a little. "But I got this."

He was off. It happened so fast that Ana barely registered he'd gone. Sprinting forward, he cleared the distance in seconds, skidding to a stop in the red dust as he bent down for his phone.

His fingers scrabbled in the dirt, trying to find a hold on the small black object.

He caught it, his feet behind him, stretching out, trying to stop his momentum and send him back across the line.

He never stood back up.

The first *crack* dropped him loosely to his knees. He looked across the line, his eyes searching for Jade.

The second *crack* propelled him face forward into the dirt. Everything seemed to soften and fall as he sank into himself on the desert floor. In an instant, Jax was gone, leaving behind an empty dark outline.

Only one thing remained defined. His right hand, wrapped around his shiny black phone. Still clinging to it: his whole life, his future, gripped tightly as everything else faded away.

27 | Jade
43:54

No more.

Jade couldn't do this. She couldn't. There was nothing left inside. All her usual go-girl platitudes were empty. Nothing helped.

For once in her life, she faced herself. It wasn't unfair or someone else's fault. She couldn't bury herself in her comfort blanket of self-pity. She had done this. She had killed Jax. He was gone.

She was curled up on the floor. Somewhere. She wasn't sure where. Someone had helped her, guided her here. Maybe Ana? Or a guy?

As she thought it, she pictured Jax. *Jax.* A guy. Her guy. Oh, god. Oh, god. Oh, god. Oh, god.

There was no coming back from this. She just wanted to go home. She wanted her beautiful mom with her stupid actor wigs and French-tip nails, floating around in her cloud of Chanel and assistants. She wanted Ruby, her annoying little sister, who followed her everywhere and copied everything she did; she even stole Jade's clothes and made a hole in her favourite Lululemon leggings. They hadn't spoken for days over that – over Lulu-fucking-lemon. Pointless.

Somehow, Jade knew, with clinical certainty, that she was never going to see them again. She was never going home.

Jax was dead. She had killed him, and soon she would be dead too. She would just lie here until the end. There was no strength in her. No will. She would fade away on this…vintage linoleum?

The pattern caught her eye. It was distinctive and oddly on-trend. A geometric repeated shape over and over. She knew this place. The reception.

There was a slight noise, some low whispers, a door banging, a chair leg scraping the floor. Someone was in here with her.

With what little strength she had, she lifted her head and looked around.

A short figure was standing by the window, their dark outline stark against the brilliant rectangle of light. Raya.

"Need anything?" Raya's voice sounded distant, as though she was speaking through a long tunnel.

"No," Jade croaked, slumping back to the floor. The linoleum was cool and had a comforting bit of bounce. It was almost pleasant. "How did I get here?"

"Alex carried you. You were out of it. You sure you don't want anything? Water?"

Jade shook her head; she didn't want anything. Not now. Not again.

"Where's Ellis? Is he here?"

"No idea. He disappeared after Jax… We're not sure what he'll do now. He's in the minority, so if we have another vote, he'll lose. We're worried he might do something stupid. So, we're going to stay in twos, in case he decides to try and pick us off one by one," she said matter-of-factly. "Ana and Alex are checking out the vent to see if it leads to Norman's hideout." Raya moved closer and sat on the floor next to Jade, her dusty DMs squeaking against the floor. "It's good news, Jade. We're going to find Norman and we're going to get out of here. We're going to be okay."

Jade heard the words but felt nothing. It was too late to be hopeful. Jax was already dead. Even if, by some miracle, she survived – her life would be over. Her reputation would be destroyed. She was a killer; the kind that true-crime TV loved – young and beautiful.

"For what it's worth, I'm sorry," Raya added, her voice uncharacteristically soft. "Jax didn't deserve that."

Jade didn't move. There was no answer. She knew Jax didn't deserve it more than anyone. She had killed him. She had thrown his phone over the line because she was stupid and selfish. She should have died, not him.

A thought had been circling amid the guilt – something hard to reach. Jade didn't know if she had the words to express it. She wasn't even sure she understood it fully. But somehow, she had to put it out there.

"It's why I'm here, isn't it? It's karma. Because of what I did to Karl Hunt."

Raya didn't speak, but her dark-rimmed eyes watched Jade thoughtfully.

"Jax's death, the white line, all this bad stuff is happening to me because the fire was *my* fault, wasn't it?" She looked at Raya, searching for a sign of agreement. But Raya gave nothing away.

Jade carried on. She had to. She was too far into this. It needed to be said.

"I humiliated Karl Hunt in the locker room. I wanted to make him pay because he embarrassed me – following me around, thinking I would ever be interested in someone like him. It was mortifying. Everyone was laughing at me. I hated it so much. He had no right to make me feel that way. So, I hurt him – I wanted to. The next day…he hurt me back. Not just me…all of us. I know I didn't light the match, but I think I was there – in his head. I was the reason he did what he did. And I've done it again. I took Jax for granted. I was a horrible girlfriend, you know, flirting with other people, with Alex, right in front of him. I cheated on him too. More than once. He didn't deserve it. He was always just…Jax. And now he's dead because of me. It's karma. I'm being punished because I'm bad. I've done cruel, bad things. Now I'm paying for them."

Jade pushed herself to sitting. Tears had pooled in the corners of her eyes. They flowed freely down her cheeks, leaving streaks on her face.

"I'm going to die here, Raya. I know it. I'm going to die, and there's nothing I can do to stop it from happening because I deserve to die…"

She broke into full hard sobs. It was the end. Her end. She knew it. No coming back.

"So, you're guilty. Big whoop." Raya's voice pulled Jade up short. "This isn't *The Jade Show*. We're all guilty. We're all in this karmic hellhole for a reason. We've got to find a way to get over that, or we might as well just throw ourselves over the line now. Save everyone the trouble."

Jade sniffed. Hearing it said like that – just casually put out there, made it seem smaller somehow. *You're guilty. Big whoop.*

For a moment they sat together silently, lost in their own thoughts. The room was heavy with heat, dust drifting slowly in the air, circling through strips of sunlight. A fly buzzed lazily above them. It was oppressive and yet oddly reassuring, as though time was slowing, the future held at bay, at least for a moment.

"I wasn't at the gym when the fire started," Raya said, so quietly Jade almost missed it. "I was *lucky*, everyone said."

Jade glanced sideways at Raya. There was something in her expression, her voice, that was unfamiliar. This wasn't the usual irritatingly politically correct Raya. She seemed different somehow.

"See, the thing is…it wasn't luck." Raya turned her face away, towards the window.

Jade was confused. What was Raya trying to tell her?

"Karl came to see Caden that night, at half-time," Raya continued. "Caden and I were hanging in the back of his Candyvan. Karl seemed okay, a bit wired, but not dangerous or anything; he just wanted to get off his face. He was blowing off steam, ranting about how he'd just been suspended, how the school was full of evil queen bitches and bullies. Going on and on."

Jade did the math. It was the day after the locker room incident. He was talking about her. *An evil queen bitch.* That was her.

"Caden left; he hated drama in his Candyvan. Messed with his head. But Karl didn't stop – he kept ranting about how school sucked." Raya paused, considering her next words carefully. "The thing is…he told me that in the third quarter…he was going to light up 'the whole fucking place'…"

Raya's words tailed off. She closed her eyes.

Jade's brain was two steps behind. She sat, frowning, processing what she was hearing. Finally, the pieces fell into place, her mouth dropping open as she realized just what Raya was telling her.

"*You knew?*" she half-whispered.

Raya shifted uncomfortably.

"I didn't think it was real, okay? I thought he was just trying to get some attention, to look cool. Honest to god. It was a moment. We were hanging out and chatting and he was being a dick. I didn't know he meant it. How could I?" Raya was talking around in circles, trying to convince herself more than anyone.

Jade got it. Kids at school talked shit all the time. Jesus, if any adults saw their social media posts, half of them would have been locked away by now. It was all out there; a whole secret, tawdry world open to those media savvy enough to dig for it and young enough to care, buried in an endless stream of pouting snaps and flexed biceps. Jade knew that as well as anyone. She lived for it.

"So, what's the problem?" Jade asked, confused. "You didn't believe him, so big deal."

Raya gave a short sharp laugh.

"Here's the problem. I thought he was full of shit. But then… when half-time was up…I couldn't go back in the gym. Some instinct told me not to. It's like, somehow, I *knew*…so I just left. My friends were still inside. Ana was inside…and I just…I left. I didn't text or warn anyone. *I just left them.* I drove to the mall and hung out. For the longest time, I thought I was being stupid. I was so mad at myself for being pathetic, I was embarrassed…right up until I heard the sirens."

Raya stood up abruptly and walked over to the window. She stared out, arms folded across her chest.

"I've been telling myself for over a year now that it wasn't my fault – that I couldn't have known Karl really meant all that bullshit." Raya turned and for the first time faced Jade, looking her squarely in the eyes. "But actions speak louder than words, right? If I'd trusted my instincts, I could have stopped the whole thing.

Danny and Maia would be alive..."

Raya rubbed at her eyes vigorously, her hand coming away black, smudged with eyeliner and dirt.

"So, yeah, Jade. What you said about karma...I agree. Maybe we didn't light the match then or now, but we *are* guilty. Both of us. If I'd been a better person, no one would have died that day. You might have been the one to push Karl over the edge by being a complete bitch." Jade mumbled a weak protest, but Raya continued. "The thing is, Jade, maybe this is karma, the universe avenging itself on us weak, stupid fools. Maybe we do deserve to ride the red truck. Fuck it."

Raya looked down at her feet and kicked angrily at the floor. Jade crumpled up her nose. Well, that hadn't helped. Wasn't Raya meant to make her feel better?

A slow clapping made them both jump.

"Well done," said a low voice. Ellis was standing in the doorway.

Instantly Jade felt unnerved. There was something wild about his expression, something she hadn't seen before. The prince seemed almost...predatory. Like a tiger looking for an easy kill.

"Nice story." Ellis walked forward slowly. He had one hand behind his back, hidden from view. "Makes perfect sense. Running away. Hiding. Cowardice. All classic Raya Mori."

Raya must have sensed the danger. She was watching Ellis nervously.

"Cathartic, isn't it? Confessing your sins. Admitting your guilt," Ellis said.

"Yeah, you should try it sometime, dickhead," Raya shot back.

Ellis was staying close to the door, close enough that he could use his superior speed to cut her off if she tried to leave.

Jade was too nervous to speak. Even in her messed-up state she could tell this was not going to end well. Ellis was searching for a new victim. Her instincts told her he was gunning for Raya, but she wasn't sure about anything any more. Their secret pact must have expired now that Jax was gone. No more two-for-one deal. She started to feel very small, squeezing herself against the counter as though it could swallow her up and offer some protection.

Raya pushed herself up, standing as tall as her diminutive build allowed, her hands balled into tight fists.

"Where are the others?" Ellis said coldly.

"They're searching the outbuildings. I was just going to go and help them." There was a slight waver in her voice.

"Sure."

Raya took a tentative step towards the door. Ellis didn't move from the doorway. He just stood there, both hands behind his back now.

Raya took another step, watching Ellis closely. He turned almost infinitesimally as though to let her pass; his back came into Jade's view for the first time. She gasped. In his right hand, he was gripping a plastic zip tie. This was not good. Not good at all. Her instincts were right. Ellis meant trouble.

Raya took her chance. She stepped forward and grabbed the rusty old door handle pushing down hard on it. The door creaked open. She backed into the open doorway, still facing Ellis. Her relief was palpable and premature.

"Before you go, I just want to say thank you," Ellis said. His back was now fully turned towards Jade. She could see his fingers playing with the zip tie.

"For what?" Raya asked suspiciously.

"For making this easier."

"What the hell are you talking about, Ellis?" Raya looked like she wanted to end this and get out of here. She shuffled backwards impatiently, every inch of her leaning towards escape.

"Well, now I know your guilty secret, I won't feel so bad about this." He smoothly brought his hand in front of him, holding up the zip tie.

A look of shock crossed Raya's face. There were no words. She fell back into the glaring sunlight and turned to run.

That was all it took. Ellis moved in, his right hand swinging forward, his left reaching up and around, fast and efficient. Raya didn't stand a chance. In seconds she was pinned on the ground, her hands bound. Ellis had her exactly where he wanted her.

She tried to scream, to call for help, but Ellis's full weight was on her.

"STOP! Oh my god! Just stop!" Jade was on her feet. She wanted to run at Ellis, to hit him and scream at him. But she couldn't. Her feet wouldn't move. Fear coursed through her. If she tried to fight him, he would kill her. She knew it.

"Jade, sit back down and shut the fuck up," Ellis growled. "Just focus on my voice and do what I'm telling you. You'll be all right if you do exactly what I say. *Sit down.*"

Jade sunk to her knees, sobbing, hands tight at her sides. She could see Raya, pinned on the dirt, unmoving.

"Wha…what are you going to do to her?" she whispered.

"What do you think?"

"But…we can…Ana said—"

"What?" Ellis's voice was cutting. "What do you want, Jade? To search for fairies and fucking unicorns until we all get blown up? Or do you want to live? Danny's sister doesn't want to face the truth, so she's going to lead anyone stupid enough to follow her straight to their death. The only way any of us walk away from this goddamn motel is if we play the game, and right now, that means Mori has to cross the line. Do you hear what I'm saying, Jade?"

Jade nodded; she couldn't find words.

"Good. Then listen carefully. I will get us both out of here alive. Do you hear me, Jade? I have a plan for us, okay? For you and me. Right now, the only question you need to ask yourself is: do you want to live or die?"

Through his legs, Jade could see Raya's face. Her eyes were open, staring at Jade, imploring. Dirt was smeared across her face, in her hair.

"What's it to be, Jade?"

Jade was shaking, her whole body quivering with shock. Too much horror. She couldn't hold a thought.

"Jade?" Ellis barked at her.

"Live." Her response startled her. "I...I want to live. I'm sorry, I'm so sorry, Raya. I'm sorry..."

"Good choice." Ellis turned abruptly.

"Jade...please..." Raya's words were muffled. "Jade, help..."

Jade put her hands over her ears. She couldn't hear this. She couldn't watch. She couldn't...

Pulling Raya to her feet, Ellis dragged her away from the building, heading towards the line. Towards the death machine.

There was nothing else for it. It was too much. Too much. She couldn't do this any more. No more.

Jade closed her eyes and screamed over and over and over.

Karma.

28 | Ana
29:27

Nothing.

How was it possible? Had she been wrong all along?

Ana pushed the thought away. Too much depended on her theory that Norman had a secret hideout under one of the outbuildings. If she'd made a mistake…it didn't bear thinking about what would happen next.

They'd started in the food store. It didn't have any secrets. She'd searched every inch with Alex, starting at the air vent and working their way out. No hiding psychos, no secret doors into hidden lairs. No cameras or microphones; clearly Norman hadn't wasted time wiring the locked outbuildings. Nothing at all, just the vent, a cool breeze whistling through it.

There was only one other outbuilding close enough to be connected to the vent.

Now she was standing in it, with Alex.

This one must have been the motel dumping ground. It was packed full of furniture piled in dangerously teetering stacks. Bed frames, mattresses, tables and chairs, shelves and shelves of dust-covered appliances and boxes filled with yellowed sheets and towels.

There was a single three-foot-wide pathway meandering about thirty feet into the dark. Shafts of brilliant sunlight broke through rusty cracks in the corrugated metal roof, spearing through the air. The curved walls echoed every sound back and forth.

Ana switched off her phone flashlight and quickly checked the time, a sinking feeling in her stomach. Less than half an hour and counting. Too little time. Always too little time.

Junk – a shack full of junk. It didn't seem possible that anyone would be hiding here. Alex must be feeling it too. He hadn't spoken to her since they'd arrived. She glanced over at his back. He was squatting down, looking under pieces of furniture and boxes, moving them out of the way, checking behind them for something, anything.

"I'll take the right side, okay?" Ana said, trying to keep her voice upbeat. She walked over to an insurmountable wall of metal bed frames and started nosing around, moving things, peeking around. She wasn't expecting to find anything, but she would use the time to think. No way around it, she needed to come up with a plan B before Ellis did.

For several minutes they worked in silence, shifting piles as they made their way deeper into the dark space. Despair settled on Ana like sweat and dust – she pushed it away.

A loud crack was followed by an immense crash as an entire pile of chairs fell, wooden legs and arms splintering on the floor. Alex jumped out of the way.

"Shit, sorry," he muttered.

"Are you okay?" Ana moved over to see him. He was standing in one of the shafts of light, spotlit from above.

Hopelessness. It hung on him like a shadow. Ana could see it weighing him down. He pushed his hair back, tucking it behind his ear, then letting it fall forward again as he nodded.

Ana watched him. Every fibre in her wanted to walk over to him, to curl up in his arms and sink down on the floor. To sit, wrapped together, in that one pool of golden light and stay for ever. No more strength or fear. No more sadness or guilt. They could give up the fight. They could let the clock run out on them.

They could just be.

But even as she thought it, she knew she couldn't. Giving up, as delicious as it felt, meant giving up on Alex and Raya. That wasn't going to happen.

"Come on," she said. "Let's look back there." She nodded towards the darkness at the far end of the building. "If I was trying to hide, I'd start in the shadows."

She forced a smile. Alex nodded and climbed out of the pile of broken debris.

They started digging around, this time working side by side. Passing things back and forward, lifting heavy pieces out of the way together. They covered the area in sections, five feet, ten. Keeping busy. Ana's mind was wandering again, pushing at the edges, trying to figure out who could be behind this. One thing kept coming back to her. Whoever it was knew them – knew their guilty secrets. But who?

"Alex, you know the mandatory school counselling?"

Alex paused, chair leg in hand, and looked across at her.

"Yeah. Why are you thinking about that now? It was such a waste of time."

"I know. Dankman's incompetent."

"I reckon he's worse than that. He kept trying to get me to say stuff that I just wasn't ready to say. You know? About Danny. About my feelings." Alex rubbed his hand over his face, pushing the sweat out of his eyes. "Then…I don't know. It's like when I finally talked to him, he just did nothing. Wrote me a prescription I didn't bother filling and thought his job was done. Told me to come back if I was having suicidal ideation. I'm not sure I even know what that means."

Ana nodded. No question, Dankman could do more harm than good. He was totally unqualified to help a group of kids dealing with real trauma and very real grief. But he had got her talking, and from the sounds of it, Alex too. Maybe they weren't the only ones?

"Do you think the others told him stuff too? Secrets and things?"

"Ana, you don't think *Dankman* is behind this, do you?" Alex was watching her. His scepticism was obvious.

"I don't know. I mean, I know it sounds silly, but he knows us. He talked to all of us." Ana blushed. Her suspicions about Dankman had been growing. But now, saying it out loud – it just sounded stupid. Dankman – the slobby school psychologist who spent most of their sessions playing solitaire on his phone. A criminal mastermind? That sounded like too much hard work for a man who wheeled himself around his office in his desk chair so he wouldn't have to actually stand up. Besides, he had no reason to do this. From what she'd seen, his only motivation in life was to avoid having to do anything.

"Well, who do you think it might be?" she asked, quickly redirecting the conversation.

"I did have this crazy thought…" It was Alex's turn to blush. "It's stupid. It's just something that Caden said about how Benny's death didn't look right. He reckoned there wasn't enough guts and stuff for a high-velocity rifle shot. So, I had this idea…what if Benny faked his own death? What if he's actually the one behind this?"

"*Benny?*" Okay, now Ana didn't feel as ridiculous. They were both reaching and knew it.

"Yeah, I know. Stupid idea," Alex said. "Just forget it." He bent down to pick up a lamp, hiding his face.

"No, it's a good idea. Certainly, no stupider than thinking Dankman's behind this," Ana said kindly. "You know, I sort of wish one of us was right. I'm pretty sure we could outrun Benny if it came to it, and Dankman wouldn't get too far chasing us in his chair." They laughed. Somehow talking about it made Norman seem a little less scary – a little more human.

For a few more minutes, they dug around in silence, shifting furniture and peering behind shelves. Reluctantly Ana forced herself to check the time:

23:12

She put her phone away and took a deep breath. Panicking wouldn't help. There was still enough time – everything would be okay. With renewed effort, she clambered over a large pile of stacked chairs to check behind them. Nothing there.

"I hope Raya's doing okay," she muttered, half to herself. It felt wrong to split up, but Jade wasn't capable of walking, let alone searching a building, and with Ellis on the loose, it wasn't safe for anyone to be alone.

"You know, I got to hang out with her today," Alex said, sounding oddly nervous. "She's nice. I never really spoke to her much before. We talked about…stuff."

"Yeah? What stuff?" Ana said with what she thought was an air of nonchalance. It was silly, but her curiosity was piqued. Alex balanced a pink lamp on top of a crate and smiled at her.

"You."

Ana flushed a little, stupidly pleased at the thought that her two best friends had been talking about her. She picked up a box and threw it to one side, hoping to hide her expression.

"Raya had this idea…" Alex said, looking for all the world like an awkward middle-schooler. "She thinks…that maybe, you and I…"

Ana's heart started beating fast. Was this *that* moment? Was this happening? She silently thanked Raya for sticking her nose in, willing Alex to finish the sentence. But he fell quiet, turning inwards to his thoughts. Ana could have kicked him. *Don't stop now!*

For a painful minute they both poked around in the piles surrounding them, the air heavy with unresolved business. Ana's brain stewed with thoughts: prompts she could give to get Alex to keep talking. Before she got the chance though, she felt a hand touch lightly on her arm. A musician's hand.

Alex had stopped digging and was next to her, looking at her; his soft brown eyes had an urgency in them. Ana's stomach flipped. She could feel his fingers, resting gently on her skin. There was fire in his touch. Her eyes held his look.

"Raya said…that we…that you…maybe."

Oh, god. Just say it! Ana nodded encouragingly. It was like squeezing water from a stone. Her heart was pounding; it seemed impossible he couldn't hear it, feel it. Thank goodness there were no cameras in here, spying on this moment, watching them.

"Raya thinks we like each other," Alex said, the words finally coming to him. "But…I mean, that's just stupid, isn't it? I mean, you're Ana, as in Danny's sister, and I'm, like, you know…just Alex." The bubble burst. Alex dropped his hand and stepped back from her, turning away. He started picking at the junk around him again.

Ana was frozen to the spot. Her whole body tingling as the feelings faded, her heart throbbing painfully. Disappointment crushed her. What had just happened?

She forced herself to turn away too – no way she wanted Alex to see her expression. Questions raced through her mind, formed on her tongue, then fell away. Was she wrong? Was Raya wrong? Had Alex unceremoniously tried to let her know he didn't feel the same way about her? Frustration and mortification rose in equal parts.

She shoved a box hard. It fell back, opening a pathway into a dark corner behind a bookshelf. Stepping over, she moved into the shadows, grateful for an excuse to hide her face from Alex.

From her hidden spot, she dared to sneak a peek at Alex. He had stopped digging again and was sitting on an upended box. His face seemed tight, racked with thought. She didn't get him. What was he trying to do here? Let her down gently, or tell her he loved her? It was one of the two.

"Ana, I need to tell you something, and I really need you to just listen."

Here we go again.

"Sure." She kept her voice neutral, but the mental barriers were dropping into place. Her moment of weakness had passed, and she needed to protect herself and move on. Keep digging. Keep busy.

"Do you remember the night Danny died, at the hospital?"

Ana remembered every painful detail, whether she wanted to or not. The red plastic row of chairs, the green walls. The waiting families. Maia's parents in matching NASA hoodies, huddled together in the corner, waiting in terrified silence. Karl's dad standing by the window – apart from the others, hands deep in his pockets, shoulders hunched. Disinfectant. Masks. Announcements, as people bustled past crinkling in their blue gowns. Slamming through the swing doors into surgery, out of surgery. Gurneys. Police. Noise.

"You know, that was the last time we really talked, until this trip," Alex said. "The next day, I came to find you. I knocked on your door, but you didn't answer. It was okay, I understood. But then the days went by and became weeks. I'd walk into the hall, and you'd hide. At the bus stop, you'd walk half a mile to catch a different bus. You dropped the one class we were in together. I get it. It's not your fault. You didn't want anything to do with me."

The barriers were firmly in place and locked down in Ana's head now. She kept moving, shifting boxes, one after another, mindlessly working so the words wouldn't get inside, wouldn't break through.

"The thing is, Ana, I understand. I know it was my fault that Hunt did what he did. My song killed Danny. My song broke us. I know you can never forgive me. I don't blame you, Ana. I'll never forgive myself. Not as long as I live."

Ana was surprised to feel tears on her cheeks. Somehow, she had stopped moving, a box still in her arms, frozen in place. His words were pushing her. A jumble of images merged and danced in her head. The beep of the heart monitor. Alex knocking softly on the front door. Her mother sobbing at the yellow kitchen table while food burned on the stovetop.

It hurt. It hurt. It never went away.

Alex stood up and moved behind the bookshelf. He was behind her, the darkness swallowing them both, hiding their pain.

His voice was so soft she barely heard his next words.

"Raya had it right – about me, anyway. I do like you, Ana. A lot. I think...I always have. But I totally understand if you don't feel the same. I don't blame you. What I did to you and your family can never be forgiven. I'm so sorry…"

Ana turned. The walls fell away. *How could he blame himself?* How could he think she blamed him? She was the one. She was the guilty one. Never him. Never Alex.

"Alex. What happened wasn't your fault. I have *never* blamed you. Ever. How could I? I…" She looked up at him. They were so close now, she could feel his breath on her skin, the warmth of his body. She felt herself move towards him, leaning in, the back of her hand brushing his fingers, her knee touching his leg.

She came up to his chin, to the neck of his T-shirt, his skin smooth and dark, damp with sweat.

"Raya was right about both of us." A whisper was all she could manage. It was enough.

Alex looked down at her. His face so close. His brown eyes, warm with love. His soft, sweet lips smiling.

She wanted him so badly. She wanted to pull him down to her and kiss him. She wanted to fold into his arms and never leave.

It was the moment. *The moment* – right up until she saw it.

Ana gasped. Stepping away, her arms dropped to her sides.

Alex seemed momentarily surprised and disappointed, but then seeing her expression, he turned and followed her gaze.

There it was, in the dark – the faintest white glow catching the corner of a large crate. Blink and you'd miss it.

Was this it? Was this weak light the thing they'd been searching so hard for? Or was it another false hope? Ana walked over to the crate and shoved it hard, pushing it aside, revealing the source of the light.

A large metal box frame was bolted to the floor, topped with a hatch door. There was a handle on one side next to a glowing rectangular keypad, the white letters standing out starkly in the darkness, its bright light illuminating the walls and boxes strewn about it.

Ana kneeled down; her fingers touched the metal hatch. So, this was it. It was real. She had been right all along.

Norman had been here all this time, hiding behind the hatch – and they'd finally found him.

29 | Alex
17:15

They'd almost kissed.

Alex stood by the hatch, his thoughts firmly fixed on one thing: *Ana*. She'd gone to fetch Raya and the others, while he'd stayed behind to kick-start their next life-or-death challenge – getting the hatch open.

The moment replayed itself in his mind – exploring what had just happened. *Almost happened.* They had been so close, he could still feel her – her dark skin shiny with a thin layer of sweat, dusted lightly with sand; her ever-changing, unknowable eyes looking up at him, into him. She was beautiful – and more powerful than he'd ever seen her before. Something in this god-awful place had opened her up, let her step out of Danny's shadow and be herself. Ana. His Ana. Alex smiled.

The keypad on the hatch glowed brilliantly in the darkness; he felt a deep swell of optimism. They were going to survive – he was sure of it. They'd found the hatch; they'd found the door that would take them behind the curtain. This was their first real chance to stop Norman. There was hope.

Of course, it had seemed improbable that they would make it

this far. Alex was acutely aware of how unprepared they were for whatever was inside the hatch. Someone armed and dangerous might be standing behind the door, waiting for them to unlock it. Maybe a whole squad of murderous, bodybuilding meatheads with semi-automatics was lurking inside. They already knew that Norman wasn't working alone. If the cowboys were on the outside, who knew how many minions he might have on the inside. *Then again...* they could find a completely empty lair with a functioning satellite phone, a fully stocked fridge, and a TV subscription so they could binge-watch *Friends* while waiting to be rescued. There was no point in worrying. Not yet.

Besides, they didn't have a choice, did they? The truth was, at this stage in the game, with barely fifteen minutes to go until the next hour ended, it didn't matter. There was nothing for them out here except more death and horror. Whatever was inside the hatch, at least they would have a chance, no matter how slim – and they would be together.

That's all he wanted. That was enough.

They just had to guess the four-letter code. How hard could that be?

Bending down, he studied the keypad; it looked new and shiny compared to the metal hatch lid, which was pretty scratched-up and rusty. The lock must have been recently installed – and recently used from the looks of it. The surface was dust-free, with the full alphabet, a hash key and a delete button.

He wasn't the best at math, but he knew that if the code was random, it would be impossible to break in time. But Ana was convinced that the code would be part of the game. If they made it this far, Norman wouldn't miss the chance to taunt them with another twisted little manipulation – the whole set-up at the motel was so meticulous; there was nothing random. No. There would be some clever connection, there had to be, if they could just figure out what.

Leaning forward, he took a deep breath and tentatively typed in four letters: A B C D, then hash. There was a short beep; the keypad flashed white. The code he'd entered disappeared. Okay, so that was how this worked. It seemed pretty straightforward.

On his second attempt, he paused to think. What could the actual code be? What four letters might be the key to unlocking the hatch? He reached out and typed: C O D E.

Beep. The keypad reset. Yeah, maybe that was too obvious. He needed to think harder – what would Norman choose? What would a psychotic murderer choose?

Nervously he keyed in: K I L L.

Beep. This time the keypad flashed red. A countdown appeared on the small screen: sixty, fifty-nine... Okay, so those were the rules. Three wrong tries gave you a one-minute time penalty. Alex was relieved – it could have been worse. One minute wasn't the end of the world. It just meant they needed to think things through and not waste time on random guesses.

So, what could it be? Four letters. Think, think... He started with A.

Ants, apps, acne... His mind blanked. He felt the same mild panic he got during exams. *Back, ball, bear...* None of the random four-letter words that popped into his head made any sense. *Cars, cats...eggs...* This was stupid, they had no connection to Norman or the motel. He wished Ana was the one doing this – if anyone had a chance of figuring this out, it would be her.

It wouldn't be long, he reminded himself. She'd be back soon, with the others. Between them, they would stand a fighting chance of guessing the code. They'd get it. They could put together a list of ideas and—

Bang.

Alex jumped, falling back from the hatch.

Even though the sound was unmistakable, his mind pushed it away. It couldn't be. No. Something had fallen. A box on a shelf that they'd dislodged earlier…or maybe it was Ana coming back?

Every nerve was on high alert, straining to listen. Faintly he thought he heard muffled footsteps, distant shouts, crying. No – no, this was all wrong. They had found the hatch. They were going to figure out the code and escape. No one else was going to die today. *No one.*

He tried to hold down the rising wave of panic.

Awkwardly fumbling, he reached into his pocket and pulled out his phone. The screen shone back at him, green numbers lighting up the dark, confirming his worst fears:

59:48

A new hour had begun.

Someone had crossed the line. Someone had been shot. *Someone else was dead.*

Without hesitation, Alex leaped to his feet and ran for the door, stumbling over boxes and broken furniture. He had one thought only: *Ana is out there…somewhere.*

He had to get to her.

Crashing through the heavy metal doors, he tripped forward, sprawling onto the ground. Desperately he looked around, squinting against the glaring sunlight. Where had the shot come from? *Where?*

There was a quick movement off to one side. Ellis walked out from behind the pool enclosure, shoulders hunched, heading away from the road sign, from the death machine. He was clenching and unclenching his hands, over and over.

What had he done?

Alex ran fast, fear and adrenaline surging through him, heading for the sign. Another one of them was dead – and it wasn't Ellis. But it didn't have to be Ana. *It didn't have to be Ana.*

As he rounded the corner of the pool fence, he skidded to a dead stop. There it was – a long line of dust on the horizon. The red truck was already heading their way. His heart was in his throat. His legs were heavy and for a moment he couldn't move.

A dark shape lay on the ground, across the line.

It didn't have to be Ana.

Slowly, disjointedly, he forced himself to walk towards the line; his movements felt clumsy as though his limbs weren't connected right. As he got closer, he could make out the small, dark mass huddled in the dirt, arms zip-tied to the rope that had dragged her across the line.

He almost stumbled and fell. He heard a low wail from somewhere behind him, desperate footsteps running for the line. There was no breath. Nothing left. Just a hollow sensation, tinged with the smallest shameful flash of relief.

A gust of wind pulled at the body.

A lock of short, black hair caught the wind.

Raya was dead.

30 | Alex
55:15

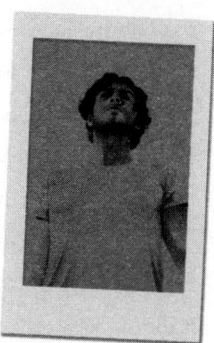

Ana kneeled on the line where she had collapsed, mere feet from her best friend's body.

One inch would push her over. From the look of her, she probably wouldn't care. Alex put his arms around her and tried to edge her gently away from the line, pull her back to safety. He tried to keep his eyes away from the small figure lying, curled up in the dirt like a fragile, dead bird. Discarded.

"No, please, god, no…" Ana was sobbing.

Alex wrestled her away, dragging her back out of harm's reach. The red truck was getting uncomfortably close.

"Not Raya. No…please…not Raya…" She kept fighting him, reaching for Raya. It was all he could do to keep her on this side of the line.

"Raya's gone," he whispered in her ear. "She's gone. That's not her, Ana. Not any more. There's nothing you can do."

"No, no…please…"

He engulfed her in his arms and held her tight, willing her to be okay. She was shaking from head to toe. He bent his head down, burying his face into her hair, breathing in the soft scent of her, just moments before so intoxicating, now laced with grief and sorrow.

How could this be happening? They had found the hatch. They were going to get out of here. All of them. What the hell went wrong?

The truck was close now. They didn't need to see this. Alex scooped Ana up in his arms and turned them both away, heading back to the motel.

The sound of the truck pulling up followed them. Voices, doors slamming, thuds and bangs, everything tinged with a sense of horror. This wasn't the way it should end – not for Raya. Not for anyone. But especially not Raya.

Alex's room was close, the door left open, flies buzzing around the entrance in a lazy cloud.

There was no fight left in Ana. He felt her strength leave her, her weight bearing on him more and more as they walked away from their friend for the last time. He half-carried her into the dim room, kicking the door shut behind them as they both collapsed onto the bed.

Alex felt tears behind his eyes. Furious tears of grief and frustration. They'd had a chance, a real chance to get out of here. Why now? After everything they'd been through, what was the point?

He looked down at Ana. She was curled up, her dark skin unnaturally pale, her eyes closed. He knew that expression. Shock.

It had been on all their faces a year ago. All the kids, teachers, even the firefighters and paramedics as they'd faced the horror in the gym. He'd been in the restroom when the fire started, one building down from the old gym block. He hadn't seen the things

Ana and the others had seen. But he had heard the sounds and felt the sheer terror.

They were kept well away, behind cordons, a wall of police holding them back. Rows of waiting ambulances and police cars lined the car park, well behind the front line – the fire trucks, flashing lights, sirens screaming.

He had stood there, scanning the faces of the kids running from the flames, desperately searching for a familiar face, a flash of dark hair, a red hoodie. Danny and Ana. They had to be there. They had to.

He hadn't known then. It was only later, much later, that the rumours started. Messages cutting into the fear. Texts, snaps, desperate calls. Rumours that became a reality. He had never deleted the texts he got that day – the moment he knew:

Ana:
plz come to the hospital

Ana:
its danny

Grabbing a pillow, he gently tucked it under Ana's head, fully aware of the futility of the gesture. She didn't even know he was there.

He stroked her forehead softly. She felt cold and clammy despite the heat. He knew this. They'd been here before. The green hospital corridor. The red plastic chairs. Sitting together, waiting. She hadn't spoken then; she wouldn't speak now.

Her breathing was shallow and fast, her fists clenched, just like last time; after the doors from surgery swung open, after the doctor walked over and asked if Danny's mother had arrived yet, after she took Ana's hand and said she was very sorry.

Ana had gone to the same dark place, beyond his reach, beyond anyone's reach. There was nothing he could do then – or now.

Alex just had to be there and wait.

As long as she needed. He would wait.

31 | Ana

One Year Ago

Ana sat on the top row of the bleachers and sighed.

Damn Danny. He'd disappeared the second they arrived so he could chase after his latest conquest – Isaiah, the ridiculously hot, absurdly tall centre from the junior varsity team.

She was only here because of Danny. One of his many friends had promised to drive them both home after the game, so she'd reluctantly stuck around, hoping to avoid an hour-long bus ride. Bad idea. She'd be lucky to be home before midnight at this rate.

"No! I reckon Ellis is losing it," Alex said. "He just took number nine down. That's a foul, for sure." Alex had stayed to keep her company, probably out of kindness. She wasn't much fun to watch a game with – she knew little and cared less about sports.

Sneaking a sideways look at Alex, she smiled to herself. He was wearing his little-boy-on-game-day face – a slight frown, intense concentration in his big brown eyes. There wasn't a sporty bone in Alex's body, but he loved basketball. He was a Lakers fan for life. That was how he'd bonded with Danny when they first met – in elementary school, over ice cream and a shared love for LeBron.

The ref was shouting something about technicals. Ellis Locke, the point guard, was standing on the sidelines in his Wolves jersey, frustration pouring off him like sweat. His team were still down. Ellis's minions of the day were jumping up and down in the front row, chanting: "Ref, you suck; ref, you suck!" Ana recognized Jade Clark and a handful of other beautiful people, heckling anyone who moved into their orbit. Jax Patel was zooming around them, filming the game over his shoulder, smiling for his invisible fans.

Maybe she should just go.

It wasn't like she'd be missed. She glanced at the door at the back of the gym where Danny had disappeared half an hour ago, heading to the locker room. He wouldn't be back anytime soon – not if Isaiah had anything to do with it. Her one unsporty ally – Raya – had ditched her halfway through the first quarter and was probably smoking weed in Caden Loftus's Candyvan. And though he'd never admit it, Alex would enjoy the game a lot more without having to babysit her.

No, it was time to cut her losses and catch the bus home. Taking out her phone, she shot Danny a quick text.

"Hey, I'm just going to the bathroom." Alex stood up. "I don't want to miss the end of the quarter. This game's brutal." He paused, focusing on her for a moment. "You hungry? Want me to pick up a hot dog or something on my way back?"

He would make someone a really great boyfriend someday, Ana thought (not for the first time).

"I'm good. Actually, I'm going to head out and catch the bus. I've got a stack of homework due," she added.

"Really? You sure?"

"Yeah." *Be free*, she thought. *Enjoy the game.*

"Okay," Alex said, putting on a good show of disappointment.

"If that's what you want, I guess. See you tomorrow?" He clambered down the bleachers. The game resumed; there was more shouting, squeaking shoes and loud cheering. The noises were starting to get to her – chants echoing around the old gym walls, louder and louder.

Throwing her stuff in her backpack, she gave Alex a head start, then climbed down after him, heading for the exit.

Her phone beeped:

Danny:
sorry sis my bad omw

Damn it. Now she wasn't sure if she should go or wait for Danny. Why did he have to do everything at the last minute? God, he could be annoying!

She was so focused on her phone that she wasn't paying attention to where she was going and walked smack into someone moving fast in the opposite direction, catching a flash of grey and orange.

"Uh, sorry, Karl," she muttered awkwardly, but Karl Hunt just grunted, moving on, heading for the back of the gym.

More grey and orange caught her eye in the bleachers; Maia Walsh and her debate team boys. They'd won their debate this afternoon and were celebrating with hot dogs bought by Maia's excessively proud parents. Each year a different parent sponsored the team and each year the uniforms became more ostentatious. Last year had been head-to-toe NASA, courtesy of the Walshes. This year, Matt Hunt – Karl's dad – had sponsored the team, with striped polo shirts that looked like they were straight out of a maximum-security prison, the words HUNT TECH blazoned across the team's backs. Hideous, and mortifying. Ana had taken her uniform off and buried it at the bottom of her backpack the second the debate ended.

Maia was waving her over, but Ana pretended not to notice. The debate team weren't the most sociable group and Ana wasn't up for trying to make awkward conversation. Better to leave them to it. She kept her eyes down and walked on.

"Banana!"

And there he was. The man himself. Danny had appeared at the back of the gym, looking a heady mixture of shifty and self-satisfied.

Ana grinned – she couldn't help herself (even though he was the single most irritating human being alive) and walked in his direction.

She had only made it a few feet when it started. The smell came first. It was distinctive – not a woodsy campfire smell. More of an acrid chemical odour, the kind that sets alarm bells ringing in your mind. Something was on fire that wasn't supposed to be.

Maybe it was just a bonfire outside. The old gym building didn't have any ventilation, so smoke was probably blowing inside and getting trapped. Probably nothing.

"Hey, banana brain." Danny grinned at her. His usually tan skin looked a little red. That's what he got for kissing random, unshaven boys in locker rooms. "You're not leaving, are you?"

"Where have you been? You ditched me."

"Yeah – sorry, sis. Isaiah had something in his locker he wanted to show me." Danny grinned so widely that Ana laughed. Another boy. Another love. Another head-over-heels, passionate drama. She wanted to hug him. He lived on a different planet from the rest of them – a rolling, free-falling joy ride. No fear. Just fun.

The fun twin.

"I think I'm going to head out. I've got a stack of homework," she said half-heartedly. She already knew she'd be staying. Danny wouldn't let her off a night out. Not for something as unimportant as homework.

"Aw, don't go yet. It's early. Let's grab a hot dog and find Alex."

A few people were coughing now. The burning smell was getting stronger.

Ana looked around. Was it her imagination, or was it looking a little hazy in here? There was a faint halo in the air around the lights.

She wasn't the only one who'd noticed. There was a wave of muttering in the crowd. Ellis had stopped playing and was standing in the middle of the court, ball in hand staring towards the back wall. The scoreboard was flickering.

"What's with all the smoke?" Danny asked, his smile fading a little.

"No idea. It just started." There were no fire alarms or sprinklers going off, but there was definitely a cloud of smoke building up in the rafters. Uneasy laughter broke from the bleachers behind them. No one wanted to be the first to react. It had to be nothing – didn't it?

A few shouts broke out from the seats near the back of the gym. People were standing and pointing to the wall. Tendrils of dark smoke were curling through the air vents. A fire alarm gave out a half-hearted series of chirps before falling ominously silent.

Ana stood still, watching things play out around her. There was a disconnect somewhere in her head. It didn't look real somehow, and yet there was no question – the fire was *inside* the building and growing by the second. A deep creaking, moaning sound could be heard beneath the voices, as though the old building itself was shifting.

Suddenly the scoreboard cracked loudly and went out, in a shower of sparks.

It was as if a switch flicked. Simultaneously, everyone knew it was time to get out. Not panic, not run and be laughed at for the rest of high school. Just a swift-but-cool exit, joking about how stupid this was on the way out. Teachers shouted orders, bags were gathered, phones filmed the drama. A heightened, fake-jovial atmosphere filled the gym as people hustled towards the front doors. This was so stupid. But just in case…

Ana looked at Danny. They shrugged. Better go.

"Let me get my bag – I left it in the locker room," Danny said, heading towards the back of the gym. Ana followed him, even though it didn't feel right – everyone was heading the other way.

They got as far as the back door when it happened.

The wall behind the scoreboard exploded. Fire streaked into the gym; bricks crashed down around them. A searing, roaring heat lashed out across the roof, through the air – flames burning viciously like a living beast, writhing in fury.

All sense left. Screams and horror replaced the nervousness of moments before.

Big things happened, one after the other. A swell of people broke free, running for the front doors. A row of high windows shattered, one after another, raining shards of glass over everything. A bank of spotlights swung down wildly across the court, suspended at one end, flames streaking behind it.

Half the court was filled with screaming figures, the front doors blocked by a wave of bodies. The gym had transformed into a death trap, cattle driven through it, trapped within its walls.

They needed to get out. Now.

Ana looked around desperately. They were on the furthest side of the gym from the front doors, with a wall of people blocking their way. They would be the last ones out – assuming they made it in time. She looked at the flames now burning wildly across the rafters. Large panels of roofing were peeling back; pieces dropped to the floor in flames. Kids scattered beneath them, screaming.

It was happening so fast. Too fast.

Panic coursed through her. They would have to run *underneath* the fire. The whole roof was burning. What if it collapsed on them? They would be trapped. There was nowhere to go – there was no time.

There had to be another way out. She grabbed Danny's hand.

"There's another door. A fire door." Danny looked at her, confused. She pointed behind them, at the door to the locker rooms and back hallway. "There's a fire exit at the end of the hall. We can get outside from there!"

It went against every instinct to head in the opposite direction to everyone else, but they were already here. The fire exit was so close – just through the door. They could make it. They would be outside in moments.

Danny nodded. He understood. He turned and ran to the back door, pushing through it, Ana at his heels.

The air in the hallway was black with smoke. Coughing and spluttering, eyes burning, they made their way to the end, feeling their way along the walls, until they found the fire door. Relieved, they slammed into the panic bars. The door cracked open, but then stopped. Something was blocking it. Danny shoved it hard, rattling it. Something on the outside held firm.

"Fuck! Ana, help me!" Both of them crashed their shoulders

against the door, together. Over and over. It wouldn't budge. Through the crack they could see a heavy chain padlocked between the handles. There was no way they could break through it.

The smoke was unbearable; Ana's throat was burning with every choking breath. The hallway seemed to be getting hotter and hotter. The fire must be getting closer. *Was it in the hallway?* They had to get out. Now. They had to.

She banged on the door. Through the glass panel, they could see the dark night outside, figures moving, staring at their trapped faces, pointing. So near, but so far.

"Help us!" Ana shouted to them. "Please!"

"Open the door!" Danny rattled hard on it. Useless.

The figures moved closer, pulling at the chain on the other side. It wouldn't budge. Scared faces, heads shaking desperately, voices.

"We can't open it!" "We'll get help." "Just stay there."

Just stay there...? Where the hell else were they supposed to go?

A wave of intense heat caught the back of Ana's neck. Slowly she turned, terrified to look back. The fire was at the far end of the hallway, fingers of flame reaching, burning towards them. The air was unbreathable; they were choking, coughing, gasping for air. They didn't have time to wait.

The door back to the gym was blocked by the flames now. There was no way out, short of running through the fire. They were trapped.

The locker room.

There were windows in there. Weren't there? Ana wasn't sure. She tried to focus, to concentrate, to picture the locker room in her mind. Yes – there was daylight. She was sure of it.

"Locker room. We need to get to the locker room!" Ana tried to shout, her voice stolen by the roar of the flames. She broke into a spasm of coughing as she pointed desperately behind them. With every breath she was inhaling more smoke, less air, her chest burned.

Danny shook his head.

"No. They'll come. They'll open the door."

Flames filled half the hallway now, violently lashing around, racing through the space. It was like nothing Ana had ever experienced. Wild, terrifying, consuming. Closer and closer. A lick of flame brushed over her. She smelled the hairs on her arm burn. They were going to die if they stayed here.

"Danny, we can't wait!" Ana forced the words out, forced them through the coughing. "A window…in the locker room. *A window.*"

"No. They'll come." Danny shook his head, turning back to the door, rattling on it, clinging to the handles.

Ana grabbed his T-shirt, turning him to face her. She had to make him understand.

"Danny – we'll die here. You need to trust me."

Their matching eyes locked together. A second, maybe two – that was all it took to seal their fate. He nodded. The decision was made. It was easy. Ana was the brains. Danny trusted her. Always.

"Go!"

They pushed away from the exit towards the locker-room door. Danny went in first, holding the door open for her. Ana was about to follow him when a scream stopped her in her tracks.

Maia Walsh was standing in front of the burning gym door. She must have followed them into the hallway.

She was rigid, her arms clinging to her backpack, her face locked in a grimace of fear, mouth open. Her curly dark hair was gone, replaced by a wild curtain of flames. She was on fire.

"MAIA!" Ana ran across the hallway, her hand reaching for Maia's arm. But her fingers never reached her.

Maia staggered backwards, half-falling; her silhouette lit up in flames as she fell through the gym doorway. The fire surged around her, swallowing her whole.

Ana fell back. Horror cut through the fear. She almost dropped to the ground. Almost. The image of Maia was seared into her eyes. She couldn't think. *She couldn't*.

"*Ana!*" Danny's voice cut through the noise. She had to get to the locker room. She turned, willing her limbs to work, to get her out of this, away from here. Danny was in the doorway, still waiting for her. The flames were everywhere. It was too much. She shook her head, desperate to clear her thoughts.

Move, she thought. *Move*. But her legs weren't behaving.

"ANA!" Danny shouted. "Listen to my voice. *You need to come now!*"

His voice released her, unlocking her fear. Suddenly she was back. She started moving, started towards the locker room, towards Danny. Started.

But it was too late.

It happened so fast. The ceiling tiles near them caught fire, lighting up like a match. Flames ripped along the hallway ceiling. A wall of heat knocked Ana over. She fell to the ground, away from the locker-room door as the entire ceiling collapsed, crashing inches from her feet, blocking the doorway. Coughing, terrified, she crawled back, away from the flames, in the only direction left to her – back to the locked exit door.

Reaching out, she grabbed the panic bars desperately. The metal was burning hot now, and pain seared through her hands, her skin. She gasped, falling back into the corner of the door frame, holding her scorched hands protectively to her. Fire everywhere. Smoke everywhere. This was it. She was going to die here. She sank to the ground, curled up into a ball. She could smell her burned skin, as the fire reached for her. Terror coursed through her.

She was going to die. She was going to die.

She didn't hear when the exit door crashed open, prised apart by someone with a crowbar. She didn't feel the hands dragging her outside. Just her. Alone. Into the cold, night air. Coughing and coughing.

Smoke followed her, pouring through the doorway behind her. There were voices, people. Everything was a blur. Nothing registered, except one thing, one desperate thought – *Danny is still inside.*

Pulling herself to her feet, Ana turned to go back, but hands stopped her. There was no door any more, just a burning maw, tongues of flame licking out at them. Taunting them.

"Help my brother...locker room...have to go back..." She was coughing, spluttering, but too many hands held her back.

"Too late." "Can't go back." "So sorry..."

"No...no, please!" She was begging – desperate.

The locker-room window. Where was it? She scanned the high gym wall, looking for the window, finally seeing it, almost hidden in the heavy smoke. There it was – high up. A small, narrow clerestory window. Too small. Too narrow. *Too high.*

There was no way someone could reach it, let alone escape through it. Why had she not remembered that? *Why?*

Thick, black smoke poured through the broken glass. It moved like an animal, light flickered at its edges – the fire was inside the locker room. There was no way out. No escape. Danny was trapped.

Ana writhed free of the hands holding her and, stumbling, ran to the wall. Her fingers clawed at the brickwork – at the one thing separating her from her brother, trying to climb up, to break through, anything. *She tried.* With every part of her. With everything she had. *She tried.* Her fingers bled, seizing in pain, her burned skin shredded on the wall.

"Danny… *Danny*…"

The hands were back – gloved now, firm. A voice was talking to her.

"It's okay, kid. Come with me. I've got you."

"My brother…"

"There's nothing we can do. We need to go. We need to get you out of here."

She tried to pull away, but her legs gave out and she fell. The ground was cold. Wet earth mixed with broken shards of glass. An empty paint can lay on its side, feet from her, dried green paint spilled across dead leaves.

Leaves, broken glass, a can of green paint.

The voice was talking, the gloves were on her arm, her face. Questions, words. But there was darkness at the edges, closing in over her head. Burying her. Everything was losing focus as she stayed like that – unmoving.

Leaves, broken glass, a can of green paint.

She should have died then. She wished she had died then. Every day since, she wished that everything had just stopped, ended – that she had closed her eyes and let the darkness take her too, swallow her whole.

Leaves, broken glass, a can of green paint.

At some point the strong arms must have lifted her up, must have carried her away from the wall, away from Danny. For the last time.

But it wasn't over. It would never be over now. With a certainty that was forged in that moment of pure, bitter grief, she knew one thing. For as long as she lived, as long as she breathed, she would never forgive herself for what she'd done. She had sent her brother to his death. He had trusted her, and he had died because of her. There would be no absolution, no respite, no hope. Not for her. Her guilt was damning.

She had killed her brother.

There would be no redemption.

32 | Ana
47:06

"I killed Danny."

After a year, it was odd how easily the words came out. Ana couldn't bring herself to look up at Alex. She didn't want to see his reaction. But it was time.

The shock of losing Raya had shaken something loose inside her. No more hiding. No more cowering, barely breathing, under the weight of guilt.

Until this moment, the only other time she'd spoken about it was during that one therapy session with Dankman. She hadn't told anyone else what had happened – what she'd done. Her mom, Raya, Alex…she couldn't break it to them. They were grieving Danny's loss. How could she tell them that she had caused it – that it had been her stupid idea to go into the locker room, that Danny had wanted to wait, that he would be alive now if it wasn't for her? How could she tell them that when Danny had needed her the most, she had let him down – she had let him die?

Now, here in this motel from hell, it had happened again. Raya was gone. *Raya.*

Ana's chest burned with pain. She tried to hold an image of

Raya's face in her mind, but it was forced out by the shape on the desert floor, black hair blowing in the wind. A hollow nothingness thrown down, cast away.

Somewhere in the darkness of her mind Ana knew they'd already lost. Whether they opened the hatch and made it out or not, the game was over. Raya was dead. Danny was dead. There was no reason to hide any more. There was nothing left to lose.

Almost nothing. There was still Alex.

It was time she told him the truth.

She fixed her eyes on a particularly nasty stain on the carpet and talked. Her voice sounded scratchy and dry to her. She went back to that day and forced herself to recount every detail – no hiding from it. No sugar-coating the ugly raw truth. Just the facts laid bare.

When she was done, she realized her shaking had stopped. There was an odd sensation in her arms and legs. Lightness, maybe? As though somehow the weight of it all had been lifted almost imperceptibly.

So, there it was. The truth. Hanging in the musty air between them. She had killed Danny. Now Alex knew.

There wasn't a sound in the room. Alex hadn't moved. Ana didn't dare face him.

She took a long deep breath. It was her turn to wait.

It seemed an eternity before Alex stirred. He stood up and walked over to the wall where he had propped his guitar. Picking it up, he gently touched the wood, the strings.

Ana kept her eyes away from his face. She didn't want to see his expression. What if he hated her? What would be the point?

Alex sat back down and started strumming, his fingers playing softly, finding their notes.

"I wrote this a few months after…" Alex sounded tired. He started picking slowly, a melancholy tune finding itself in his fingers. A slow rhythm picking up, like a heartbeat.

His voice was quiet, barely above a whisper. Ana turned slightly to listen.

"Give my own life just to have you back
Give it all up just to see you here
Throw it all away just for one last chance.
Give my own life just to have you back
Fall on the ground now and never stand
Lose my whole world just to save yours.
Just don't let me fall.
Throw it all away
End it all today
Please don't let me go.
Just don't hide away.

Give my own life just to have you back
Give it all up just to see you here
Throw it all away just for one last chance.

Don't let me go
Don't let me fall
Don't let me go."

Alex stopped, his fingers hovering over the strings, silenced. He had spoken the best way he knew how.

Tears ran down Ana's face. She turned to face him.

"For Danny. You wrote that for Danny." She could barely hold her emotions together. The words stung, they bit into her soul. *Give my own life just to have you back.* If only she could. *If only she could.*

"No," Alex said, lowering his guitar to the ground. "I wrote it for you."

Ana glanced at him, momentarily confused.

"For...me?"

Alex nodded. He looked at his hands, as if wishing they could speak for him.

"What happened to Danny...we couldn't...no one could change that. We all had a part to play, you know? Yeah, we're all guilty, or could have done something differently. But not really. Not if you think about it. We loved Danny. Ana, we still do. We would never, *ever* have tried to hurt him. Wherever he is now...he knows that."

Wherever he is now. Ana closed her eyes, her mind reaching, searching for her twin.

"I wrote the song for you, Ana. When Danny died, I didn't just lose my best friend. I lost both of you...and it was too much." Alex reached out his hand and gently took hers. For the first time, Ana dared to look up at him; his eyes held hers. "I loved Danny. But I loved you too. I've always loved you." His thumb softly stroked the palm of her hand.

For once, Ana didn't feel the need to pull away. Her mind was racing, processing. She'd told him everything – her horrific secret, and he was still here.

"You don't...hate me?" She had to say it.

Alex shook his head and smiled. "You have to ask?"

A year. It was a long time to carry this. It wouldn't go away, ever.

But the weight was lifting. *Wherever Danny is now he knows I love him. He knows.*

For the first time in a year, Ana felt like the broken parts of her were pulling together. Not complete. Not a whole. But close enough to feel just the smallest corner of herself, of who she had been before.

Alex leaned into her, his head falling on her shoulder, his curly hair on her cheek. She breathed him in, deeply. She remembered him. She remembered herself. The way he made her feel.

Like coming home after a long, dark journey.

There was no stopping it. Ana turned into Alex's arms. Their lips found each other. They pushed together, clinging to each other; passion, desire and grief shared between them.

Wrapped up into each other, they fell back, fingers curling into hair, breathing each other in.

No words were needed.

Soon enough they would have to face what was in front of them. The next hour would tick away and bring whatever sick cocktail of pain and fear was waiting for them. But just for now – for this moment in time – there was only love.

No more, no less.

❋

33 | Ana
36:56

Ana stood shoulder to shoulder with Alex in the baking-hot storage shack, looking down at the hatch.

The small flashing keypad winked at them tantalizingly. On and off. Stay or go. If they stayed, three of them would die before the sun set. If they figured out the code and got out of here – out of the "balloon" – they had a fighting chance.

There was no more thought about what they might find inside the hatch. There was no time for that. Maybe it would be empty – maybe not. Maybe whatever was inside was worse than anything they would face out here. Maybe it would kill them. They didn't know. All they could do right now was focus on the next step. On getting the hatch open. Whatever came next, they would figure it out when the time came.

Game on, Norman.

No sign of Ellis or Jade. They were probably lurking around, watching from a safe spot. Ana felt her jaw set. Even if she somehow guessed the code, it was too late for Team Ellis. They'd lost their chance to escape with her when they killed Raya.

Her fingers were in her pocket; she touched the cool surface of

Raya's Zippo, feeling the texture of the etched letters. RM.

Not now. Later, the grief would come, but right now their mission was clear. Find the four-letter code that would open the hatch and get inside. Ana kneeled by the keypad and, taking a deep breath, typed L O B A, followed by the hash. Beep. A white light flashed. Okay. That would have been too easy, but she had to try.

She looked at Alex. He shook his head and shrugged.

"I don't know. Maybe 'Hunt'?"

Ana's hands shook as she entered H U N T. If Norman had chosen the name of the kid who'd deliberately started the fire, what would that say about him? She was almost relieved when the beep sounded.

K A R L. Nope. Phew.

Beep. Three wrong guesses. The keypad turned red, and a countdown appeared on the screen. Sixty seconds, ticking down. Sixty seconds to think. Sixty seconds lost.

At the one-minute mark, the pad turned green.

S F H S – maybe St Francis High School?

F I R E

L I N E

No luck. They were locked out. Another precious minute wasted. Ana looked nervously at her phone:

33:06

They couldn't keep messing up like this. They couldn't afford to.

Squatting next to each other on the floor, they both took turns keying in guesses. Alex found a pencil on a shelf, and they scribbled ideas on the side of a crate next to them. Brainstorming, as fast as they could. Scratching out the worst ideas. Trying out the better ones:

YEAR

LOST

HOPE

On and on. Time was ticking away. They could both feel it. Their guesses were getting wilder, off target. Desperate. This wasn't working. Norman didn't play that way. There had to be something more, something they were missing.

EXIT

DEAD

SIGN

Panic was setting in. They had wasted well over ten minutes and were no closer. They were running out of ideas and had given up writing words on the crate, instead taking turns to enter any words that entered their heads.

She looked at Alex. He was bent over the keypad, his hand hovering over the glowing keys. His long fingers were shaking.

Oh, god, what if she had made a mistake? What if the code was random?

The thought sent a bolt of fear through her. If her plan didn't work, it was too late to try something else. They'd put all their eggs in this one basket. Was Alex going to die because of her – because of one of her stupid ideas? Just like Danny. Was it happening again?

No! Not this time. She closed her eyes and took a deep steady breath. *Focus.*

Norman could have gone with a standard numeric lock. It would have had tens of thousands of combinations, compared to this alphabet lock. Or if he'd wanted to be really secure, he could have used biometrics – money didn't seem to be a problem for him. No – Norman chose an alphabetic cypher for a reason. It wasn't random. There was a word that would unlock the hatch. A four-letter word that meant something.

Maybe it was a name or a clue. Maybe it was something personal to Norman. But the lock was new, which meant it must have been deliberately installed as part of the set-up for the Balloon Game. It was all connected. The code had to mean something, it had to be part of the game.

Which meant it was guessable. They could do this. They would do this.

A loud metallic clang shook her from her thoughts. Someone was banging on the door to the shed.

Ana turned to Alex. They'd had the forethought to bar the door by wedging a steel pole through the handles in case Ellis came for them – which was only a matter of time. It was getting close to the end of the hour, hunting time.

"I'll go see if the door's holding," Ana said, looking around and finding a long wooden pole resting against a shelf. "Keep trying, okay? Maybe it's something we've seen, or a word, a name. It has to have meaning."

Alex nodded. Their eyes locked, a grim determination in their expressions. There was no time for drama. They were in the fight for survival here. He squatted in the dirt by the hatch and entered another word.

A L E X. Wrong.

Ana clambered over the piles of junk towards the door. More loud bangs and clattering noises.

A chair leg poked through the gap and splintered as it was levered sideways in an attempt to prise the door open. There was more loud clanging as dents appeared in the corrugated metal.

Something heavy was being thrown at the door, over and over.

Ana checked out the makeshift lock. They were surprisingly lucky – the handles were D-shapes of solid metal, welded to the door frame. The bar wedged through them was holding. It would take a supreme effort to break it down. It would take time.

They needed a distraction.

"Nice try, Ellis," Ana shouted.

There was a pause. A shadow appeared under the doorway. Ellis was right outside the door.

"Need help?" Ellis called out. "You've been in there a while, so I'm guessing you found the hatch."

"Lucky guess."

"So, what's up? Is it locked? Can't get inside? I'm pretty good at puzzles. Let me in and I'll give you a hand. You know what they say, teamwork makes the dream work."

"Thanks for the offer, but as we're not playing for the same team, I think we'll pass."

She could see glimpses of Ellis through the cracks. Up and down, examining everything – the door, the hinges, looking for a chink in their armour.

"Okay. Well, have it your way." Ellis's voice sounded distracted. She wasn't the only one killing time. "You know we have less than twenty minutes left?"

Twenty minutes? How had the time gone so fast? Ana felt a bolt of fear. Twenty minutes and they were no closer to figuring out the code. What if they didn't guess it in time? What next? Give up? Leave the outbuilding and let Ellis pick them off one by one? Or stay in here and die? Some choice.

Things were silent outside. The shadow had moved away. Ana

listened carefully, trying to figure out which way Ellis was heading. She mentally ran through his options. There were skylights on the curved roof, but it would be next to impossible to climb up over the blistering hot sheet metal. Most likely Ellis had already scouted around for any holes he could crawl through. He must have decided the door was his best option.

Where was he?

"Ana, I got nothing," Alex sounded panicked. "I'm blanking."

Ana looked for any sign of Ellis. Still nothing. She had a bad feeling about this, but there wasn't anything she could do. There was no way around it – their only hope was to open the hatch. If they failed to crack the code before the hour was up...well, she couldn't let herself think about what would happen. They had to. It was that simple.

"Let's swap," she called back, heading to the hatch again. "I've no idea what Ellis is up to. Be careful."

As they changed positions, Alex briefly caught Ana's hand. The warmth of his fingers on her skin – soft against her scars, stopped her. *That feeling.* She pushed gently against him, and they stood for a moment, stealing precious seconds as they held each other – close together. She closed her eyes. They were not dying today. Not like this. Not now.

That was when it hit them.

There was no mistaking it. The all-too-familiar smell of smoke. The smell of fire – the bitter scent of burned rubber, paint and plastic. The smell of death.

"No!" Ana jumped back. Was Ellis really doing this? Was he going to smoke them out and then pick them off? Or let them burn to death then throw their charred bodies across the line? How could he? What was *wrong* with him?

"That bastard," Alex said, running his fingers through his hair, turning to look at the door. Smoke was billowing under it; a flicker of flame licked the edges of the metal frame.

It took just seconds for the smoke to spread throughout the shed. They would have minutes before they wouldn't be able to breathe. Outgunned. Ellis had won. He'd figured out that if there was only one way in, there was only one way out. They were trapped unless they opened the hatch.

This was bad. Really bad.

Ana's hands were shaking. She was transfixed by the fire, the flames. She couldn't do this. She couldn't go through this again. She froze on the spot, unable to move, barely breathing.

Seeing her face, Alex turned and squatted down by the keypad.

DOOR

LOCK

HELP

Red light. The one-minute countdown started. Alex stood up.

"I'm going to the door. If it comes to it, I'll fight him. Okay?" Alex said, picking up the stick Ana had dropped. He pulled her around to face him. "Ana, I'm out of ideas. I need you to take over. You're the smart one. You're our only hope. Out there we lose." Alex was talking gently, but his words had a finality to them. "Don't look at the fire. Just don't look at it. This is different from last time. I promise."

Ana got it. No time for weakness. No time to remember. They both had their part to play. Their lives depended on it.

She nodded, shaking herself out of it, shaking it off.

"I've got this. Go," she muttered, turning away, and dropping to her knees to study the lock.

The minute was almost up. The smoke was getting thicker by the second.

A clue. A word. Four letters. Was it something in the anniversary card? Maybe the invitation? What was it? She closed her eyes and pictured the motel, the rooms, the pool... It had to be there somewhere, hiding in plain sight. *Four letters...* What wasn't she getting? *What?*

Suddenly, she had it.

It was so obvious – it had been in front of them this whole time, flashing brightly, taunting them. The road sign: four letters. It had clearly been recently repaired – and not very well, as two of the letters were out of sync. Why had Norman gone to the effort to repair the sign at all? He hadn't bothered to fix anything else around the motel. Just the four-letter sign, winking at them over and over.

The motel name was the clue. It had to be, right?

She heard Alex coughing. Her eyes were stinging. There were all kinds of noises, creaking metal, crackling fire. When she looked around, she could barely make out Alex's outline through the smoke.

The keypad lit up. This was their last shot, their last three guesses. They couldn't last much longer in this hellhole.

She focused on the name. They had already tried L O B A. No luck. That would have been too obvious. But Loba meant wolf in Spanish. Wolf. Why wolf? This wasn't an area with wolves. That must mean something. Why else would Norman choose wolf?

Leaning over the keypad she typed carefully, her eyes smarting from the smoke.

W O L F

Beep. Red light. Her heart was beating too hard, she felt sick.

Only two chances left; she had to get it right. Something to do with the sign. *Think!*

Maybe she had it the wrong way around? Maybe it wasn't what the motel name had been changed to – maybe it was the old name?

Quickly, she reached into her pocket and pulled out the coaster, turning it over to look at the image on the front. She peered at it in the smoky dark, scanning the faded photo of the old motel. The road sign was cut in half under the image of the rose in the corner. Only the first two letters were visible – R and O. Could it be? She looked back at the rose image. There were pink roses all over the motel – on the curtains, the dodgy wall art, the cheap laminate countertops. Could it be *The Rose Motel*?

That must be it!

Her hand was shaking as she typed the letters:

R O S E

Beep. Red light. Wrong again.

A rush of panic hit her. They had one last chance. What could it be? They'd tried everything! She'd been so sure it was the motel's name. It was the last thing to try, the last thing that made sense.

The smoke caught her, and she coughed hard. It was impossible to breathe. But she had to. She could hear Alex coughing at the door, and something else that sounded like shouting. Light was cutting through the smoke. *Was the door open?*

Ana pushed the thought away. She couldn't screw this up. Alex was depending on her. There was only one way they both survived this. She stared at the glowing keys, her eyes watering, coughing hard.

Motel Loba, Wolf Motel, Rose Motel... What was she missing? She pictured the road sign. That stupid, miserable light, looming over everything from the moment they had arrived. Flashing over and over, the red and yellow lights out of sync. MOTEL L B, MOTEL O A, MOTEL L B. Two of the letters newly replaced in a mismatched font. Two of the old letters – something O, something A.

Ana gasped. Suddenly she had it – she knew the motel's old name. She had been so close. Just one letter off. It must be the code. It had to be – *it had to*.

It was impossible not to cough. She pulled her shirt over her mouth and held it in place with her left hand. With her right hand she reached for the keypad.

This time her fingers didn't shake.

She brushed the ash off the keys and carefully typed four letters.

Something O, something A.

R O S A

The Motel Rosa. The pink motel.

Click.

The lock released. She'd done it – she'd cracked the code.

Without hesitating, Ana pulled on the handle and lifted. The hatch lid was heavy steel, but it moved a crack. She heaved harder, coughing incessantly. Finally, the lid was open enough for her to flip it over. It fell back, revealing a black hole with a clang.

"Alex!" Ana shouted. But the words were barely audible. She broke into a spasm of coughing. "Alex!" What was wrong with her voice? It was croaky, weak.

She turned to find him. But the smoke had thickened into an impenetrable blanket. She tried to wave it away, scrabbling to her feet. Her legs felt strange, limp. There just wasn't enough air.

She had to get Alex now.

"Al…" she gasped.

A figure was moving towards her, barely visible in the ashen air.

"Here!" She waved at him desperately. "Alex…over here…" Coughing violently, she dropped to her knees. Everything was starting to spin.

The figure was closer. Tall. Too tall. Its face masked with fabric wrapped around it. Something in its hand. Something metal.

It was Ellis.

He moved towards her, one arm reaching up, a metal crowbar raised high over his head. He wasn't coming to talk. He was ending this.

Ana raised her hand to block him, but her arm didn't move right. It fell limply as she slumped backwards. There was nothing she could do. She gasped desperately for air. Nothing left. Her vision was closing in on her, narrowing, pulling her towards blissful unconsciousness.

Ellis was just feet away and moving in for the kill. This was it. Game over.

Suddenly she felt something grab her from behind. Strong hands lifted her and dragged her backwards. She felt herself falling, into the hatch.

A cool, welcome darkness overwhelmed her, closing in on her as she slipped away, her mind shutting down until there was nothing left but silence.

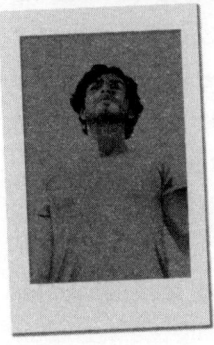

34 | Alex
11:19

Alex was lying face down in the red dust, the burning shed several feet behind him. He watched sideways as smoke billowed out and was quickly taken by the desert wind.

Where was Ana? Had she made it out?

His head hurt where Ellis had smacked him hard with something. He could feel gravel burns on his legs and arms from being dragged. Everything was blurry – inside and out, all the pieces missing, jumbled up in his head.

Wriggling awkwardly onto his side, he tried to sit up. His hands were roughly tied behind his back with a lamp cord – the old lamp was still attached and banged against him when he moved.

Slowly, awkwardly, he manoeuvred himself into a sitting position. He must have been lying there a while; the fire was burning itself out. Wind sucked ash out of the building, sweeping it skywards, momentarily giving him a clear view of the hole where the door had been.

He stared into the darkness, searching for movement, willing Ana to come out.

Where was she? Was she okay? Had Ellis got to her? Where was Ellis?

"An..." He spluttered into a round of violent coughing. His chest hurt – he'd breathed in so much smoke, it felt like someone had put their hands around his neck and tried to choke the life out of him.

It took minutes for the coughing to subside. He sunk back onto the ground, light-headed, everything spinning. It was all he could do to lie there and try to hold on. A wave of nausea followed the dizziness.

Just sit it out. Hold on.

It was hard to know how long he stayed like that. Time was passing in waves. Tentatively he opened his eyes, red and smarting from the fire.

A pair of disconcertingly clean Kobe sneakers were inches from his face. One reached forward and nudged him hard in the shoulder.

"You awake?" Ellis said, his voice clear and untouched by the smoke.

Alex felt his senses snap into place. Ellis was alive; they were still in danger. He tried to sit up again. This time it was a little easier.

"Where...Ana?" He broke into another fit of coughing.

"She didn't make it," Ellis said calmly.

The words hit Alex before the meaning could sink in. Didn't make it. What did that mean? Didn't make what?

"Ana...?"

"She's gone, doofus. Which just leaves the three of us. You, me and Jade." Ellis watched him as he spoke, his expression cold.

Alex shook his head, trying to wake himself up, trying to make sense of the words. Gone. Ana didn't make it. Ana was gone. *She was gone.*

It was as though a bucket of ice-cold water had been thrown over him, cutting through the mess in his head, smacking him hard between the eyes.

A sensation crept over him – a familiar one, something he'd hoped he would never, ever feel again. Not after the first time, last year, in that hospital corridor when the doctor told them that Danny had died. What was it? Fear? Grief? There wasn't one word that summed it up. It was as though the pit of your stomach was being ripped out of you and there was no hope, no light left. No breath.

Ana hadn't made it. Danny. Raya. All gone.

They had lost. Ellis had won. The game was over.

Alex closed his eyes, sinking back to the ground. The fight left him. The horrors of the last day melted into an emptiness that he willingly accepted. The raw burning in his throat could take him. He could just stop breathing, just let his struggling lungs give up and die.

"Oh, for fuck's sake, stop feeling sorry for yourself," Ellis barked, kicking him with the toe of his shoe. "You may get a reprieve for now. I'm honestly not sure I can stand another hour with Jade. She's gone completely mental."

Alex felt tears well in his eyes, stinging as they mixed with ash. He wanted to hide his face – not give Ellis the satisfaction of seeing him cry, but he couldn't move or turn away. He had nothing left in him.

A sharp laugh, and something grabbed him roughly by his shirt, pulling him up.

"Snap out of it." Ellis shook him. "Don't get me wrong, I like men who cry. Shows strength of character to wear your heart on your sleeve. But we haven't got all day, have we? I've got a game to win, then I'm going home. So, *get the fuck up*. We need to find Motel Barbie and end this."

Alex was no match for the point guard's powerful basketball-trained physique. He was manhandled to his feet and dragged, half-stumbling after Ellis, the lamp swinging wildly off the cord, bashing into his legs.

No need to guess where they were headed.

Ellis's hand-crafted place of execution.

As they rounded the corner of the pool fence, they got their first unobstructed view of the death machine, instantly stopping them in their tracks.

Jade was standing near the rusty old tractor, her feet inches from the line, muttering to herself. Her platinum-blonde hair was standing up in a bird's nest on the back of her head. Carefully constructed make-up streaked her face in morbidly fleshy colours. She shifted from side to side, a grimace of a smile plastered on her face.

"Like I said," Ellis half-whispered. "Completely fucking mental."

Alex instinctively nodded in agreement.

They walked forward. Ellis waved at Jade with his free hand.

"Oh my god – is that Alex?" Jade's words sounded strange, disjointed, almost childlike. "We thought you were dead." She was pulling at the bird's nest with one hand – hard – taking great handfuls at a time. It must have hurt.

"Not dead yet, but don't get too attached," Ellis said.

"Oh…no, no. We don't like that. Don't like that at all." Jade turned back to face the desert and started muttering to herself again in a baby voice. She kept staring at Jax's phone. The small rectangle lay where he'd dropped it, where he'd died, about ten feet beyond her.

When they got close to the death machine, Ellis pushed Alex to the ground, and sighed.

"What do you think, Jade? Shall we let Alex cross the line next, or stick with tradition and go with ladies first?"

Jade seemed flustered. She kept moving around, uncomfortably close to the line. One hand was firmly knotted into her hair; the other swatted the air in Ellis's direction, as though she could magic him away.

"Not nice…not nice…" she muttered. "…is too hot…we want boba…no sugar…always too much sugar…"

"Oh, for fuck's sake," Ellis muttered under his breath. "Some people really don't handle stress well." Ellis squatted down next to Alex. "She's talking herself into a one-way ride over the line. I'm not putting up with this shit for another hour."

"We like boba…right? It's our favourite. Right, Jax?" Jade was clearly talking to the phone.

Alex looked up at her. Had she said Jax? Wow, she was really out of it.

Ellis seemed to have noticed too. He stood up and walked over to her; as he got close, she wrapped her arms around her body defensively.

"Jade, can you tell me where Jax is?"

Jade just looked at the phone; its broken screen caught the bright sunlight. She didn't need to say what she was thinking. Ellis gave a short bark of a laugh.

"Well, I guess that wouldn't surprise me. If Jax did come back to haunt us, he'd probably be reincarnated as an iPhone." He was grinning.

Alex looked down at the dirt – it was like rubbernecking the scene of an accident. He wouldn't feel sorry for Jade, he told himself. Even if she had completely lost the plot and thought she was talking to her dead boyfriend. She was with Raya the last time they saw her alive. Whatever happened, whatever Ellis did, she must have sat back and let it happen. She wasn't a victim.

"Oh, look! There he is." Ellis waved at the phone. "Hey, Jax – looking good. What's that…? Uh huh…sure…okay." He turned to Jade and leaned forward conspiratorially. "Jax says you should go to him." He caught Alex's eye behind Jade's back and winked. "He says he's waiting for you."

Jade shuddered. She kept her face firmly turned away from Ellis.

"I'm not…I'm not…" Jade looked at the phone. Somewhere inside the mess in her head, she must still be registering danger. Alex felt relieved.

Ellis must have picked up on the same vibe. He stopped grinning and slipped his hands into his pockets, his brow creased in thought. He was alert, looking around taking in everything. Jade's proximity to the line, her body language. Alex was in no doubt – Ellis had chosen his next victim. The only thing left was deciding how to do it.

Did Jade understand what was happening? Did she know that Ellis was coming for her? Would she fight it? Alex's eyes searched Jade's face for something, anything. But all he saw was fear and confusion.

"Ja—" Alex broke off into a violent, hacking cough. His throat felt raw, each cough sending a spasm of pain through his chest. He fell back, struggling to catch his breath.

Ellis watched him dispassionately for a moment, before turning his attention back to Jade: "Jax says he wants you to come to him.

He wants to tell you something." Ellis feigned a kind of sad-awkward expression. "He says…he forgives you."

This was low. Even for Ellis.

Jade's lip quivered; her eyes filled with tears. Her entire body was shaking violently.

"I'm so sorry…so sorry…I never meant…" Her whole fragile figure seemed to shrink into itself – like a lost child. She started to cry.

"It's okay, I know." Ellis stepped forward and gently, almost tenderly, placed his hand on her shoulder. Jade instantly recoiled, spinning around to face him, her expression taut with fear. Her tears were flowing freely now, her heels pushed deep into the line's white paint. Ellis dropped his hand. "I know you didn't mean to kill Jax, or let Raya die to save yourself. No matter what everyone else will think – I know you're not a murderer. You're just doing what you have to – what we all have to. You're not a bad person." Was he talking to himself? It was like watching a snake carefully coil itself around an unsuspecting victim.

"Don't listen…" Alex's words were barely croaks. Awkwardly, he shifted himself forward, onto his knees, the lamp cord cutting into his wrists as he pulled against it.

Ellis shot him a dark warning look before turning to check the time. A steely expression crossed his face. They must be down to the final minutes of the hour by now.

"You need to go to Jax now. Go to him and this will all be over," Ellis said, moving incrementally closer to her. His voice had a new urgency.

Jade was transfixed. Her sobbing dried up; she was staring at the phone as though she could see Jax, smiling his big smile, filming the moment. A strange look of calm flickered across her face.

"Go," Ellis whispered encouragingly. "Jax needs you." He had her. Alex could see the trap close. So smoothly, so easily. *He had her.*

"Jade, stop…" Alex pushed himself to standing, dragging the lamp behind him. "Jax isn't there…Jax is…"

In two steps, Ellis covered the distance between them. He grabbed Alex by his shirt and flung him back down on the ground, locking his arm firmly around his neck. Alex gasped for air, struggling against the tight grip, choking.

"Jade, listen to me." The sweetness was gone. Ellis was done playing. In one of his hands, he was gripping a plastic zip tie. Plan B. "It's easy. You have two options. You can turn around and walk across the line to Jax. You can ride off into the fucking sunset together. Just the two of you. No more pain, just love. Or you can stay here…with me." He held out the zip tie like an offering.

Time almost stopped as Jade looked at Ellis, then the phone, then back to Ellis. There wasn't much to choose between. She could stay here with her guilt and fear – with Ellis and his death machine – until he strapped her to it and dragged her over the line. Or she could walk over to the phone, to Jax, who loved her, who forgave her. If she wanted it to be so, it would be. Jax was waiting for her. He was smiling and waving, calling to her. Did anything else matter? Did the truth matter? Right here, in this moment, this was her truth.

As it turned out, Ellis was right. It was easy. She chose Jax.

The shaking stopped as she stepped over the line, a soft smile on her face. She seemed for all the world like vintage Jade Clark again, every inch a movie-star's daughter. As she walked towards the phone, her hair caught the late afternoon sunlight and rippled softly in the wind. She was golden, immaculate. Everyone wanted to be her, everyone loved her, desired her. She was one of the beautiful people. Like Jax. Like her Jax.

She didn't look down. She didn't look back. No hesitation. Jax was smiling. They were magnets. She could feel the pull of him, the need for him. They couldn't fight it. It was her place. Her destiny.

Alex closed his eyes and slumped back against Ellis's grip. He couldn't watch.

Ellis had won, again.

35 | Ana
51:53

Ana woke with a jolt. She sat bolt upright, her hands pulling at her shirt. It felt as though something was tight around her neck. But there was nothing there.

She coughed several times – a dry, rasping cough. Everything hurt. Her head was spinning, her eyes burned. Her throat felt like she'd swallowed sandpaper.

Instinct told her to pull herself together; danger was still here. But her body responded sluggishly. Her eyes wouldn't focus, darkness pulled at the edge of her vision; she kept coughing in violent bouts.

She was sitting on something soft; it had the downy feel of a sleeping bag. Was she on a bed? Was she back in her room? Where was Alex?

Her mind was slowly pulling itself together, remembering bits and pieces. The smoke, Alex at the door, Ellis coming towards her...
Someone had grabbed her and pulled her backwards. She remembered it now, the feeling of strong hands dragging her into the hatch.

The hatch! She was inside the hatch!

Fuck. She jumped to her feet, all senses kicked into gear as she scanned the room, searching for Norman. Where was he? Where? He had to be here – he'd carried her here and left her on this sleeping bag. *Where was he?* For several terrifying moments she checked every corner, every shadow, picking out shapes in the dark – but there was no one there.

Taking a deep breath, she forced herself to look at her surroundings.

The long, narrow room was dark and had the musty, earthy smell of a damp basement. A string of bulbs lit up the curved corrugated roof above her, giving off a weak yellow glow. There was a small, curtained area with the lid of a camping toilet peeking out behind it. A modest kitchenette was installed at the end wall with a single gas burner; utensils and plates were lined up neatly on a shelf above the counter, with food stacked below in labelled plastic containers. To her right she could just make out a large crate pushed up against the side wall. A chessboard was set out on top, a single chair to one side.

There was no sign of a way in, or out.

Everything was utilitarian and meticulously organized, like some prepper's underground bunker – built for survival. Ana swallowed nervously. *Who was this person?* Who built this whole set-up? Who spent time carefully lining up their plates in a neat row, right before kidnapping seven teenagers?

Nervously, she scanned the shadows one more time. At the far end, she could only make out vague angular shapes in the weak light – maybe a desk? A chair? It was hard to tell what was down there, but it wasn't human. She was alone.

Her thoughts flashed to Alex. He was outside somewhere, with Ellis – and if Norman wasn't in the bunker right now, then he had to be out there too, probably armed. If she didn't do something soon, before the hour was up, Ellis would make damn sure Alex crossed the line...and Norman would be there to finish things off.

There must be so little time left! She had no idea how long she had been unconscious. Quickly, she pulled out her phone:

49:14

For a moment she was disorientated. That couldn't be right. It was too long – after the bunker and the code. It should have been closer to the end of the hour. Then it hit her like a hard punch in the gut.

It was a new hour.

The timer had restarted. While she was unconscious, someone must have crossed the line. Someone else was dead.

Ellis, Jade or...Alex? Who was it? Panic hit her. *Please not Alex.* Ellis would have got rid of him first if he had the chance. Had Alex crossed the line? Was Alex already dead? Was this all for nothing? She couldn't go on. Not without Alex.

Stop it, she told herself sharply. *Alex is alive.*

She could feel it in her heart – she could feel him. Alex was fine and she was going to find a way out of this trap. Everything was going to be all right – he was going to be all right.

With a self-control she didn't know she had, Ana switched her thoughts over to the job at hand. She was in Norman's secret lair. There had to be something she could do from here, something that would end the game once and for all.

Barely aware she was doing it, Ana's hands curled into fists. She checked around – a set of free weights were lined up in a neat row next to the mattress. Reaching for the middle weight, she hefted it in her hands. Light enough to swing. Heavy enough to do some damage.

The other end of the bunker was emitting an eerie blue glow. Armed with the weight, she walked slowly towards the light, nervously triple-checking the shadows as she passed. She carefully edged around the crate with the chessboard set out on top; there was a game in progress – it looked like checkmate. Norman liked his games and liked to win. No surprises there.

The blue glow was coming from a bank of monitors covering one wall, tidily arranged above a desk with a grey coffee cup next to a row of matching grey pens. The desk was stained with several cup rings. Whoever had been sitting there really liked coffee.

As Ana moved closer, the screens came into view.

All but one were switched on, grainy images from around the motel lining the wall: the pool area and reception, the flashing motel sign lording over everything. Several familiar rooms appeared as the images changed, views constantly switched around.

Every corner, every angle of the motel was there in front of her. Several blank screens cycled in and out – maybe where they'd successfully destroyed some of the cameras, and there were no images of bathrooms. But there must have been so many more cameras than any of them ever suspected. Eyes everywhere, following their every move.

It was hard to believe that someone had stood right where she was now standing, and had seen and heard everything that happened to them. That they'd watched the bus arrive, watched them laughing at the poolside, crying on the line. They'd heard them in their rooms, talking, sleeping, kissing… Alex.

She sat in the chair and pulled herself closer to the desk, setting the free weight on the desktop within easy reach. Then she studied the screens one by one, searching for any sign of Alex. The images were on a cycle, maybe ten, fifteen seconds before they flicked to another view. It could take precious minutes waiting until he showed up on one of them.

Ana half-watched, glancing around her when she could, searching for anything else she could use. Maybe there was a radio or some way to reach the outside world and call for help.

The end wall was barely visible in the gloom.

A pale rectangular shape could just be made out. Ana's curiosity got the better of her and she pushed her chair towards it. It was a large cork board; several photos were pinned to it alongside a crumpled twenty-dollar bill.

It took a moment, but as her eyes adjusted to the darkness, she could see the images, materializing one by one – faces. Seven school photos, with the familiar St Francis High logo, were neatly arranged around one picture in the centre of the board.

Ana stood up and walked over to the board, reaching out to touch the picture in the middle.

It was an ordinary-looking boy, smiling awkwardly. Blue eyes and sandy-blond hair, wearing his grey-and-orange striped debate team shirt. He looked so young, raw. He might have been good-looking when he was older, when he'd escaped high school, if he had lived long enough.

Karl Hunt.

Ana looked at the other photos: Raya, with her home-cut mullet back in her BTS phase, Caden grinning lopsidedly, Ellis in his green-and-yellow varsity jacket, Jade and Jax, all smiles. Then there was Alex, his hair cropped short, pre-glow up. Sweet and young, achingly familiar.

Her eyes briefly found her own photo – Ana Reyes, smiling

shyly. She looked away, not wanting to remember the way she used to be. That girl was long gone.

Everyone was there. All seven. The motel seven. All the happy, innocent faces. They were so much younger then – the photos were from the year before the fire. Before the Motel Loba or Rosa, or whatever the hell it was called. Before anything really, truly bad had happened to any of them. Grinning stupidly, on the edge of unimaginable darkness.

They wouldn't have been smiling if they'd known.

She turned back to the desk. The coffee cup and pens had logos on them – the letters HT in bright orange. Instinctively she touched the cup, feeling the temperature. It wasn't hot, but there was a little warmth left. It had been used recently.

Returning to her search, she studied the monitors, a new-found resolve as she scanned from left to right, looking for Alex. He would have to show up at some point. He had to. Over and again the screens kept flicking from view to view. Where was he? *Where was Alex?*

She didn't know what it was – maybe it was a slight shuffle, or a flicker of a shadow, but something made her freeze. The hairs on the back of her neck stood up; every sense was on high alert. Nothing tangible, but her instincts were on fire. She leaned back in her chair, her hand moved to the weight, her fingers curling around it ready.

Somehow, she knew, without a doubt, that she was no longer alone.

Very slowly she turned around.

Standing in the centre of the bunker, backlit by one of the bare light bulbs, was the dark outline of a man.

36 | Ana

"Water?"

The man's voice was low, almost a growl. Ana's heart was beating fast. This was it. This was Norman – the puppet master. The one who was killing them off one by one and filming it so he could enjoy the show.

A white mask hid his face, the eyes cut out, revealing ominous black holes, a creepy bland smile on the white surface. Around the edges she could see signs of the man hidden beneath. Dark-blond hair, tan skin with freckles. The hands were a little wrinkled, he was older – middle-aged, at a guess.

In one hand, he held a bottle of water. The other hand was raised placatingly in front of him. He had what looked like a radio clipped to his belt.

"You must be thirsty, after all that smoke." He reached out, offering the water to her. "Here, take it." The voice was unfamiliar, muffled by the mask. Ana tried to place him – Dankman? Benny? She couldn't fit the pieces together; her thoughts were all over the place.

Ana didn't know what to do. Here she was, alone and face to face with the man who wanted to kill them. She suddenly became very aware of the danger of her situation. Underground, in a locked bunker with a psychopath. No one else knew the code to get in.

Odds were, she wouldn't leave here alive.

The man moved towards her, very slowly, water still held out in front of him, other hand raised as though he was approaching a cornered animal.

Fight or flight time. Ana looked around, her vision sharpened, her instincts kicked in.

She swung around, holding the free weight in front of her like a weapon.

"Stay back!" Her voice cracked – it was raspy from the smoke. She fought the impulse to cough.

The figure stopped. He was less than five feet away. One of the bulbs was directly above his head now, illuminating him. For the first time, Ana could see him clearly.

He was wearing baggy sweatpants and white trainers with a grey collared shirt. There was still nothing remotely familiar about him. He was unnervingly average. Ana was surprised – somehow in her head Norman had grown into mythic proportions. She would have been less surprised if a chainsaw-wielding murderer had jumped out at her. Not this.

But then, weren't serial killers often nondescript dad-next-door types who befriended their victims right before chopping them up for breakfast? She'd listened to enough true-crime podcasts to know not to let her guard down. This man had watched them suffer. He was a sick, twisted psycho and there was no telling what he was capable of in person.

She tightened her grip on the weight.

"Okay. I won't come any closer," he said. His accent was middle-American, nothing distinctive. He bent forward and put the water bottle on the floor. Her mind raced. She needed to play for time and figure this out. She scanned the roof and walls searching for the hatch but there was nothing. How had he appeared from nowhere? The exit had to be on his side.

She nodded at the water bottle.

"I...I'd like water. But you need to move back. You're too close." Her voice sounded weak from all the coughing. But that could work for her – if he thought she was injured it might create a false sense of security.

The man nodded and moved away, walking backwards around the crate, his eyes on her at all times. When he reached the chair, he sat down and unclipped his radio from his belt, setting it on the chessboard in front of him. He propped his elbows on the board next to it, still facing her, his white mask glowing like a macabre, grinning face in the artificial light.

Ana took a quick step forward. Resting the weight on the floor within easy reach, she picked up the water and took a long grateful sip.

"Thank you," she said when she was done, putting the bottle down again and retrieving the weight. It seemed ridiculous to thank a psychotic killer for giving her water, but it felt right. He would like it; it would appeal to his ego and show compliance – she was playing his game.

He was about ten feet away. At that distance, she'd have a head start if he came for her.

"I should say I'm not surprised that you figured out the code. You always were a smart one – by far the best on the debate team.

I always thought you'd be the one to watch out for," he added, nodding to himself. "And now, finally…here we are. I've been looking forward to this moment for a long time – Ana Reyes."

She started at the sound of her name. Of course he knew her. He knew all of them, didn't he? He even knew what she'd done and exactly why she was here. The man sat back in the chair and stretched out his arms, making himself comfortable. The light caught him at an angle, and for the first time Ana noticed there were thin orange stripes on his grey shirt and a small orange logo on his chest pocket. Two letters: *HT*.

She gasped; her heart was beating so loudly she was sure he could hear it. Orange and grey. *Orange-and-grey striped polo shirts.* The eighth photo on the board.

Suddenly she had it. She'd seen him before. Things fell into place, like dominos in a row, one after the other. It all made sense.

She knew who he was. She knew who Norman was.

Ana fixed him with her eyes, her expression cold.

"I wish I could say the same. Is it Norman…or should I call you Mr Hunt?"

37 | Alex
39:41

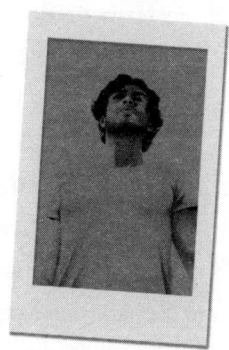

As Ellis tied the lamp cord to the knot on the death machine, Alex watched disinterestedly, as though from a distance. He was calm and silent, wrapped up in his thoughts.

An idea had grabbed hold of him. Something he'd thought about a lot after Danny died.

There had to be grace in death. What else was there? When there was no hope left, when you faced the end. There could only be grace. Danny had died so quickly, so brutally, he'd had no control. But Alex could die with dignity.

He wouldn't fight Ellis. What would be the point? He couldn't win. Besides, what would life be like without love, without friends? All he'd have were the memories, the ghosts, and he didn't want to live with them.

But there was still something within his control. He could choose to be true to himself, right up until the end. That was all he had left to him. That was his grace.

Ellis's hands worked fast and efficiently. He kept glancing up at Alex, studying his face.

"You know what I'm doing?" Ellis said as he tied the last knot.

Alex nodded.

Ellis stood up, stepping back to admire his handiwork. He seemed bothered by Alex's lack of interest.

"You do understand that you're about to die?"

Again, Alex nodded calmly. He gazed out across the desert. It was changing. They had been so wrapped up in the day, he hadn't noticed the passing of time. The air was cooling, there were colours in the sand and in the sky. Colours that hadn't been there before. If you stopped to look, it was as though time was unfolding in front of you. It was stark, but beautiful. A good place to die.

Ellis walked over to the tractor and sat on the upended chassis, the front wheel within easy reach. He wriggled a little, settling himself, legs astride, like a cowboy riding a metal steed. His fingers reached out and rested poignantly on the wheel. He set his phone carefully against the metal, propped so the countdown numbers were visible, ticking away the final hour.

"I don't get you, Alex. All I need to do is turn this wheel and your life is over. *Your life*. Everything gone. Don't you give a fuck?"

Alex shrugged. He didn't have to make conversation.

"Fine." Ellis seemed irritated by the lack of response. He grabbed the wheel, jerking it around hard. The rope tightened on the cord, pulling Alex's hands up and dragging him a few feet closer to the line.

Abruptly, Ellis stopped. The rope stopped moving.

A cat toying with a mouse before eating it. Alex shuffled himself back into a sitting position and turned back to the desert. He wouldn't show fear. He wouldn't give Ellis the satisfaction of breaking him.

After all, this couldn't go on much longer. Everyone was gone now. It was just the two of them. This was the final countdown, and Ellis would be free to leave as soon as Alex was in the back of the red truck. There was no reason to stretch this out, other than for the sadistic pleasure of taunting Alex with imminent death, and if he didn't respond, it would get boring quickly. How long would a cat keep playing if the mouse just lay still?

Ellis jumped off the tractor and started pacing, glancing across at Alex from time to time. He checked his Rolex for the fiftieth time.

"See this watch?" Ellis held his wrist up so Alex could see it. "This was a gift from my father. He gave it to me when I was ten and I came out to him. He told me I was going to need to be tougher, faster and smarter than everyone around me because I would never be accepted otherwise." Ellis gave a short, sharp laugh, and rubbed the face of the expensive watch lovingly. "Well, this Rolex is the last present my father ever gave me. It was the year my mother died. Oh, I've had random generic gifts ordered by his assistants for my birthdays. But nothing more from the big man himself. Always too busy saving the fucking world to remember he has a son." Ellis walked up to Alex and sat down in the sand next to him.

Alex stayed quiet. Relieved. It was strangely comforting listening to Ellis's self-indulgent ramblings. It gave him something to think about other than imminent death.

"Do you want to know something? After the fire, my dear father never even came to the hospital. I could have died, but he didn't give a fuck. All he's ever cared about is his job. The truth is, Alex, I disappoint him. I can see it in his eyes. No matter what I say or do, it's not good enough for him."

Alex bit his lip, willing himself to stay quiet. It was all too human. Too flawed. Ellis had systematically brought them down because he had a massive chip on his shoulder.

"You poor kids have it so easy." Ellis was still ranting, enjoying his captive audience. "No one expects anything of you. You so much as scratch your ass; they give you a fucking medal. The whole system is skewed in your favour, set up to scrape you off the bottom and give you every chance – and you know what else? It's skewed against people like me, just because I wasn't born in the gutter. It's designed to cut me off at the knees and bring me down to the level of every other broke loser out there. I could cure cancer and it wouldn't matter. It will never be enough. *I* will never be enough."

Alex laughed. He couldn't help it.

"You think it's *funny*?" Ellis shouted. He leaped up; Alex half-expected him to walk over and end the game right here, right now with his bare hands. Maybe a part of him wanted it.

But instead, Ellis started pacing again. *Why didn't he just get on with it? What was he waiting for?*

"You know, I saw your place once. When I picked Danny up from his apartment. We went over to see if you were home. Your abuela opened the door. She offered us cookies. Nice lady." Ellis had recovered his composure a little.

Alex felt a shot of nerves. Where was Ellis going with this? Was he moving on to the psychological torture phase? Not enjoying the physical threat enough and trying a new approach? He felt queasy. This was much more dangerous territory.

Ellis walked closer, squatting down by Alex's sandy Converse. He faced him directly, pushing close, staring into his eyes. There was nowhere for Alex to hide.

"The thing is, Alex, you think of yourself as poor, one of life's victims. But you're not. Sitting on the ratty couch in your poky little living room felt good. Coming home to that sweet old lady and her fresh baked cookies – that's not poor. That's fucking rich. That's a real home. Something I've never had. You know, I would honestly give up everything for a life like yours. I would voluntarily live in a shithole, rented apartment in Receida, if it meant I could have a family that gave a fuck about me; someone to ask about my day or notice when I'm home late. Someone to bake me *cookies*."

It was working. Ellis was getting under his skin. Alex ached inside at the thought of home, of Abuela. Losing him would destroy her. He was all she had left.

Ellis must have sensed his power. He smiled.

"Like it or not, Alex, out of all of us here, you're one of the lucky ones. People care about you, and when you're dead, someone out there is going to actually give a fuck. It's almost tragic. Your old abuela was a nice lady – decent, kind. She's really going to miss you when she finds out you're dead…her little Alejandro. But don't worry, I'll tell her you died quickly and with honour. I won't give her the gruesome details. I'll visit her in person, hold her hand while she cries…eat some more of those damn fine cookies…"

That crossed the line. Alex met Ellis's eyes squarely for the first time.

He was done listening.

"You really think you're a victim, Ellis?" His voice was still croaky from the smoke. "We all have shit to deal with. When I was growing up, my dad drank. A few years ago, he lost his job and was so down about it, he'd get off his face then come home and take it out on my mom and me. One time, he was ragging on me…my mom tried to stop him, and he beat her so badly, she nearly died.

He got a five-year sentence, but my mom…she was never the same again. It broke something in her, and she left. My abuela took me in but is too sick to work and can't afford to look after us. I work three part-time jobs to pay for our food and rent, and even then, sometimes it's not enough. But you know what? You were right about one thing. It is a real home. A shit one, but a real one, because I love my abuela, I love my mom, wherever she is…and, god help me, I love my dad – even though I would give *anything* not to."

Tears of frustration filled his eyes. He could hear *that* song playing in his head, all the anger, the rage and desperate frustration. Look where that had got him. Too much pain in the world. Too much hurt. You could only do your best. Grace.

His next words were quiet, almost whispered.

"I get so angry sometimes. *So angry.* But I can't choose what my dad did, or my mom. I can't control what happened to my family, but I can choose not to be bitter. I can do that. That's my choice. Sometimes, that's all I have. So, you want to sit here and have a pity party – you go right ahead. No one cares about you, Ellis, because you don't care about anyone else. If you don't have a real home, it's because you never made one. Don't you see? Living with all the anger, surviving by any means necessary, doing the things you've done…that's not strength. It's not how long you live that matters – it's *how* you live. It's what you do with the time that's given to you, however short."

He'd said his piece. He was done.

He looked back out across the line, away from Ellis, away from the Motel Loba. A deep feeling of heaviness settled over him. Exhaustion. If he could just close his eyes and let this play out. Once and for all.

"Nicely played." Ellis's voice cut into Alex's thoughts. "You almost had me. Right up until the end." Ellis stood abruptly and walked over to the death machine, swinging his long legs over the top. "I'd never pegged you as a manipulator, Alex. Always thought you were a bit clueless to be honest. But that speech – that was masterful. Do the right thing, Ellis. Make good choices, Ellis. Did you think that would make me change my mind? That I would do what? Spare you? Sacrifice myself? Die with honour? Fuck that."

Ellis's hand was back on the wheel. His fingers twitching restlessly.

"You see, the problem with your lovely speech is…I can't do the right thing, or make a cookie-filled home, or even make my dear father love me if I'm dead, now, can I?"

Alex didn't bother turning to look at him. He locked his eyes on the horizon.

"Whatever, Ellis. Do what you have to do. Tell yourself what you have to hear. Let's get this over with." He closed his eyes. "*Just do it.*"

The longer this took, the harder it was. Thoughts kept sneaking into his head, messing with him. Little chinks of hope or memories, pieces of who he was, kept rising up. Fear of dying, of ending like this, tore at him. He didn't want to die. He wanted to live. Desperately. He knew that as surely as he knew anything in this moment. But he couldn't make that choice. He could only choose grace.

Hold on to yourself. Hold on to your truth. He had to. It was all he had left.

He listened for the sound of the wheel turning, a gentle creak as the rope extended and started to pull. But there was nothing. Still nothing.

"Just do it, Ellis."

Any second now. The wheel would start. He felt the sun on his face, one last time. He breathed in the cooling air, the salty desert wind. If he licked his lips, he could almost taste it. One last time.

Still nothing.

What was Ellis waiting for? What?

Why wasn't he dead yet? It didn't make any sense. He was the last. After he crossed the line, the game would be over. Ellis would be free to go. The victor. There was no reason to stretch this out. No reason to keep it going. Unless…

Alex suddenly laughed.

"I'm so stupid. Of course, it's obvious, isn't it?" He shook his head. Why had it taken him so long to figure this out? "You can't kill me yet, can you? There's a reason why I'm still alive. The game isn't over when I cross the line because I'm not the last one…" Alex paused here. Could he say it aloud? Did he dare? "She's not dead… is she? Ana's still alive…"

"I don't know," Ellis said quietly.

The way he said it – Alex believed him.

"You didn't find a body. You didn't find Ana." Alex's mind was racing. "Jesus, she made it! She figured out the code and made it into the bunker. She's alive!" He started laughing so hard, he broke into a fit of coughing. He didn't care. There was still a chance. Still hope.

"I said, *I don't fucking know*. She probably burned to a crisp in the fire. Just because I didn't find a body, doesn't mean she's not dead." Ellis jumped to his feet and kicked at the dirt. He looked furious.

Alex was still laughing. He knew Ana. If there was no body, then she was still alive. She was too smart to die like that. He had to believe that, to believe in her.

Ellis looked like he was ready to spin the wheel and be done. But he couldn't yet. He needed to keep his hostage alive for as long as possible, just in case Ana showed up. It could prove to be a tactical advantage; Ana would never do anything to hurt Alex, and Ellis knew it.

"Does it fucking matter? Even if she survived, which is unlikely, she won't survive the next hour." He turned to face Alex squarely. "You see, you're her weak spot, Alex. She'll come out of hiding for you – and when she does, I'm going to finish the game. Once and for all."

Alex just shrugged. The power had shifted.

"Whatever, Ellis. Maybe I can't stand up to you and win. But Ana? She's beaten you at every turn. She's smarter and stronger than you will ever be. If she's alive, if she made it to the bunker, then you're the one who needs to be afraid, because she's mad at you, Ellis – for Raya, for what you're doing to me. She's so mad…and you want to know something else? When she comes – and she will come, it won't be for me." Alex turned to look at Ellis through his curtain of dark hair, a smile on his lips. "She'll be coming for you."

38 | Ana
34:23

Matt Hunt reached up and pulled off his mask.

"No need for this any more." He threw the mask on the bunker floor next to him and looked at Ana. She hadn't dared move and was still standing in the middle of the floor, clinging to the weight with both hands.

The dim light caught his features, vaguely familiar but softened by age and grief since the last time she'd seen him – a year ago, standing in the hospital hallway, hands in pockets, waiting to hear that Karl was dead. She knew him from the all-school debates; the sad widower who'd sponsored the debate team and showed up to every event, no matter how small, to support his only son. The only son who had walked into the gym a year ago, poured gasoline everywhere and set himself and the building on fire.

Instinctively, Ana glanced behind her at the photo in the centre of the cork board. Karl's young, anxious face peeked out at them, smiling into the mess that his actions had created.

"You finally figured out who I am. So, what was it? What gave me away?" Hunt was sitting on the edge of the chair now.

"The debate team uniform." Ana nodded at his striped shirt and orange "HT" logo. "Your company, Hunt Tech, sponsored the debate team. Whoever was doing this had to have some tech skills – decent enough to hack the school portal. That was kind of obvious, don't you think?" she added. It had been anything but obvious, but she didn't need to tell him that. She'd got there in the end.

"Ha, yes. My rather chic shirt." Hunt chuckled; he was enjoying himself. "I did indeed sponsor the debate team. When Karl was put on probation by the school, they required him to join the team. He was miserable, so I figured I'd support him in any way I could – show him I was proud of him. What else did you manage to figure out?"

Ana tried to project calm control, her mind racing.

"The Balloon Game. It was the debate team warm-up."

"Yes! Karl loved that game when he was little. We played it endlessly on car drives. He was the one who suggested it to the debate team, you know," he added proudly. "A moral quandary. Who should live and who should die – it seemed like a fitting metaphor for this place. Good. Anything else?" He was smiling. Ana felt a flash of hot anger. *How dare he smile?*

"The Motel Loba." Ana was winging it now, putting two and two together on the fly. "The Wolf Motel. In honour of Karl's old basketball team – the St Francis Wolves, I assume?"

"Hmmpf...close." Hunt shook his head. "I did rename the Motel Loba after the Wolves, but certainly not in their honour. They don't deserve to be honoured." A coldness had crept into Hunt's tone. He threw out a quick smile. "Well, Ana Reyes. You answered my questions. I believe you have earned the right to ask me some questions now."

"Is Alex alive?" Ana didn't hesitate. She had to know. Her knees felt inexplicably weak. She held her breath. What if the answer was no. What then?

Hunt nodded curtly. "Alex is alive."

That was all she needed to hear. There was still a chance. It was like a drug coursing through her veins, a powerful burst of hope, exploding inside her, pushing fear away. There was still a chance.

"Next question," Hunt said, smile still fixed smugly on his face.

How can you do this to us, you loser-freak? Ana bit back the words. It wouldn't help. To beat him, she would have to think like him.

"Why are you doing this?"

Hunt's smile dropped. It was as though a shadow fell over him. He looked away from Ana, one hand reaching out to gently touch a chess piece, fingertips resting on the queen.

"Two years ago, my beautiful wife, Karl's loving mother…died." He moved his hand across to the white king and pushed it to the centre of the board, then carefully picked out a knight and stood it alongside the king. "It was hard for Karl, losing his mother that young. He had…struggles – challenges. He rejected his family and got into drugs and all sorts of trouble. Getting kicked off the Wolves was the lowest point for him. Basketball was his life, the one thing that kept him going. You would have thought they'd have given him a break. He'd lost his mother, for Christ's sake. But no. One strike and you're out."

Ana had heard it all before. Karl's motive for starting the fire during the big game – avenging himself on the team that had rejected him. She didn't want to listen to Hunt making excuses for his son's behaviour; not after today, not after everything he'd put them through.

While he was distracted, she took a closer look at Hunt's radio.

It was propped on the chessboard, inches from his hands – he was keeping it close. From here it was impossible to tell if it was a satellite phone, or just some kind of fancy walkie-talkie, but she hadn't seen anything else in the bunker that looked like a communication device. It had to be the way Hunt kept in contact with the outside world. Which meant it was her way to call for help.

Hunt was still talking: "Things were getting better, slowly. Karl got help – therapists, doctors, support groups. He was taking anti-depressants and they were making a difference. I took time off work to be with him. He had started working out and was beginning to feel like himself again, for the first time since his mother died. The night before the fire, we were planning a European vacation, booking hotels and flights. He was so excited about the trip, about his future. No matter what anyone says, I know that my son did not want to die. *I know.*"

Hunt's focus was on the chessboard. He wasn't looking at her. Ana suddenly became aware of the weight still in her hand. All she needed to do was walk up and smack the weight into his head, take his radio and call for help.

This would be over.

She felt nauseous at the thought. She wasn't a killer – she'd never hurt anyone in her life. Could she really do this? Would she be physically able to hit him? To kill him? Even as she thought it, a brief, unwelcome image of Caden flashed into her thoughts – standing on the line, begging not to go. Maybe she was capable of more than she wanted to admit.

"But then, there was the fire. I got a call and went straight to the hospital…and waited. For so long…waiting for them to tell me it was over. My boy was gone. Time of death: 9.58 p.m." Hunt picked up the knight and cradled it in the palm of his hand. There was an edge to his voice. "*Murder-suicide* – that's what they called it. They said Karl started the fire deliberately – that he'd wanted to die and take the basketball team down with him. They called him a *monster*, a killer...my sweet boy. I tried to tell them that they had it wrong; that for whatever reason he lit that fire, Karl wasn't suicidal, and he would never, ever have done anything to hurt anyone else. Not deliberately. I tried to tell them, but no one would believe me. It was easier to make Karl the villain rather than look at what really happened that night."

Ana watched the top of his head, the side of his profile, his neck, taut with emotion. She felt her muscles tense. Her hands were sweating. She tried to imagine it, tried to picture herself stepping forward, raising the weight up high.

Hunt was lost in his own thoughts: "...could have given up. I was tempted to. I could have ended it all then and gone to be with my wife and son. But the one thing that kept me going was the thought that my boy's memory was tainted, vilely torn apart by lies. I had to prove his innocence. I had to show the world what really happened that night. I had to find the truth. For Karl and for my wife. For Rosa."

Rosa. The Motel Rosa. R O S A. Ana almost laughed. So that was the reason he'd picked this place and dragged them all the way out here. The reason he picked the code for the hatch. It was named after his dead wife. Great.

All the pieces were finally dropping into place. *Only the truth will set you free.* Handwritten in the anniversary card. It made sense at last. They were the guilty. Each harbouring a dark secret from that fateful night. A secret that could free Karl Hunt from the blame of deliberately killing and injuring his classmates. A secret like her own.

"So how did you do it? How did you find out who was guilty?" *Keep him talking,* Ana told herself. Keep him distracted. It wouldn't be too hard. Hunt was making the most of his villain's monologue. He must have spent a few too many nights eating ramen alone in the dark bunker.

"It's easy if you know where to look. I spent months hacking into everything, digging my way through people's private lives – their social media, their bank accounts. Everything from police records to the La Cholla school system – privacy is an outmoded concept these days. There was one place where I found some delightfully sordid, nasty little secrets. Indeed, the school psychologist's reports were interesting reading...very interesting."

Of course. Suddenly it all made sense. She had been right all along – Dankman *was* the source of their guilty secrets. Maybe he hadn't done it deliberately, but at the end of the day, was there a difference? They had trusted him and he had let them down. She hadn't been the only one to confess her "guilt". All seven of them must have had something to say – something Hunt found when he hacked into Dankman's files and read everything. *Everything.*

Shame washed over her. *This man had read her confession.* He knew that she had led her own brother to his death. That Danny hadn't died because Karl started the fire – that he had died because of her stupid, arrogant belief that she knew best. Hunt knew what she was and maybe he was right about her. Maybe she deserved every bad thing that had happened here.

Hunt's eyes were on her – he was watching her closely. She wanted to turn away from him, not give him the satisfaction of seeing her doubt, but she didn't move. The time for hiding was over. She had faced her worst fear and confessed to Alex, to someone she loved, and he had forgiven her. She needed nothing from this man. She straightened, standing taller.

Alex.

Her hand tightened around the weight. She needed to distract Hunt one last time. This time she would do what had to be done. Alex was going to live. She would make sure of it.

She took a few steps towards the chessboard. The smell of smoke was more noticeable here.

"Okay, so you found out what we did. You know that we all messed up in some way a year ago. Why not just release what you found to the police or the press?"

"Oh, I wanted to – I would have liked nothing more than to send all your dirty secrets to the press. But no one would have believed me – my proof was illegally sourced; I didn't have a neat little paper trail that would stand up in court. I was just the killer's grieving dad, making up a bunch of lies because I couldn't accept the truth about Karl."

"So, you came up with the Balloon Game. You hand-picked the guilty and brought us here to force us to confess."

"I had to. I had to create irrefutable evidence, and this was the perfect way to do it." Hunt gestured towards the wall of screens. "I have recorded confessions from each of you, acknowledging your role in what happened. Confessing to the bullying, drug dealing and cowardice that led to the fire. Admitting that it was your own negligence and Jax Patel's selfishness that resulted in two unneccesary deaths – deaths that weren't caused by the fire, but by stupidity and avarice. When I release these recordings, spoken in your own words, no one can deny the truth of what really happened one year ago. My son did not kill anyone – and once I have the final confession, the big one, I will have absolute proof that my son *did not kill himself.*"

"Ellis..."

"Indeed. Ellis Locke. The grand finale. I might never have found out what his secret was, if I hadn't seen his lawyer visiting him at the hospital on the day of the fire. Why would an innocent teenage boy need a lawyer? And why so soon? What was the hurry? That's when I knew Ellis Locke had something to hide – something big. I left Ellis a special message in the anniversary card. A warning, you might say."

"The twenty-dollar bill? That was for Ellis? I...I don't understand..."

"No, you wouldn't. But what matters is that Ellis will."

He looked around, his eyes locking on to Ana's, his expression dark.

Ana moved the weight behind her, wondering if he sensed what she had been thinking of doing, scrabbling to say something to distract him.

"So...you win. You get your confessions. Why kill us? You have what you need. Why did we have to die too? We're just kids..."

"*My son was a kid!* You're not innocent because you're young. I had to make the stakes high, or you would have never confessed," Hunt snapped. Instinctively, Ana backed away. His movements were becoming more erratic. She would have to act soon.

"What about the adults? What about the police who accused Karl, or the press who pushed the story that Karl was a monster? What about the custodian who locked the wrong exit doors and got off with just a reprimand? *What about the school?* The fire safety system completely failed and no one was held accountable. They claimed it was a faulty electrical panel – a freak equipment failure, and no one was prosecuted. *No one.* Why aren't you punishing them? Why us?"

"Oh, don't worry, Ana. They're next. That's the sequel." He grinned and bent down, his hand reaching under the chessboard. This was her chance.

Ana jumped forward; the weight raised in the air.

No thinking. Do it. For Alex. For Raya.

Before she even got half the distance, before she could bring the weight down on him, Hunt stepped back, something dark and shiny in his hand. He was pointing a gun at her.

Ana dropped the weight heavily on the ground. It landed with a dull *thwack*. She froze, unsure what to do. She'd had her chance and blown it. He had her, he was too far away – if she ran at him, he would have all the time he needed to simply pull the trigger and the next hour would start. Her body would be left down here, unfound. The bunker would become her tomb.

"Nice try." Hunt was laughing at her. *Laughing.* "Much as I have enjoyed our little chat, I must get going. I really don't want to miss the finale. Now turn around and get down on your knees."

The gun went up.

She considered refusing, but there would be nothing to stop him from shooting her right there and then. He clearly had no problem with killing teenagers. Reluctantly she turned around and dropped to the floor. The hairs on the back of her neck stood up as she listened for sound, aware that at any second, if he wanted to, he could pull the trigger and be done with her.

There was a rustle of movement. She felt her hands roughly pulled behind her and crudely zip-tied together. Then her ankles. The ties cut into her skin, but she didn't care. Hunt half-dragged her back against the wall.

The gun's cold, steely eye was directed at her face now. His finger rested on the trigger.

"Can I ask you something, Ana? After all of this…the motel, the Balloon Game…do you feel better?" Hunt's expression was oddly soft. He must enjoy this part – the power he had over her.

She would not give him the satisfaction.

"*Better?*" she spat the word. "How can you say that? How? You have tortured us and killed us. You executed Raya, my best friend. You killed Benny and Caden and Jax. Now you're trying to kill Alex. How dare you? *How dare you?*" She was shaking with fear or anger, she didn't know or care which.

"That's not answering the question. I've watched you for months, Ana. I've tracked everything you've done. I've seen you barely existing in a cloud of guilt and grief, struggling to even get out of bed and make it through each day. You destroyed your relationships, your grades, you threw away any future you might have had. All because you were broken, living under the shadow of guilt. All because in your heart you believed that you killed your brother."

Ana recoiled from him. She couldn't do this. Not any more.

"Go to hell!" It wasn't sophisticated, or clever. But she was spent. Every last ounce of her was done. Hunt wanted one last victory. He wanted more than death, he wanted to see her destroyed. She wasn't playing any more.

"One last time, Ana. Now that you've confessed your guilt, now that you've faced death once more, and actively chosen that you want to go on – *do you feel better?"*

The simple answer was yes. Yes, she had been pushed to the edge and chosen to fight. Yes, she had found Alex and Raya again. Yes, she was feeling more like herself than she had in a year, and, yes – she had faced the consuming guilt that had been eating away at her every day. But for what? Only to have everything viciously ripped away again, to watch the only people in the world she loved suffer and die in this godforsaken hole.

"Humph. That's what I thought." Ana could sense his smugness; he was proud of what he'd done here. He was enjoying his cruel game. Anger coursed through her, pushing away the fatigue. She was done playing.

"Go on, then. What are you waiting for?" Ana raised her chin defiantly and stared down the gun barrel. *"Just do it."*

"As you wish, Ana Reyes. As you wish…"

She closed her eyes, grateful for the darkness. A numb sensation settled over her. Not fear. Just dullness, as though her senses were shutting down. The end of the road.

The roar was back, louder than ever. Crushing her. There were faint sounds, movements, but they were quickly lost in the all-consuming noise in her head. This time, she would let the roar take her, like an ocean wave crashing on the shore and pulling her back with it, away from life, into the sea. Into nothing. This last time, she would go willingly.

She thought of Danny. Is this what it felt like? Had he known that his time was up – that he was going to die? Did he hear the roar? *Would she see him again?*

Rustling, a creak, the strong smell of smoke. Fragments cutting through the noise. Why was she still alive? What was Hunt waiting for? Every nerve was on edge, waiting for the end. Would it hurt? Where would it hit her? Why was it taking so long? *Just do it. Just fucking do it. Get it over with.*

She almost turned. Almost opened her eyes to see. Almost.

A deafening crack reverberated off the walls. The sharp sound echoed around the bunker, fading away until there was nothing left.

39 | Ana
24:05

Was it over? Was she dead? Ana scrabbled to pull her senses together, scanning her body for pain, but felt nothing. She was thinking – how could she be thinking if she was dead?

At the edges of her mind, she became aware of a faint sound – the dull repetitive hum of the air-conditioning unit. Air conditioning? In the afterlife?

Carefully she opened her eyes and peered around. The bunker came into focus. Hunt was gone. He had taken the radio with him.

She gasped, sucking in gulps of air. She was alive. Hunt had left her alive – for now. Relief flooded through her.

She was curled up on the mercifully cold concrete floor, squeezing her knees to her chest. The shock faded as she focused on her breath, in and out. Her heart started to beat normally in her chest; her shaking subsided.

There was no way to tell how long she lay there. Time had ceased to flow in this godforsaken bunker. But, bit by bit, thoughts started to cut through the mess in her head, nudging her, pushing her to get up, to move. There was something she needed to do – an imperative; something more important than her.

She had to get to Alex. She checked her phone. The timer was still counting down the next hour. Twenty-three minutes remaining.

Alex was still alive. Ellis was still playing the game. Hunt was still hunting. This was not over.

Pulling hard on the zip ties, she tested them out. They were just small bits of plastic, but surprisingly tough. They cut into her wrists but didn't stretch or flex. There was no question in her mind that she was getting out of here. No pieces of plastic would hold her back now. Not after everything she'd faced today.

Her mind raced as she looked around, sizing up her options. Suddenly she smiled.

Time to fight fire with fire. Carefully she pulled her knees up, pushing her body close to her tied hands. Her fingers grasped at the pocket of her jeans. It was awkward and painful; she could feel something slippery on her fingers. Blood from the zip ties cutting into her wrists. She didn't care. She was so close. Her fingertips brushed the top of Raya's lighter.

A last push and she stretched herself further than she thought possible. Her fingers reached down and just like that, she had it. The Zippo was in her hand, behind her back, her thumb felt the letters: RM.

Feeling her way around, she flicked the lighter open, testing out the wheel. This was going to hurt – for sure, but what were her options?

She manoeuvred her hands behind her, guiding herself by touch only, the Zippo cradled in her fingers. In her head, it felt right – the angles worked. If she lit it here, she could melt the ties.

Taking a short sharp breath, she flicked the wheel.

Ouch! The flame burned straight up onto her skin. She almost dropped the lighter. Breathing deeply through the pain, she bent forward and adjusted the angle. Before she could think about it too hard, she lit it again.

Fuck. It hurt so badly, but this time she smelled the sizzle of plastic. Taking a deep breath, she pulled her hands apart with all the strength she could muster.

Snap. The tie split. She brought her hands forward and, bending down, used the Zippo to free her feet. There was a nasty black burn on her left hand, the smell of burned flesh, but she brushed it off – she was past caring.

Rolling onto her knees, she pushed herself up and looked around.

The chessboard and pieces must have fallen off the crate they were resting on and were now scattered across the bunker floor. A small crack had appeared between the side of the crate and the wall; a strong smell of smoke was coming from it. Ana kneeled by the crate and ran her fingers along the crack. Air was whistling through it. Her heart jumped.

Everything was starting to make sense. The loud crack wasn't a gunshot, it was the heavy crate slamming shut behind Hunt when he left the bunker. This was the exit. The way out. She prised the side of the crate open and peered inside.

A small dark tunnel led off to the right; the space was tight with barely enough room to crawl. At the far end, shafts of light cut through heavy, smoky air. That must be where the hatch and keypad were. That must be the way back into the outbuilding.

She was going to get out of here.

But first, there was something she needed to do. Running over to the desk, she checked the screens, searching for Alex. The images flashed up, changing over and over, set on the timed loop.

Where was he? Her eyes flicked left to right, searching. If she could just find Alex – if she could get to him in time before it was too late. Before Ellis.

As she scanned the wall of screens, she noticed multiple wires leading down from each of them into a plastic conduit that disappeared beneath the desk. Of course, Hunt didn't have cellular either; everything in this bunker was likely hard wired.

Instinctively she ducked under the desk and followed the conduit. It led behind the desk drawer. Ana pulled the drawer out and using her phone flashlight, looked for the source of the wires.

Hidden behind the drawer was a laptop. So, this was where Hunt was recording the video feeds. This was it – everything was saved here on this laptop. She reached in and pulled it out, then set it on the floor and flipped it open. The screen woke up instantly – revealing a single open window.

As Ana stared at it, her jaw dropped open. She slumped down on her knees. It took several moments to register what she was seeing, and several more moments to understand it.

Then it hit her.

Hard.

She jumped back, her mind racing. Recalibrating. For the first time all day, she felt completely lost, with no idea what to do next. Only one thing stood out in her mind. One person.

She needed to get to Alex. Now.

It was as though the wind caught her; looking around she saw the free weight lying on the floor where she'd dropped it. Reaching for it, she crawled back under the desk, and raising it high, smashed it into the laptop. Hard. Over and over.

Pieces of plastic, keys, wires went flying in all directions. When she was sure it was unsalvageable, she stood up, breathing hard. She picked up the smashed laptop and placed it on the desk in front of the monitors.

Pulling the lighter out of her pocket, she balanced it carefully on top, the letters RM facing forward. *For Raya.*

Fuck Hunt. He didn't get to own their confessions. He didn't get to control them, to show the world their secrets. He didn't get to win his own game. For the first time in a long time, Ana smiled. She turned to the cork board and pulled Karl's photo off, folding it in half. Reaching over to the desk, she carefully nudged a grey pen into the fold and wrapped it up, slipping the package into her back pocket.

It was time to get the hell out of there.

Clambering down into the small opening behind the crate, she army-crawled through the tight tunnel back to the hatch. In the time she'd spent trapped in the bunker, the fire must have burned out. The heavy hatch lid was already open, the metal warped and blackened by flames. The keypad had completely melted – Hunt wasn't going to be able to lock himself safely away in the bunker again. Ana climbed into the smoke-damaged shack above. Shoving debris out of the way, she leaped over still-smouldering bits of furniture, finally finding her feet on free ground and taking off in a sprint.

There was no hesitation or thought. She knew what she needed to do and where she needed to be.

Rounding the corner of the pool fence, Ana ran as fast as her legs would carry her. Straight to the death machine.

40 | Ellis
17:41

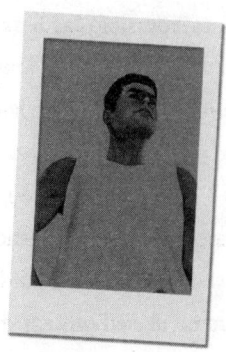

What's wrong with me? Ellis wondered. There was no emotion. No horror, no fear, no remorse. He was sitting on an upturned tractor, holding a metal wheel that could end the life of one of his classmates – his ex-friend – and yet he felt nothing.

Did that make him a sociopath? No – a sociopath would be enjoying this. Lacking in empathy? Probably.

Ellis released the wheel and flexed his hands, opening and closing them. Something was wrong with his hands. Ever since Caden had crossed the line, his palms had felt tight, uncomfortable, as though ants were crawling under the skin. He shook them out.

Alex was panting for breath. He was lying awkwardly, hands over the line, pulled tight by the rope. His body was stretched out behind him in the red dirt, still safe inside the circle. That's where Ellis left him hanging.

Ellis watched as Alex struggled to hold himself up, struggled to hold on. Alex seemed very invested, pulling against the ropes, trying to twist himself upright. It reminded Ellis of an animal caught in a trap, trying to gnaw its own leg off to escape, to survive.

Well, it wasn't going to be Alex's choice. The hour was almost up. They had sat here baking in the lowering rays of late afternoon sunlight, waiting, just in case Ana was still alive. Just to be sure. If she didn't show up soon, Ellis was going to call it.

Of course, she was probably dead.

The last he'd seen of Ana was her dark outline through the heavy smoke in the outbuilding. She was low to the ground, coughing. It should have been so easy – he'd reached out to grab her, but his hand closed on empty air, just as the fire took hold and a section of shelving collapsed over them. He had barely got out of the way in time. Ana had almost certainly died in the fire, trapped under those shelves. But as the flames had forced him out before he could be certain, there was always a slight possibility that she had somehow escaped – either snuck out of the burning building before him, or (and this was where he felt a little nervous) she'd made it through the hatch.

Ellis was all too aware of the risks if Ana had survived. He wasn't afraid of a confrontation. One on one, he would easily win. What he was desperately afraid of was that she would stay hidden until the final hour was up. They would both die, and all of this, all the things he'd done, would be for nothing. He wouldn't put it past her – to sacrifice herself just to make sure he didn't walk away. Especially after the next hour ended and Alex took his one-way ride on the red truck.

No, most likely she was toast. If he'd had time to sift through the ashes of the outbuilding, he would have found her under some burned-out shelf – or, at least, what was left of her. But even if every instinct told him that she was dead, he would anticipate the worst, right up until this was over – that there were three of them still alive, still playing the game. That the game was still very far from won.

"How much time is left?" It was the first thing Alex had said in a while.

"Enough," Ellis said, his eyes flicking over to where his phone was lying propped up on the tractor. Just over sixteen minutes. Good.

So close. He should wait until the very end – just leave enough time to drag Alex over the line with a small margin for error. Then maybe that would be it. No more countdowns or trucks. Maybe this whole thing would be over, once and for all. Ellis pushed the thought away. He didn't deal in hope – it made you careless. Hope was for losers. As far as Ellis was concerned, your destiny was in your hands, make of it what you will.

A pale violet colour tinted the distant mountains – the first hint that this hellish day was coming to an end. The wind had a refreshing coolness to it at long last. The desert looked the way it had when the bus had first arrived. Had it only been twenty-four hours? It felt like a miserable lifetime.

Damn it; what was going on with his hands? The fingers kept seizing up as though he was cramping or something. He rubbed them together forcefully trying to shake it off.

There they went again – his fingers locking into a claw shape.

It was ten times worse after Raya went. She'd really struggled. Even though she was tied up and weighed about as much as a small cat, it had been brutal forcing her over the line.

Sharp jolts of pain seared up his forearms. He must have pulled a muscle or something. What if his hands wouldn't let him turn the wheel? What if they seized up completely? He rested them on the wheel and tested himself, gripping and releasing the metal.

He had to distract himself.

"Damn, look at the time. I guess Ana's a no-show," Ellis said flatly. "Must be dead, or maybe hiding. Maybe she decided you weren't worth risking her life for."

There was no reaction from Alex.

"It doesn't matter. When you're dead, if the clock resets, I'll go hunting."

Still nothing.

"You know, I liked you, Alex. You're a good guy. Genuinely. I'm sorry it had to end this way."

Nothing. Damn it. Ellis's fingers seized again. What was wrong with him? He was in the final stretch; the game was his to win. So, why did he feel...off? It was as though his body was betraying him.

He pictured a flash of cloth in his hands, camo stretched through his fingers. Black hair, grabbed firmly in his fist.

Fuck it.

He grabbed the wheel and yanked on it hard.

There was a loud clank, followed by a creaking noise. The rope was moving, the cord cutting into Alex's wrists as he pulled against it, then suddenly stopping again. Alex's arms were over the line now. Ellis wondered how much of him had to cross over before they would shoot him. Head? Head and chest? Or whole body?

He should wait. There was still time. It was the smart thing to do. It was just so hard. He was spiralling.

"Fucking say something, Alex," he barked. It was reasonable. If Alex wanted to live for the remainder of the hour, he would have to put the work in. "Amuse me. Talk." Anything that would stop the thoughts.

But Alex did nothing. He didn't even look in Ellis's direction. There was something calm about the way he held himself, as though the deepest part of him had already crossed the line, was already free.

Envy. It came out of nowhere. To face your death with such courage, strength. Alex was going to die, but he was clean, his hands were clean. He had lived well and knew it. There was no fear left. No guilt. No shame.

Not like Ellis.

Both hands seized up. Caden's T-shirt slipping in his fingers. Raya's hair falling from his fist. When death came for Ellis, now or in a hundred years, there would be no peace, no absolution. No redemption.

Lucky Alex.

That was it. Enough.

"Fine. Have it your way." He couldn't do this any longer, his thoughts eating away at him, his hands failing him. He needed this to be over one way or another. He needed to go home. *Now.*

"It's been nice knowing you, Alex. See you on the other side," he muttered darkly, grabbing the wheel firmly and turning.

41 | Ana
11:28

"STOP!"

Ana skidded to a halt, her feet kicking up a small cloud of red dust.

As far as dramatic entrances went, this was a good one. She couldn't tell who was more shocked to see her – Alex, lying halfway across the white line, or Ellis, caught red-handed, mid-murder.

Ellis released the wheel and turned around on his tractor-throne to face her. The old tractor clanged and creaked as the rope stopped moving. Alex's head and arms were across the line already, but he was safe for now.

"Ana…" Alex muttered. He seemed so lost, so vulnerable. Ana wished she could run over and kiss him, hold him, untie the rope, and tell him everything was going to be okay. But first, she had a job to do.

She had to get this right. Everything depended on it. She flashed him a quick smile, hoping he could take something more from it, read into it. She had to save her words for the final round of the game. She had to win.

One hand was behind her back, her fingers gripping tightly to a long metal bolt she'd grabbed from the floor of the outbuilding.

"Danny's *nobody* sister. Nice of you to return to the land of the living. I thought we'd lost you back there." Ellis's voice was neutral, but the expression in his eyes was different from before. He was wary – almost respectful. Maybe he'd finally realized just how dangerous Danny's nobody sister could be. Pity, Ana thought, his consistent arrogance and underestimation of her had been a big advantage. "So, did you crack the code and enter the dragon's lair? Did you find Norman?"

Ana didn't respond. She had no intention of telling him about the bunker. She was holding all the cards right now. All the cards – but one.

She glanced over at Alex. He was lying halfway across the line, his position precarious. It wouldn't take much to push him over. It was no accident that Ellis was keeping within arm's reach of the wheel.

"So, I guess this is it," she said, slowly moving forward, closer to Alex, her back to Ellis. "The finale. Two of us will *die* and then the game will be over. It could be me or Alex, or even you, Ellis – because I promise you, we will not go down easily."

While she spoke, she moved around Ellis and stood between him and Alex. Her phone was tucked into the waistband of her jeans, the camera poking out discreetly; she had started recording while her back was turned to Ellis. Whatever happened next, she wanted a record of it.

Ellis laughed outright. "Seriously? I was coming around to thinking you were *actually* smart." He was a picture of cool control. "I'll be the winner, and I'll tell you why. Because since we arrived in this shithole, I've been the only person with enough fucking balls to play the game. I have done what had to be done. I have got my hands dirty because no one else could do it. No one else was strong enough."

This was the opening she'd been waiting for. Her heart was racing. She had to play it perfectly.

"Done what had to be done? What are you talking about, Ellis?"

Ellis was laughing hard, reeking of cocky smug arrogance. Ana resisted the urge to walk up and slap his perfect face. They were talking about people *dying*, and he thought it was funny – there was something seriously wrong with him. She wouldn't stop short of a full confession.

"Why are you laughing?" Ana said, trying to sound innocently confused. "I don't understand…"

"No, of course you don't. Because people like you don't think outside of the box. You live your sad, wasted little lives obeying rules and being nice to everybody until – if you're lucky – you die old and decrepit in some pit of a nursing home." Ellis was on his soapbox now, ranting, right where she wanted him. Ana folded her arms and leaned back, letting him dig his own grave. "I'm alive because I played the game. I kept myself one step ahead at every fucking turn. I read each play. Benny was so stupid, it was easy to convince him to go. Jade was so guilty over murdering Jax, she just needed a little psychological shove in her Lululemons. To be fair, Jax's death was a surprise – killed by his iPhone-wielding girlfriend, but I had the foresight to pivot off the back of it and catch you all off guard."

He might just as well have been giving a play-by-play of his last Wolves game. There was no emotion as he described each death. No feeling at all.

"Now, Caden – that's an interesting one. I think, to be fair, we should share the credit for that one." Ellis smiled slyly in her direction. "Who would have thought you had it in you to cold-bloodedly lie to his face like that. I'll be one hundred per cent honest here – I underestimated you, Danny's sister. You can be fucking evil when you want to."

Ana avoided his eyes. Was he right? Had she killed Caden? She'd lied to his face, that was true. The hypocrisy of the situation hit her. She'd thought she was the good guy, but hadn't she done the same thing as Ellis? The hard truth was, she'd manipulated Caden into crossing the line, and he had died because of it.

No. It was Caden or Alex. She'd just done what she had to do. She wasn't trying to save herself, choosing her own life over others. That had to be different, right? Briefly her mind wandered off-task, she glanced at Alex, momentarily confused.

Alex was still hanging on to the rope. He was listening but seemed tired. His wrists were red raw from the lamp cord; there was a cut on his forehead. His skin glistened with sweat and dirt – he looked rough, broken somehow. He nodded to her.

That was all she needed. She knew what she was fighting for. There would be time enough for recriminations after this was over. After they went home.

There was just one last thing she had to do. Her fingers closed around the metal bolt; her palms were sweating.

"What about Raya?" She turned back to Ellis. Her voice was ice-cold. She didn't want to hear this, but it needed to be said on camera.

Ellis looked at her, a half-smile on his lips. He paused thoughtfully, fully aware of the impact his next words would have – the pain they would hold for Ana.

"Raya cried." Ellis stated it drily, like he was ordering pizza. Ana felt as though an icy knife had been plunged into her chest. *Raya cried.* "I know," Ellis said, watching her face closely. "I was surprised too. I thought she'd have more guts than that. But, in the end, true colours show through. Though to her credit, she didn't beg for her life…" Ellis paused relishing the moment, the power, "…she begged for *yours*."

It felt like the world had stopped, for a moment. Everything froze in place, locked down inside and out. Ellis's words hung in the air. As she'd faced her death, Raya had been thinking of someone else, thinking of Ana. Something clenched tight in her chest, making it nearly impossible to breathe.

Ellis was right about one thing – in the end, true colours do show through. Raya had died the way she'd lived – with love. Even death couldn't take that from her.

A single tear fell, mixing with the dirt and ash on Ana's cheek. A new-found resolve was rising inside her, anger mingled with grief and love. *End this.*

For Raya. *Once and for all, end this.*

Her fists balled up; the metal bolt held firmly in her right hand. Her head dropped low, dangerously. She tensed, ready for the final leap, the final run. Raw anger seared through her.

End this.

Ellis was ten feet away, still perched lightly on the tractor. He watched her, his measured athletic eye assessing her body language. There was no question he could sense the rising danger; no doubt he wasn't afraid. He wanted her to take a run at him. His hand rested easily on the wheel, his fingers drumming up and down, playing with it. Playing with life and death.

Neither of them spoke.

Timing was everything. Ana's thumb pushed into the rusty metal. No time for self-doubt. She took a deep breath and did it.

Three steps towards Ellis. He rose up, ready for the attack. One hand gripped the wheel and turned.

Suddenly Ana swerved, changing direction, sprinting to the front of the tractor. The metal creaked as the gears strained to turn. Ana bent low, reaching under the hot metal hood.

Ellis looked thrown: he was expecting a full-blown attack, ready to defend his position.

Before he could reset, Ana opened her fist and rammed the bolt hard into the rusty gears. There was an ear-splitting shriek as the metal was ground up, wedging itself firmly in place. The entire tractor groaned, straining, but the bolt held.

The rope stopped moving, the death machine ground to a halt. It had worked!

As Ana pulled back, straightening up, her relief was short-lived.

In two long bounds, Ellis covered the distance from the wheel to where she was standing. Before she could react, he grabbed her by the hair, pulling her roughly away from the machine. She strained at his grip, but his hand was firm.

Ellis glanced across at the gears, the top of the bolt sticking out between the teeth. He smiled.

"Once again, I underestimated you." He pulled her close to him. Ana could feel his breath, fast and hard on her face. "Last time I make that mistake."

Slowly Ellis extended the arm that was holding her, stretching until she was held at arm's length. His other hand reached out to grab her neck, his fingers nearly circling it, closing tightly.

She'd fucked up. She knew it with complete certainty. All the time she'd been focused on Ellis's weakness, she'd made the exact same mistake. She'd underestimated him and what he was capable of.

This was it. This was how she was going to die. Strangled, choking for air on the desert floor. She couldn't speak, her hands reached out for anything she could grab. But Ellis held her firmly. There was nothing she could do.

Ellis tightened his grip. Ana choked and gasped, her vision darkened.

"So long, Danny's sister," Ellis said coldly. "It's been a trip."

Ana closed her eyes. Game over.

42 | Alex
08:52

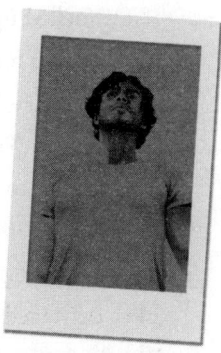

How did football players do it?

Alex was lying on the desert floor after taking down Ellis in a spectacularly clumsy headlong tackle. He'd somehow completely upended Ellis and sent him flying backwards while simultaneously flipping himself hard onto the death machine.

Everything hurt – his head, his shoulder – he was too winded to talk.

There was something wrong with his right ankle. He glanced down and saw that it was resting at an odd angle. He must have cracked it on the rusted tractor when he fell. He tried to move his toes and a searing pain shot up his leg. He gasped and winced, squeezing his eyes shut. This was not good. But he'd done what he needed to do. He'd taken down Ellis before he could hurt Ana.

The good thing about lamp cords – they didn't make very tight knots. While Ellis had been killing time on the tractor prattling on about his dad, Alex had worked at the knot over and over, loosening it just enough that when Ana was still talking, he managed to wiggle one hand free. Just in time.

He looked around for Ana – she was on the ground next to Ellis, pulling herself to her knees, shaking her head and neck.

Ellis was flat on his back. He must have been winded too – he wasn't moving, for now. They had a chance, if they were fast, Ana might be able to make a run for it before Ellis woke up.

As if to emphasize the danger, Ellis moaned and stirred slightly – one arm lifting and then dropping again to his side. There was no time to waste.

"Ana," Alex said, rolling to his stomach. Every movement hurt; breathtaking jolts of pain shot up his leg. He didn't want to think about it, but his ankle had to be broken. "Ana, are you okay?"

Ana looked around groggily. Her eyes focused on Alex.

"Shit, Alex. What happened? Are you hurt?" She scrambled over to him, her eyes round with concern.

Alex nodded at his leg. His shoe had come off, and the right foot was turned inwards at an unnatural angle. Ana sunk down to the ground next to him. Whatever happened now, he wasn't going anywhere.

"You…you should go. Run. Get somewhere safe, hide somewhere where Ellis won't find you. Quick – before he wakes up." Sweat was breaking out on his forehead – he bit his lower lip.

On cue, Ellis groaned and shifted slightly. They didn't have long.

They were in trouble. Alex knew it. If it came to a two-against-one fight, he was realistic enough to know that the odds would still be in Ellis's favour, especially now with his ankle. There had to be something he could do – anything. He looked around desperately. There was a large rock under the death machine. Large enough.

"Go, and I'll take care of Ellis…I'll stop him. I'll…I'll…" He felt sickened at himself for even thinking it. He didn't know if he had it in him to kill someone in cold blood, or how he would live with himself after. But he had to try. For Ana. He had to end this game.

"No, Alex!" Ana sat up. "No, you can't hurt Ellis. I can't explain now – there's no time. I need you to do what I say, okay? Even if it doesn't make sense..." She looked up at him, her eyes imploring.

Alex nodded. Whatever she needed.

Ellis groaned again. His hands were working now, flopping around. They had moments, at most.

"Quickly – I'll help you up." Ana's voice was shaky but clear. "We need to get to the line."

"*The line?*" Alex paused. That was the last place they should go. If they were on the line Ellis could force them over. It didn't make sense. They should go as far away from the line as possible.

"Alex. I need you to listen. I need you to trust me. Can you do that?"

Alex smiled for the first time in a long time and nodded. That would be the easiest thing he'd done all day. He trusted her. Always.

Bending down, she reached her arms around his waist and gently helped him up. His head fell against her shoulder. The pain was breathtaking. A wave of dizziness and nausea swept over him. He could feel her hand pressed against his chest, his heart beating hard and fast against it.

"It's going to be okay, Alex. We can do this," she said. Half-walking, half-carrying him, they staggered towards the line.

Just in time.

Ellis rolled onto his front. He was struggling to get his arms and knees under him, to push himself up. He was mumbling a little, unintelligible words. Slowly, he turned his head sideways. His unfocused eyes found them.

Time was up.

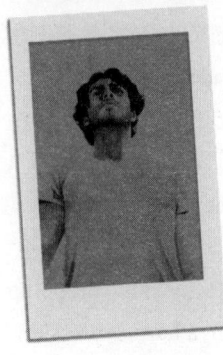

43 | Alex
07:35

Ana was holding Alex up, his arm over her shoulder. He could feel how hard it was for her even just standing there, supporting his weight. He pulled her closer.

"Ow," Ellis said, rubbing his neck and glaring at them both. "You should have tried out for the football team, Alex."

"Hurts less than being strangled to death," Ana said sharply.

"Fair point." Ellis was looking around, his eyes scanning everything. The loose lamp cord, Alex's ankle, the defunct death machine. He smiled and gave a small, sharp bark of a laugh. "Well, here we are again. Time's almost up and – no offence intended – I think I have the upper hand when it comes to speed. How's this going to play out?"

"You're going to cross the line," Ana said calmly.

Ellis stood still, an amused half-smile on his face.

"Okay, interesting. Let's run with this. Um, why exactly am I going to cross the line?" Ellis raised his eyebrows.

"Because your life is already over," Ana said. She was speaking slowly, choosing her words carefully. Ellis's smile slipped a minuscule amount.

"Explain."

"When we were chatting earlier, I never got the chance to mention that I met Norman, or should I say Matt Hunt – Karl's dad. He's an interesting man – a little bitter."

Alex glanced at her face in surprise. Norman was *Karl Hunt's* dad? Why would he do this to them? Hadn't his son done enough damage – caused enough pain?

Ellis had gone very quiet. His face shut down, a hard expression settled in.

"He had a lot to say about you – about what you did a year ago." Ana shrugged as best she could with Alex's arm over her shoulder.

A muscle in Ellis's jaw was twitching. His pale eyes were working, left to right, processing this new information.

"Did you think you'd get away with it, Ellis? Did you think no one would find out?" Ana laughed. "Bad news. Hunt has evidence and when all this is over, he's planning on releasing it to the police."

"What evidence?" Ellis said, his voice suspicious.

"Enough to ruin you and destroy your reputation. When people find out what you really did…your life out there, as you know it, will be over. There's nothing left for you to go back to, Ellis. Just shame and humiliation. Think about your father, the great Grant Locke, what he'll think of his only son when he finds out what you did."

"What did I do? Tell me, what is it I'm supposed to have done?" Ellis was testing her.

Alex was weakening, he could feel his strength going, his good leg was shaking. Ana propped him higher, putting more weight on her shoulders. One way or another, this would be over soon.

"You know what you did, Ellis, and the only way you can redeem yourself now is if you do something truly heroic. Something that people will choose to remember you for. Something that will make your dad proud."

Ellis started laughing loudly.

"Something like…throw myself across the line to save the poor lovers? Is that really your final play?" Ellis snarled. His old confidence seemed to be returning. "Redemption? Do you think I give a fuck about *redemption*? I only care about *surviving*." He paused almost imperceptibly. "I've got to say I am disappointed in you. I would have expected more from Danny's sister. There are some major flaws in your plan. Firstly, you're bluffing. You clearly have no idea what I did. Secondly, my father already knows everything, and guess what? He already loathes me…" He opened and closed his hands, rubbing them against his pants. "But you are right about one thing. I'll give you that. Hunt does know my oh-so-guilty secret. I figured that out when we arrived. You see, he left me a little clue in the anniversary card. A warning. I knew I was in trouble right then." He reached into his pocket and pulled out the twenty-dollar bill.

Alex frowned. What did twenty dollars have to do with any of this?

"Why don't you tell us, Ellis?" Ana met his eyes squarely. "Why don't you tell us what the money means; tell us what you did a year ago? You've already won. At least we'll die knowing the truth." Ellis's eyes narrowed. He cocked his head to one side and focused on Ana. Alex had the feeling that there was some kind of shared understanding between them that he wasn't a part of.

Ana shifted forward slightly: "Are you getting it now, Ellis? Do you understand the message in the card: *Only the truth will set you free*? It was for you, Ellis. All of this. The card, the message, the money…this whole damn place. It was all for you. Hunt's not going to let you leave until you confess before the cameras. Even if you're the last one standing, even if you win the whole damn game. It's over, Ellis. Whatever you did a year ago, it has to come out, one way or another, or all of this – everything you've done today, will be for nothing."

Ellis shook his head and gave a short nervous laugh.

"Okay. Sure, you want to hear what I did? That's how you want to spend your last moments alive? Fine, why the fuck not? You'll be dead soon enough. You listening, Hunt? I'll give you what you want, all right?" he shouted, turning around, arms raised.

Despite his bravado, he seemed to be struggling to find the words. "The game…a year ago…that was my one shot. Scouts were there from all the big schools, and I had to look good, or all the years I'd put into basketball wouldn't mean shit. Even my father came. It was the one fucking time he showed up. The one time…and… I choked."

Ellis's grey eyes were cold and hollow – he was pacing again, up and down, always within reach of them, just in case.

"At half-time, I was done. I didn't know what to do. I panicked. It felt like everything was slipping away. I went out for some air and sat in my car. I thought about leaving. Just driving away, making up some excuse later. But they'd know that I lost it and ran away. That would be a deal breaker. A lousy player and mentally weak – no one would ever sign me. I didn't know what to do. But then…I saw Karl. He was kicking around fuming about some girl. He wanted to buy one of Caden's pink pills, but he was out of money. It just felt like karma or something… He needed money and I needed a way out…"

"Ellis, what did you do?"

"I did what I had to do." Ellis sniffed; his strong profile turned to them – his bravado was faltering. His next words were almost a whisper. "I paid Hunt twenty dollars to start the fire."

Alex felt the air leave him. He could barely stand it – the thought of Ellis slipping a twenty-dollar bill to Karl, telling him to set fire to the school gym. How could Ellis have done that? Over a lousy basketball game?

"You *paid* Karl to do it?" Ana looked equally shocked. "*You paid him twenty dollars?* How could you, Ellis?"

For all the world, it seemed as though Ellis, the prince, was about to cry.

"I didn't...I didn't mean for any of this to happen...I thought, a small fire, the alarms would go off, sprinklers...there would be no way we could keep playing after that... When I saw what was happening, I tried to stop it. I tried...but the fire..." Ellis rubbed his hand over his shoulder, touching the rough skin, the burn scars. Ellis the hero, rushing into the flames to try and save people. Now it all made sense. He was trying to fix his mistake before it was too late.

"Jesus..." Ana dropped her head.

There it was – the final piece of truth. All of this, all the grief and pain, all the death, the loss, Danny...it all came down to a twenty-dollar bill. Karl hadn't meant to kill himself or anyone else. It wasn't suicide or murder, it was an accident, a stupid thoughtless, unnecessary accident.

There was a long silence. The wind had picked up and was whistling across the plains. The rusty windmill was spinning wildly, clacking loudly. Clouds were massing over the distant mountains. This day was done.

"Does anyone else know what you did?" Ana asked at last.

"Only my father and his legal assistant. After...in the hospital; I called and told him everything. I didn't know what to do. I thought I should tell someone what really happened – what I did. But he said to tell no one; that he would take care of everything." Ellis kept his eyes down throughout his speech – on his shoes, on the ground, anywhere but on them. "My father didn't visit me in the hospital, you know. Not once. His legal assistant came – several times, just to make sure I had my story straight. But not my father. We never spoke about it again after that first call. In fact, since that day he hasn't...he hasn't looked me in the eyes. What happened...what I did...I disgust him." Ellis rubbed his eyes. "I sometimes wonder... I wonder if he wished I'd died in the fire that day...so he wouldn't have to live with the disappointment."

Alex caught Ana's eye. Her expression was hard to read. Ellis's confession was coming so late in the day, after everything they had been through. Everything that had been done. Was there a place for pity?

Ana straightened up.

"Look at me." Her voice was unnervingly calm. Ellis kept his eyes downturned, fixed on the ground.

"I said, *look at me!*" Ana pulled herself forward. Reluctantly Ellis looked up. They locked eyes – adversaries at the final showdown. The air between them crackled with danger, anger – grief. In that second, they were connected by something wider, something deeper than them.

"You did what you did. It happened. Now it's time to move on."

Surprised, Alex glanced at Ana. She was calmer than anyone had a right to be as they faced their own death. She knew what she was saying and meant it.

"Ellis, I forgive you." Her last words were barely above a whisper.

Ellis stared at her, his expression written over with confusion and pain. He hadn't expected this and didn't know what to do with it. Ana held his gaze.

"*I forgive you.*"

Slowly Ellis started to fold in on himself. He started to cry. The tears that he had been holding back released in a flood. Shaky, ragged breaths racked through him as he stood fixed on the spot.

"Fuck you, Ana. *Fuck you!*"

Angrily he pushed away at his tears, at his emotions, with the back of his hand. He fought with himself, battling for control.

"If you think that changes anything, you're fucking wrong," he shouted, taking several threatening steps towards her.

Alex instinctively pulled Ana closer.

"GO! Or I will *fucking kill you!*" He held his fists in the air; his outpouring of emotion suppressed under a new-found fury. He was livid. He was dangerous.

This was it. Alex's heart sank as it finally hit him that Ana's plan, whatever it was, must have failed.

There was nothing for it. Nothing they could do – not with his leg. Alex knew he'd rather get shot by some random stranger a hundred times over than let Ellis strangle them both with his bare hands.

His head dropped: he was slipping a little, the pain was overwhelming him. He buried his face in Ana's hair for a moment, closing his eyes and breathing in.

"NOW!" Ellis stepped towards them, his voice, his movements laced with rage.

"Together, okay? We go together. Our way," Ana whispered to him.

Alex's heart was beating wildly. He didn't want to die. Every fibre of his body wanted to pull away, to run, to live. There were so many things he'd never do, places he'd never see, songs he'd never hear. So much of life ahead, now gone.

Ana turned her face to him, tears running down her cheek. She smiled sadly and in that moment, it was just the two of them, alone in the world. This was the only way now, their path. Their end.

"I'm scared," he whispered.

"Do you trust me?" she asked.

"Always." He gently leaned forward, his lips touched hers, soft at first, then with passion and fire, pulling them close, enveloping them in something powerful and deep. Something eternal, that couldn't be stolen by death. They would die with grace. They would die with love. They would die together.

"Oh, for fuck's sake." Ellis moved closer, fists held out threateningly.

This was it. Their finale. Together, they turned their backs on Ellis, the Motel Loba and the Balloon Game for the last time.

"It's time to let go," Ana whispered, as though to herself. Her words were lost in the sage-scented air. Alex nodded. At last, after everything, it was time.

Half-carrying him, Ana stepped over the line. The first step, then the next. It felt easy, like nothing – after all the fear. She kept them both moving along, heading towards the highest peak in the distance. Alex focused his eyes on it. The view from there must be beautiful. You'd be able to see for miles. The motel would look so small, like a kid's toy. A game.

Crack.

Ana fell; her full weight instantly filled his arms, pulling them both down. Alex wished he'd gone first. Gently he laid her on the ground. Her eyes were already closed – too soon. Gone so easily, so quickly. Just like that.

His fingers brushed her cheek and gently pushed her dark hair back. He leaned forward and tenderly kissed her lips one last time.

He was ready. He wanted to go now. He wanted to be with her again – for this all to end. Slowly he straightened up, his hand still holding Ana's. He sat back; inviting, waiting, ready – and closed his eyes.

44 | Ellis

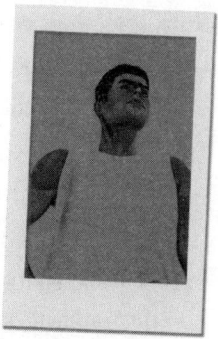

The sharp report of the final gunshot echoed around the cluster of buildings long after Alex had fallen. Ellis stood, immobile, staring at Ana's and Alex's bodies.

His hands were clenched tight, locked in place. He carried his weight forward on his toes ready for action, but it wasn't needed any more. They were dead. All of them. The fight was over. Like that. So quick, so easy.

Their outlines were entwined together, Alex's arm had fallen over Ana – protective, even in death. Every ripple of breeze lightly picked up wisps of hair or played with the fabric on a shirt. A lizard skittered into their convenient shade. They had fallen with their faces turned away from him, and he felt a flash of disappointment. Something in him wanted to see their expressions, to look into their lifeless eyes. He wanted to see them empty – the sparkle gone. No more fight, no more tears, no more love.

He wanted to see their eyes and know death.

Ellis pulled himself up. He needed to keep it together, now more than ever. He couldn't let his guard down. Not when he was so close, so *damn* close. He would only allow himself to relax after the truck took their dead bodies away. Then, and only then would he savour it – the sharp bitter taste of victory.

There was nothing on his phone. No countdown. No messages. That had to be good. He started pacing along the line, his eyes scanning the horizon searching for the telltale cloud of dust.

It didn't take long. The red truck appeared in the far distance, barely visible at first, then steadily growing larger.

Ellis watched dispassionately, with just a passing thought that this shitty truck wasn't fitting. It should have been a hearse, or even a slick, shiny, air-conditioned limo. Something more significant to mark the moment of his victory. His win.

The truck rattled up, pulling alongside the bodies. The two cowboys got out without so much as a glance in Ellis's direction. They got straight to business, pulling on their work gloves, and walking over to the bodies. Ellis thought he saw them pause and whisper something to each other; maybe they were surprised that there were two bodies this time. Maybe they were thinking what a shame for a young couple to wind up like roadkill at their feet. Young dead love. How adorable.

They grabbed Alex first, by the wrists and dragged his body over to the flatbed. Then one of them, the big cowboy, scooped Ana up in his arms and placed her in the truck next to Alex, slamming the tailgate shut for the last time.

The deal was done.

"Hey." Ellis found his voice. Time to end this. "Hey, you. What now? What do I do now?"

The men ignored him and climbed into the truck.

"I *won*. Do you hear me? I won the game. How do I get out of here?"

Nothing. They started the engine and swung the truck around, kicking up a wall of dust in their wake.

"Hey, wait. Where the fuck are you going? I said *wait*."

For a split second Ellis wanted to step over the line and run full tilt after the disappearing truck – force them to give him a ride, to get him the hell out of this nightmare once and for all.

But he couldn't. His toe was in the dust, touching the white paint. He kicked at the line, carefully, like there was an invisible wall in front of him. That stupid, scrappy line had meant death, and every nerve told him to step back, step away. Do not cross.

A dizzying jumble of thoughts slammed him. What if the sniper hadn't got the memo that this was over? What if Karl's father was never planning on letting him survive? What if this was all a trick?

Ellis indulged himself briefly, letting fear and doubt race through him, feeling his heart beating hard with terror. He allowed himself five seconds of weakness – he counted them off in his head. Then he turned his cold eyes up, away from the line, and focused on the distant horizon.

He wasn't a coward, no matter what his father thought. He was done being jerked around like some weak puppet. He was the winner, the survivor, the fucking prince – and he was getting the hell out of here.

He lifted his right foot high, with a deliberate motion, his bright green Kobe suspended in the air over the line. All he had to do was put his foot down, test it out. Then he could go home. He could do this.

I forgive you.

He jumped back. Fuck, it was like the words were stuck in his head. He could hear them, in Ana's voice, as clearly as if she was standing in front of him.

"I don't care," he shouted into the wind. "Do you hear me? I don't fucking care."

If anyone was watching, they'd think he was crazy. But the others were already dead. He pushed past the words, burying them inside. How dare she forgive him. She had no right to do that. No right.

Pulling himself up tall, he turned to face the line again.

He would forget her words. He would forget Ana. He would put this whole nightmare behind him. He had to believe that. Because if he didn't, then he'd lost the game – and Ellis didn't lose.

The white line stood out starkly against the red earth. He shook out his stiff hands, his arms, and stepped up to the edge again. This was the only way out. He could do this. Raising his foot one more time, he held it over the line. Fear caught at him, doubt – but this time he didn't move back.

Breathing deeply, trying to calm himself the way he'd been trained to, standing on the free throw line before thousands of cheering people. He had complete control…

He stepped over the line.

Nothing.

No crack of a bullet splitting the air. No explosion of dust at his feet. Nothing. He moved forward, one step, then another. His heart beating violently. Still nothing.

It was over.

Slowly Ellis unclenched his fists and dropped his shoulders. The tightness in his chest released, he breathed in deeply. A smile crept over his face.

It was over.

Exhilaration smacked him out of his stupor. He punched the air, spinning around like he'd just won MVP.

"Woohoo! Yaaaas!" He started running hard and fast. Anything in his path got kicked or slammed aside. He grabbed a rock as he passed the Motel Loba sign.

"Fuck you," he shouted, flinging the rock hard at the glowing letters. There was a loud crunch and the "A" flickered out.

There he was – on the far side. He was free.

Closing his eyes, he sank to his knees, spreadeagling across the stony ground. There was steady heat radiating from the earth. It felt comforting, as though the ground was protecting him, warming him.

He lay there for a long time – he didn't know how long. No matter. He wasn't on the clock any more. He owned his time now. He owned his future.

When he finally opened his eyes, evening colours had caught the edges of the sky; the vast desolate landscape was fading into dusk. He was the last survivor of the Balloon Game.

Pushing himself to his feet, he faced the motel. He should go back, even though the thought made him nauseous. Who knew how far he'd have to walk before he got rescued. He'd need water, snacks, a hat if he could find one. No point in dying of heatstroke after everything he'd been through.

But as he looked back at the motel, its pink walls glowing innocently in the softening light, he thought he could see them; shadows moving about, echoes in the cold evening. They were all still there, in the motel: Jade and Jax by the fire, Caden under the tree, Alex with his guitar set on his knee, Ana and Raya whispering together at the far end of the pool. He could hear soft music on the night air, see the firelight catching their faces.

Memories. The air was filled with them. Joking. Laughing. Alive.

They were all there, and they would never be leaving. This was their tomb now, their graveyard.

Ghosts.

Ellis recoiled. His hands knotted up.

He couldn't do it. He couldn't go back across that line – back to the Motel Loba. Not now. Not ever. Even if he died of thirst in the godforsaken desert, he would never go back. It was time to leave this cursed place – once and for all.

Backing away, almost falling over his feet, he ran for the road – the same road that had brought them here just twenty-four hours ago. He was going to walk along that road until he put the Motel Loba far behind him, until he found some gas station or truck stop, where he would buy an ice-cold drink and call his father to come and get him.

He would walk and he would keep walking for as long as it took, and he would never, ever look back.

He was going home.

Distant lights. A row of yellow dots, a flicker of red and green above, twinkling through the darkness.

Ellis checked his Rolex.

It was close to five in the morning. After an interminable night walking in soul-sucking darkness, his spirits were picking up at last. He was thirsty as all hell, and his hands were numb from the chilly night air. But the motel was far behind him, and now, after all this time, he was about to be rewarded. There were signs of life ahead. The lights meant buildings, people, rescue. This was almost over.

He picked up the pace.

Dead teenagers from LA would be a big deal. When he told people what had happened to him, there would be drama. Sirens and flashing lights, ambulances, news vans, helicopters. He knew what to expect. He'd had the best of it after the school fire. He made a good victim. Good-looking, clean-cut; he spoke well and had mastered the art of casting his eyes down, even tearing up a little.

Poor Ellis. Brave kid.

As he daydreamed, he walked faster.

The lights were closer now. He could probably cover the distance in ten, fifteen minutes. A small thrill of relief pulsed through him.

The small red and green dots were forming into a shape – maybe a sign? Vague structures could be made out below, faintly illuminated by the row of yellow lights. He couldn't tell what kind of buildings they were yet. But they were lit up, that had to be a good sign.

His thoughts spun off wildly. Maybe it was the gas station. Food! Cold drinks! He would start with an ice-cold Red Bull, or a slushie, or even go classic with a Coke. Maybe they'd have some hot dogs on the go. Jesus – hot food. His stomach growled with pleasure.

It was fun thinking about his rescue, but Ellis knew he had to pull himself back into the moment. There was one last thing he needed to do before he could relax. He needed to get his story straight.

Hunt could still post the silent footage from the cameras, so Ellis would have to play it very carefully. He should keep his lies as close to the truth as possible, just alter one or two key facts. That way it would be easier not to get caught out.

Luckily, he'd removed the cameras by the death machine, which made things a lot easier to explain away. He could just tell the truth, with a small twist – he would take himself out of the narrative. Caden, Jax, Raya, Jade...all of them died playing the game. Poor Ellis hadn't wanted it to happen, he'd even tried to stop them. But the others played by the rules and died by the rules. Tragic, really.

There was just one loose end.

Ana and Alex. This was where he had to be careful. After all, he'd survived, and they'd died. The suspicion would be on him.

Had they accidentally wandered over the line? Had they held hands and skipped to their death in a burst of glory?

He ran through permutations, but nothing fitted. Unless...

Of course – Ana. She'd be the perfect fall guy. No one even knew who she was back in the real world. Her only friends were her dead brother, Raya, and Alex. And guess what – they were dead too. Maybe she was a little crazy after losing her twin, and now this. Yes, she would make the perfect scapegoat.

It was all Ana. She'd tricked Alex and lured him close to the line, then she'd attempted to push him over and in the struggle, they both fell.

I forgive you, he thought darkly. Well, screw her. She might not be so forgiving if she knew that he was going to destroy her reputation. Throw her under the bus once and for all. Her short life over, her memory shredded, destroyed. A monster better forgotten, erased from history. Like Karl Hunt. The firestarter.

A monster.

Ellis faltered, stumbling a little on the dark road. The cold must be getting to him, messing with his head – his hands were seizing up again.

The sign was readable now. GAS STOP, it declared

unimaginatively. He could just make out the buildings. There was another smaller sign on one of them. What did it say? He strained his eyes, squinting to make out the words.

D…something…something…DI…he could almost make it out…DIN…

His heart leaped. DINER. Holy sweet Jesus. There would be food. Real, cooked food: milkshakes, burgers, fries. Life had just got so fucking sweet.

He broke into a run, heading for the lights. No more wasting time. No more thinking. He was ready to be rescued – ready for all of this to be over. He was going to open that door and walk into a new life. He was going to put the Motel Loba far behind him. He would forget. He would move on. He would.

And, like it or not, his father would have to accept the undeniable truth – that his misunderstood son was not a cowardly disappointment, a taint on the family name. His son was a survivor, once and for all. Nothing was going to change that now.

The brightly lit diner was decorated joyfully in pastel colours and vintage signs invitingly promising: "Homestyle Food", "Free Pies with Fries", and "Early Bird Specials!" The place was open – there was even movement inside, shadowy outlines of figures obscured by cafe-style net curtains. It seemed surprisingly full, considering there were no cars parked outside.

As Ellis approached the door, he could hear noises – conversation, TV, music; the place was lively. An army cot was set up on the porch near the door, a large plastic jug of water on the ground next to it. Probably for anyone too drunk to make the drive home. Must be a bunch of country rednecks with nothing better to do than hang at the nowhere-diner all night.

He paused at the door, mentally checking himself one last time. He had one shot to get this right. No fuck-ups. He was innocent, a victim in need of rescue...and food. Lots of food. Taking a deep breath, he pushed the door open and stepped inside.

Blinking in the bright light, his eyes slowly adjusted after hours on the dark road. The first thing that hit him was the comforting smell of toasted bread and cheese. It was intoxicating. His stomach rumbled. It smelled like heaven.

The next thing he noticed was that the diner had fallen silent. The buzz of conversation ended abruptly the moment he stepped into the room. There were only muffled noises coming from an ancient boxy TV fixed high on the wall behind the long, tiled counter.

But the thing that stopped him dead in his tracks was the group of dusty, dishevelled customers who had all dropped whatever they were doing and turned to face him.

There were no strangers here.

He knew all six of them better than he could ever want to. Six faces he'd thought he would never see again, not in this lifetime.

One of them stood up from a booth seat and, pushing her messy, dark hair away from her all-too-familiar face, looked directly at him, smiling.

"Long time no see, Ellis," said Ana.

45 | Ana

Ana enjoyed the look on Ellis's face.

No traces of his usual smug arrogance. Even the cruel twist at the corners of his mouth disappeared as his jaw dropped, a shocked flush brushing his cheeks.

He knew he was fucked. She could see it in his eyes.

Everyone had fallen silent; the only sound was the TV playing in the background, the cheesy theme from some vintage sitcom, plinking happily away, scoring the moments until Ellis could speak again.

"What the— You all died...I saw you..." Ellis stammered.

"Died?" Ana cocked her head and looked at him. "No. I think some of us might say we were murdered." She smiled and caught Alex's eye. Despite the pain from his ankle, he appeared to be enjoying this as much as she was.

Ana imagined Ellis's brain was jumping through hoops right now, trying to recalibrate, trying to process the unthinkable.

They'd all been through it when they first arrived at the diner.

Caden had had the hardest time of it.

He was the first across the line, and the first to be dropped off at the diner. When he woke up, lying on an army cot on the porch, alone and off his face, he'd convinced himself this was the afterlife. In true Caden style he went for a little explore around the deserted diner, made himself a grilled cheese sandwich and went back to sleep on a comfy booth.

The sound of the red truck pulling up outside woke him. He'd watched as the two bandana-wearing cowboys carefully lifted Jax out of the back and placed him on the cot, before silently driving off to collect the next victim.

When Jax woke up, he rocked Caden's world view. They spent the first hour arguing about whether they were in purgatory or California. A small distinction.

About two minutes after arriving, Raya had the whole thing figured out.

Each hour, on the hour, the red truck would arrive, and the cowboys would drop another sleeping student on the cot and hightail it out of there.

They contemplated ambushing the cowboys upon their next delivery and demanding they take them home. But no one was up for it – the memory of being shot was too recent. They'd survived this far, no need to push their luck.

There was no cell reception at the diner and no way to call for help, so Raya worked up the courage to ask the cowboys if they possibly had a radio that she could borrow for a minute. They just ignored her, and she backed away as fast as she could.

They came up with a plan. They would wait for the next hour to pass, grilling up the rest of the cheese toasties and making sodas from a box of flavoured syrups they'd found behind the counter. Then they'd feed the new arrival – the food seemed to settle them a little and help with the disorientation.

When they were calm enough to listen, Raya would take the lead and explain what was happening: "It's okay, you're not dead. They shot us with some kind of tranquillizer. You're safe. Here, have some more grilled cheese."

As they waited, the mood was subdued. There had been no time to deep-dive into processing what had happened to them. They just knew that they were alive – they had walked through fire, twice. They were survivors.

By the time Jade arrived, a sense of heightened anticipation settled in as they realized that it was down to the final three, it was almost over. In a few short hours, the Balloon Game would have played out. This fucked-up, miserable day would be at an end.

Unwelcome thoughts started to seep in through the cracks. Flashes from the last few hours – jumbled, messy images. Eyes flicked down; faces turned away as memories played out in their heads – choices made as they faced their darkest moments. Things they'd done as they died.

Unknowingly, they drifted apart, finding separate corners of the diner to hide out in. Jade moved to a booth near the door, curling into a tight ball next to the window, arms wrapped around her knees as if holding herself together. Jax followed, sitting uncharacteristically still on the seat across from her, hands playing with the salt and pepper shakers. Caden tuned the old TV to an even older show and sat at the counter, his back turned to the rest of them, resolutely facing the screen.

Raya went outside and sat on the edge of the concrete porch alone, staring blankly out at the desert skyline, as she counted down the minutes until the next hour was up – waiting for the next delivery.

The memory of being tied up and dragged across the line was too vivid, too visceral. Right now, Ellis was out there in what he thought was a life-or-death battle against Ana and Alex. More than anyone, Raya knew what he was capable of and that if it came to it, he would have no qualms about throwing someone over the line, alive or dead.

This wasn't over yet. Someone could actually die.

Raya was sitting in the exact same spot when the red truck pulled up again, and she watched as not one, but two bodies were carried over to the porch. The cowboys set Alex down on the cot, carefully avoiding his ankle. Ana was placed on a blanket on the ground next to him.

As they walked back to their truck, one of the cowboys paused, half-turning to Raya.

"Help will be here at dawn," he said, his voice muffled by his bandana. "It's over, kid." He gave a short nod – and that was it. Their job was done. The cowboys climbed into the truck, slamming the doors shut. She could hear loud country music playing as they pulled away one last time, leaving the familiar trail of dust far behind them, lit up red in the glow of their receding tail lights.

It's over, kid. That fucking easy.

Raya forced her bitter anger down – Ana and Alex were alive. In this moment, that was all that mattered. She would worry about the rest tomorrow.

One by one, the others came out of the diner. They gathered around the final two, waiting as they woke up, eager to be the first to tell them the good news. *You're not dead. You survived.*

The funny thing was – it wasn't a surprise.

When Ana sat up and looked around, she smiled happily at all the faces surrounding her, took a sip of offered water and then said calmly: "Well, thank fuck that's over!"

Now, several hours later, they were all finally here.

The survivors were spread around the diner, facing Ellis – the last man standing, the winner of a prize no one wanted any more. He had fought too hard. By the time he'd finally stepped over the white line, he had crossed many more lines, ones that should never be crossed. Ones you can't come back from.

Voices on the TV chatted away happily. The grill crackled and spat as another forgotten toastie turned deliciously black. In the far distance, underneath everything else, was a new noise. The faint wail of a siren.

It was a new day. Help was on the way at last.

"You ain't welcome here." Caden had been sitting sullenly by the bar, still watching the TV. He stood and turned to face Ellis, his sheer bulk making him appear to loom over the point guard.

Ellis flinched. He was breaking a sweat, shifting from foot to foot.

"You hear? Or you deaf?" Caden shuffled closer to him. His face had turned red, his fists tightly clenched at his waist.

Maybe for the first time in his life, Ellis took it. He didn't speak. He didn't move, his head hung low, as he watched Caden warily.

"Caden's right." Raya's voice surprised Ana. She'd been sitting quietly in a booth by herself since Ana's arrival. She was unnaturally subdued – whatever had happened on the line must have been terrifying. Raya rubbed her wrists unconsciously; raw, red welts cut into them from Ellis's zip ties. "You should go, Ellis. Now. Before we do something we'll regret." Her voice was shaky, shock and anger registering in equal parts.

Ellis looked around, taking in the circle of faces surrounding him. He flexed his hands, over and over. His eyes sought out Jade, then Jax – there was desperation there.

"I…I didn't…" He was struggling, reaching for anything that could help him. "Raya, I never…"

"Yes, you did!" Raya turned to where Ana was standing and pointed to Ana's phone. "May I?" Ana nodded. It only took a moment to find what she was looking for. She turned the volume up and pressed play, holding it out for all to see.

Ellis's voice rang out: *"Raya cried… I know. I was surprised too. I thought she'd have more guts than that. But in the end, true colours show through…"*

Ellis was shaking almost imperceptibly. His head was down again, eyes too, hands balled tightly. There was nothing left for him to say. The voice on the phone had said it all for him. Raya put the phone back on the table.

"Busted," she said, smiling – her first genuine smile since she'd died on the line.

"We won't…forgive you… Never." Jade's voice was stilted, as though she kept losing her train of thought. Her eyes were ringed red, and her blonde hair still stood up at the back in a wild bird's nest. "You're sick, you are. You need help." She looked at Jax, but he just shrugged.

"What? Ellis didn't kill me. *You* did, babe…" Jax muttered, grinning, clearly pleased with himself. But Jade stared at him blankly, as though she couldn't make sense of his words. Jax shifted on the spot sheepishly. "Just sayin'…"

Alex was sitting in the booth next to Ana, his leg propped on the seat opposite, bundled in a pile of dish towels. He nodded in agreement. He didn't say anything. He didn't need to. The message was clear.

Ellis looked deflated, a cloud of desperation sinking over him. He couldn't defend himself. Not this time. Thanks to Ana, his own words, his actions had followed him out into the world. There was no way he could take them back now.

His balloon had crash-landed, and he knew it.

He looked around wildly. His eyes found Ana's and locked on; the darkness had faded, replaced by a hooded, unreadable expression.

Words ran through Ana's mind. There were so many things she wanted to say. She wanted to scream at him for hurting Raya and Alex, for setting fire to the outbuilding, for trying to strangle her on the line – she could still feel his hands tightening around her neck. She wanted him to know that all his cruelty had been for nothing, that he hadn't escaped the Motel Loba – not really. He never would now. It would follow him for ever.

But as she met his stare, something gripped her inside. There was genuine fear behind his guarded expression. He was a seventeen-year-old who had just realized his future was over. *This* was his moment on the white line – *this* was his time to face the end. He could see no way out; he had fought for his life, for his future – and he had lost it all.

Caden edged forward, pushing Ellis towards the door.

Ellis nodded – he understood. It was over. Hands shaking, he reached for the handle and pulled the door open. The bell dinged; the wail of the distant sirens drifted in on the cold night air. Without pausing, without looking back, he walked through the doorway into darkness.

There was a *clack-clack* as the screen door creaked shut behind him.

The atmosphere in the diner felt instantly lighter, a collective release – they could breathe again.

One by one, they turned away from the door, moving back to their respective corners. Caden retrieved his burned toast and started munching on it loudly, back turned to the others. Raya slumped onto her booth seat with a sigh. Jade curled up in her corner again and resumed staring vacantly out of the dark window.

A deep feeling of exhaustion hit Ana. This didn't feel right. They'd prevailed – Ellis had finally been forced to face what he'd done, to look into the eyes of the people he had hurt. Justly – Ellis was a sadistic jerk. No question. Not to mention an arrogant, self-serving, selfish bastard.

But at the end of the day, this wasn't all on him. Hunt had known all along that Ellis's secret was the key to proving Karl's innocence. He could have just taken Ellis and played his cruel game with him alone. But Hunt had chosen to come after all of them, like some sick, power-hungry, avenging angel. They had all been forced into a corner and made to fight their way out. Hunt had done this to them – no one else – and while it didn't excuse Ellis's actions, on some level, he was a victim too.

Ana looked around at the faces, all turned away, unable to face each other. They were just kids, every one of them. Some she'd barely known before this trip, but now they were forever tied together, their futures, their paths entwined.

There had to be hope that they would move on, put this behind them and live well. Otherwise, what was the point? When did it end? Fear, pain and loss followed by grief, hopelessness and guilt. The vicious cycle that had started with the fire, with everything that had come before it, with everything that Matt Hunt had revived in his sick and twisted game – it was all still playing out. It had to stop somewhere.

Didn't it?

Instinctively she picked up her phone and scrolled through Ellis's confession. She watched as the distorted image caught Ellis, moving backwards and forwards, in and out of view, flexing his hands as he confessed to causing the fire, his face distraught.

Would they ever truly be able to put that night at the gym behind them and live with their terrible mistakes, or would part of them stay trapped for ever in the past – trapped in the motel, inside the white circle? Was this going to be their story? Or would they forgive themselves and move on? The cycle had to end. But it would only stop when they made it stop.

It would only stop when they made it stop.

Suddenly she knew what she had to do – she just wasn't sure if she could do it. She turned to Alex. He had been watching her silently.

"Alex…I think I need to go after him," she said, searching his face for a reaction, half-expecting him to try to stop her. But Alex just smiled.

"Yeah, I know." His soft eyes were warm. He nodded. He understood.

That was all she needed. Grabbing her phone, she jumped to her feet and ran to the door, out into the night one last time.

46 | Ana

"Ellis, wait!" The diner door creaked shut behind her. Ana walked forward, her phone in her hand.

Ellis was standing next to a gas pump, his tall outline caught in a circle of orange light, spotlit from above. His back was turned to her, head down; his powerful shoulders slumped forward, like a beautiful but damaged Greek statue.

As she looked at him, Ana felt a wave of emotions. All the fear, loathing and hatred that he had embodied, contained in that single figure. The way his hair caught the light, his broad chest, his hands gripped at his sides – it burned through her. She could feel those hands holding her by the neck, the sheer horror as his fingers tightened.

Her resolve wavered. What was she doing out here? Ellis had made his own bed, let him lie in it. She should just turn around, head back to the diner, to Alex and Raya. Screw Ellis.

But then she heard it.

"I'm sorry."

Was she imagining it? It almost sounded like the wind.

Ellis half-turned; his profile was briefly illuminated, his cheeks streaked with tears.

"I'm...so sorry..."

"Sorry won't bring Danny back." Ana didn't know where the words came from, just that she had to say it. They couldn't be here, at the end of everything, and not remember who this had all begun with. Her brother. Ellis's friend and lover. Somehow, throughout everything that they had been through in the past day and a half, Danny had always been there, standing between the two of them – the missing link.

Ellis nodded; he was crying. She watched as he sobbed, his powerful frame bent and cowed by his grief. There was nothing for her to say. This was on Ellis; this was his shame and regret. His pain. He needed to feel this. He *needed* to.

For several moments they stood there, lit from above, as though on an empty stage. Time was finally slowing down – she could feel it. No more countdowns. No more endings. Just the rest of their lives stretching ahead, for better or for worse.

As Ellis's tears subsided, he sniffed and wiped his arm across his face.

"For what it's worth...I loved him too." Ellis's voice was soft; he kept his eyes fixed on the ground. Taking a deep, shaky breath, he nodded to himself as if he had decided something. Slowly, he turned away from her, away from the diner and started walking towards the dark road.

Ana watched his retreating back. She could just let him go. It was what he deserved, after everything he'd done, after all the grief and pain he'd caused. She owed him nothing.

But for the last time that day, she heard it – the question that was always with her: *what would Danny do?* Only this time she already knew the answer. With one hundred per cent certainty, she knew.

Her resolve strengthened. She took a deep breath. She knew what to do, she just needed the strength to do it. For Danny.

"You can come back from this, Ellis," Ana said. Her voice caught in the night air.

Ellis stopped, head down, and turned to face her.

"No...I can't." He was holding something in his hand. Almost gently, he held it out for her to see. The twenty-dollar bill. "I can't come back from *this*, Ana – from what I did a year ago, or from what I did here – from *who I am*. I can never come back from this." He sounded broken.

Ana looked at him. His grey eyes were unnaturally soft and clouded with remorse. The angry energy was gone. The prince was gone. There was just Ellis.

It was time. It wasn't going to be easy, but it had to be done. They had to end this cycle once and for all.

"Can't you?" She reached into the pocket of her jeans. Unlocking her cell phone, she tossed it to him lightly. His baller instincts kicked in and he caught it in the air with ease. Holding it in his hand, he looked at the phone, then at Ana, shock on his face.

Their eyes held. They stood, together but apart, on the gas-stained concrete. This is what it had all come to. This one final play in the game. This one final act.

The ball was in his court now.

With nothing left to say, Ana turned away.

The exhaustion was back – bone deep. She felt like she could lie down on the concrete right here and sleep for a hundred years. She walked back to the diner, pausing only when she reached the door – unable to resist the urge to look back one last time.

Her cell phone lay on the concrete where Ellis had been standing

– the crumpled twenty-dollar bill on the ground next to it.

Ellis was gone.

This was an ending of sorts, for Ellis, at least. Whether he'd deleted the phone recording or not – it was done, his future had been set in motion. He had his second chance.

Would he have the courage to face what he had done; to take responsibility for the fire and for all the pain he had caused in his desperate fight for survival? Would he have the strength to change, to grow from this and become a better person? Would he ever forgive himself, or was this the start of a life filled with bitter anger and denial? She didn't know. She didn't care. The one thing she did know – the one thing that mattered, was that it was up to Ellis now.

His call. His choice. His life.

The wind caught at the twenty-dollar bill, lifting it lightly into the air, before tumbling it back down on the concrete, flipping it over, stealing it away. Ana watched as it made its slow journey, out of the circle of light, heading for the endless desert, heading into darkness.

There were no winners here. Not today.

The game was finally over.

EPILOGUE

"How are you doing?" Ana dropped her head onto Alex's shoulder.

"Been better," Alex said, smiling.

The two of them were sitting side by side on the concrete forecourt, foil blankets wrapped around their shoulders, keeping out the last of the chill night air.

The gas station had become a staging area for the rescue operation. Lights flashed, radios crackled, uniformed figures scurried here and there. Ambulances were lined up in a row in front of them, backs open, contents spilling out. A whirr of news helicopters flying overhead created a constant background hum, like angry mosquitoes swooping over again and again. There was a buzz of nervous energy. Everyone was trying to help. Everyone wanted a part to play.

It was overwhelming. Ever since the police had received an anonymous tip-off, it was all systems go. The local town was on standby. An emergency response area had been set up outside the hospital. Parents and school administrators had been flown in on a donated private jet (apparently Mr Dankman's kind offer to join them was politely declined). They were all in town now, just waiting for *the motel seven* to arrive.

Without a shadow of doubt, Ana knew her mom would be there; probably front and centre, anxiously checking each ambulance as it arrived, bothering everyone in uniform for news of her daughter. It didn't matter that they had barely spoken in weeks; when Carmen Reyes heard that Ana was in trouble, she would come. Ana held this thought close as she contemplated what she had to do – it was time for the truth, no more secrets. It was time to tell her mom what she had done a year ago, in the fire – about Danny's death. Whatever came of it, she was finally ready.

Turning away from the chaos, Ana looked out across the all-too-familiar desert. Dawn light was creeping over the distant mountain range. A new day.

Three hundred and sixty-six.

Next to her, Alex shifted, groaning as he adjusted his ankle. The EMT hadn't taken any chances, and his entire lower leg was wrapped and bundled into an immense plastic splint.

"Does it hurt much?" Ana nodded at his leg.

"I'm good," Alex said. "It looks worse than it is, and the pain meds are pretty awesome." His voice sounded tired. She took his hand, their fingers entwining. It felt natural, being here with him – by his side. After everything, it felt right.

"Hey, lovers." Raya walked up and scootched onto the ground next to them. "Did you hear they found the motel? It was burned to the ground."

Ana wasn't surprised: "Probably Hunt trying to cover his tracks and destroy any evidence of the Balloon Game, in case he's caught." It wouldn't work. When the police had first arrived, Ana handed them a small package: a photo of Karl folded around a grey pen with the HT logo, covered in Matt Hunt's fingerprints. Between that and Alex's phone, containing copies of a dozen photos Ana had taken inside the now destroyed bunker, they had all the proof they needed of what Hunt had done to them at the Motel Loba – evidence he couldn't burn. *Checkmate.*

"What if they don't catch him?" Alex's voice had an edge to it.

They all felt it. The man who had kidnapped and tortured them was still out there somewhere – still free. The thought was terrifying. At the end of the day, thanks to Ana destroying his laptop, Hunt had failed to save the confessions he had gone to such cruel lengths to obtain. What would stop him from coming after them again?

"They'll catch him," Raya said, projecting a confidence they all needed to hear. "One of the cops told me there's a huge manhunt underway. They've got the whole area on lockdown. No one's getting away."

"Wouldn't want to be driving a red truck today," Ana added, wondering what else the police might catch in their net. Two cowboys and a lost basketball player, maybe? She briefly pictured Ellis, wandering alone down some long desert road, desperately trying to get cell reception so he could call his father.

Raya snorted. "Personally, I'm not staying in another motel anytime soon." Her voice sounded different – worn down, as though some of the fight had gone out of her. Ana looked at her friend. Her face was streaked with dirt, her hair sticking out in clumps. She was clearly trying to be okay, pushing through, but she wasn't fooling anyone.

"Raya, I'm so sorry I wasn't there when Ellis…" Ana didn't know how to finish the sentence: *When Ellis killed you? When he tied you up and dragged you to your death?*

Raya shook her head dismissively.

"No. Don't go there. It was a freaking mess. We all had to face shit today. There'll be plenty of time to cry about it later." Raya forced a short smile, changing the subject. "Besides, you're the dark horse, aren't you? The only one to make it into Hunt's lair. What was he like? Did he have creepy beer-bottle glasses and a comb-over?"

"No," Ana said thoughtfully. "He was kind of ordinary, a basic, boring dad type. Even when he talked. I mean, he was obviously ridiculously smart and all, but he almost seemed...pleasant. Like he'd be selling cookies at a bake sale or something."

"Yikes. Somehow that seems worse. If you can't tell a psycho from their looks, they could be any one of us." As Raya said it, Caden walked out from behind a police car and lumbered across in front of them, heading for a nurse handing out free Gatorade.

Ana and Alex laughed.

"Stop it!" Raya remonstrated gently. "Caden's all right. I mean, his heart's in the right place, even if his head's not always."

"You know, gotta give him credit," Alex said. "Caden was the only one who figured out that we weren't really being shot at. He knew there was something fake about the way Benny died. I totally missed that. I was sure Benny was dead – there was all that blood, and his eyes were wide open. I still don't get it."

"I can help with that," Ana said quickly. In the time she'd spent hanging out in the diner, waiting for Ellis to arrive, she'd managed to put together some of the missing pieces of Hunt's puzzle. "Benny was a ringer. It was a set-up. They faked his death so convincingly that none of us would question if we were actually being shot or not."

"Benny? *Our Benny* was in on it? Dang," Raya said. "I liked Benny. What gave him away?"

"A few things. Benny's keychain had the letters HT in orange on it. I thought it was for the 'Happy Travels Bus Co'. But when I was in the bunker, I saw the exact same logo – HT for *Hunt Tech*. Why would Benny have a company keychain unless he was working for Hunt? Also, when we were on the line and Benny was about to go, he promised that we would be all right, *all of us*. I swear he was trying to let us know it wasn't real – to warn us."

"Oh, yeah, and what was with that fake accent?" Raya said. "New Joy-sey meets Fla-ri-dah? I'm guessing he's a gig actor who's not too good at his day job."

They all laughed. Even though Benny was a fake, somehow it was still a relief knowing that he hadn't died. One less thing to be sad about.

It felt oddly natural – the three of them sitting on the ground together, hanging out and talking. Almost as if it was just a regular school day. Not the day they had died. The day everything had been lost, and then found again.

Ana glanced from Alex to Raya, drinking in their faces, the closeness. This was everything, and she'd come so close to losing it all. It was a ridiculous thing to say, but she almost felt *lucky*. Not everyone got a second chance – she knew that better than most people. But here it was – a do-over, and this time she would not lose sight of what mattered most in the world. She would not lose them again.

"I love you guys," she said quietly.

"Okay, much though I love you back, I'm not into threesomes," Raya said, climbing to her feet. "I'm going to find myself an air-conditioned ambulance and get the heck out of this overheated hellhole. Catch you later." She winked and walked away, heading after Caden. "Wait up, Big C. Don't suppose you have any spare smokes kicking around?"

One of the ambulances started up, slowly reversing out of the line, and pulling away. Probably Jade and Jax's ride. The two of them had barely spoken since waking up at the diner. Nothing like a near-murder experience to test your relationship. A hollowness had crept into the space between them – a crack in their veneer. Hopefully it would heal and *The Jade and Jax Show* would be back in full swing, posted for all to see. Maybe the damage didn't run too deep. But even as she thought it, Ana pictured Jade's face at the diner – the empty look in her eyes as though something was disconnected inside her – broken. Whatever came next for them, it was going to be a long road ahead.

Ana watched the ambulance go, lights flashing as it pulled away from the gas station heading into town. It would be their turn to leave soon – to ride away and leave all this behind. To see her mom and Alex's abuela. To pick up and start over – again.

"Okay?" Alex asked, rubbing her shoulder.

"Yup. All good. Considering." Ana stretched – she was feeling a bit numb from sitting in one position for so long. A deep, pervasive tiredness was settling over her as the adrenaline wore off. She would sleep for a week, given half a chance.

"Ana...there's something I wanted to ask you when we were alone." Alex sounded a little on edge. "On the line, you knew we weren't going to die, didn't you? I just...why didn't you tell me?"

She had been wondering when this would come up. It had been one of the hardest things she had had to do in a very bad day – letting Alex believe that they were going to die.

"Alex, I'm *so* sorry." Ana looked away, avoiding his eyes. She would never forget the look on his face as they crossed the line – if only she could have spared him that. "I wanted to tell you more than anything, there was just no way to do it without Ellis finding out too. In the bunker there was a video feed from inside the diner on the laptop. I knew everyone was alive and if we could just cross the line, we'd be okay. But Ellis was dangerous – he could have hurt you, or worse. I had to let him think he'd won. If there had been any other way, I would have told you. I'm so sorry for putting you through that."

"It's okay," Alex said, pulling her close. "It wasn't on you. I get it. To be honest, I thought you were pulling a *Romeo and Juliet*. Leading us to our death. I'm sorry – I underestimated you."

"That's the theme of the day." Ana laughed. But as she said it, another thought occurred to her. There had been another theme, an undercurrent that had carried them through everything.

The truth will set you free.

The final step in Hunt's cruel game. He had brought them here to torture them into confessing their parts in the fire and clear Karl's name. But his plan had failed, the confessions had been destroyed by Ana, and rather than clearing his son's name, he had revealed himself to be the very thing his son was accused of – a monster. Even if the truth about Karl's role in the fire eventually came out, the Hunt family name would now forever be tainted with evil.

But, ironically, for the survivors, after everything that they had been through, after confessing their guilt and accepting their fate – in some strange way the truth *had* actually set them free. Each of them had been given something that Danny, Maia and Karl never had – *a second chance.*

Ana nestled her head into Alex's shoulder, looking out across the desert.

The first rays of dawn light clipped the top of the distant mountains and cut through the sky, turning the world gold and purple. The lightness inside her soared for a moment. A new day was beginning – a brilliant day filled with colour and life and love.

She glanced up at Alex, his face touched by the golden light, his soft brown eyes catching glimmers of the sunrise, sparkling. They had time. They had a future. Wherever it would take them; whatever came next. She could breathe again, deeply – freely.

Closing her eyes, she felt the first rays of light on her face, the warmth of a new beginning. Her skin tingled, every sense felt alive. It was as if some powerful force was hugging her, holding her close, letting her know everything was going to be okay.

But she knew it wasn't the universe or some god that she was feeling. She knew exactly who it was. She could sense him all around her now – in the wind, in the sun, in her heart. For so long she had missed him. For so long she had been shut down, held back with the weight of guilt and grief. But after all this time, after everything, in the dawn light sitting on the cracked, gas-stained concrete in the middle of nowhere – he had found her at last.

He was here with her.

Her brother. Danny.

A year ago, she had grabbed her school bag off the kitchen table and run out of the door and out of the life she knew, for ever. Since then, she had been lost, somewhere dark and lonely. But it was finally over. She wasn't alone any more.

At long last, it was time to go home.

ACKNOWLEDGEMENTS

Writing this story has been an incredible journey, from the first hint of an idea through to the finished book. Every step of the way has been supported by an amazing team of people. Thank you to each and every one of you. You made this, and I will forever be grateful to you.

Thank you to my brilliant editor, Becky Walker, whose immense compassion and grace elevates everything she touches to impossible, new heights. It has been the greatest privilege getting to know and work with you. Also, thank you to the phenomenal team at Usborne. To Amelia Mehra, Charlotte James, Jenny Glencross and Gareth Collinson for their thoughtful and considered proofreading and copyediting; to Sarah Cronin, Will Steele and Daniel Prasad for the beautiful interiors and inspired cover design that brought the characters to life so perfectly, and to the exceptional marketing and PR team: Fritha Lindqvist, Hannah Steward, Jessica Feichtlbauer and Beth Gardner. And to Aaron H. Aceves and Brennon Lane for their generous sensitivity reads.

Thank you to my amazing agent, Ludo Cinelli. Your commitment, encouragement and behind-the-scenes skills are second to none – I am so lucky that you decided to take a chance on me. Also, thanks to the dream team at Eve White Literary Agency – Eve, Steven and Emmanuel, and to all our hard-working co-agents at Curtis Brown, and Catapult Rights.

A huge thank you to Annie Berger, Gabbi Calabrese and the team at Sourcebooks for bringing *Every Last Liar* back to the US in style; and to the international publishers who have found wonderful homes for the book all around the world.

Thank you to all the booksellers, librarians, influencers and bloggers who have supported *Circle of Liars* with such generosity and enthusiasm, and to all the incredibly talented writers who took time out to review the book – just knowing that you read it was enough to make my head spin. I am truly humbled.

To my very earliest readers, thank you for your on-point feedback and much needed encouragement to keep going (you may find your name hiding in the book). A special shout-out to the immensely talented Sarah Naughton whose early faith in me gave me hope that maybe…just maybe, I could be a real writer someday.

To my folks, who gave me roots and wings…then more wings, then a jet engine and a tank of rocket fuel and a lighter. It's so easy to fly when you have air under your wings. Your unconditional faith in me has been my superpower through good times and bad. I will never be able to find the words to express my gratitude to you, and I know you will never need to hear it. You are, quite simply, the best.

When clouds blocked my sun, thank you to the people who walked by my side until the sun came out again. To Susie, for being the best big sister in the universe, and for carrying me when I couldn't stand alone; to my brothers Bob and Paul, for their unconditional love and support; to Lindy, who had my back when I needed it the most, and Emma, Iona, Marilee and Stacy for letting me ugly-cry on their shoulders. To Becky, Ray, Aidan, Jo, the Aussie Francises and to my endlessly supportive friends, family and colleagues who have cheered me on from both sides of both ponds. There in the darkness, here in the light. I love you all.

Above all, thank you to my kids. You are my all and everything. To Nat, whose brilliant ideas have shaped every part of this book – I will never forget the endless hours of listening, laughing and plotting together; to Jack, whose gentle strength and unwavering confidence have carried me through so many writer's ups and downs and in-betweens; and to Gemma, whose passion and heart have inspired so much of this story and pushed me to be a better writer (and human). This book is for you…if you ever actually read it!

And of course, to Shaggy, who was always the better writer. You would have laughed and laughed (…and laughed). Looking forward to toasting you from our old haunt on the fifth floor of Waterstones. I miss you, my friend.

Finally, at the very end of the journey, there is you, the amazing reader. I am so grateful that you made space in your day for this book. This journey would mean nothing without you, and I hope that you enjoy the ride as much as I have. With all my heart – thank you.

Kate Francis is an English-American writer and architect. She graduated from Edinburgh University and the Bartlett School of Architecture, and worked as an architect for several top design firms in London. She now lives in California with her three kids. When she's not building something, she enjoys kayaking, walking the dog, and crafting interesting ways to kill off fictional teenagers.